Author of:

LIVVY

To my two grandchildren, Jessica and Ryan, who bring a special meaning to my life.

ACKNOWLEDGEMENTS

A special thank you to Nadia McKechnie and Debbie Eagleson-Pepper for assisting in the editing process. And to Sara Ye, for her help in formatting, due to my limited knowledge of word-processing.

PROLOGUE

THE FEAR THAT HAD overwhelmed her just a short time earlier had left her now. The medication had taken its effect and she rested calmly, eyes closed, uttering a silent prayer. She had been brought to the emergency ward of the Metropolitan Hospital at ten minutes past midnight. Her husband had been with her in the ambulance and was still with her in the sterile room six hours later. She had been in a state of panic, unable to walk and in unbearable pain. The hospital staff had reacted quickly, pushing and probing, taking blood and X-rays, and finally ordering an ultrasound, in order to determine the nature of the large mass they had identified in her lower abdomen.

At daybreak, the doctor informed her they would be operating within two hours and despite all his assurances of a successful outcome, he had stopped at guarantees. The medical jargon passed over her head; she couldn't cope with the words, only with her own thoughts of fear and pain and possible death.

Moments after the doctor's departure, she was being prepared for the operation and was given more medication to sedate her. She struggled to maintain her conscious state, terrified that this would be the last thing she would remember. Slowly her mind clouded over and her life began to pass before her, drifting backwards through events she had long forgotten, or wanted to forget, and other wonderfully happy times she wanted to hold onto until the day she died…

CHAPTER 1

ABIGAIL JANE PARKINSON WAS born in Oakfield, Ontario on a bright September morning in the year nineteen hundred and twenty eight. Her mother, Emily, was only fifteen years old, having been seduced by a boy of sixteen who she had walked to school with every day for almost two years and thought of as a trusted friend. Because of the trauma of the incident and Emily's youth, marriage was out of the question. In a small town like Oakfield in the twenties, where an unwed mother was the object of cruel gossip and forced to suffer untold humiliation, poor Emily could not overcome the shame she felt.

Soon after the birth of her baby, Emily ran away from home and despite her family's desperate attempts to find her, she was never seen or heard from again. Emily's mother, a widow, was approaching her sixtieth year and did not expect to have to raise another child but she doted on the new baby and decided to call her Abigail. Meanwhile her other two daughters, Lillian and Adeline, already in their early thirties and still unmarried, were just as enamoured with the new addition to the family and anxious to help out as much as they could.

As the years passed, Abigail grew into a beautiful child and at the age of seven everyone commented on her large sparkling blue eyes and dark curly hair. She was taller than the other children in her class, very bright and the pride of her family, but it was at this tender age that she experienced the first tragedy in her life when her grandmother passed away and her Aunt Lillian took charge of the household.

After a week of mourning, Abigail went back to school and soon reverted to the happy child she had once been but she knew she was different from the other children. She was well liked by her schoolmates, who had now taken to calling her Abby, but when they talked about their parents, she experienced an emptiness that she couldn't explain. She adored her aunt Lillian and fantasized that she was her real mother and when, in later years, she learned the true circumstances of her birth her emptiness changed to anger and she never felt any desire to search out her natural parents.

By the time Abby was thirteen, she had attained a unique sense of independence and felt ready for any challenge that life could bring. The death of her Aunt Adeline the following year only seemed to strengthen her, at the same time bringing her closer to Lillian whose whole existence centred around her niece.

CHAPTER 2

THE NEXT FIVE YEARS passed without incident and now that Abby was a young woman, she and Lillian spent many happy hours together chattering while they shared the household chores, cooking, sewing and puttering in the tiny garden. They truly enjoyed each other's company and did not consider for a moment that their sheltered world would ever change.

Lillian was only fifty-one years old when, like her sister before her, she contracted tuberculosis. Already a frail and delicate person, she quickly lost weight and became almost bedridden. She tried desperately to put on a brave face and keep up her spirits for Abby's sake but the state of her health proved too powerful. Abby was devastated by this turn of events and spent every spare moment tending to her aunt and trying to make her as comfortable as possible. It was during this period that Abby decided to leave school and go to work in the local five and dime store. She had always intended to be a teacher and certainly had the potential for it but now this goal seemed almost impossible. She no longer had time for her studies, as her first consideration was always Lillian. She hated to leave her alone and was in danger of missing her bus on many mornings, when she fussed over Lillian's breakfast and made sure that she had everything she needed. Every weekday they had the same conversation,

"Are you sure you'll be all right, Auntie? What else can I get you? Make sure you keep warm."

Lillian would reply, "Will you just get along, you'll be late Missy. I can manage quite well until you come home" and she would look up and smile the sweet smile that Abby had come to know and love.

Early one afternoon, a traveling salesman, visiting the store, stopped by Abby's counter and stood picking through the yard goods and ribbons while secretly appraising the young girl who had caught his eye. Ed Harrison had been calling on the store for the past two years and was now a regular supplier of children's wear. At the age of twenty-one, he was of average height with a stocky build, a shock of red hair and a round boyish face. This was the first time he had seen Abby and he was enchanted with her vivid blue eyes, raven curls and the charming manner in which she treated the customers flocking around the counter. Without realizing what he was doing, he slowly advanced to the front of the line and suddenly found himself face to face with Abby. He had been so preoccupied with her beauty that he stammered helplessly and blushed to the roots of his red hair, "Hmm, hmm, I'm sorry, hmm, hmm I think I'm at the wrong counter", and with that he fled without so much as a backward glance.

Ed didn't return for nearly a month but in that time he had summoned up all his courage and this time when he finally managed to approach Abby he quickly introduced himself and apologized for his behaviour. After that encounter, he came into the store every Tuesday and Friday and after three weeks he decided to ask Abby out, "I know you're very busy Abby, but I was wondering if you'd like to go to the movies with me. I hear The Best Years of Our Lives is playing at the Palace." Abby was both flattered and delighted that Ed had asked her out. He had a shy disarming manner and as she looked him up and down noticing his stylish clothes she bowed her head demurely and replied, "I would love to go with you Ed. I haven't been to a movie in such a long time."

Leaving Lillian alone proved to be very difficult and that first evening away from home Abby was consumed with guilt. Despite the fact that she enjoyed Ed's company she was relieved when he dropped her off at her front door. "Thank you so much Ed, the movie was wonderful and it was nice of you to bring me all the way home."

Ed took her hand and raised it to his lips, "The pleasure was all mine Abby," he said, "I just hope we can do it again soon or perhaps we can have dinner together."

Abby was impressed at the gentlemanly way he treated her and agreed that they would get together again the following week.

Over the course of the next year, Ed and Abby spent many evenings together and sometimes even managed to meet on a weekend, but Lillian was always uppermost in Abby's mind and the young man took second place in her life.

One year to the day that her friendship with Ed began, Lillian took a turn for the worse and Abby, knowing that her aunt had little time left, refused to allow her to be taken to the hospital and so began what seemed to be the longest vigil of her young life. It was, in fact, only one week later when she knew in her heart that Lillian couldn't last through another night. She crawled into the bed and whispered aloud all the thoughts that she had kept to herself through the years and had never expressed, "I love you so much Auntie, and you've meant more to me than any mother ever could. I expected you to be with me forever ", and then she began to weep, "I don't know how I'll go on living without you and I'll never forget you as long as I set foot on this earth. Please don't leave me, I can't bear it." But Lillian was unable to respond and as dawn broke, she quietly slipped away.

They remained together for over an hour while Abby rocked the lifeless body back and forth staring vacantly into space. She was inconsolable, unable even to make arrangements for the funeral and it seemed as though all her reason for living had ceased. The good neighbours who took control were afraid she might harm herself in some way and they took turns watching over her. Even Ed tried desperately to talk to her but it was no use and he spent hours just sitting holding her hand and attempting to comfort her.

After a week in which Abby had eaten very little, Ed grew very angry and announced he was leaving, "Enough of this Abby, you can go on being miserable for the rest of your life or you can get over it," he said raising his voice, "I know you loved your aunt but she's gone and there's nothing you can do about it. Now, I'm going too unless you pull yourself together."

Her lack of response to his threat forced him to reconsider but he left that afternoon without his usual warm embrace and without one word about when he would be returning.

Only hours after Ed left, Abby snapped back to reality and the familiar things around her came back into focus. She had always loved the house where she had been brought up; every room reflected the warmth of her grandmother and her two aunts. She paced the living room, running her hands over the soft floral cotton of the plump chair Lillian had loved to sit in, then after picking up the small framed photographs one by one that stood on top of the old mahogany piano, she slowly began to putter around the house taking care of all the little chores that had been neglected for so long. When her closest neighbour looked in on her later she was almost her old self, although there was a reserve about her as though an invisible curtain had come down somewhere in her mind.

CHAPTER 3

ON ED'S RETURN TO Oakfield, he was overjoyed to find Abby in better spirits. Now that she didn't have the responsibility of tending to Lillian, he felt that after a suitable interlude, it would be an appropriate time to ask her to marry him. He waited patiently for two months but couldn't contain himself any longer, and late one warm July evening he finally had the courage to ask Abby to become his wife, "Abby, I have something I want to give you", he said, awkwardly pulling a small velvet box from his pocket, "I have come to love you very much and I hope you feel the same way about me. I'd like us to be married and I promise I'll be good to you and take care of you from now on. Please say you'll be my wife and make me the happiest man on earth."

Abby was shocked when Ed proposed but the emptiness of life without her beloved aunt had made her very lonely and without much thought, she accepted. It was only later when she realized how much her life would change that she became apprehensive about what lay ahead.

Ed still lived at home with his mother and father in Toronto. His father was a lawyer and had provided a good home for his family in the Riverdale area where many affluent citizens lived. John Harrison was disappointed that Ed had not followed in the footsteps of his eldest son Raymond who was also a lawyer. He had expected Ed to aspire to be someone more ambitious than a traveling salesman but he was a gentle man and tried not to interfere with his childrens' lives. Meanwhile, Ed's mother, Martha, doted on both her sons and wouldn't hear one bad word said against either of them. When Ed told his parents that he had met the girl of his dreams and wanted to get married his mother was astounded, "Who is this girl?" she demanded, "Why haven't you mentioned her before?"

Ed put his hand gently on Martha's shoulder, "I didn't mention her before because the minute I met her I thought she was special and too good to be true, Mom. I wanted to tell you about her but I decided to wait until I knew we could have a future together. Two days ago, I asked her to marry me and happily she agreed to be my wife. I know you will just love her too, Mom."

Martha was not easily swayed, "That's all very well Ed, but we don't know anything about her. Where does she live? How old is she? Where did you meet her?"

"Slow down, Mom", replied Ed grinning, knowing all along that he would be getting the third degree, "Her name is Abigail Parkinson and she lives in Oakfield. She's twenty years old and works behind the yard goods counter in the local department store and that's where I met her."

John Harrison, sighed but kept silent, once again disappointed that Ed had not found someone with more lofty ambitions but Martha wanted to know more, "What about her parents, what do they do?"

Ed was apprehensive when he was obliged to tell his mother that his fiancé had never known her parents and had been brought up by an aunt who had recently passed away. As expected, Martha frowned remarking, "This seems all highly unusual son, are you sure she's the right girl for you?"

Ed had more patience than most men and taking his mother's hand replied, "Mom, I love her and she loves me and when you meet her you will love her too. I'll be bringing her to meet you next weekend and I know you'll welcome her with open arms."

Martha glanced across at her husband who sat motionless taking it all in and then when he quietly nodded, she turned back to Ed, "All right Ed, we just want you to be happy and we look forward to meeting her."

Ed hugged his mother, "Thanks Mom, you're the best."

CHAPTER 4

WHEN ABBY ARRIVED AT the Riverdale house the following Sunday for lunch with the Harrisons', she found both John and Martha waiting eagerly on the front steps. Ed had driven to Oakfield to pick her up and she was sitting nervously in the passenger seat as they approached the house, which she noticed was a large Tudor style home with beautiful leaded glass windows and a large front porch. She had dressed in her finest muslin blouse with its ruffled collar, her best pearl grey knee length skirt and matching sling-back high heeled shoes with grosgrain bows. She had felt confident before she left her house, but as she stepped out of Ed's four-year-old Buick Roadmaster she was visibly shaking.

Ed, sensing her distress, took her hand and walked her slowly up the pathway towards his parents who were quietly appraising the young woman who was to become their daughter-in-law. John only noticed the lovely face with the amazing blue eyes, the wide generous mouth and the soft dark hair curling over the slim shoulders, while Martha was more interested in what Abby was wearing and she couldn't help but approve. Abby was surprised to see that Ed's father was above average height, slim with a rugged but handsome weather-beaten face and thick silver hair while his mother was short, plump, rather plain and had short curly hair the same shade of red as her son.

Ed pushed Abby gently forward, "I want you to meet Abigail Parkinson, Mom and Dad", and then turning to Abby, "This is my dad, John and my mother, Martha."

Abby had stopped shaking but her voice had a slight tremor as she held out her hand, "I am so pleased to meet you Mr. & Mrs. Harrison, and please call me Abby."

Martha and John both shook Abby's hand and then after a little hesitation, Martha suddenly stepped forward and gave her a hug, "It's so nice to see you, my dear," she said, "Ed has told us so much about you. Please come in the house and make yourself comfortable. Lunch is already on the table and I'm sure you must be hungry after that long drive".

Ed smiled broadly at his mother, grateful that she had tried to make Abby feel so welcome and over a lunch of fresh smoked salmon, shrimp, tossed salad and seasoned ripe red tomatoes, John and Martha came to know a lot more about the girl who was to become Ed's wife.

It was difficult for Abby to talk about her Aunt Lillian as she still felt lost without her but she knew that Ed's parents were anxious to learn about her life and she decided to be totally honest with them, and even told them about the circumstances of her birth. Rather than being judgmental, Martha was empathetic, realizing that through no fault of her own Abby had been the victim and deserved to be treated with compassion.

After lunch, they settled in the living room and Abby was impressed. It was obvious that the Harrisons' were affluent people and could afford to decorate their home with fine antiques, beautiful rose velvet couches, floor length damask drapes and a wonderful Aubusson carpet in shades of ecru, rose and apple green.

"I love this room." Abby remarked, "You have exquisite taste, Mrs. Harrison."

Martha puffed out her ample chest with pride, "Thank you Abby. We've lived in this house since we were married so both of our boys were brought up here."

"Tell me about your other son."

"Raymond? Well, he's a lawyer just like his dad; he got married three years ago to one of the young ladies who worked in the law office. He doesn't have any children yet but his dad and I are hoping there will be one on the way soon; we are so looking forward to becoming grandparents. Have you and Ed discussed how many children you want Abby?"

Abby blushed and bowed her head avoiding Ed's eyes, "Actually we haven't discussed that, Mrs. Harrison but I do love children. I always wanted to be a teacher but I had to look after Aunt Lillian so there was no way I could pursue my studies."

Martha got up and went to sit beside Abby, "I think it's admirable that you sacrificed your career for your aunt my dear, you must have been very close."

Abby suddenly got very teary eyed and fished for a handkerchief from her purse, "Yes, we were close. She was like a mother to me and I really miss her."

At the sight of Abby distraught, John looked a little embarrassed and Ed rose from his seat to cross the room and take Abby's hand, "Now look what you've done Mom, you've made her cry."

Martha was mortified, “I’m so sorry Abby, please forgive me,” she begged.

“No need to apologize” said Abby beginning to smile, “I like to think of Aunt Lillian often and crying helps. Each time it gets a little easier to bear.”

CHAPTER 5

ABBY WAS THE SOLE heir to Lillian's estate and it took her almost three months before she was able to sell the house and dispose of all of her aunt's possessions. This was a particularly painful time for Abby and the more she thought about leaving Oakfield for good, the more anxious she became. An antique dealer from a neighbouring town purchased most of the furniture and as each piece was removed from the house, Abby felt as though Lillian was being stricken from her life forever. It was when Abby saw Lillian's favourite chair being lifted into the van that she finally broke down in tears and seriously questioned her decision to marry Ed.

All that was left in the house were a few of Lillian's things that Abby wanted to keep and her own personal belongings including the single bed and dresser in her bedroom. This would be the last night that she would spend in her own room and as she lay awake thinking about her life, she knew that she had to go forward and honour her commitment to Ed.

"Please God," she whispered, "Let me be a good wife."

The next morning at 10 o'clock, Ed arrived with a pick-up truck, borrowed from a friend, to help Abby move her bed, dresser and all of the packing cases to his parent's basement for storage. Abby would be staying with the Harrisons' until the wedding at Christmas and then she and Ed would be moving into their own Victorian house just a few blocks away. The house was a gift from the Harrisons' and Abby was overwhelmed with their generosity. As Abby climbed into the truck and looked up at the window of her room where she had spent every night of her life, she felt tremendous sadness and it was an effort not to break down. Ed was completely oblivious to Abby's state of mind and after stopping off at the realtor to give him the keys he chattered almost non-stop about their future together all the way to Toronto.

The next two months were spent in a whirlwind of activity, not only was there a wedding to prepare for but Abby was also expected to pick out all the furniture for the new house. Without Martha's help there was no way she could have coped and they spent hours together shopping for the wedding and pouring over House & Garden. Martha seemed to have boundless energy and Abby was content to let her do most of the planning. The two women got along well and spent so much time together that Ed began to feel neglected. It was difficult enough with Abby living in the same house and not being able to show her any real affection in front of his parents. He knew that Abby was a virgin and fantasized daily about their wedding night while Abby, on the other hand, attempted to push the whole idea out of her mind.

The only close friend of Abby's was a schoolmate from her hometown of Oakfield. Marion Preston was the complete opposite of Abby in appearance, short of stature with honey blonde hair, fair skin and green eyes. She wasn't particularly pretty but she was a kind, thoughtful girl with a good sense of humour and well liked by everyone with whom she became acquainted. When Abby asked her to be matron-of-honour at her wedding, Marion graciously accepted and was secretly thrilled at the prospect of visiting Toronto.

Martha felt that they should have at least one bridesmaid in the wedding party and suggested Raymond's wife Julia. Abby was not particularly fond of Julia but didn't feel comfortable voicing her opinion to Ed or anyone else. From the moment she had met her future sister-in-law, she had the distinct impression that Julia did not approve of her. Unlike Abby, she was rather sophisticated, always well groomed, dressed in the finest clothes and adorned with jewellery. Exceedingly thin, with raven hair pulled into a chignon and bright red lips, she reminded Abby of the wicked queen in Snow White and Abby suspected that when crossed, she could be just as evil. Julia was not exactly pleased at the idea of being a bridesmaid and convinced both Martha and Abby that she should have the role of matron of honour while Marion would suit the lesser role. When she got her way, she immediately began to dictate exactly the style of dress she wanted to wear and selected a high neck, halter style, bias cut in lavender silk. This posed a problem for Abby as she had no idea what to do about Marion, but Julia, always in a take-charge mode, suggested a rose silk in a more youthful style. When Marion arrived in Toronto for a fitting Abby had to admit that Julia had good taste. She almost found herself asking Julia for advice on her own bridal gown but she fell in love with an ivory taffeta dress with a square neckline and full bouffant skirt that she saw in a department store window and had it duplicated by Martha's dressmaker.

CHAPTER 6

THE WEDDING TOOK PLACE one week before Christmas in the small church that John and Martha attended every Sunday. Raymond, who was the best man, was surprised to see that his brother was perfectly calm while getting dressed in his dove grey tuxedo, pure white shirt and dark grey silk tie. "Aren't you nervous?" he asked.

"No, not at all. Should I be?" Ed replied with a frown.

Raymond tried to be tactful, "Well, this is a real commitment and there's still time to change your mind. I know you love Abby and she seems like a great girl but are you sure you want to settle down with her for the rest of your life?"

Ed rested his hand on Raymond's shoulder, "I have never been more sure of anything in my life so I hope you're going to wish me well."

At the same time, Abby was sitting in Martha's bedroom fully dressed in her bridal gown and veil staring into the mirror, while Marion and Julia fussed in the background with their own outfits. Abby was holding a lace handkerchief and twisting it around in her fingers attempting to overcome the anxiety she was feeling. Not only was she nervous about being the centre of attention on this particular day but she was having second thoughts about marrying Ed. She knew he was a good person, kind, thoughtful and generous and she did love him but she wanted to feel passion and excitement when she was with him and that had never happened. Martha bustled into the room in a beige lace dress and wide brimmed hat, "Come on girls, you need to get a move on. The cars will be here any minute to take us to the church."

Abby rose from her seat and turned to face Martha with tears in her eyes.

"You look absolutely beautiful my dear." said Martha and then she noticed the tears. "Oh my goodness, what is it Abby? Are you feeling ill or are you just nervous."

Abby tried to cover up what she had been thinking and took both of Martha's hands in her own, "I'm sorry, I was just thinking about Aunt Lillian and how much I wish she could see me now."

Martha released her hands and embraced Abby, "That's understandable, dear. I'm sure she's looking down on you right now and feeling very, very proud."

Julia had been listening and was getting impatient. "Don't you think we should get going, or we'll be late? Don't forget your bouquet Abby, it's on the dresser."

When Ed saw Abby coming down the aisle of the church on his father's arm, he was overwhelmed with love for her. He had always imagined finding the girl of his dreams and now she was walking towards him and about to become his wife.

When Abby had to recite her vows, she wasn't sure she could get through the rest of the ceremony but Ed's reassuring smile gave her the strength and it only seemed like minutes had passed before the minister pronounced them husband and wife.

The reception at the Harrison's home was magical. Martha had decorated the house in all the Christmas finery but most of the accents were in white. Even the tree was covered in artificial snow and there were miniature twinkling white lights everywhere. There were fifty guests, mostly relatives and friends of the Harrison's, while Abby only had one guest, her friend Marion. Despite this she played the perfect hostess along with Martha encouraging everyone to indulge in the extravagant buffet set up in the dining room and she drank just enough wine to take the edge off her nerves and allow her to enjoy herself. It was only when she thought about the night to come that she began to feel anxious again.

Just before midnight Ed and Abby left the party to drive to the Park Plaza Hotel. Abby had changed into a two-piece powder blue suit, which accented her eyes, and as they left the house, all of the guests gathered on the front lawn to wave them off and wish them well. They had arranged to stay in Toronto for the first night of their honeymoon then drive to Montreal for the next five days with the intention of being home in time for New Year's Eve. Ed was obviously excited about finally being alone with Abby and kept stealing glances at her as he drove into the centre of the city, "You looked so beautiful today, Abby, I couldn't take my eyes off you when you were coming down the aisle."

Abby smiled and put her hand gently on Ed's thigh, "Well, you didn't look so bad yourself."

Abby's gesture made Ed even more excited and he could hardly wait to get to the hotel and finally be able to make love to her.

Checking in at the reception desk brought reality home to Abby when Ed signed them in as Mr. & Mrs. Ed Harrison. She was actually married to this man and she vowed to try and make him happy.

Once in the room, Ed had no desire to open the bottle of champagne that John and Martha had sent and immediately disappeared into the bathroom while urging Abby to change into her nightclothes. When he finally emerged dressed in burgundy silk pajamas, Abby was still sitting on the chaise longue in her blue suit.

Ed came and sat beside her, "Abby, why aren't you changing?"

Once again tears sprang to Abby's eyes, "Just give me a few moments, please Ed."

"My darling, don't be frightened. I know this is all new to you but I promise I won't hurt you. I promise I'll be very gentle and if you want me to stop you just have to say so."

Minutes later, Abby retired to the bathroom and when she emerged she was wearing a full-length white lace nightgown. The low neckline was trimmed with pink ribbon and she looked even more beautiful than she had looked in her wedding dress. Ed, who was sitting in bed with the bedclothes drawn up to his chest, gasped at the sight of her, "Oh Abby darling, you look amazing. Come over here, I want to see you in the light."

Abby slowly walked over to the bed and when Ed pulled back the covers she gingerly crawled in beside him. When he began to kiss her, it felt different than all the times before when they had kissed and she knew she was about to experience the mystery of what went on between a husband and wife behind closed doors. As Ed became more passionate, he forced his tongue between her lips and when his hands roamed roughly over her breasts she was more frightened than excited but did not have the heart to tell him to stop. It was only when he quickly discarded his pajama bottoms then lifted her nightgown and thrust himself into her that she felt she couldn't endure any more and cried out, "Please Ed, stop, please stop." But it was too late for Ed, he was too aroused to stop now and continued thrusting himself in and out and it was then that Abby realized the pain had subsided but she still desperately wanted it over with. Finally with a great shudder, Ed collapsed on top of her and a moment later rolled over onto his back, "Wow, that was great Abby, I hope you enjoyed it too. Better get some sleep now, we have a long drive tomorrow," and with that he turned away from her and minutes later was sound asleep and snoring softly.

After ten minutes, Abby crept out of bed and into the bathroom to wash away all evidence of their lovemaking. She wondered how people could actually call it that because it reminded her of the farm animals she had sometimes seen mating in Oakfield. She finally concluded that this must be the way it was for everyone and she might just as well get used to it.

CHAPTER 7

ON NEW YEAR'S EVE after returning from their honeymoon, Ed and Abby spent a joyous evening with John and Martha at the Palais Royal. Everyone was dressed in long evening gowns, dancing to an eleven-piece swing band, and the buffet was overflowing with hot and cold entrees and all kinds of desserts, which were hard to resist.

Abby had actually enjoyed her honeymoon in Montreal despite having to endure Ed's constant attempts at lovemaking. They had toured the city enjoying the French ambience and had eaten in some of the finest restaurants. They had even driven to the Laurentians, spent a night in a lodge and tried skiing. To Abby, the pure white snow and the mountains made it seem like a fairyland and she came to realize how little of the world she had seen growing up in Oakfield. Now back home in Toronto after only one day they were having a wonderful evening but Abby knew that as the New Year began, she would be facing the reality of her life with Ed.

Abby was still in the process of decorating their house but was already thinking about going back to work. Ed was not pleased with this idea and wanted Abby at home. He had come from a traditional household where his mother had never worked and had always been at the beck and call of his father. Martha maintained a spotless home and every night when John came home from his office, no matter what the time, Martha had a hot meal waiting for him.

In the two months that Abby had spent at the Harrisons' before her marriage, she should have realized that this was what Ed had expected and she was disappointed when he didn't understand that she needed to do something more constructive than housekeeping. Her disappointment was short lived when in late February she began to experience morning sickness and suspected that she might be pregnant. When the family doctor confirmed her suspicions, Ed was ecstatic and John and Martha were over the moon at the prospect of becoming grandparents. Only Julia was cynical about the coming event, "Boy, you didn't waste any time," she remarked with a smirk, "fed up with each other's company already?"

Ed was used to Julia's sarcasm but this was beyond acceptable, "What's the matter Julia, feeling a little jealous, are we? Isn't it about time you and Raymond thought about having a family?"

Julia's eyes blazed, "For your information, I don't want any snotty nosed little kids around. Raymond and I are quite happy by ourselves."

Ed knew this wasn't true and was well aware that his brother had always wanted children but deciding not to interfere any further, he shrugged and walked away.

Ten months, almost to the day of their marriage, their first child was born. Like Ed, he had red hair, light green eyes and Abby's slim build and she adored him from the moment she set eyes on him. Abby's pregnancy had been difficult, she had a urinary infection that just wouldn't seem to go away and she was fatigued most of the time but the actual birth had been surprisingly quick. Just three hours after her first contraction, her son entered the world.

Abby had never felt such tremendous love for any other human being before. Even while he slept, she would sit gazing at his tiny face just waiting for him to wake up so that she could pamper him. She named him Daniel in spite of Ed's minor objection and decided that with this addition to the family, life couldn't get any better.

When Daniel was just over a year old and beginning to take his first steps, Abby became pregnant again. At first she felt deprived as though someone was trying to take her attention away from her precious little son but as the months passed she began to look forward to the new baby. While the first birth had been relatively easy, there were complications with the second delivery and after eighteen exhausting hours of labor, Kate Lillian Harrison was born.

Abby couldn't believe her good fortune. She realized that caring for her husband and children brought her great contentment and she settled into a daily routine just as she had with Aunt Lillian. She no longer had the desire to work outside of the home and Ed, being fairly successful, provided well for his family while Martha spent many happy hours with Abby helping to care for the children.

CHAPTER 8

AS DANIEL APPROACHED HIS eighth birthday he began to develop a real charm. The excessive love his mother had given him seemed to bounce right back onto anyone who came into contact with him. He had a smile that would melt the heart of the most disagreeable individual but at the same time he was slightly reserved, overly polite and almost a little too old for his years. Meanwhile, his sister Kate was a bundle of energy, always laughing and totally independent since she had learned to cope in her own little world without all the doting attention of her mother. At six-years-old, Kate had inherited Abby's looks with dark curly hair and bright blue eyes and she was slightly built but taller than most children her age. Being the less favoured child one would have thought she would feel some animosity towards her brother but she was so good natured and had such generosity of spirit that she paid him almost as much attention as her mother did. Ed was well aware of the situation involving his children and tried to focus on Kate whenever he was home but he worked long hours and often traveled out of town so Kate rarely saw her father.

Abby had decided that Daniel's eighth birthday was going to be an exceptional occasion and she began busying herself with arrangements for a large party. She invited several of Daniel's school friends and some of the neighbor's children as well as his grandparents, his Uncle Raymond and Aunt Julia. While John and Martha had played an important role in Daniel's young life, Raymond tended to stay out of the picture and Abby was positive that Julia was to blame. True to her word, Julia remained childless and was adamant that it would stay that way and she tried to avoid children at all costs. Abby was, therefore, somewhat surprised when Julia accepted her invitation to the party and wondered how she would cope with the noise and all the little hands covered with ice cream and chocolate cake.

On the day of the party, the house was festooned with balloons and ribbons and Abby was surrounded with heaping plates of sandwiches and cookies which she had spent all morning preparing. Too busy to make a birthday cake, she had purchased an oversized chocolate cake covered in mounds of frosting from the local bakery and hid it in her bedroom closet while the refrigerator housed a bowl of strawberry jello and two tubs of ice cream, one vanilla and one mocha.

It was a cool fall day but hot in the kitchen and Abby suddenly felt weary and decided to put her feet up for a while. Two hours before the party was about to begin, she settled into her favourite chair and closed her eyes. Ed, meanwhile was making a last minute pickup of pop and other odd items needed for the party and Abby had deliberately arranged for Daniel and Kate to visit with their next door neighbor, who had just acquired a new pet rabbit, so that they would be out of the way and not have any idea about the surprise to come at home.

The sound of sirens woke Abby from her nap. She looked at her watch and realized she had been asleep for less than fifteen minutes but she felt an immediate sense of alarm and tiptoed slowly to the living room window, which looked out onto the street. Nothing looked out of place but the normal peacefulness of the neighbourhood was assaulted with the sound of voices yelling, and then suddenly a fire engine passed by with its bell clanging. Abby propelled herself towards the front door and out onto the street praying that nothing serious had happened. She noticed the ambulance as well as the fire engine and when she saw Ed sitting on the sidewalk with his head in his hands she had a sudden feeling of dread.

Jane Manning, Abby's neighbour, saw her come out of the house and immediately started running towards her. When she reached her, she grasped both of Abby's hands and tried to turn her away, "Don't go there Abby, you don't want to see. Please come into the house."

Abby pulled her hands away, "Why, what's happened?" she cried.

Jane persisted, "Please Abby, I beg you, come into the house and we can talk about it."

Abby shoved Jane roughly to one side and began to run towards the crowd of people that had gathered in the middle of the road. As she approached, the crowd seemed to sense her arrival and drew apart so that she became aware of the tiny figure with the mop of red hair lying lifeless on the ground and the paramedics surrounding it. When she realized it was Daniel, she screamed a primal scream that all mothers who had experienced great tragedy would recognize and fell to her knees throwing herself across the tiny body. It was only with coaxing and tender words that the paramedics were finally able to pull her away and explain that there was nothing they could do. There was no possible way that Abby could accept that her beloved Daniel was dead and merciful oblivion took over her mind and body as she slumped into a heap on the floor.

Abby remained in a state of shock for six long weeks. She accepted the condolences of family and friends and attended the funeral suitably dressed in a plain black dress with a touch of white at the throat, but she resembled a robot programmed to do all the right things without any expression or feeling. The result of a stupid accident had deprived her of her dearest possession and she was consumed with grief. It was when she learned the details of what had happened that she found it even more difficult to cope. Daniel had run out into the road, chasing the neighbor's wayward rabbit. Darting between two parked cars he ran right into the path of his father, who had just turned the corner after completing his errands. Daniel didn't stand a chance against any vehicle, let alone the heavy family station wagon. Ed was not to blame; there was no way he could have stopped in time to avoid his son and if Abby was having a difficult time, Ed was forced to deal with guilt as well as loss.

With both parents preoccupied in their own private worlds, Kate, in her struggle for survival and recognition, found love and solace with her grandparents and even Julia managed to hold out a helping hand to her niece.

CHAPTER 9

ONE YEAR LATER ON the anniversary of Daniel's death and what would have been his ninth birthday, Kate was lying curled up asleep on the rose velvet chesterfield in her grandparent's house. Martha sat close by in the matching wing chair quietly knitting while John sat opposite reading the daily newspaper. Every few minutes Martha would glance over at Kate and audibly sigh. Usually her knitting soothed any anxiety she felt. She had been making multicoloured scarves for several years and took great pleasure in giving them away every winter to the homeless who dropped in for coffee, cookies and sometimes a slice of cake every Tuesday afternoon, at the local church. The click of her needles used to annoy John but he had become used to it and took comfort in seeing his wife indulging in such a satisfying pastime.

After an hour of silence except for the clicking and the constant sighing Martha suddenly dropped her knitting into her lap, "I can't stand this anymore. I'm going to give that daughter-in-law of mine a piece of my mind."

John scowled as he peered over his reading glasses, "I don't think that's a very good idea, you can't go interfering, you might make things worse."

"How can I possibly make things worse? Kate is obviously being neglected and I can't bear to see her so unhappy."

Martha had been concerned when Abby had dropped Kate off at the front door early that morning. She claimed she had a nagging headache and needed some peace and quiet and as soon as Martha had ushered Kate into the house, Abby had jumped into her car and driven off without uttering another word. Kate had immediately begun to cry and stamped her foot in frustration, "Mommy hates me," she said and started sobbing uncontrollably.

Martha was shocked and put her arm around Kate's shoulders, "Oh darling girl, what brought this on?"

Kate continued to cry for a moment and then looked up at her grandmother; her eyes still brimming with tears, "She hates me, she's never liked me but she always kissed me goodbye. Why did Daniel have to die? Everything was better when he was here even though he was always her favourite."

Martha embraced the small body, stroking her hair over and over in an attempt to comfort her, "Oh Kate, I'm sure your Mommy loves you, it's just that she's terribly sad."

"No," Kate protested, "I think she hates Daddy too. She never talks to him anymore."

"Well dear, Mommy and Daddy have been through a lot but I'm sure things are going to get better."

"No they won't. Daddy sometimes stays out all night and when he's home he just sits around drinking beer and then he talks all funny. And this morning Mommy baked a cake for Daniel's birthday but he's dead. He can't eat the cake," and Kate began to cry again.

Martha was so disturbed at this turn of events that she had no idea what to say or do. It was only later after she had calmed Kate down and persuaded her to rest that she began to think about what course of action she should take.

Martha arrived at her son's house and wasted no time in marching up to the front door and ringing the bell. After several moments when Abby did not appear, she pushed the bell again, letting it ring continuously and it took very little time before her persistence paid off. Abby threw open the door and seeing it was Martha all alone on the doorstep she immediately thought some other tragedy had occurred and something had happened to Kate. "Martha," she cried, "Where's Kate, why isn't she with you?"

"Like you really care," replied Martha pushing her way passed Abby into the house.

Abby followed her mother-in-law, as she made her way into the living room, and then turned on her heel with her hands on her hips, her lips drawn together in a scowl.

"I don't know what you mean, of course I care. Where is she?"

"She's fast asleep on the chesterfield in my house after crying her eyes out," Martha replied raising her voice, "She thinks you hate her and I can see why. You come over and dump her onto John and me claiming to have a headache and you don't even say goodbye to her let alone give her a hug or a kiss. You lavished all your attention on Daniel while he was alive and you're still paying him more attention than Kate. She told me about the cake you made for Daniel's birthday. What is wrong with you Abby?

Daniel is dead and it's time you recognized that fact and realize that you have another child who needs you."

Abby, who had sunk into one of the deep chintz armchairs while Martha was berating her, looked stricken and her mouth began to tremble.

Martha had no intention of allowing Abby to feel sorry for herself, "Don't you dare cry, there's been enough of that. Daniel's been dead for a year and we have all suffered but that poor girl has suffered more than all of us. If it weren't for her grandfather and me, and even Julia, she wouldn't get any love at all."

Abby was stunned. From the time she had first met her mother-in-law, she had always thought of her as a mild mannered, kind and thoughtful woman. It was hard for her to equate that image with the person who stood looking down on her now with her hands on her hips.

"I don't know what to say," she stammered, "I had no idea that Kate was so unhappy."

"How could you possibly know when you hardly even know she's there? Yes, you feed her, clothe her, and drive her to school but you don't see her. She's only seven-years-old for goodness sake and she needs her mother. As for Ed, I have no idea what's going on there but I intend to find out. No son of mine is going to treat my grandchild as though she doesn't exist."

Abby could no longer hold back her tears, "Oh Martha, I am so sorry. I've been living in the past and I know it has to stop, I miss Daniel so much."

Martha showed no sympathy, "You're right, it has to stop. You have to make a decision, either you go on being miserable for the rest of your life or you start right this minute changing your outlook. I expect you to pick up

Kate by suppertime and bring her home then you can start making it up to her."

Abby rose to her feet but had trouble looking Martha in the eye, "I'll be there, I promise."

"Well, make sure you are," and with that Martha headed for the front door, "and I'll be talking to Ed about all this."

Abby followed and as Martha was about to close the door behind her, she quietly muttered, "Thank you."

When Martha arrived back home she was surprised to learn that Julia, having arrived half an hour before, had taken Kate to the park to play on the swings. She was well aware that her niece was being neglected but she didn't expect Martha to confront Abby.

"How did it go, dear?" John asked in his usual quiet manner.

"First of all, what did you tell Julia?"

"Just that you couldn't stand to see Kate so unhappy any longer and were going to talk to her mother."

Martha looked puzzled, "I just can't get over the way Julia has changed. When she's around Kate, she's like a different person."

John had always been a discerning man, "I think you might be seeing the real Julia. I know she had a difficult childhood and so she's learned to be a fighter. She puts on this veneer but I believe it's all a cover up for her insecurities. She probably relates Kate's situation to her own as a little girl, anyway I'm glad to see the softer side of her."

Martha nodded, "You know John, Raymond always told us we didn't really know her. When he told me she was a loving and caring person, I thought he had to be joking. From the first time I met her, I always felt there was a wall between us."

John put down his paper and removed his glasses, "Perhaps we shouldn't judge people so easily but you still haven't told me what happened with Abby."

Martha proceeded to tell John about the confrontation, and as she did so he looked more and more uncomfortable, "I think you were a little harsh dear," he remarked when she had finally finished.

"Nonsense, it was just what she needed. I hope it was a wake up call because if there isn't any change I'm going to do something about it?"

John felt a sense of alarm, "What do you intend to do?"

"Why, I'll try and get custody of Kate, of course!"

"Now you are being overly dramatic. I'm sure things will be better from now on."

Martha shrugged, "Well, they'd better be. I'm not placing all the blame on Abby. That son of yours needs a good talking to."

John smiled, "Oh, so he's just my son now when he's in the doghouse."

Martha sat on the arm of John's chair and smiled back, "You know what I mean dear."

John patted her hand and settled back to finish his paper but his mind was on Martha. He had been married to her for over thirty-five years and he loved her even more than the day they had said their wedding vows. She had been an exceptional wife, always there when he got home from the office, ready to attend to his needs and listen to him when he wanted to talk. Being a lawyer, there was so much that he couldn't discuss with her but she sensed when he was working on a hard case and made an extra effort to make him feel at ease in his own home. He wished that both of his sons could have been so lucky in their choice of a wife.

When Abby arrived to pick Kate up, she was surprised to find her sitting at the dining room table playing a game of Go Fish with Julia. After greeting Martha silently at the front door and acknowledging John she stood quietly watching her sister-in-law and her daughter from the entrance to the dining room. Julia was so engrossed in the game that it was minutes later before she finally noticed Abby and immediately rose from her chair, "Abby," she said, "how nice to see you," then turning to Kate she continued, "Kate, look your Mommy is here to take you home."

Kate looked up petulantly at her mother, "I don't want to go home. I want to stay here with you Aunt Julia."

Julia approached Abby and touched her lightly on the shoulder, "It's all right," she whispered, "She'll come around in a minute."

Abby bowed her head, "I don't blame her for not wanting to come home. I've been thinking a lot about what Martha said to me."

Julia shook her head and ushered Abby towards the living room while calling to Kate, "Stay here honey, I'll be back soon, Mommy and I are just going to have a little chat."

Once in the living room, Abby noticed that John and Martha were nowhere to be seen and she had a sense of apprehension. She sought protection behind John's wing chair resting her hands, one on top of the other, on the high back, "I don't understand, Julia," she said, "it's no secret that we've never exactly been friends. Why are you suddenly so interested in Kate?"

Julia smiled and sat down on the piano stool, "I know I've always said I didn't want any kids and I haven't spent much time around them but over the years I've noticed Kate has grown into a sweet and thoughtful child. Then since Daniel's death, she's been so lost and I can't help feeling sorry for her. My own parents were drowned in a boating accident when I was Kate's age and I was brought up in an orphanage so I know what it feels like to be abandoned. Maybe I've come off pretty harsh at times and if so I apologize but I really want to help Kate, and you too if you will let me."

Abby was caught off guard, "I had no idea about your childhood Julia, I am so sorry."

"No need to be sorry, I didn't tell you about myself for sympathy Abby. I just want you to know that I understand, not only about Kate because she feels abandoned but you too because you lost your son."

Abby came out from behind the chair and walked over to Julia, "Thank you Julia, I really appreciate your concern and I want you to know that I'm going to do my utmost to make it up to Kate."

It was then that Martha arrived and Julia decided it was time Abby had a little break, "Abby's just leaving," she said and with that she took Abby by the arm and led her back to Kate. "Okay Kate, time to go home, Mommy has a surprise for you."

Kate was cautious but young enough to be tempted and slowly got out of her chair. It was then that Abby took her hand and led her towards the front door frowning at Julia over the child's head.

Julie mouthed the words, "Ice cream, Rocky Road!"

That day, two women had come to an understanding that proved to be the beginning of a life long friendship neither of them expected. And that evening turned out to be a new beginning for Abby and Kate.

CHAPTER 10

IT TOOK ABBY LESS than a week to change the relationship with Kate. On their first night home alone together, with Ed out of town, Abby tried to assure Kate that she was now the single most important person in her life. When Kate was securely tucked up in bed, Abby didn't just pat the bedclothes and murmur "Goodnight" and then leave the room, she sat down on the side of the bed and gently stroked Kate's hair, "Things are going to be different from now on Kate," she said, "I know I haven't been a very good mother since Daniel died and I'm going to make it up to you. You mean more than the world to me and I love you very, very much. We are going to start doing things together starting tomorrow."

Kate peered up at her mother in the semi darkness, "But why did you hate me so much Mommy, I don't understand?"

"Oh Katie darling," Abby sighed, "I could never ever hate you. I was just so depressed when your brother died and I forgot how to be happy. I've been living in the past and although I'll never forget Daniel, I have to accept the fact that he's gone but you are here, my precious girl."

"But why did you make Daniel a cake today? I know it would have been his birthday but he's dead Mommy."

"I can't explain that Kate; I'm just so sorry for everything and I hope you'll forgive me."

Kate reached up and threw her little arms around Abby's neck. "I forgive you Mommy, now what are we going to do together tomorrow?"

Abby had tears in her eyes but she couldn't help smiling at Kate's practical change of subject, "Well, it's Sunday so we have all day to think of stuff, but how about we talk about changing your whole room?"

Kate's eyes lit up, "Oh could I have a bed like Ellie? She has a bed with posts and frilly curtains and I just love it."

"It's called a canopy bed and yes you may have one, but if you go to sleep now, right after breakfast tomorrow, we'll come back here and talk about everything."

"Oh Mommy I don't think I'll be able to sleep, I'm so excited."

Abby leaned over and kissed Kate gently on the cheek, "I'm sure you'll be in dreamland in a few minutes, but in those few minutes just remember that I love you and I always will. Goodnight honey."

Abby felt a tremendous sense of relief when she left Kate's room and the unrelenting depression she had been experiencing seemed to have lifted but she knew she still had work to do. It was time to talk to Ed about his frequent absences, his drinking and his indifference towards his family. The fact that he was away from home on this particular Saturday night didn't make sense. He was supposed to be on a business trip in Ottawa but there was no explanation for him to be away on a weekend and he hadn't bothered to phone. Abby wasn't worried about him; she had no illusions that he had been in an accident or was physically ill. He had done this so many times in the last year that she had begun to suspect that he might be having an affair and she considered confronting him about it.

Ed finally arrived home on Sunday night after Abby and Kate had spent the day listing all the changes Kate wanted to make to her room. Kate had already gone to bed, thrilled to know that she would soon be sleeping in a pink wonderland full of frills and flounces with a sky blue ceiling full of clouds and small twinkling stars that would dance overhead at night. Abby didn't bother to get up when Ed entered the living room, throwing his briefcase onto an occasional table that stood just inside the entranceway. He barely glanced at Abby as he headed for the kitchen, retrieved a beer from the refrigerator and then sauntered back nonchalantly, "How's it going?" he asked.

Abby turned to look at him and couldn't hide her disdain, "How do you think it's going? I spent yesterday with your mother on my case about the way I was treating Kate and I can't say I blame her. She was right and she gave me the wakeup call I needed."

"Wait a minute," Ed intervened, "Are you telling me my mother starting interfering in our lives?"

"There's no need to be indignant, she had every right, after all she is Kate's grandmother. She taught me a valuable lesson and I intend to change things for the better. I've done nothing but mire in my own self-pity since Daniel died, but he's gone and life has to go on. Kate and I spent the whole day together today and although I haven't been paying much attention to how she felt before, she seemed happy today. Now it's your turn to start putting some effort into this marriage Ed, and to start giving Kate the love she deserves."

Ed had been standing shaking his head while Abby spoke, "Are you suggesting I'm a rotten husband and father?" he asked, his voice rising.

"Yes, that's exactly what I'm suggesting. Where have you been all weekend and where have you been all those other times you haven't come home? When are you going to stop drinking and when are you going to show Kate and me some affection?"

Ed slammed his beer down, spilling some of the contents, "I've been working, for your information. Who do you think pays for everything around here? Hey, I didn't come home to listen to this crap, I'm going to bed."

Abby immediately jumped up and grabbed his arm, "You just can't walk away Ed, this is important."

Ed was surprised at Abby's aggressive behaviour, "Get your hands off me, lady," he growled and raised his hand as if to strike her.

Abby was so taken back that she retreated behind the chair she had been sitting in, "What are you going to do now Ed," she cried, "Start knocking me around?"

Ed glared back at Abby then turned on his heel and stomped out of the room and up the stairs. Meanwhile, Abby stared hopelessly after him wondering what had become of the kind, gentle man she had married.

CHAPTER 11

IN THE FOLLOWING FEW weeks Abby kept herself busy redecorating Kate's bedroom. She decided to take on the whole project by herself in order to save money and take her mind off the growing distance developing with Ed. His erratic behaviour had increased to the point where he was drinking daily and staying away from home several nights each week. They barely spoke to each other and the intimate side of their marriage had ceased to exist.

Abby was desperately unhappy but had no idea how to handle the situation and she rejected the idea of going to Martha for help. Even though her mother-in-law had indicated that she was going to confront Ed, Abby was sure that John had talked her out of any interference. Meanwhile the relationship between Abby and Kate grew stronger as they spent more and more time together. Often after supper, when Abby had helped with Kate's homework, they would go for a walk, watch TV or play a card game. On weekends, because it was November and the weather was getting colder, they would go to a movie and stop by Fran's where they would feast on grilled cheese or western sandwiches followed by apple pie or an ice cream sundae. Kate had come out of her shell and relished this time with her mother. Sometimes she would be almost glad that Daniel was gone and she had Abby all to herself, but then she would feel guilty and pray silently for Daniel's forgiveness.

On the weekend before Christmas, Abby and Kate had spent all day Sunday decorating the tree that John had delivered the week before, and stringing up streamers and sprigs of holly all around the living room. They were both exhausted and looking forward to the roast chicken supper that Abby had prepared early that morning and then watching television, when suddenly Abby heard the front door open. She hadn't expected to see Ed as he had just left late on Saturday evening and it was rare for him to be away for just one night. She was aware of him opening the closet door to put his heavy overcoat away and going directly to the kitchen where she expected him to be looking for his favourite beer. She continued to hang the last crystal ball on the tree and turning to Kate said, "Kate darling, why don't you go and say hi to Daddy."

Kate took Abby's hand, "No Mommy, I don't want to. He's gone to get drunk again and I don't like him like that because he gets all quiet and sort of mean."

"Oh, honey," Abby said kneeling down so that she was at eye level with Kate, "I think it will be okay tonight. We have to be nice to Daddy and then he won't be mean."

Kate was just about to protest again when Ed walked into the room and flopped down in his favorite chair balancing his bottle of beer precariously on the arm.

"Hello Daddy", Kate said, half hiding behind her mother's skirt.

"What's the matter Kate, don't I get a hug anymore?" said Ed scowling.

Kate stepped tentatively forward and attempted to put her arms around her father's neck but she recoiled at the smell on his breath. Ed sensing her reluctance to embrace him grabbed her arm. "Why don't you sit on my knee princess?" he said smiling.

Abby reacted immediately and pulled Kate away, "It's her bed time Ed, she's had a long day helping with all the decorations and she's very tired".

Kate looked up gratefully at her mother avoiding the annoyed look on her father's face, "Yes, I do feel tired Mommy and I have school tomorrow."

"Come along then Kate, we'll get you washed and into your pajamas," and with that Abby hustled Kate out of the room.

After tucking Kate up in bed and reading to her from her favourite book, The Wind in the Willows, Abby made her way downstairs only to find that Ed had fallen asleep. There was so much she wanted to say to him but knowing he'd been drinking, anything she said would probably antagonize him so she sat down quietly opposite him and picked up a magazine. Her attempt to engross herself in her reading was futile and she found herself staring at the man she had married so many years ago. Ed was never a handsome man but he had always had a boyish appeal about him until the loss of his son and the onset of his habitual drinking. Now his once red hair was unkempt; his face was puffy with distinct bags under the eyes and he stooped over like an old man.

Abby had changed too, she had gained a little weight and taken less interest in her appearance, but her hair was still dark without a hint of gray and she had noticed on many occasions that men she passed on the street often gave her a second glance.

Ed began to stir and then almost as though he became aware of Abby staring at him he opened his eyes and muttered, "What are you looking at?"

Abby dropped her gaze to the magazine that was resting in her lap, "I was just thinking, that's all."

"Oh yeah, what about?"

Abby resigned herself to the fact that she needed to tell Ed how she really felt, "I was thinking about us Ed and what's happened to our marriage. I know that since Daniel died I haven't exactly been easy to live with but then neither have you. You're hardly ever here, you drink all the time and when you are here, you're like a stranger in your own home."

Ed leaned forward in his chair bristling with anger, "So you're blaming me for everything, is that right?"

Abby lowered her voice, "No Ed, I already admitted that I've been somewhat to blame."

"Doesn't sound like that to me. I'm not home a lot because I'm busy making money to put food on the table and have a couple of beers now and then, so what?"

"That's not altogether true Ed, I know you work hard but there's no excuse for you to be away from home on weekends and you drink a lot more than a couple of beers. Go look in the garbage and you'll see an empty scotch bottle plus a half full one in the cupboard."

Ed got up and stood menacingly over Abby, "So you're keeping tabs on what I'm drinking now. Well, what I do is my business and if I want to stay out on a weekend, I'll damn well do that too."

Abby was almost speechless but managed to whisper, "Is there someone else, Ed?"

Ed's face turned red and he took a step back, "No way lady, I have enough problems coping with you and my mother?"

"What do you mean? " Abby asked, "What has your mother done?"

"She was on my back for weeks until I finally stopped going over there. I don't need the aggravation and I don't need your nagging."

"I'm not nagging Ed, I just want things to go back to the way they were before Daniel died. I thought we were happy then."

Ed sighed and flopped down in his chair again, "Things will never be the same Abby, now let's just drop the subject I'm tired."

Abby persisted, "You can't just leave things like this Ed, we need help. Maybe we should go to a marriage counsellor or talk to someone at the church."

She was totally unprepared when Ed shot up and stalked towards her with his eyes blazing, "Enough," he yelled, "I've had enough, just shut your mouth lady or I'll shut it for you."

Abby cowered and threw her arm protectively over her face, "Don't you dare touch me Ed," she screamed.

Ed tried to pull her arm away, "Yeah, and what are you going to do about it?"

Abby struggled out of his grip and ran out of the room towards the stairwell where to her horror she saw Kate sitting on one of the steps staring through the banister with tears in her eyes. She ran quickly up the stairs and scooping Kate up in her arms she murmured, "Oh honey, please don't cry, everything's going to be alright."

Kate buried her head in Abby's shoulder, "But why is Daddy yelling, it's making me scared?"

Abby took Kate into her room and laid her gently on the bed, "We were just having a little argument that's all and there's no need to be afraid."

"I saw him Mommy, he was going to hit you," Kate protested.

Abby took Kate's hands in her own, "No honey, Daddy wouldn't hit me, he's just tired, he had a bad day. There's no need for you to worry, it's time you were asleep and you have school in the morning."

Kate pulled on her mother's hands, "Please lie down next to me Mommy," she begged.

Abby stretched out beside the small body and wrapped her arms around her, "I'm here and I'm not going away until I hear you snoring."

Kate giggled, "I don't snore Mommy."

"Well it must have been the Sandman that I heard."

"Who's the Sandman Mommy?"

"He's a spirit who brings sleep and wonderful dreams by sprinkling magic sand on sleeping children."

"Can I see him tonight?"

"No Kate, nobody ever sees him, if they did he wouldn't be magic. Now go to sleep or he won't come."

"Okay Mommy, night, night," and Kate closed her eyes while Abby stared at the twinkling stars that now illuminated the bedroom and vowed to keep her precious daughter safe.

CHAPTER 12

IN THE FOLLOWING WEEK leading up to Christmas, Abby did her best to stay out of Ed's way. Uncharacteristically he was at home for supper every night, but rather than sitting at the dining room table with Abby and Kate, he parked himself in front of the TV balancing his plate on his knees and with the ever present bottle of beer close at hand. Abby was relieved that she didn't have to deal with his moods, but she felt sad for Kate who once again had to settle for indifference from one of her parents.

Abby decided that despite the problems within her marriage, she was determined not to let it spoil the coming holiday. The whole family was gathering at Martha and John's on Christmas Day, as they had every year since Ed and Raymond were small children. Not only was the immediate family invited but also Martha's younger brother Hugh, his wife Betty and their two teenage children, Alex and Jessie. Abby knew just how excited Kate was and not wanting her to be disappointed, she decided to remind Ed that he should buy a gift for his daughter but he merely threw a few dollar bills at her and suggested she take care of the problem.

On Christmas morning when Kate opened her gifts, she was thrilled with the new clothes that her mother had bought, and when Ed came down for breakfast, she quickly kissed him on the cheek thanking him for her new Barbie doll with the three new outfits, including a prom gown of pink organza. Thankfully, she had no idea that her father had made no effort to find a gift for her.

Late in the afternoon, the family assembled for Christmas dinner and Martha, as always, had prepared a feast. She was never content to serve the traditional turkey with two or three vegetables and plum pudding for dessert. Abby, who was helping to bring the dishes to the table, thought Martha must have been up all night cooking. Not only was there turkey with onion dressing and thick savoury gravy but honey glazed ham, both mashed and roast potatoes, yams, peas, carrots, Brussel sprouts and for dessert, plum pudding, brandied fruitcake and lemon meringue pie.

Kate was happy to see Alex and Jessie again. She hadn't seen them since the previous April, when Uncle Hugh and Aunt Betty, as she called them, had been at her grandmother's for an Easter celebration. Although the teenagers were years older than Kate, she felt more comfortable not having to be the only child at the table and she was a little in awe of Jessie who was wearing a crimson dress and wearing her honey blond hair in a sleek pageboy style.

Julia, who had arrived in style with Raymond bearing an armful of gifts for everyone, looked particularly stunning in a straight dark green velvet skirt and off the shoulder black sweater. Her hair was in its usual chignon and she wore long drop earrings of gold intertwined with pearls. Abby felt positively dowdy beside her, but she had dispensed with any negative feelings about her sister-in-law since the day she realized how much Julia cared for Kate.

Dinner was a happy occasion except for one somber moment when John proposed a toast to absent family and friends, and everyone's thoughts turned to Daniel who had always been the life and soul of the party. Abby's eyes were filled with tears but she struggled to overcome her sadness for Kate's sake.

Ed had begun drinking long before they had arrived at his parent's house and he continued to drink all through dinner, forsaking his usual beer for white wine and champagne. By the time dinner was over and dishes were already being cleared from the table, he was obviously drunk but appeared to be in a jovial mood. It was when he started telling rather ribald jokes that Martha scowled at him in disapproval, "Okay son, I think we've heard enough of that," she said.

Ed just grinned and shook his head, "What's the matter Ma, too ripe for ya?"

John, realizing things might be getting out of hand, spoke up, "I think you've had enough to drink Ed, why don't I get you a cup of coffee?"

"Yes, that's a good idea," agreed Julia, "I'll go and make some, in fact I think we can all use a cup."

"Now hold on little lady," Ed countered rising from his seat and barring Julia's way into the kitchen, "Since when did you take over?"

Julia looked towards her husband for support but Raymond merely shook his head. She then stared Ed directly in the eyes and said, "Get out of my way Ed," but Ed stood his ground.

Abby, feeling she might be able to defuse the situation, gently took Ed's arm and whispered, "Let's go home," but he merely shook her off and continued staring back at Julia. It was only when his father, who was normally a very quiet and unassuming man, stepped between them that he began to back away. "I suggest you get out of here now son and go home. Abby and Kate will stay here until I'm sure you've had enough time to sober up."

Kate, who had been sitting open-mouthed watching the scenario unfold, had never seen her grandfather assert himself before and Abby was praying that her father-in-law had enough influence over Ed to make him leave the house. She was surprised when without a word Ed turned on his heels and slammed out of the front door, but when she heard the squeal of tires as he drove away, she began to wonder if he was too drunk to drive. Martha became very agitated and began wringing her hands together, "Oh my goodness John, what have you done? He shouldn't be driving, he could get in an accident."

John put his arm around Martha's shoulders, "Don't worry dear, he wasn't staggering, he was just drunk enough to be disruptive and disrespectful and I won't put up with that in our house."

"Quite right," Julia agreed, "Don't you think so, Raymond?" but her husband merely nodded then lowered his head. He had no intention in getting involved with a family problem.

An hour later as Abby was preparing to return home with Kate, Julia cornered her in the kitchen, "I hope you're going to be all right Abby," she said.

"Thank you Julia, but I'm hoping he's fallen asleep like he usually does after he's been drinking."

"Well, if there's a problem I want you to call me and don't be shy about it."

Abby was grateful for Julia's concern but she was still having difficulty accepting the change in her attitude after so many years of indifference. She decided to take the bull by the horns, "Why are you being so kind to me Julia?" she asked.

Julia smiled, "I don't have any ulterior motive, believe me. Look Abby, why don't we get together on Wednesday for lunch? I know Kate isn't at school this week but maybe you can drop her off here. We could go to that lovely little French restaurant a couple of blocks from my house and have a nice chat."

"I would really like that," Abby replied, "I haven't been to a decent restaurant for a long time."

"Good, let's make it one o'clock. I'll pick you up first then drop Kate off here and we'll be on our way."

Abby was relieved that for once she didn't have to make any decisions, "Thank you Julia, I look forward to it. I'll just go and make sure it's alright with Martha."

CHAPTER 13

JULIA AND ABBY WERE seated at a table for two next to a roaring fireplace in the Pandora Bistro. Even though it was the middle of the day, the restaurant had a dark, intimate atmosphere. Candles glowed on all of the tables, which were covered in deep red tablecloths to represent the Christmas season and the paintings of the French countryside hanging on the walls were draped in gleaming gold streamers and sprigs of holly.

From where she sat Abby, could see beyond the beautiful classic bay window onto the rear garden, which looked like a fairyland after the heavy snowfall that morning. All of the trees were twinkling with hundreds of fairy lights and the snow was still falling in large fluffy flakes.

Abby sighed, "This is just lovely Julia, thank you so much for asking me to lunch with you."

Julia was pleased with Abby's reaction. This was one of her favorite restaurants and she ate there often as was evident by the waiter's greeting when he approached their table, "Good afternoon, Madame Harrison, it's good to see you again," he remarked in a heavy French accent.

"Ah, Henri," Julia replied smiling up at him, "I am well. This is my sister-in-law and this is the first time she's been here, so I hope you are going to impress her."

"Of course Madame," he responded, "As always, we try to impress. Now may I get you both something to drink?"

"Yes," said Julia taking over, "Please bring us a bottle of your De Neuville Sauvignon".

"Right away Madame, an excellent suggestion," and Henri shuffled away with a mincing walk that made Abby chuckle quietly to herself.

"I hope you didn't mind me ordering for you Abby?" Julia asked.

"No, not at all. I'm afraid I'm a little out of touch with the finer things of life."

"Well, I won't begin to assume what you 'd like from the menu but I would recommend the Crevettes Mignonettes and the Crêpe François."

Abby briefly studied the menu but decided to defer to Julia's suggestions, "That sounds wonderful, that's what I'll have."

"Perfect," said Julia closing her own menu and placing it on the edge of the table, "Let's enjoy our food and then we can really talk."

After all dishes were cleared from the table and Abby sat back feeling full and contented with her cup of rich black coffee, she looked across the table at Julie and grinned, "That was one of the best lunches I've eaten. It's nice to try something new and I want to thank you for bringing me here."

"It was my pleasure," Julia beamed, "We will have to do this again but now we need to talk Abby."

"But we have been talking, haven't we?"

"Yes, about everything under the sun but your marriage and mine."

Abby looked shocked, “What do you mean, your marriage?”

“Later Abby, first we need to talk about Ed, I’m worried for you and Kate.”

“I know Ed is going to get better Julia, things can’t go on like this. I know he’s still suffering because of Daniel’s death but he’ll get through it just like I did.”

“It’s been too long and I hate to do this Abby, but you have to know the truth about Ed.”

Abby became a little defensive, “I don’t understand what you mean Julia and I still don’t understand why you’ve changed so much. I always thought you disliked me.”

Julia shook her head, “No Abby, you are so wrong. I never disliked you, I always envied you.”

“Envied me?’ Abby was incredulous. “Why on earth would you envy me, Julia? You’re a beautiful and successful woman. You have a good marriage, a wonderful home and there is very little you can’t afford. If the truth be known, I should envy you.”

Julia’s eyes teared up, “Those are only the things you see on the surface Abby. I’d give up everything to have a child like Kate and as for my marriage, it’s a sham.”

“Oh Julia,” Abby said leaning forward and clasping Julia’s hand,” I had no idea, you were always so adamant that you didn’t want any children.”

“It was all a lie, I can’t have children. I just put on an act to cover up the pain. That harsh woman you’ve always seen isn’t really the person I am. I always tried to block the idea of being a mother out of my mind but as I’ve gotten to know Kate and grown to love her, I’ve come to realize what I’m missing from my life.”

"But have you tried everything? What do the doctor's say? Surely there's something that can be done?"

"No, it's hopeless, I gave up years ago."

"What about adoption? There are a lot of children out there that need parents."

Julie shook her head, "I thought about that a lot but I just can't do it. I told you, my marriage is a sham and it wouldn't be fair on any child."

"I don't understand Julia," Abby said, "I thought you and Raymond were happy."

Julie smirked, "Happy? I'm miserable and I don't know how he feels but honestly I don't think he feels anything. It's like being tied down to a zombie, the only thing he shows any interest in is his job, and because we work together that's all he can talk about. He never wants to socialize with our friends anymore and I'm beginning to feel isolated. As for our sex life, well I can't remember the last time he even kissed me."

Abby began to look a little uncomfortable, "I am so sorry Julia. I always thought Raymond was a quiet man, rather like his father and he's always been a gentleman but it must be very difficult for you. Why are you staying with him if you are so unhappy?"

"That's just it, I'm not," Julia replied suddenly looking very determined, "Right after New Year and the company get-together I'm walking out."

"Really, does Raymond have any idea?"

"No, of course not, he's blind to everything except his damn job. Oops, sorry I didn't mean to curse."

Abby grinned and then looked concerned, "That's okay, but where are you going to go? What about the house and what about your job? Surely you can't go on working in the same law firm?"

Julia's mood suddenly seemed to change and she almost appeared excited, "I'll deal with the house later but I've found a wonderful little cottage style place to rent in the Beaches. It's so cute Abby and I can't wait to move in. As for my job, well I've applied to another law firm downtown and I'm almost positive that they're going to hire me."

"My goodness Julia, you've certainly been busy and I must say I have to admire you for your courage, I'm not sure I could be so brave."

"Of course you could," Julie said grasping Abby's hand, "And that's what I really wanted to talk to you about. Meanwhile all we've talked about are my problems."

Abby began to shake her head but Julia squeezed her hand, "No Abby, you have to listen. I hate to be the one to tell you this but I care about you and I particularly care about Kate. I can see your marriage going downhill and it's having a bad effect on both of you. I'm scared Abby that one of these days Ed is going to get violent with you. I've already seen how he can get when he's drunk."

"If you're talking about the other day," Abby protested, "he was just angry that's all. When I got home he was fast asleep and he stayed that way for the rest of the day."

"You don't understand Abby," Julia insisted, "I've actually seen him get violent. Three weeks ago, Raymond saw him in a bar with some brassy looking blonde and he was really drunk. Raymond tried to get him to go home and he was going to drive him but he ended up punching Raymond in the face and then he fell down in a stupor. It took three men to put him in our car and he stayed the night at our house. When he finally woke up, he didn't remember anything but he was furious. He told his brother that he had no right to interfere with his life and if he wanted to drink, it was his business."

Abby slumped in her chair, "Why didn't you tell me this before?" she asked.

"Raymond asked me not to get involved and if the truth be known, I'm surprised he even approached Ed in the first place. The less Raymond has to deal with personal issues, the better he likes it. Anyway, I decided to keep quiet until that fiasco at Christmas. You have to be very careful Abby and if you ever need any help, you know where to come."

Abby was barely listening; she couldn't get the picture of Ed with another woman out of her mind. There had been brief moments when she thought he might be cheating on her but Julia had made it a reality, "I think I'd like to go home now Julia, if you don't mind," she whispered.

"Oh Abby," Julia whispered back, "I am so sorry to have upset you but I had to warn you. I'll gladly drive you home whenever you're ready."

"I'll be ready as soon as we pay the bill," said Abby.

"I'll take care of it," Julia insisted as she waved Henri over to the table, "and I don't want any argument."

"Thank you so much," Abby said forcing a smile, "You've been so kind. I'll go and get our coats."

Abby was very quiet on the drive home and Julia decided to allow her time to absorb what she had told her, and when they arrived at Abby's house they briefly embraced and promised they would stay in touch.

The house was eerily quiet when Abby opened the front door but she was glad to have some time to herself before Martha brought Kate home for supper. She made herself a cup of coffee and walked out to the sunroom, which they had added onto the back of the house just after Daniel was born. It looked out onto the garden, which was now covered in a blanket of snow and Abby's thoughts turned back to the all the wonderful summers when she had spent hours tending to the flowerbeds. Daniel had loved the flowers and plants and she could remember the times when he wanted to help her, digging with his little trowel and insisting on watering everything in sight with his little plastic watering can. For the first time, Abby began to smile thinking about Daniel. She knew that she would always grieve for him but she would never again sink into the depths of despair that had taken a year out of her life and cost her daughter so dearly.

Placing her cup of coffee on the small wicker table she was about to sit down on one of the comfy padded chairs when she heard footsteps. As she hadn't expected anyone to be home it surprised her when Ed appeared in the doorway, "Oh Ed," she sighed with relief holding her hand over her heart, "You scared me. I didn't think you'd be home until tomorrow."

"Is that why you were off gallivanting somewhere and where's Kate?" he asked with a hint of sarcasm in his voice.

Abby noticed that he had obviously been drinking and his words were a little slurred, "I was with Julia, we had lunch together and Kate is at your mother's."

"With Julia," he smirked, "that's priceless. I thought you two didn't like each other. What does that bitch want?"

"She didn't want anything Ed," Abby replied trying to defuse the situation, "we've gotten to know each other a little better and I actually quite like her."

"So you decided to go to lunch together, eh?"

"Yes and we had a very nice time; we went to a lovely French restaurant near Julia's house."

"And I suppose this so called restaurant was damn expensive," said Ed, his voice rising.

"Yes, but….," Abby didn't get the chance to finish.

"Hah! So you go off gallivanting when I'm not around, palming Kate off on my mother and spending all my money in some fancy restaurant," Ed yelled as he stalked towards Abby.

Abby tried to back up but she had nowhere to go, "It wasn't like that Ed," she said nervously, "Julia paid."

"I hate that bitch and you're getting just like her. I forbid you to see her again, do you hear me?" he roared as he came even closer.

Abby was terrified but suddenly something inside her snapped and she took a step forward and stared Ed in the face, "I heard you Ed but I'm your wife, not your slave. You can't tell me whom I can or cannot see. If I want to see Julia, I will and you can't stop me," and with that she tried to get past him but he grasped her wrist and twisted her arm behind her back.

Ed's eyes were bulging but Abby continued to stare him down, "You think you're pretty smart, don't you?" he screamed, "Well nobody gets the better of me."

Abby didn't remember much after that; she was only aware of a pounding headache as she opened her eyes and tried to sit up from her position on the sunroom floor. She noticed the wicker table was toppled over and her cup lay shattered beside her with its contents spilled on the terrazzo tiles. Resting in a sitting position against the chair, she gingerly felt the back of her head and noticed a distinct bump, which was tender to the touch, but there was no blood. She could only imagine that Ed had pushed her and she had fallen hard, hitting her head as she met the floor but now he was nowhere to be seen.

Glancing at her watch Abby realized that Martha would be arriving with Kate within the next thirty minutes and she had to be sure that neither her mother-in-law nor her daughter had any idea what had transpired. Slowly she struggled to her feet but feeling light headed, she was forced to sit down for a few moments. She listened for sounds of Ed in the house but heard no one and she prayed that he had gone off somewhere and would not return until he was completely sober. It was hard for her to equate the person she had just encountered with the man she had known before Daniel died. Living with him was no longer an option but she had no idea where to go or how she would manage. The only job she had ever had was in the five and dime store in Oakfield, but she knew in order for her and Kate to survive, she needed to find work and start saving for the future and then she could plan her escape from her marriage and find her independence. There was nobody she could ask for help. Martha would take her son's side; she was sure of that, and according to Julia his brother had no interest in anything other than his job. Then she realized, Julia might be the one friend she had who would support her despite the rocky start to their relationship. It was then that she decided to ask Julia for help.

CHAPTER 14

THE NEXT DAY AFTER speaking to Julia briefly on the telephone, Abby arranged to meet her for coffee and asked her neighbour, Jane Manning if she would look after Kate for an hour or two. Kate had been to Jane's house often and liked to play with Jane's six-year-old daughter Mandy, and although Abby felt guilty taking time away from Kate during the holiday, she had too much on her mind to let the opportunity of speaking to Julia go by.

When Martha had brought Kate home the day before, Abby had managed to compose herself sufficiently that Martha had no idea what had occurred earlier. She chattered away about the wonderful time they had at Riverdale Park throwing snowballs and feeding the animals in the small zoo and it was all Abby could do to concentrate. All she wanted to do was to spend time alone with Kate, almost as though she was her only lifeline and when Martha finally left, she hugged Kate so tightly that Kate pulled away and looking up at her mother asked, "What's wrong Mommy, are you okay?"

"Yes, darling," Abby replied smiling even though her head was still throbbing, "I'm just glad to see you that's all. I had a lovely lunch with Aunt Julia but I missed you."

And now here she was sitting across from Julia at a small table in the local coffee shop.

"Obviously you have a problem Abby, something must have happened since lunch yesterday," Julia determined.

"It's Ed, he's drinking so much, he's becoming violent and I don't know what to do."

Julia gasped and reached across for Abby's hand, "Oh no, did he hit you, what happened?"

Abby's eyes filled with tears, "I'm not sure whether he hit me or pushed me but I woke up on the floor, and I must have hit my head because I have a bump and I had a serious headache."

"But why? Were you arguing at the time," Julia asked.

"Actually we were arguing about my meeting you for lunch yesterday. I know it's no secret that you're not fond of each other…"

"You can say that again," interrupted Julia.

"Well, he accused me of wasting his money on a fancy restaurant and he wouldn't listen when I told him you paid for lunch. He's out of control Julia and I can't take it any more. He needs help but he thinks all therapists are crazy so I can't see how he'll ever get better. I need to get out but I have to be able to support Kate and myself so I need to get a job. I'm asking for your advice Julia, what should I do?"

Julia moved her chair so that she would be closer to Abby, "Well, if you separated, you're entitled to support, and then if you divorce, you should be able to get money from the proceeds of the house. I know his parents gave you the house as a wedding gift and I know it's in Ed's name but that won't matter when it comes to splitting your assets. Anyway, all that's a long way off because you should really get a job before you even think of moving out. Chances are Ed will fight you every step of the way, so you need to be able to support yourself without any help from him."

Abby shook her head, "I do have some money my Aunt Lillian left me and I've had it in a savings account since we were married, but I'll need that for Kate's education down the road. I've never had a real job that pays well; I haven't had much schooling and I've had no real work experience. I wouldn't even know where to begin."

"I really want to help you Abby, but I need to think about this. I agree you should get out of the house not just for your sake but for Kate's too. Isn't it ironic that both of our marriages are falling apart at the same time?"

"Yes, it is," Abby agreed, "but I know you'll be all right Julia. You're a sophisticated, intelligent woman while I still have a lot of the country mouse in me."

"Nonsense," snorted Julia, "you're smart Abby and you can do a lot of things I can't do, like cooking and sewing and decorating."

"Thank you Julia, but I don't think those things will help me find work anywhere."

"I'm not so sure and I really want to think about this some more. After New Year will be the perfect time to start looking for a job and I already have a an idea in my head, but can you wait until after the holidays and then I may be able to help you?"

"Oh Julia, of course I can wait, I don't know how to thank you."

Julia grinned, "Don't thank me yet, and just keep your fingers crossed."

"Oh I will, I will," said Abby.

CHAPTER 15

NEW YEAR'S EVE PASSED without incident. In the years before Daniel's death, Abby and Ed had always celebrated at a fancy restaurant, either alone or with associates from Ed's company. On this particular New Year's Eve, Ed was nowhere to be found and Abby was quite happy to spend the time alone with Kate.

Martha had invited the family to join them for a special supper but Abby preferred that her mother-in-law knew nothing about Ed's absence and diplomatically declined the offer suggesting that they would be spending the evening with friends. Julia had called briefly to wish Abby well before she went off to attend the annual company get-together. She also had some news she wanted to share but it had to wait until after the holiday.

On New Year's Day when it was quiet in the house, and Abby and Kate decided to take a walk, Abby couldn't help wondering what Julia wanted to tell her. She felt sure it had something to do with her decision to find a job and leave Ed. She was still thinking about it after they had eaten supper. Kate was tucked up in bed and she couldn't concentrate on the television program she was trying to watch, a retrospect of the previous year's events. She was just about to switch the television off and read a book when she heard Ed's key in the door. Never knowing what his mood was likely to be at any given time, she decided to stay where she was and let him make the first move. When there was no further sound from the hall or the kitchen where Ed usually headed for his beer as soon as he arrived home, Abby waited a few moments and then called out, "Ed, is that you?"

When there was no reply, she got up and walked out of the living room only to find that Ed wasn't in the hall or the kitchen or any other room on the main floor of the house. Thinking he must have gone upstairs, she decided to check the bedrooms but he was not in their own room, or Kate's. Holding her breath, she slowly opened the door to Daniel's old room, which still held most of his possessions, and there was Ed lying on the bed crying uncontrollably. Suddenly, Abby felt a deep compassion for this man who was unable to deal with the loss of his son but she wasn't sure how he would react if she attempted to console him. Finally, when he continued to sob with gut wrenching howls she automatically went to him and tried to pull him into her arms.

Ed became aware of Abby immediately and pushed her away, "Go away," he screamed, "leave me alone."

"No Ed, I'm not going anywhere," Abby responded, backing away slightly from the bed, "this has to stop. You need help to get over your grief. You're destroying this family and I can't let you do that."

Ed sat up, his eyes red and his words slurring, "This family's already destroyed. Don't you get it? Daniel's dead."

Abby felt angry now, "Oh I get it alright, Daniel was my son too. I've done enough grieving but I have to be a mother to Kate now and you have to start being a father again. I'm sick of seeing you like this and I'm not putting up with it any more."

Ed came right up off the bed at Abby's words, "So what do you intend to do about it?" he smirked.

Abby was trembling but she knew she had to speak up, "I'm getting a job and when I can afford it, I'm leaving with Kate."

Ed started to laugh, "Ha, what a joke. You haven't got the guts lady and who would hire you anyway."

"Julia's going to help me," Abby snapped back defiantly, but as soon as she said the words she knew she had made a big mistake.

Ed let out a roar and slapped Abby hard on the face leaving a red welt, "You don't talk to her, you hear me? If I catch you talking to that bitch again you'll be sorry," and pushing Abby to one side, he stormed from the room.

Abby was reeling from the blow but she refused to cry. Sitting on the bed she held her head in her hands. She was now convinced that she had to leave and no matter what Ed said, she needed to talk to Julia. Exhausted, she finally laid down on Daniel's bed and cuddling the pillow he loved so much, she drifted off to sleep.

Abby got a call from Julia exactly one week later but only after a frantic Martha telephoned to say that Julia had left Raymond. Abby admitted that she knew Julia wasn't happy in her marriage but she claimed no knowledge of Julia's plans to move out. Martha was devastated and just couldn't understand what the problem was. According to Raymond, he was perfectly content and it came as a complete surprise to discover that his wife was leaving him. Naturally, Martha had no idea that her son was such a poor communicator, despite being a lawyer, and that he hadn't an emotional bone in his body. She had always perceived him as being a rather quiet but very kind and gentlemanly type and most of his friends and acquaintances saw him that way too. The problem was that none of these people were sharing, or attempting to share, an intimate relationship with him and after so many years of apathy, Julia had had enough.

Abby avoided any discussion with Ed concerning his brother's problems, in fact any time Ed was home, she avoided him as much as possible and only spoke to him when absolutely necessary. His total indifference towards Kate was more upsetting than his attitude towards her, but Kate appeared to have come to accept it and drew closer and closer to her mother.

When Julia finally called, Abby had just returned from her neighbor Jane's house where they had been out in the back yard along with Kate and Mandy putting the finishing touches on a giant snowman. Abby was just settling down with a cup of hot chocolate to warm her up when the phone rang, "Hello?" she said tentatively wondering if it could be Martha again.

Julia's voice came through loud and clear and she sounded particularly upbeat, "Hi Abby, it's Julia. How are you?' then without waiting for an answer she continued, "I'm sure you must have heard from Martha that I've already left Raymond, I know she's pretty upset."

"Oh, Julia it's so good to hear from you, "Abby said, "yes Martha called me and I had to play dumb. She just can't understand why you would leave her precious son. Can't imagine how she's going to react when I leave too."

"So you're still intending to go ahead with it? Has something else happened, Abby?"

Abby sighed, "I'm afraid he got a little violent again, nothing too serious but now we aren't speaking. He's still drinking and staying away a lot so there's nothing to keep me here. Anyway enough about me, where are you Julia?"

"Well, I've moved into the house at the beaches and it's fabulous Abby and I'm so close to the lake that, even though it's really cold out, it's so great walking along the boardwalk. I got the job with that other law firm so tomorrow I'm giving in my notice."

"Of course, I forgot about you changing jobs too, did Raymond know about that?" Abby questioned.

"Yes, I told him but he didn't react too much, in fact he hardly reacted to anything I said. I don't know why I should be surprised after all these years. I have to give him credit though, he was concerned about whether I could manage on my own and suggested that we talk about selling the house so that he can give me half of the equity."

"I bet you were relieved that he took it so well but what happened when you actually walked out of the door?"

Julia paused and then replied in a whisper, "He kissed me on the cheek and then I noticed he actually had tears in his eyes. I have to admit it was rather sad because he is a good man but I just don't love him any more."

"I am sorry, Julia," Abby sympathized, "you know I wish you well and I hope we can get together really soon, I would love to see where you're living."

"Well that's really why I called, I want you and Kate to come on Sunday. You know I'm not a great cook so we'll order in a pizza or go out and eat. I want to talk to you about your situation. You remember, I said I had an idea but wanted to think about it?"

"Yes, of course I do," Abby replied anxiously.

"That's what I want to talk about, so why don't I pick you up at around four o'clock on Sunday. Ed won't be home will he?"

Abby had no idea when Ed would be home and she didn't want him to see Julia or to know where she was going, "I think it would be better if we wait at the corner of the block just in case," she suggested.

"Okay, I won't be late, I wouldn't want you two freezing to death," Julia said chuckling to herself.

CHAPTER 16

EARLY ON SUNDAY MORNING, Julia walked through the rooms of her rented house and smiled to herself. This house was so different from the one she had shared with Raymond, and even though she didn't own it, she felt as though it was truly hers. It was a small house, fully furnished and filled with wonderful old furniture in a myriad of styles that all seemed to come together. The owners of the house were a rather eccentric couple who had retired and spent years traveling the world collecting all kinds of treasures. They had suddenly decided to join the Peace Corps and go on a mission to Africa for two years and luckily Julia had heard about the house through a mutual acquaintance.

When Abby and Kate stepped out of Julia's car later that day and saw the house, they couldn't wait to go inside and explore and Julia couldn't wait to show them around.

"It's fabulous Julia," Abby remarked," you're so lucky to have found this place."

"Yes, I know," said Julia, "it's just what I was looking for. It's so different from my old house, Raymond and I used to rattle around in there. It was way too big for just the two of us while this place is just right; in fact two or three people could be really cozy here."

"Why, are you thinking of getting a roommate or two?"

Julia pulled Katie towards her and sat her on her lap, "As a matter of fact I am and you'll never guess who," Julia replied grinning from ear to ear.

Kate bounced up and down impatiently, "Who is it? Who is it? Tell us Aunt Julia please, "She whined.

Julia just kept on grinning and Abby frowned while she tried to puzzle out who Julia was talking about. Then suddenly a light bulb went on in head, "It's me and Kate, isn't it?"

Julia nodded and slipped her arm around Kate's shoulders, "Yes, it's you and Kate, I want you to come and live here with me at least until you are able to manage on your own. I'm worried about you both and I don't think you should stay in that house."

Kate ran to Abby and threw her arms around her mother's neck, "Mommy why do we have to leave our house. Where's Daddy going to live?"

Abby pulled Kate onto her lap and held her face in her hands, "I am so sorry, but your Aunt Julia is right we need to move. You know Daddy has some problems and he needs to stay where he is and work things out."

Kate began to cry, "But he'll be all alone and I'll never see him again."

Abby began to rock Kate gently trying to comfort her, "He won't be alone darling, he has Grandma and Granddad and of course you'll see him again. He will always be your Daddy and he loves you very much."

Kate continued to cry while Julia slowly shook her head, "I guess I didn't handle that very well Abby. I should have spoken to you alone first, please forgive me."

"There's nothing to forgive, you meant well and I'm grateful for the offer Julia, but may I think about it for a few days?"

"Yes, of course," replied Julia, "but that isn't all. I just hope I haven't assumed too much."

"Why what else is there Julia?" Abby asked.

"Well you were talking about getting a job and I happened to be buying a plant at a florists just a couple of blocks from here on Queen Street. I noticed there was a sign in the window that they needed an assistant so I spoke to the owner about it. He was there with his wife and they desperately need help. I would guess them to be in their seventies and they both have strong accents which I couldn't quite put my finger on. Anyway the wife is rather frail and can't help out much any more so they need someone to take her place. You absolutely love gardening Abby. You know a lot about flowers and I heard you worked behind a counter once so you do have some sales experience. Anyway I told them you'd be interested and that you would call them and arrange for an interview."

Abby looked shocked, "My goodness Julia, you certainly have been busy, haven't you?"

Julia bowed her head as she felt her cheeks flush, "Yes," she whispered, "I guess I have."

Abby sat Kate down and walked over to her sister-in-law, "You are a treasure Julia," she said placing her hand on Julia's shoulder.

Within two days Abby had made up her mind what she needed to do after another violent confrontation with Ed. Fearful of what might happen if she told him of her plans, she decided to just leave the house with Kate while he was away and take only their personal belongings. Abby had never been materialistic and had only developed a connection with certain items around the house that she had lovingly furnished with Martha's help soon after her marriage. Knowing how Ed would react finding both his wife and daughter gone, she couldn't risk adding to his fury by removing anything from the house. Only the single bed that she had brought from her Aunt's house in Oakfield and which was now stored in the basement caused her to pause and think about what she was leaving behind, and she was overwhelmed with nostalgia for the days she had shared with Lillian.

On Friday afternoon, Abby paid a visit to the principal of Kate's school and explained why Kate would not be coming back. It had been difficult telling her daughter that she would be going to a new school and would be moving away from her friends, but now Kate appeared to be curiously indifferent about leaving familiar surroundings and her father. Abby had no idea that Kate had been witness to the latest violent confrontation she had with Ed and seeing her father's behaviour had frightened her.

Just before supper and right after Abby had packed two large suitcases full of clothes, Julia picked them up and drove them to her house in the beaches. When Kate learned that she had to share a bedroom with her mother she began to come out of her shell, "Mommy, this will be fun sleeping in the same room," she said.

Abby looked around the room with its twin beds covered in plump Laura Ashley comforters and matching curtains on the bay window, "Yes honey, it will be lots of fun. I think Aunt Julia has gone to a lot of trouble to make this room comfortable for us. It would be nice if you gave her a hug and thanked her."

Kate jumped onto one of the single beds, "I will Mommy but why is she being so nice to us?"

"She just wants to help us," Abby replied.

"Yes I know but you didn't like her before. I heard you tell Daddy once that she reminded you of the witch in Snow White."

Abby ran over and knelt in front of Kate putting a finger to her lips, "Hush," she said, "that was before when I didn't really know her. I shouldn't have said that and don't you repeat it. Your Aunt Julia is a kind and generous person and we should be very grateful to her. She's given up part of her home so that we can move in here and she's even helping Mommy to find a job."

"Are you going to work in the flower shop Mommy?"

"I'm not sure yet. I'm going to go and see the people who own the store and see if they'll hire me."

"What do you mean, hire you?"

Abby smiled and sat down beside Kate, "It means that they may let me work for them, then again they may not. They may not like me so we'll just have to see."

"Of course they'll like you Mommy," said Kate throwing her arms around Abby's neck, "in fact they'll love you."

Abby couldn't help laughing, "Well I hope you're right. Now let's go and see what Aunt Julia's doing. I think we may all be going out to supper."

CHAPTER 17

ABBY AND KATE SETTLED in over the weekend and on Sunday afternoon Julia took them on a drive almost an hour east of the city to the Bowmanville Zoo. Both women and Kate had a particular affection for animals even though none of them had ever owned a pet. Julia was mulling this over on the drive home and suddenly announced, "I think we're going to get a cat!"

Kate, who was in the back seat, jumped up and leaning over Julia's shoulder yelled in her ear, "What did you say Aunt Julia? Did you say we were going to get a cat?"

Julia reached back and patted Kate's hand, "That's what I said young lady. We'll go to the Humane Society and pick out a kitten."

"When, when?" screamed Kate excitedly.

Abby turned and motioned for Kate to sit down, "Take it easy Kate." Then frowning at Julia she said, "Do you really mean it Julia?"

"Yes I do, I've never had a pet and I've always wanted one. We weren't allowed to have them in the orphanage and after I left there, I lived in buildings where they didn't allow any pets."

"Why didn't you get a dog or a cat when you were with Raymond?"

"Believe it or not, he's allergic to the hair. Any time we got close to a dog, even in the park, he would begin to sneeze. Come to think of it, a cat would be a good excuse to keep him from visiting," said Julia giggling at the thought.

After they arrived home and enjoyed a homemade turkey casserole that Abby had prepared and some store bought pecan pie, Abby and Julia settled down to watch a little television while Kate sat at the dining room table with her colouring book. They had planned to have a peaceful evening but Julia was suddenly alerted to a car pulling into the driveway. When she peered out of the window and recognized the green Chevy Bel Air, she immediately ran over to Abby and grabbed her arm at the same time gesturing to Kate, "It's Ed, you'd better go into the bedroom and let me handle this."

"I want to see Daddy," Kate announced pouting.

"I know Kate but it would be better if I saw him first," said Julia looking at Abby for support.

Abby took Kate's hand just as the doorbell rang and pulled her out of the room, "Your Aunt Julia's right. Let's just see if Daddy's in a good mood and if he is, I promise I'll let you see him."

Julia opened the door with her head held high, "Hello Ed, I'm surprised to see you here."

Ed looked Julia up and down and sneered, "I bet you are, where's Abby?"

"How would I know?" Julia replied with a toss of her head.

Ed advanced a step but Julia didn't back up, "Where else would she go? Let me tell you something lady, when I get hold of her there it'll be hell to pay. Now are you going to get her or do I have to barge my way in."

Julia refused to be intimidated, "Take one step inside this door and I'm calling the police, now get lost."

Ed's eyes were blazing as he stared back at Julia, "I always knew you were a bitch but you haven't heard the last of me. You tell my wife that we're finished and she gets nothing, I'll make sure of that."

"You've made yourself perfectly clear Ed," said Julia in clipped tones, "you can speak to Abby's lawyer. We'll have him get in touch with you."

Ed took another step forward and Julia put up a hand protectively, "Damn you, you'll pay for this too. She won't get away with this, she thinks she can just walk out and take Kate with her. Well we'll see about that."

"Go away Ed and leave us alone!" Julia screamed as she backed up and started to close the door. Ed paused and considered pushing his way into the house, but on second thoughts he climbed into his car and backed out of the driveway with a squeal of brakes.

Julia was shaking when she came back into the living room and Abby came out to hug her, "I heard every word Julia," she said, "you were so brave."

Julia was about to reply when they heard the sound of crying.

Kate stood in the doorway with her fists pressed against her eyes sobbing her heart out, "Daddy doesn't love us any more," she managed to sputter out, "he's never coming back again."

It took Abby some time to calm Kate down eventually slipping into bed beside her until she fell asleep. She wondered if she had done the right thing by leaving Ed and as she lay staring at the plain white ceiling, she wondered where the stars had gone. When Abby finally returned to the living room she found Julia waiting patiently reading a magazine, "Hi Abby," she said, "is everything all right?"

Abby sank down onto the chesterfield, "Well, she's asleep and I think I was able to make her understand but it's so difficult. I don't want to say anything bad about Ed, after all he is her father."

"You sound as though you might be having second thoughts, are you?"

Abby got up and wandered over to the window, "I just don't know Julia," she replied peering out into the darkness, "maybe I should give him another chance."

Julia rose and joined Abby at the window; "I think you would be making a big mistake by going back Abby. Why don't you give it a week or two? I know it's a big change for both of you. If you stay it means enrolling Kate in her new school and going back to work after all these years, but you can't go on exposing Kate to the life you were living. It's better for her to have one loving parent than two that are fighting all the time, especially when there's violence involved."

Abby's shoulders slumped, "I know you're right, it's just that I'm a little scared. I haven't worked for a long time and I haven't had to fend for myself before."

"You'll be fine Abby, I promise," Julia insisted, "you're a strong woman and things will work out, you'll see. Now why don't you come and sit down and I'll make us some coffee."

Abby smiled and took Julia's hand, "That sounds like a great idea, thank you for everything Julia. I don't know how I'm ever going to repay you."

"Well when you start working at that florist shop you can help out with a few dollars," Julia said chuckling, "now sit down and I'll get the coffee."

Abby watched as her sister-in-law went to the kitchen and noticed how different she seemed. She had cut her long black hair so that it now fell in waves to her shoulders and she no longer wore it in the chignon that had been her trademark. Even her make up was lighter, the crimson lips now a soft pink and the eyeliner she used to wear was almost non-existent and her clothes were less severe too. She still looked very business-like when she went to the office but the dark suits were now stored away at the back of her closet and at home she was usually in jeans and cotton sweaters. Abby had always thought of Julia as exotic and sophisticated but now she was a natural beauty and it was obvious that leaving Raymond had brought about other changes in her life.

When Julia returned with two mugs of steaming coffee and a plate of digestive biscuits, Abby couldn't help commenting on the change, "Julia, I hope you don't mind me saying this but you look so much nicer than before. Don't get me wrong, I always thought you were lovely but now you look even lovelier. The new hairstyle really suits you. You look so natural and a lot more relaxed."

"Why, thank you Abby. Raymond always liked me to look like what he called "a lawyer's wife" always done up like a dog's dinner. It took a lot of work to look like that and I'm glad I don't have to do it any more. "

Abby chewed on her lower lip self-consciously. "Maybe you can help me to look better Julia. I need to lose a few pounds and my clothes aren't exactly the height of fashion."

"Well you could come to the gym with me, I go twice a week and we could go jogging on the weekend. I know it's pretty cold out right now but if you dress for it you won't even notice it. As for anything else Abby, I think you should take one step at a time. Maybe later you should cut your hair, it would look lovely a bit shorter and curlier and if you put some red highlights in it, it would look fabulous."

Abby walked over to the mirror that hung over the mantle and peered at her image. Her hair, which was still very thick and straight, fell well beyond her shoulders and she tried to imagine herself with a different style, "Maybe you're right Julia, I could do with a real change. I just feel so dowdy right now especially when I look at you, you look so radiant lately."

"Nonsense," said Julia shaking her head, "all you need is a little updating. You are one of the most attractive women I know; you have exceptional blue eyes and wonderful skin. Once you get on your feet and get a new wardrobe you'll have all the men chasing after you."

Abby started to laugh, "Fat chance of that and if I don't get to bed early every night I'll have bags under my eyes as big as potato sacks!"

Julia chuckled," I guess that means you're ready to turn in. Well, finish up your coffee and say goodnight because I'm off to bed too," and with cup in hand she headed to the kitchen.

Abby took the last mouthful of coffee and called out to Julia, "Goodnight Julia, sleep well."

CHAPTER 18

ON MONDAY AFTER JULIA left for the office driving the 1954 Chevy Corvette that Raymond had generously given her as a birthday gift, Abby walked to the local school to enrol Kate even though she wasn't absolutely sure that their move would be permanent.

Rather than leaving Kate at school for the rest of the day, Abby decided to give her a little more vacation time and take her to lunch and then to see the movie, Old Yeller, a story about a boy and his dog, that was playing at a small theatre downtown. Abby was nervous about staying in the house without Julia and had visions of Ed returning and pounding on the door but she also knew that she couldn't keep avoiding him by leaving the house every time Julia went off to work.

At four o'clock, after returning home, Abby started preparing supper. She had always been a good cook and had enjoyed creating new recipes for her family although, since Daniel's death, she had lost interest and most of the meals she served were dull and unimaginative. Tonight she decided to make a pasta dish with shrimps and scallops and a salad garnished with feta cheese, tomatoes and pine nuts. Kate wasn't particularly fond of pasta but there was a promise of a trip to the Dairy Queen for dessert if she ate every scrap on her plate.

Abby was half way through her preparations when she heard the phone ringing in the living room. Kate who had also heard it tugged on her mother's apron, "The phone's ringing Mommy."

Abby hesitated, "I'm not sure if I should answer it, it's probably for Julia."

"But maybe it's Daddy," said Kate hopefully.

Abby hesitated, and then wiping her hands on a tea towel she went to answer the phone which was still ringing incessantly, "Hello," she whispered.

"Oh Abby, you're there. I'm so glad I managed to get hold of you. I've been calling all day and I've been frantic with worry. Ed was here last night and he told me you and Kate had gone. What's happening Abby, please tell me what's going on."

Abby recognized Martha's voice immediately, she sounded anxious and was breathing heavily as though she had been running. Abby knew she would have to speak to her mother-in-law sooner or later but she didn't expect her to call Julia's house this soon, "Hello Martha," she replied, "I'm sorry you're so upset but I didn't really have any choice about leaving. You're Ed's mother so I don't want to say anything bad about him. What did he tell you?"

"Well, I have to be honest Abby, he was pretty drunk when he came here and I couldn't make much sense of what he was saying. John was furious that he came barging in here late at night in that state, in fact he drove him home and actually put him to bed. Is that what the problem is Abby, is it Ed's drinking?"

Abby didn't know how to handle the situation with Martha. She was, after all, Kate's grandmother and she didn't want to jeopardize that relationship. On the spur of the moment she decided to stall for time, "Martha, why don't you come over tonight and visit and then we can talk?" she suggested.

Martha sighed, "Thank you Abby, I would love to do that and I want to see Kate. Raymond must have told Ed where Julia lived and I know it's in the beaches but I don't have the address."

After giving Martha directions, Abby sat down on one of the comfy chairs near the fireplace and put her head in her hands. A moment later she felt a tiny hand on her shoulder, "What's wrong Mommy, did Grandma upset you."

Abby pulled Kate onto her lap, "No honey, not at all. Didn't you hear me invite her around tonight? I know she really wants to see you and I'm sure you want to see her too."

"I do Mommy, but what about Daddy, Is he coming too?"

Abby folded her arms around Kate and rested her cheek on the top of her head of chestnut curls, "No, I'm afraid not tonight but maybe sometime soon. I don't expect you to understand Kate, but you can always talk to me. You can ask me anything you like and I'll try to answer just like I'm going to try and answer Grandma when she gets here. I know you both love Daddy very much, so it's hard for me to explain why we left home. Just trust me honey and everything will be all right."

When Kate didn't respond, Abby turned her around so that she could see her face, "Do you know what I'm saying?"

Kate nodded and slipped silently off of her mother's lap. "Good," said Abby, "now I'd better go and finish supper or it won't be ready when your Aunt Julia gets home."

Martha had already dished out supper for John and left it warming in the oven while she picked at her own meal. It wasn't her usual practice to go ahead and eat without him but she knew he would be home late after an earlier phone call. He had called to tell her that he was leaving the office and going over to see Ed to make sure he was all right after the episode the night before. Martha became anxious as she waited but she needed to know the situation with Ed before she visited with Abby. Just a few minutes before seven o'clock John walked through the door and was immediately greeted by Martha who had become more and more impatient, "Oh John, I'm so glad you're home," she said kissing him on the cheek, "what happened? Is Ed all right, I've been so worried?"

John took Martha's hand, led her into the dining room and then patting her on the shoulder, took his place at the table. When Martha made a motion to go to the kitchen, he held up his hand indicating he wanted her to stay, "Why don't you sit down for a minute dear, supper can wait."

Martha frowned and then sat down, "It's bad isn't it John?"

"Well, I guess you could say that," John replied,

"When I got there he was slumped on the sofa with a beer. He obviously hadn't bothered to shower or shave and his clothes were a mess, and I noticed a load of dirty dishes in the kitchen as I walked by. When I tried to talk some sense into him about his drinking, he refused to discuss it and blamed Abby for all his problems but he wouldn't say what those problems were. Then he blamed me for favoring Raymond and if that wasn't enough he excused his behavior on trying to cope with Daniel's death. He's so angry; I've never seen him like this before."

Martha slowly shook her head, "Maybe I should go over there and help him clean up the house."

John sighed, "Martha, you don't understand. A dirty house isn't the problem; Ed's just sunk to rock bottom and the only person that can help him is himself. I don't know what went on between him and Abby and he won't tell me but he's adamant about not taking her back."

Martha was shocked, "What? I can't believe that and what about Kate?"

"He didn't want to talk about Kate. Maybe when you go over to see Abby tonight you'll find out exactly what happened. Perhaps I should come with you."

"No, I think it would be better if I went alone," Martha replied rising from the table, "why don't you just have your supper and I'll get ready and go."

Back at Julia's house, Kate was whining, "When are we going to the Dairy Queen? You promised if I ate all my supper we could go and now it's nearly time for bed."

Julia looked over Kate's head at Abby and rolled her eyes; "Grandma will be here any minute so we can't go right now."

"But Mommy said we could," Kate persisted stamping her foot, "it's not fair."

Abby intervened, "Enough of that Kate, if Grandma agrees we'll all go but if she doesn't, then we'll go tomorrow."

"Not fair," Kate repeated collapsing into a sitting position on the living room rug and folding her arms across her chest defiantly.

Abby glanced helplessly at Julia just as the doorbell rang and before either one of them had a chance to react Kate rushed to the door, opened it and threw herself into Martha's arms, "Hi Grandma," she yelled, "can we all go to the Dairy Queen now?"

Martha patted Kate on the head, "Hold on a minute missy, let your old grandma get in the door."

Kate backed away as Abby came forward to embrace Martha, "Come in Martha, sorry about that but I promised Kate we would go if she ate all her supper."

"Well, then I guess we should leave right away then," said Martha grinning back at Kate.

"Whoopee," Kate yelled, "I'll go and get my things on".

After Kate raced to the closed-in patio at the back of the house to find her parka and boots, Martha looked around the room, "This is lovely Abby, such a cozy room."

"Yes, Julia fell in love with the whole house when she saw it."

"Where is Julia?"

"She went out to the kitchen when she heard the doorbell to clear up the supper dishes. Let's see if she wants to come out with us."

Just as they reached the kitchen door, Julia appeared with a tray, a pot of coffee and a plate of shortcake cookies, "Oh, hi Martha, it's good to see you. Thought you might like some coffee to warm you up."

"Sorry Julia," Abby intervened, "but we're going to the Dairy Queen and we have to go now because it's getting late and it's Kate's first day at her new school tomorrow. You are coming with us, aren't you?"

"Of course," Julia replied placing the tray on the dining room table, "I'll make some fresh coffee when we get back."

As the three women left the house with Kate skipping happily in the lead, Abby whispered to Martha, "We'll have to talk later."

CHAPTER 19

SITTING IN THE CAR overlooking the Bloor Viaduct eating ice cream while the temperature outside was almost at freezing point didn't seem to make much sense. The three women were wrapped up in their own thoughts while Kate attacked her banana split as though it was her last meal. Many cars were parked on top of the hill, which was the place to be to get the best view of the city, and on this particular night it looked like a winter wonderland. It was Kate who finally, realizing how silent it was, suddenly spoke up, "How come no one's talking?"

Abby who was sitting next to her in the back seat hesitated then replied, "We were just too busy enjoying our ice cream honey," and then turning to look at Kate she couldn't help smiling, "and by the state of your face, you really loved that banana split."

Kate wiped her sleeve across her mouth before Abby had a chance to react, "Yes, it was yummy. Can I have another one?"

At that everyone was reduced to giggles and the sombre mood of earlier changed but the night was still young and Abby still needed to talk to Martha about her failed marriage.

Once back at the house, when Kate had finally fallen asleep after nagging Martha to read her a bedtime story, Julia made fresh coffee and suggested that Abby and Martha might want to be alone.

Abby persuaded Julia to stay, feeling that she might need some moral support if her mother-in-law decided to take Ed's side but at the same time she was still reluctant to tell the whole truth.

Martha had always liked Abby; in fact she had become very fond of her and thought of her as a daughter. She had no intention of alienating her and she knew that her relationship with her granddaughter would be in jeopardy if she left tonight on bad terms, "What happened between you and Ed, Abby?" she asked gently.

Abby was nervous and feeling a little shaky. She put her cup down, "I don't really know Martha, he's completely changed from the man I used to know. I know he blamed himself for Daniel's death and he just can't seem to forgive himself. At first, he was just depressed but then he started drinking and now I really believe he's become an alcoholic."

Seeing tears come into Martha's eyes, Abby moved over to sit beside her, "We hardly say a word to each other any more and he's so angry most of the time. To be truthful, I was happiest when he was not at home and that became more and more often. As for Kate, he's completely abandoned her emotionally and I know I did the same thing but thank God you gave me a wake up call and I'll be forever grateful for that."

"So do you think there's any hope of you getting back together?" Martha whispered dabbing at her eyes with a tissue.

Abby took Martha's hand, "I'm not sure but I can't go back now, at least not until Ed gets some help and gets rid of his demons. Look Martha, I don't know what Ed's told you, if anything, I've tried my best to make it work but I can't get through to him. For now, Kate and I will stay with Julia. I've enrolled Kate in a new school and tomorrow I'm going to apply for a job."

Martha looked across at Julia, "What do you think of all this, Julia?"

Julia had been contemplating whether to tell Martha about Ed's violent behaviour but decided against it, "I think Abby's doing the right thing. They need time apart and maybe there's a possibility that they can make their marriage work once Ed straightens himself out"

Martha nodded, "And what about your marriage Julia?"

Julia sighed, "I'm afraid that really is over. Raymond's a good man, he's kind and generous but we just don't communicate. He has such problems showing any emotion and that's very hard to live with. I'll understand if you're upset with me but I had to get away and Raymond's been really decent about it. We parted on very amicable terms and I wish only the best for him."

"I guess times have really changed," said Martha sadly, "couples used to put up with each other. John tends to hide his emotions too but I learned to live with it. We've been married for so long and now both our sons are left to fend for themselves."

"Raymond will be all right, we always had a housekeeper to clean the house and he can always hire a cook, although he's perfectly capable of cooking himself. As for Ed, well that's another story."

Abby stood up and walked over to the window then turned to face Martha, "Don't baby Ed, please Martha. He's a grown man and he has to stand on his own two feet. Maybe the one thing you can do is to persuade him to get counselling, but that's all. If you go over there and start making his meals and taking care of the house he'll never make an effort."

At that moment Martha could only imagine her youngest son lying drunk in squalor on the living room floor surrounded by beer bottles and she started to cry in earnest, "My poor Ed, he accused John of favoring Raymond and he's right. I've tried to make it up to him all his life but a son needs the approval of his father."

Julia got up and knelt down in front of Martha, "Enough!" she snapped and Abby saw a glimmer of the old Julia she used to know. "Ed is an adult and he should get over it. He's not just a drunkard but he's also abusive."

Martha gasped while Abby ran forward and grasped Julia by the shoulder, "No Julia, don't," she begged.

Julia shook off Abby's hand and grasped Martha's arm, "You have to know the truth if Ed's going to get well. He's been hitting Abby."

Abby let out a sigh and sank down onto the chesterfield while Martha leaned back in the chair exhausted, "Why didn't you tell me this before?" she asked.

"Because Abby didn't want to hurt you and neither did I but if you're going to try and get Ed help then you need to know the truth. His drinking has made him violent; he gets so angry he just lashes out. Once he gets the drinking under control and gets grief counselling too then the anger will go away. It won't happen overnight Martha, I can promise you that. Working in a law firm, I've been exposed to dozens of cases like this and some people turn their lives around and some don't. Just remember that none of this is your fault or John's. You're not responsible for Ed any more but you can try to encourage him to get help."

Martha leaned forward and gently patted Julia's face, "Thank you for telling me Julia, that was very brave of you," then slowly getting to her feet and staring at Abby said, "I think I'll go home now."

Abby jumped up and put her arm around Martha, "I'm so sorry, are you sure you'll be all right driving home?"

"Yes dear, if you'll just get my coat I'll be on my way."

At the front door both Julia and Abby hugged Martha and kissed her on the cheek, "You will come visit John and me, won't you?" she said, her voice wavering, "and you'll bring Kate too?"

"Of course, we will," Julia replied smiling, "and you can come visit us any time you like, you're always welcome here Martha."

CHAPTER 20

THE FOLLOWING MORNING BEFORE Julia left for the office she spent a few moments lingering over breakfast in an attempt to reassure Kate that her new school would be a good experience and the place to make a lot of new friends. Kate sat silently playing with her cereal and swinging her legs back and forth, it was obvious she was not happy.

Abby, who had just finished dressing, arrived at the table just in time to hear Julia's attempt to encourage Kate, "Now come on Kate, let's not look so glum and finish up those cornflakes otherwise we'll be late."

Kate dropped her spoon into the bowl with a clatter, "I don't want any more and I don't want to go to school," she announced.

Julia looked at Abby and raised her eyebrows, and then turning to Abby said, "Sorry Kate but you don't have any choice, every boy and girl has to go to school. I know it's going to be a little strange at first but you'll soon settle in and by the weekend you'll forget about your old school."

Kate pouted and stuck out her chin, "No I won't."

Julia reached over and took Kate's hand which she attempted to pull away, "Think of it this way Kate, we're all doing something new. I just started a new job and I didn't know anybody there until a little while ago, but now I feel like I've been there forever, and Mommy is going to start work real soon and she hasn't worked for a long time. All your life you'll have new experiences; some of them really wonderful and some not quite so good but you'll learn so much from all of them and when you grow up you'll be wise and strong."

Kate looked up at Julia, "If I'm good and go to school, can we get a kitty like you said we would?"

Julia smiled and squeezed Kate's hand, "Yes, I promise, next Saturday we'll go to the Humane Society and you can pick out a kitten yourself and Mommy and I will help."

Kate jumped up from the table and threw her arms around Julia's neck, "Oh thank you Aunt Julia, thank you, thank you," and then running to Abby she grinned up at her, "Mommy we're getting a kitty, Aunt Julia said so. I can hardly wait until Saturday, so if I go to school early maybe the week will go by faster. Hurry up and let's go Mommy, I'll run and get my coat," and she scampered out of the room.

Abby shook her head, "The logic of children! Anyway Julia, that seemed to do the trick, although I don't want her to think she's getting a reward for bad behaviour or that we're bribing her to make her go to school."

"I understand what you're saying Abby but just this once won't hurt her and she's been through a rough time," Julia responded as she rose from the table, "Look, I have to get going but good luck with the school and good luck with the florist. You are still going to see if the job's still available aren't you?"

"Yes I'm going right after lunch, as soon as I get through doing a few chores around here but I don't have a clue what to wear."

"Why don't you wear your gray wool skirt with that burgundy sweater you wore the other day? The color really suits you and it's appropriate for working in a florist."

"Yes that sounds like a good idea. You have such great dress sense," Abby remarked admiring Julia's tailored navy wool dress with its white collar and cuffs, "anyway I'd better see what Kate's up to and I'll see you tonight. Have a great day Julia."

Dropping Kate off at her new school in care of her home class teacher, Mrs. Landry, went a lot more smoothly than Abby had imagined. The promise of a kitten seemed to have defused the situation and holding her teacher's hand, Kate said goodbye to her mother without any tears or tantrums. She only needed assurance that Abby would be there to pick her up at the end of the day.

Relieved that one problem had been solved, Abby was still anxious about how the afternoon would turn out. After picking up some fresh fruit, milk and bread from the corner store, she returned home and busied herself with housework and laundry but she was nervous and considered putting off her visit to the florist until the next day. Searching through the medicine cabinet, she found some Gravol and in an effort to calm herself, she quickly swallowed one pill. An hour later when her nerves seemed to have settled, she made herself a sandwich of smoked turkey on rye with lots of mayonnaise and a cup of coffee and rehearsed what she would answer to any questions she might be asked by the owner of the shop. Julia had helped her prepare for her interview and she needed to make an impression because she had no resume to offer.

At one o'clock, walking carefully along the north side of Queen Street, because of the ice underfoot, Abby stopped and gazed across the street at the florist. A dark green door divided the shop's two windows with a sign above the larger window in gold letters that read, Charlotte's. Traffic was heavy on the street and Abby had to wait to cross with her anxiety increasing by the second. Finally the traffic cleared and she made her way to the front of the store, hesitating before going in. The larger display window was filled with dozens of vases of flowers of all varieties and the colours were breathtaking while the small window showcased potted plants, most non-flowerings like ivy, ferns and philodendrons. And there in the window was the notice "Help Wanted, Inquire Within."

CHAPTER 21

HENRICK AND GERDA VANDERVEER were in their late sixties and ready for retirement. They had immigrated to Canada one year before the Germans invaded Holland in May 1940 at the urging of Gerda's parents. Henrick had lost his parents early in life and Gerda was reluctant to leave her mother and father back in the country of her birth knowing that an invasion was imminent. After six days, Holland surrendered and although all of Gerda's family survived the war, her parents had since died, her father from coronary disease and her mother from a broken heart.

Henrick and Gerda had been childhood sweethearts and had married at a young age but Gerda was never able to conceive and they had only had each other for most of their lives. They had been brought up in farm country and loved the land especially when the tulips were in full bloom. The relocation to Toronto had been difficult, never having lived in a city before, but they persevered and after several years working for a small nursery, they decided to start their own business and opened the florist shop on Queen Street. In memory of her mother, Gerda had named the shop "Charlotte's".

Henrick had always been a jolly outgoing individual as opposed to Gerda who tended to be somewhat quiet and shy but their love for each other grew as the years passed. Even in appearance they were opposites, Henrick being of average height, at least fifty pounds overweight and with a shock of thick white hair and a ruddy complexion, while Gerda was a tiny woman, thin as a rail, pasty faced and hair still black but streaked with gray. Lately Gerda appeared to be even thinner and she had occasional lapses of memory, which caused Henrick to worry. The doctors assured him it was just a sign of aging, but he wasn't so sure and so he decided to make life easier for her by hiring someone to help in the shop. Henrick looked up when he heard the bell ring, as the front door opened, and he saw Abby in her brown wool coat with fur collar and cuffs stepping gingerly inside, "Good afternoon," he called out, "come in, come in."

Abby took one pace forward as Henrick came out from behind the counter, "Can I help you young lady?" He asked rubbing his hands together and smiling, "You must be freezing, it is very cold outside, no?"

"Yes it certainly is," replied Abby.

Henrick gestured in the direction of the display of flowers, "Stay a while and warm yourself. Were you looking for something for a special occasion?"

Abby bowed her head and nervously avoided Henrick's eyes, "No sir, I saw your notice in the window and I'd like to apply for the job. It is still available, isn't it?" she asked finally raising her head.

"Yes, yes it is but we need to discuss, yes? We can go in the back and talk but I have to get my wife to come out and mind the shop", and he bustled back to a curtained opening behind the counter, "Gerda, come, come please," he hollered, then turning to Abby whispered, "My wife, she's a little hard of hearing."

Within seconds, Gerda appeared from behind the curtain, nodded at Abby and then without a word began to busy herself with a flower arrangement. Henrick, observing Gerda's behavior grinned at Abby and shrugged his shoulders, "If you will follow me, we will go to the back where we will not be disturbed."

In the back of the shop was a cozy living room with two regency striped armchairs in brown and beige, a plump caramel coloured velvet sofa and several pieces of antique pine furniture. Abby suspected that this was part of the couple's living quarters and that the second story, which she hadn't paid much attention to from across the street, must contain the sleeping quarters.

"Do sit down, my dear," said Henrick indicating one of the armchairs, "would you like a cup of coffee or perhaps some tea?"

Abby sat down and slipped her coat from her shoulders, "No thank you, that's very kind of you."

Henrick waved his hand, "Not at all, not at all. Now perhaps I should introduce myself properly, my name is Henrick Vanderveer, and you are?"

"Abby Harrison, oh my real name is Abigail but everyone calls me Abby."

"I see," said Henrick nodding his head, "well Abby Harrison tell me what experience you have had working with flowers."

Abby swallowed then cleared her throat, "I haven't really worked with flowers, that is, I've never worked in a flower shop but I love to garden and I know a lot about flowers and plants."

Henrick paused and leaned forward looking Abby directly in the eyes, "Where did you work before?"

Abby shifted nervously in her seat, "I worked in a department store in a small town. I'm used to dealing with customers and I enjoy helping people."

"And how long ago was that?"

"A long time ago," Abby replied and got up from her seat, "I'm sorry I shouldn't be wasting your time."

Henrick suspected that Abby was having some personal problems and being a compassionate man, he immediately put out his hand to stop her from leaving, "Why don't you tell me why you need this job Abby."

Abby slowly sat down again, "I'm embarrassed to tell you."

Henrick chuckled, "I'm an old man my dear, there isn't much I haven't heard."

"Well, I just left an abusive marriage and I have a seven year old daughter. I'm staying with my sister-in-law. She's the one who told me about this job. She's been so generous but I need to contribute to the expenses and I need money for clothes for Kate and school supplies."

"What about your husband, isn't he going to help support you?"

Abby toyed with the copper pendant hanging from her neck, then gathering courage said, "It's too soon to know what's going to happen but I can't wait to find out. I need to get a job now so maybe you could hire me on a trial basis and I promise I won't disappoint you."

Henrick got up and beckoned for Abby to do the same, "Come, let's see how much you know about flowers."

Gerda looked up as Henrick came into the shop with Abby at his heels, "Who is this young lady Henrick?" she asked, no longer able to contain her curiosity.

"This is Abby, she is applying for the job Gerda and I'm just going to give her a little test."

Gerda looked Abby up and down and then moving towards her whispered, "Don't let him intimidate you my dear."

"Ha!" roared Henrick, "my wife is in good humor today. She likes to make people think that I am an ogre but she really thinks I am wonderful."

Abby was amused and realized immediately that the Vanderveers were very much in love, "Good afternoon Mrs. Vanderveer," she said extending her hand towards Gerda, "I'm very pleased to meet you and I won't let your husband intimidate me," and then she winked and Gerda grinned in response.

"Okay that is enough you two," said Henrick in a gruff voice even though he was attempting not to laugh, "I can see that you are going to get along. Now let's get started on this test."

Abby spent the next ten minutes attempting to identify every flower and plant in the shop. There were roses, lilies, orchids, azaleas, daffodils, freesias, tulips, carnations and some rare blooms that she had never seen before, but she decided to be honest and admitted that she was not familiar with every single flower.

When she finally identified the last potted plant as a Chinese Evergreen, Henrick clapped his hands with glee and turned to Gerda, "Good, good, she is very good, no?"

Gerda agreed, “Yes, she certainly knows her flowers, I think we should hire her Henrick.”

Abby’s heart began to beat a little faster when Henrick held out his hand to her and said, “I think my wife is right, when can you start working?”

“I can start right away,” Abby replied shaking Henrick’s hand, “but if it’s possible I can only work until three o’clock until I get someone to look after Kate when she finishes school.”

“No problem Abby,” said Henrick, “of course you must be there for your daughter until you find someone.”

Abby bowed her head, “May I ask how much the salary is, please Mr. Vanderveer?”

Henrick chuckled, “Of course, what was I thinking? The weekly pay is fifty-five dollars and that is for working eight hours a day for five days. I would have liked someone who could work on Saturday but as you have a daughter Gerda and I will manage.”

Abby agreed to be back at the shop at nine o’clock the next morning and as she stepped out onto the sidewalk, even though the wind had picked up and the temperature had dropped to an unbearable level, she skipped along the street as though she no longer had a care in the world.

CHAPTER 22

ABBY DROPPED KATE OFF at school the next morning and arrived at the shop fifteen minutes early. Henrik was impressed and after showing her where to hang her coat and where to put her boots, which were covered in snow, he invited her into the back room to slip on her shoes and have a cup of coffee. Gerda was nowhere to be seen and Henrik explained that she was feeling poorly and he had persuaded her to remain in bed for another hour or two. This was the routine that continued for the rest of the week with Gerda rarely appearing in the shop before ten o'clock and then doing very little other than flower arranging and watering the plants. She rarely spoke to Abby but smiled and nodded at her often and Abby was intrigued by the difference in personalities between Henrick and his wife. It was only when she finally commented on it quietly one morning when Gerda was still in bed that Henrick confessed that he was very worried about her, "She used to be so lively," he said sadly, "and now she hardly talks. The doctors can't find anything wrong with her but she is getting thinner and forgets things. I must tell you Abby that in a couple of years I want to sell the business and take my Gerda away from here. The winters are too harsh for her and she loves to sit in the sun."

Abby felt sad as she had already developed an affection for this kind old man who had shown her so much respect, "But where will you go, Henrick."

Henrick smiled as he imagined his future, "Gerda has a cousin who lives in Siesta Key in Florida, that's near Sarasota. Sofie and her husband Willem have a house right at the beach and they're always asking us to pack up everything and move in with them."

"It sounds wonderful," said Abby but she couldn't help worrying what would happen if the shop was sold and she had to start looking for another job.

By the end of the week, Abby had learned a lot about running a florist and she was grateful that Henrick had taken so much time to teach her. There was a lot to learn about buying, selling and record keeping but she picked everything up quickly and Henrick was so pleased that he let her go early on Friday even though she had found someone to care for Kate after school. Actually it was Kate who had provided the answer to the problem of where she would spend the two hours each day between the time school ended and the time Abby finished work. On the second day at school, during morning recess, she noticed one of the girls staring at her and being rather mischievous, she stared back and then grinning, stuck out her tongue. Her classmate looked a little startled for a moment and then started to giggle and Kate with hands on her hips, now looking rather intimidating, demanded, "What are you giggling at?"

The girl, who was the same height as Kate, with a mop of ash blond curls and light blue eyes tried desperately to control her laughter and finally managed to sputter, "Sorry, I didn't mean to stare but you look like my cousin Daisy."

Kate was still not amused, "And is she funny looking?"

"No, of course not but when you stuck out your tongue it was funny."

Kate seemed to relax, "I see, and what's your name?"

"Helen and what's yours?"

"Kate."

And so their friendship began that day and later that afternoon when Kate was introduced to Helen's mother, she discovered that they lived only a block away from Julia's house. That evening, she persuaded Abby to make sure she was early picking her up because then she would meet Helen's mother and maybe she could ask her if she could baby-sit her after school. Abby was rather surprised at the way Kate had thought this out and she was nervous about asking a complete stranger to take care of her daughter but the next day she rushed to pick up Kate. Just as she arrived she saw Kate with a young blonde girl talking to a rather plump woman wearing a fox fur coat and matching hat. Kate saw her mother approaching and immediately called out, "Mommy over here, come and meet Helen and her mother."

Abby smiled at the other woman and couldn't help noticing the peaches and cream complexion and twinkling green eyes, "Hello," she said, "I'm Abby Harrison."

The woman smiled back and extended her hand, "Hi," she replied in a soft voice, "I'm Dorothy Ward. I'm really pleased to meet you; Helen did nothing but chatter on about your daughter from the time she got home until the time she went to bed and I gather she wants Kate to come home with us until you get home from work every day."

Abby was stunned to learn that Helen had already put the idea in her mother's head and she had no doubt that Kate instigated the whole thing, "Oh dear, "she said shaking her head at Kate then looking back at Dorothy, "I am so sorry, Kate had no right to get Helen to ask you that."

Dorothy laid a hand on Abby's arm, "It's all right, I'd be happy to do it. As it is, I have trouble keeping Helen amused when she gets home and this way she'll have someone to play with."

"Well, I was going to ask you myself actually," Abby admitted, "I really have to thank you, that is so kind but I have to pay you for your trouble. How much would you charge?"

Dorothy frowned, "Nothing at all, happy to do it, so starting tomorrow I'll pick Kate up with Helen and take her home. Here, I'll write down my address so you can come and get her when you're ready," and she fished in her purse for a pen and paper and scribbled her address down while both Kate and Helen just stood and grinned, both very pleased with themselves.

CHAPTER 23

ON SATURDAY, EXHAUSTED BUT happy with everything she had learned at the shop, Abby reminded Julia that they had agreed to get a kitten for Kate. Julia hadn't forgotten and was surprised that Kate had only mentioned it once on Thursday night just as she was going to bed.

Over a casual breakfast of bacon, scrambled eggs and pancakes, only indulged in on weekends, Abby nudged Kate playfully just as she was about to munch on a slice of toast covered in raspberry jam, "Haven't you forgotten something?" she asked.

Now with jam smeared across her face, Kate did not look amused, "Now look what you've done Mommy," she shrieked whereupon both Abby and Julia began to chuckle.

Kate wiped her mouth with the back of her hand and scowled, "Not funny. What is it Mommy, what have I forgotten?"

Abby stopped laughing and rolled her eyes at Julia, "Well I guess it isn't important, we'll just have to think of something else to do today."

Kate suddenly jumped up from her chair and started running back and forth with excitement, "Yippee," she yelled, "it's Saturday. We're going to get a kitty today!"

Abby sighed, "So you finally remembered, your Aunt Julia and I thought you'd forgotten all about it."

Kate blushed and bowed her head, "Well, I did but only for a moment," she said in a whisper.

"I see," said Abby, "well as soon as you finish your breakfast, and I mean all of it, we'll be on our way."

Just over two hours later, they were back home again laden down with all the supplies needed for a new kitten. Julia had generously purchased a litter box, litter, food and water bowls, a velvet leopard skin cat bed and a large bag of cat chow especially for kittens. Kate couldn't wait to take the new member of their family out of her cardboard carrying case. She had poked her fingers again and again through the ventilation holes all the way home from the Humane Society while the terrified kitten meowed incessantly.

Choosing a kitten had been difficult; there were so many cats in the shelter; some very young and some in their senior years. It was the older cats that Abby and Julia felt the most compassion for, knowing their chances of being adopted were slim, but when they finally came across the tiny grey kitten asleep at the back of its cage, they just couldn't resist it. They could hardly believe their good fortune to discover that the kitten had been brought in that morning and was a rare Russian Blue. They later learned from the adoption clerk that there was no doubt that somebody else would adopt the kitten that same day if they hadn't taken her. When Kate lifted her gently out of her cage and nestled her against her chest, she couldn't believe how soft and thick her coat was and she had never seen fur that was such an unusual shade of blue-grey. As she stroked the kitten, it opened its eyes lazily and looked up at Kate. It was then Kate noticed that her eyes were green and she thought she was the most beautiful kitten in the world.

Back at the house when Abby and Julia sat fascinated watching the tiny kitten exploring the living room, Kate crept forward and tapped Julia on the arm, "Is she my kitten Aunt Julia?" she asked.

Julia took Kate's hand and smiled, "Yes honey, she's yours but you have to look after her. You have to feed her and make sure her water bowl is always full and you have to scoop out her litter box at least twice a day."

"Oh I will, I will," Kate promised bouncing up and down on the balls of her feet.

"Good, I'm glad to hear it. Now what are you going to call her?"

Kate looked to Abby for guidance, "What do you think I should call her Mommy?"

Abby shook her head, "I don't know Kate, she's your kitten and you should name her."

Kate looked thoughtful and chewed on her lower lip, "I like Pepper and Panda and Peaches and Peanuts...."

"Hold on a minute," Abby intervened, "sounds like a lot of P's to me"

Julia and Kate both giggled and then Julia suggested,

"Why don't you give her a real girl's name, something simple like Molly?"

"Mmmm, Molly, I like it Aunt Julia," Kate said and she raced over to the kitten who was scratching at the fringe on the carpet, and called out, "here Molly, here Molly."

Abby looked over at Julia and grinned, "You always say the right thing, thank you."

CHAPTER 24

OVER THE NEXT FEW weeks, life settled down into a routine. Abby had made significant progress at the shop and Henrick mentioned on a number of occasions that he was glad his instinct had been to hire her. Wanting to spend more time with Gerda, who was now only helping out during the afternoon hours, he often left her alone in the shop to tend to customers and trusted her enough to involve her in the bookkeeping.

Evenings were spent helping Kate with homework and sharing any chores with Julia, who took great pride in the upkeep of the house. At Julia's urging, Abby took out membership at the local gym and attended two nights a week and within a month she had already lost five pounds and her energy level increased. On those nights, Julia stayed with Kate and put her to bed, always reading her a story just as Abby did.

While Julia had heard from Raymond and their separation was amicable, Abby had heard nothing from Ed. Martha called two or three times to tell Abby that she hadn't seen Ed but had spoken to him on the phone and he seemed to be all right. She had tried to persuade him to get in touch with Abby and arrange to see Kate but he was noncommittal and she didn't want to alienate him so she didn't push him too hard. On one occasion, when Abby insisted that Martha come over for supper, she arrived with gifts for Kate even though it wasn't a special occasion. Abby was happy that she had kept on good terms with her mother-in-law and that Kate was able to see her grandmother and after they had eaten, she sat silently watching the interchange between Kate and Martha who was now cradling Molly in her arms and singing her a lullaby. Julia remarked afterwards that it was a Kodak moment.

Abby thought often about trying to contact Ed herself. She thought she deserved to know what he intended to do as far as supporting Kate was concerned and also felt he should make an effort to see Kate once in a while. However, even with Julia encouraging her to pick up the phone and call Ed, she just couldn't bring herself to do it.

At the beginning of March on a Saturday afternoon just as the ice was beginning to melt away and the temperature rose, Abby got an alarming phone call from John, "I need to come over and see you Abby," he said sharply, "something's happened."

Abby had always had great respect for John and knew that whatever he had to say must be serious, "Of course John, you can come over right now. I'm here alone with Kate, Julia's gone shopping."

"I see," John, said, "it would be better if Kate wasn't there. I would rather talk to you alone."

Abby thought for a moment, "Well if you could wait for an hour Julia will be back and I can ask her to take her down to the park near the lake for a short time. It's a bit cold out but she loves the swings and she likes to feed the ducks."

"That's an excellent idea Abby, I'll see you at about four o'clock then."

"Oh John, don't hang up," Abby said hoping to catch him, "is Martha coming with you?"

John let out a sigh, "Afraid not Abby, she's a bit too distraught but she'll be all right. I'd better go, see you later."

"Bye John," Abby muttered as she sat down wearily wondering what John was about to tell her.

Julia was more than happy to take Kate to the lake after she heard about John's call. She was just as curious as Abby, "I'm intrigued as to what it's all about," she said, "obviously it has something to do with Ed but I'm surprised Raymond hasn't said anything."

"Well I guess we're going to find out soon enough", Abby remarked.

John arrived right on time as Abby expected. She had always known her father-in-law to be punctual and he didn't disappoint her.

"Do come in John," she said, ushering him into the living room, "Have a seat while I bring you some tea, I already have it made."

While Abby went off to the kitchen, John remained standing and looked around the room noticing all the feminine touches that were so typical of Julia. On second thoughts, he surmised that the flowers and potted plants in the room must have been provided by Abby and he observed a number of photographs of both Abby and Julia with Kate or of Kate alone looking much more grown up than when he last saw her. Just as he was about to sit down he felt something brush past him and looking down saw Molly creeping between his legs. He bent down and picked up the tiny creature and tickled it behind its ears, "Well, well and who's this?" he asked seeing Abby walking back into the room with a tea tray.

"Ah, I see you've found Molly," Abby responded placing the tray on the coffee table, "she's Kate's new kitten. Actually she's grown quite a bit since we got her."

John put Molly down gently on the carpet, "She's very cute, quite an unusual colour. I've always liked animals, and I had a bull terrier named Buddy when I was a boy but Martha never wanted a pet in the house, not even a budgie."

Abby sat down and began pouring tea into two china cups, "That's a shame John. You know I'm really happy to see you but I'm nervous about what you have to tell me."

John took the cup that Abby handed to him and added some milk, "Abby, I'm sorry if I frightened you on the phone. Martha got me more upset than anything else and I've had a little time to think but something's happened to Ed."

Abby's hand shook and she put her cup down, "What is it, what happened?"

"Well, Martha went over to see him this morning and there was a "Sold" sign on the lawn."

Abby gasped, "What, he sold the house?"

"Yes, and nobody knows where he is. Martha talked to the neighbours including that old neighbour of yours, Jane Manning, and apparently he's been gone for two weeks. It's been about that since Martha's spoken to him and his phone was cut off, so that's why she went over there. Jane would have called you but she didn't know where you were; she said he sold all the furniture too. Some dealer came by and bought the whole lot."

Abby stood up and started pacing the room, "What about his job? Has anyone called them to find out where he is?"

"It's Saturday Abby and nobody's there, we're going to have to wait until Monday. Martha's beside herself; she thinks something terrible has happened to him but I keep telling her that he must be okay, after all he arranged the house sale and disposal of furniture, so whatever he's up to it must have been planned."

Abby rubbed her forehead and then sat down again, "Maybe Raymond knows something and he's just not talking. Julia figured it was something to do with Ed and was surprised that Raymond hadn't called her."

"Yes, you may be right but I don't think he'll talk to his mother. When Julia comes home, perhaps you can ask her to call Raymond and see what he has to say."

"I'll certainly do that John. Thank you for coming to tell me and I'm glad Kate wasn't here. I know she hasn't seen her father for a long time and I keep making excuses for him but I'm not sure how to handle this."

John put down his cup and got up, "I'd better get back home Abby, if you find out anything just call me and we'll do the same."

Abby followed John to the front door and felt incredibly sad as she hugged him and then watched him climb into his car and drive away.

When Julia returned to the house with Kate, Abby had already prepared supper and while Julia looked at her curiously intrigued to know what had transpired, Abby sent her a silent signal to wait until Kate was out of the room.

Abby had been ambitious, trying out a new recipe with pasta, shrimp, mushrooms and a thick cream sauce and although Julia was glowing with compliments, Kate announced that she would rather have macaroni and cheese. Dessert went down a lot more favourably when Abby brought three bowls of butterscotch ice cream drenched in chocolate syrup to the table and Kate ate every last bit and proceeded to lick the bowl.

"Now Kate, that isn't very ladylike," admonished Abby frowning.

Kate looked contrite and put her bowl down, "Sorry Mommy but it was so good. Can I have some more?"

"It's 'May I' not 'Can I', and no, you may not, you've had quite enough to eat. You'll end up looking like a butterball if you keep that up," she replied winking at Julia.

Kate jumped up from the table, not waiting to be excused, "I want to go to my room; I'm making something for Helen. It's her birthday soon and I think she's having a party. Can I go to it, if she has one Mommy?"

Abby and Julia had begun to clear away the dishes, "Yes, of course you can go if you're invited. What are you making?"

"Uh, uh, it's a secret," said Kate shaking her head and running off up the stairs.

Abby and Julia took the dishes to the kitchen and proceeded to clean up from supper. Now that Abby was sure that Kate couldn't hear her, she told Julia everything that John had said and suggested that maybe Raymond knew something about it. Julia didn't hesitate and immediately called Raymond but was frustrated when he didn't answer. She could only assume that he had gone out for the evening and decided to call him again just before she went to bed.

Kate was so occupied with her secret gift that it was eight o'clock before she appeared back in the living room, and Abby pushed her back upstairs to brush her teeth and change into her pajamas. She only managed to read two pages of Alice in Wonderland before Kate fell asleep and she and Julia spent the next hour speculating on where Ed could be and what he had done with the money from the sale of the house.

Julia was puzzled, "I don't understand it; how could he sell the house when John and Martha gave it to you both as a wedding present?"

Abby sighed, "Well, that's just it; it was supposed to be for both of us but it was put in his name because they bought it before we were actually married."

"Bummer," said Julia, "that probably means you have no way of getting your share of the proceeds."

"I don't care about the money Julia, I'm just concerned about Ed. No matter what he's done he's still Kate's father."

"True enough but it's hardly fair that you get nothing and he's not even supporting Kate. You're much more forgiving than I am Abby."

"I don't believe that Julia, I think you can be very forgiving and not only that you're kind and generous too. Look, can you give Raymond another call, maybe he's there only I've got a bit of headache and I'd like to go to bed."

Julia picked up the phone which was sitting on the occasional table next to her chair, "I'll see if he's home yet."

Raymond picked up on the second ring, and after a brief conversation as to how they were each faring in their lives Julia asked him about Ed. Abby watched Julia's face as she listened to Raymond but wasn't able to determine what was being said on the other end of the line. Finally after saying goodbye, Julia hung up the phone and turning to Abby gave her the bad news, "Well, there's no sense in calling his work on Monday because he's not there any more; Raymond tells me he was fired over a month ago."

Abby leaned back into the cushions on the chesterfield where she had been sitting and closed her eyes, "Go on," she whispered.

Julia hesitated for just a moment, "Not only did he lose his job because he hardly showed up for work any more but he's been gambling too. Apparently he owed so much money that he used up all the savings in your joint account and then he had to sell the house to pay his debts. Raymond only found all this out a week ago when he saw Ed again in a downtown bar, two sheets to the wind. He was staying in some sleazy hotel and talking about taking off and never coming back. Raymond didn't take him seriously but when he tried to contact him at the hotel on Thursday, he'd checked out with no forwarding address."

Abby remained perfectly still and Julia crossed the room and sat down beside her. Taking her hand, she said gently, "I'm so sorry Abby, is there anything I can do?"

Abby opened her eyes and looked tearfully at Julia, "Why didn't Raymond tell you, or at least tell his mother?"

"That's so typical of Raymond; I told you the way he is. He doesn't like to get involved in anything personal."

Abby got up and walked over to the phone, "I guess it's up to me to tell Martha."

Julia followed close behind and put her hand on Abby's shoulder, "I'll call her if you like."

"No, I'll do it, thank you anyway," said Abby wearily, "and then I'm going to bed."

CHAPTER 25

AS WINTER TURNED INTO spring and the weather got warmer, Abby spent most of her leisure hours working in the small garden at the back of the house. She loved the feel of the earth between her fingers and hardly ever wore gloves despite repeated warnings from Julia about the damage to her skin and nails.

There was no word of Ed; he appeared to have vanished from the face of the earth and Martha and John's attempts to find him had been unsuccessful. Meanwhile Abby tried to put Ed out of her mind except for those rare occasions when Kate asked about her father. After making several excuses for his absence from their lives, Julia suggested to Abby that she should tell Kate the truth but leave out the details of his drinking and abusive behavior. Eventually Abby sat Kate down and told her that her father had been suffering from depression because of Daniel's death and had just gone off somewhere to try and get better. When Kate asked solemnly if he would come back when he was better, again Abby had to be truthful and tell her that she really didn't know. Kate seemed to accept this without a word or any real show of emotion and asked if she could go to Helen's house. Kate and Helen had become so close that they spent hours together in each other's homes, and that summer Dorothy Ward asked Abby if Kate could join them on their annual month long holiday at their cottage in Muskoka. Kate was so excited about the prospect of living at the lake with her best friend that Abby couldn't refuse, although she was apprehensive about spending July alone without her.

The month without Kate seemed to drag by despite the fact that Abby was busy at the shop and didn't have to rush home to prepare supper. She took the extra time, when she wasn't gardening, to catch up on her reading. She had always been an avid reader, preferring the classics such as Bronte's 'Jane Eyre' or Austen's 'Pride and Prejudice'. She also stepped up her exercise program, turning up at the gym three times a week and occasionally jogging along the boardwalk at the edge of the lake early in the morning before the heat of the day.

Julia was caught up in an important case at her office for most of July and didn't get home until after eight o'clock on many evenings. Abby was hoping they could do some fun things together during the last week before Kate got back but Julia was invited to spend a few days with a friend in Quebec City. Reluctant to leave Abby but needing to get away, Julia left for the long drive leaving Abby completely alone, except for Molly who feeling abandoned had forsaken Kate's bed for Abby's.

When Kate returned, brown as a berry and hair lightened by the sun, she chattered on endlessly about the cottage, running about in the Ward's boat, swimming in the lake with lots of other kids and eating around the campfire. It was only later when she finally flopped exhausted into bed and realized that Molly had deserted her that she looked up at her mother tearfully and said, "Now Molly's gone and left me too."

In August, Abby and Julia decided to make the most of the rest of the summer. They took the ferry to Centre Island, had a picnic in High Park, took a swim in the lake on one very hot day when the normally frigid water left them wonderfully refreshed and treated themselves to double scoop ice cream cones. But the highlight of the month was Kate's eighth birthday when Abby decided that it was to be a special day. Her birthday had been almost overlooked in the aftermath of the tragedy in the family and the prolonged grieving process. This year Abby went all out to make it a memorable occasion and with Julia's help, they decorated the garden with streamers and balloons and set up little tables covered in colourful tablecloths depicting Disney characters. Martha and John were invited along with Henrick and Gerda, although Gerda gracefully declined because she was too tired, and Abby also contacted her old neighbour Jane and asked her to bring Mandy because Kate hadn't seen her in such a long time. Dorothy Ward and Helen arrived bringing three other schoolmates of Kate's and the house and garden rang out with the sound of happy children.

Abby made hot dogs and hamburgers with all the trimmings and fabulous sundaes topped with walnuts and chocolate syrup, but the birthday cake with its eight candles was the highlight of the party. Kate stood proudly in her new pink organdy dress with her freshly curled hair tied up in a pink ribbon, while everyone sang Happy Birthday and then after blowing out all of the candles, she turned and hugged Abby whispering, "Thank you so much Mommy; it's a lovely party but I wish Daddy was here."

CHAPTER 26

IN THE FALL, HENRICK decided to take Gerda to Florida to visit with her cousin Sophie and her husband Willem. Abby was nervous about being left alone to run the shop but Henrick had every confidence in her. They were leaving on Saturday and Abby had agreed to fill in that day but just before the Vanderveers left for the airport, she voiced her concerns, "I hope I can do this Henrick, I don't want to let you down."

Henrick patted her hand reassuringly, "My dear, I have complete faith in you. The day you crept into my shop was a special day for me, but I didn't know it then, eh?"

Abby grinned, "I didn't creep in, did I?"

"Oh yes you did," replied Henrick chuckling, "you were like a little mouse and now look at you."

"I never thought of myself as a mouse."

"Well a little chicken then, and now you are a swan."

Abby started to laugh, "I think you have your animals mixed up Henrick."

"You may be right," Henrick said scratching his head, "you'll have to forgive an old man; I get mixed up sometimes."

"You're not old," Abby protested giving him a hug, "now off you go or you'll miss your plane and then you'll be in trouble with Gerda."

Henrick frowned and then peeked out of the window, "Oops she is already sitting in the taxi, and I'd better go. Bye Abby, take care of everything and don't forget to keep your eyes open for some nice young man."

Abby shook her head and waved him out of the shop then followed him to door and stayed there while the taxi pulled away. Henrick was always teasing her about the lack of a man in her life and she took it all in good fun but sometimes she wished she had an occasional date, someone to go to the movies, or go out to dinner with. Her life seemed to be wrapped up in her work and Kate and although she was happy, something was missing. Two or three times she was aware that a customer had showed more interest in her than in the flowers or plants they were purchasing, but she had put up a wall after her experience with Ed and she had no idea when the wall would come tumbling down.

Julia, meanwhile, had been out on several casual dates. Many of the people she dated she met through her work at the law firm and that fall, she attended a number of dinner parties given by her associates. It was at one of these parties that she met Mark Lillis and the chemistry was immediate. Mark was a Professor of Mathematics at the University of Toronto and looked the part. He was Julia's height, slim with light brown hair and an intelligent face sporting a goatee and dark horn rimmed glasses. He usually dressed in jeans and a tweed jacket with leather patches on the elbows but even at a formal party he was accepted just the way he was. By Christmas, Mark had been to Julia's house on many occasions but Julia had never allowed him to stay overnight. Abby thought Mark was perfect for her sister-in-law and was curious to know where the relationship was going. Julia enlightened her, "I like him an awful lot, and in fact I think I'm falling in love with him Abby."

Abby was excited, "That's wonderful, and do you know how he feels about you?"

"I'm not really sure but I want to take it slowly. We haven't even slept together yet."

"Really?" said Abby coloring slightly, "Is it because of Kate and me being here that you don't want to invite him to stay."

"No, of course not," replied Julia rather abruptly," I could stay at his house if I wanted to. I think I have to resolve my situation with Raymond first."

"You mean, ask Raymond for a divorce?"

"Yes, that's exactly what I mean and once the divorce comes through then we'll see what happens."

"But that could take months Julia, are you prepared to wait that long?"

Julia sighed, "I'm not sure but I'm going to talk to Raymond this week and start the ball rolling."

Abby felt sad for Julia; she suspected that she wanted to take her relationship with Mark to the next level but something seemed to be holding her back. At the same time that Julia contacted Raymond to start divorce proceedings, she heard from the couple that owned the house she was renting. They had decided to stay in Africa and wanted to put the house on the market. Julia, had grown to love the house and had added so many touches of her own that she jumped at the chance to make the first offer, secure in the knowledge that she was receiving half the proceeds from the house she had owned with Raymond. When she told Abby about it she was over the moon with excitement, "Think Abby," she babbled, "our own house, isn't it fabulous?"

Abby just stood looking at Julia with disbelief, "That is fabulous," she echoed and then without any trace of malice or jealousy she continued, "but it's going to be your house not our house."

"Right, right," Julia said, "but you know what I mean. Finally I have a place I can call my own and a great sister-in-law and niece to share it with."

Abby just shook her head over and over, "You are something else Julia Harrison," she said.

CHAPTER 27

CHRISTMAS CAME AND WENT and Julia finally bought the house she so desperately wanted to call her own. The previous owners, being so far away, had no desire to haggle over the price and were more than happy to take Julia's offer even allowing her to keep all the furniture at no extra cost. Julia was elated and to celebrate, she took Mark, Abby and Kate out to supper at the Imperial Room.

Mark had uncharacteristically worn a suit and tie after Julia suggested that there was a dress code where they were going. Meanwhile Abby looked very sophisticated in a midnight blue sheath with her hair swept up and Julia was a vision in deep red velvet and with her hair waving gently over her shoulders. Even Kate was in her very best kelly green dress with a matching bow on top of her chestnut curls. Everyone was in a light-hearted mood, and Abby came to really appreciate why Julia thought so highly of Mark. He had a brilliant mind, a sharp sense of humor and seemed to be exceedingly generous. He was twelve years older than Julia and had also experienced a great tragedy in his life. His marriage to a young teacher in his early twenties was cut short when she died of a brain aneurysm leaving him with a two-year-old daughter,

Cassandra. He had struggled through the difficult years of bringing Cassandra up as a single father and now at the age of twenty-two she was married to a mystery writer and lived in Nova Scotia. Mark spoke of his daughter often and Julia wasn't surprised when she became the subject of conversation that night just as they were finishing supper.

"I had a letter from Cassandra last week," Mark announced, "and I guess I have something to celebrate too."

Julia knew that could only mean one thing, "She's pregnant, isn't she?" she asked excitedly.

Mark took Julia's hand looking across at Abby and beaming from ear to ear, "Yes, I'm so thrilled; I can hardly wait to be a grandfather."

"Does that mean she's having a baby?" Kate interjected with childlike innocence.

"Yes, and I think it's wonderful," Julia replied squeezing Mark's hand.

"I miss her so much," Mark said removing his glasses and bowing his head while he wiped the lenses with the edge of the tablecloth, "you'll have to excuse me ladies but this a little emotional for me."

Julia reached over and draped one arm around his shoulders, "We understand, you have every right to be emotional."

Mark looked up then said quietly, "I think there's something else you should know Julia."

Julia looked nervous and sat back in her chair, "What is it, you look serious."

"Maybe I should have waited until we were alone but you would have to know sooner or later."

Julia became more anxious, “Well, don’t keep me in suspense, tell me, what is it?”

Mark took her hand again, “I applied for a position at Acadia University.”

Julia pulled her hand away looking stunned while Abby feeling uncomfortable asked, “Where is that Mark?”

Julia turned to Abby and snapped, “It’s in Nova Scotia, not far from Halifax.”

Abby was taken aback at Julia’s rebuke and after hesitating for a moment she rose from the table and reached for Kate’s hand, “If you’ll excuse us, we’re going to powder our noses.”

Kate started too giggle as she stood up, “I’m not powdering my nose Mommy.”

“Come on Kate, let’s go,” Abby said impatiently and then turning to Julia and Mark she added, “I think you need a little privacy.”

When Abby returned to the table with Kate after delaying as long as she could, the tension was evident but Julia managed to rise to the occasion by turning most of her attention to Kate and asking her about anything she could think of including the latest exploits of Molly, who had now forsaken Abby and returned to Kate’s bed at night.

Mark had picked everyone up from Julia’s house earlier that evening and after they got through supper he drove them home at which point Abby and Kate said goodnight and Julia remained in the car. Abby bundled Kate upstairs to get ready for bed and then went to the kitchen to make some cocoa and wait for Julia. After almost an hour had passed, she was just considering going to bed herself when she heard the key in the lock and Julia came in looking a little dishevelled and red-eyed. Abby got up and helped Julia off with her coat, "Why don't I make you some cocoa and then we can sit and talk," she suggested.

Julia nodded, "That would be nice, thank you Abby," and she sank down into one of the comfy armchairs that flanked the sofa.

Abby returned with two mugs of cocoa and a plate of digestive biscuits. Even though they had just had a wonderful supper, she thought Julia might be in need of a little comfort food, "Tell me what's happened," she said gently peering at Julia over the top of her own mug.

"I'm sorry I snapped at you tonight Abby, please forgive me. Actually there's not much to tell, he applied for the position at Acadia and he's sure he'll get it."

"No need to apologize but tell me, is this going to mean the end of your relationship?"

"Well, he asked me if I would consider going with him….."

"What?" Abby interjected leaning forward, "well that's wonderful isn't it?"

"Hardly," Julia replied putting her mug down on the coffee table, "I've just bought this house and I don't want to give it up now. It took me years to make the break from Raymond and now I have the independence I've always wanted."

"But surely you don't want to be alone all your life?"

"Maybe, I don't know. In any case it's too soon to make any more major changes and I'm not sure I even care about Mark enough to get seriously involved with him. As a matter of fact I told him I thought we should stop seeing each other because the longer we continue this relationship the harder it will be when he leaves Toronto and makes a new life for himself out East."

"I'm so sorry Julia," Abby said, "and this evening was supposed to be a celebration. I hope Mark didn't spoil it too much for you."

Julia got up shaking her head, "I'm just not going to let it bother me," she replied, but Julia could see the tears in her eyes as she headed for the stairs and called out quietly, "Goodnight Abby, see you in the morning."

Mark and Julia occasionally kept in touch by telephone but they agreed not to see each other. Then in late spring, Mark informed her that he was going to Halifax to visit Cassandra and look at available properties in the area. Julia was relieved to know that he was finally leaving even if only on vacation. It was a prelude to the time when he would truly be out of her life and she could stop thinking about what might have been.

During the months leading up to Mark's departure, Julia had spent many of her leisure hours with Abby and Kate. On weekends they would go to a movie, visit the museum, toboggan in High Park or spend an afternoon with Martha and John. Neither Raymond nor his parents had heard from Ed and still had no idea where he was. It had taken a toll on Martha and she had lost quite a bit of weight but John was philosophical about the whole affair and maintained that no news was good news.

Martha wasn't the only one that had lost weight, by early summer Abby was almost as slim as Julia and now that she had become a little more sophisticated and Julia had softened her appearance; they were often mistaken for sisters. Abby had taken Julia's advice and highlighted her dark hair with auburn streaks and every morning she carefully made up her face in the way that Julia had taught her. Even Henrick remarked on her transformation and suggested that she might be ready to expand her horizons. When Julia questioned Henrick as to what he actually meant, he complimented her again on how much she had learned working at Charlotte's and that he felt she was ready to attend the annual florist convention in Kansas City. Having never been out of Ontario, let alone Canada, Abby was terrified at the thought but Henrick continued to encourage her and in mid summer she found herself on a plane flying to Missouri. Traveling alone and staying in a hotel was a liberating experience for Abby and she returned home three days later feeling much more confident than ever before. When Julia greeted her at the door after her limousine ride from the airport, she could already sense a change in Abby and she looked radiant. In a rare few hours of leisure time during the convention she had gone shopping in an upscale store and purchased a light weight summer suit in pale yellow and was wearing it with all white accessories including a heavy beaded necklace and sunglasses. Julia stepped back as she came through the door, "Wow, look at you," she exclaimed then running to the bottom of the stairs she called out, "Kate, come and look at Mommy, she looks like a movie star."

Abby had just reached the end of the hallway when Kate came racing down the stairs, "Mommy, Mommy," she yelled throwing herself into her mother's arms.

"Hello honey, "said Abby tenderly holding Kate at arms length and looking into her eyes, "I missed you so much."

"I missed you too Mommy but Aunt Julia and I had lots of fun. I like your necklace Mommy," she said tugging on the beads at Abby's throat, "you look really pretty."

"I think she looks beautiful," said Julia, "come Abby put your suitcase down and I'll put the kettle on. We'll have a cup of tea and I want to hear all about Kansas City."

Abby smiled, "Not too much to tell really," then she leaned towards Julia and whispered, "I didn't meet any sexy men, if that's what you want to know."

"Why are you whispering," Kate demanded.

"Grown up talk," replied Julia, "but you can stay and listen if you like."

"No thanks," said Kate, "it's boring, I think I'll go and play with Molly."

CHAPTER 28

THE FOLLOWING FEBRUARY, ONE frigid Friday morning, Julia had just come downstairs to the kitchen to make coffee when the telephone rang. She was surprised to hear Henrick's voice at such an early hour and felt a growing concern when he quietly asked for Abby. "It's Julia, Henrick," she said, "is something wrong?"

Henrick's voice betrayed his anxiety, "Yes, it's Gerda, she's had a stroke and it doesn't look so good. I really need to speak to Abby."

"Oh Henrick, I'm so sorry, I'll get her for you, just hold on a minute," and Julia put down the phone and ran to the bottom of the stairs calling for Abby who, after hearing the phone ring, was already poised on the landing anticipating bad news.

"It's Gerda, she's had a stroke. Henrick sounds pretty upset; he needs to speak to you."

"Oh goodness," Abby remarked as she rushed down and picked up the phone, "Henrick, it's Abby. Julia told me about Gerda, how bad is it?"

Henrick sighed, "It's very bad; she had a massive stroke and she's in a coma. She's in intensive care at St. Michaels".

"And where are you Henrick"

"I'm at the hospital," Henrick replied as his voice broke, "I can't lose her Abby, I just can't lose her."

"Oh Henrick," Abby whispered, "I'm sure they'll do all they can for her. What can I do to help?"

"Just take care of the shop and if you can open up tomorrow too I would be grateful."

"Of course, anything you need. I'll get ready and go over right away and as soon as I lock up tonight I'll come over to the hospital."

For the next week, Abby took over the whole operation of Charlotte's and even though she was bone tired at the end of the day she spent at least two hours every evening keeping Henrick company while he remained at the hospital watching over Gerda. Abby didn't know how he could keep going every day on very little food or sleep, and she encouraged him to eat and go home to his own bed but he refused to budge. Even after visiting hours, he would sit and doze in the main lobby of the hospital and no amount of cajoling would do any good.

Gerda never regained consciousness and ten days after she was first brought to the hospital, she quietly passed away. Henrick was inconsolable and Abby, in an attempt to ease his suffering, closed up the shop and helped with all of the funeral arrangements.

It was a simple ceremony in a chapel on Glebe Road with a small number in attendance. Abby, Julia and Kate sat quietly beside Henrick along with Sofie and Willem who had flown up from Florida and a few regular customers from the shop. The burial at Mount Pleasant cemetery proved to be the most difficult time for Henrick. It was snowing heavily and the wind was howling bending the trees all around them. As Abby watched this man, who had become like a father to her, stooped over in despair and wiping away his tears, she was filled with compassion. What would happen to him now, she wondered.

When everybody returned to Julia's house, the mood was sombre but after serving bowls of hot potato soup, sausage rolls, small egg tartlets and red wine, even Henrick seemed to brighten a little. He started to reminisce about Gerda and all the wonderful times they had spent together and at times he even smiled at his own thoughts. It was only after Sofie and Willem left for their hotel and the other guests had said their goodbyes that he approached Abby about the shop, "Come," he said guiding her by the arm and sitting down beside her on the sofa, "we need to talk about what we are going to do about Charlotte's."

"Yes, I've been wondering about that," said Abby gently, "are you going to sell?"

"Yes," replied Henrick nodding, "and I want you to buy it…."

"What?" Abby interjected, "How can I? The only savings I have are for Kate's education and I just can't touch those funds Henrick."

"But you don't have to pay me right away, you can pay me out of the profits every quarter or every six months, Abby."

Abby got up and started pacing the floor, "Why are you doing this Henrick? You know you can sell to somebody else and get enough money to make your life a lot easier, and anyway what are you going to do now? Are you just going to stay home and grieve because I won't let you do that?"

Henrick got up and took Abby by both hands, "My dear, you have been like a daughter to me and you're the only person I trust to take over Charlotte's. Gerda and I struggled to make a life here and opening the shop was the answer to our dreams. I just can't let it go to a stranger no matter how much they might pay me. You'll need to hire someone else to help you but I know you can do it; you're smart and the customers love you and you can take over the living quarters or rent them out. As for me, well I'm taking these weary old bones to Florida. Sofie has offered to take me in and I'm going, it's what my Gerda would have wanted."

Abby threw her arms around Henrick, "I don't know what to say, I can't believe you're doing this for me and I'm going to miss you so much."

Henrick hugged Abby back and tears formed in his eyes, "Well maybe you can come visit. Kate would love it at the beach and you're going to need a vacation yourself after running the shop for a while."

"It sounds wonderful," said Abby stepping out of Henricks arms and placing her hand gently on his cheek, "I love you, you know."

"And I love you more," Henrick replied.

When Abby told Julia about her conversation later that night, Julia encouraged her to take Henrick's offer, "This is a chance in a lifetime Abby and you can't afford to turn it down and anyway you'd break an old man's heart if you did."

"Trust you to say the right thing again," Abby remarked, "I wouldn't want to upset Henrick and it is a wonderful opportunity but I'm not sure about moving in upstairs above the shop."

"I don't want you to do that, it's not suitable enough for you and Kate," advised Julia, "in fact I've been meaning to talk to you about giving Kate a room of her own."

Abby frowned, "How do you propose to do that, there aren't any extra rooms here?"

"Ah but there could be," replied Julia pursing her lips and nodding, "we could divide up part of the patio area that runs along the back of the house or turn the attic into a bedroom. The attic would probably be better because it will be closer to you and it will make a nice cozy room once it's been renovated."

"But it will cost so much," protested Abby.

"Maybe," Julia agreed, "but it will just add to the value of the house, so stop being negative and put that creative mind of yours to work and think about how you are going to decorate it."

CHAPTER 29

BY EARLY SUMMER, ABBY had already spent the last three months running Charlotte's and could hardly believe that she actually owned the shop. She considered changing the name but in deference to Gerda's memory and her affection for Henrick, she decided against it.

Henrick had settled in Siesta Key with Sofie and Willem and was already beginning to enjoy his new life. He phoned Abby often wanting to know how she was getting along and if she needed any advice and at the same time regaling her with tales of deep sea fishing and playing golf at least three times a week with Willem. He had joined the local country club and Abby smiled to herself when she began to read through the lines after he had mentioned a certain lady named Ginny on a number of occasions. Through Sofie, she learned that Ginny was a widow and a barrel of laughs and she had certainly put the smile back on Henrick's face.

Spending so much time at the shop meant that Abby had to rely more and more on Dorothy Ward and Julia to help out with Kate and even though she had hired someone to help, it was impossible to run the business without devoting many more hours to it than ever before.

Pauline Barton applied for the position of assistant after Abby advertised in the Toronto Star. She was one of many applicants but Abby took a liking to her immediately even though she had little knowledge of flowers or plants. She was in her late thirties, married with two teenage children and had a motherly quality about her. Short in stature and rather plump with short brown hair she reminded Abby of Martha except that she wore hippy style clothes, large dark framed glasses and oversize hoop earrings. Pauline lived with her family in a house in Corktown, an old area of Toronto close to the lake, and moving to the rooms above the store was out of the question. The rooms had remained empty and although Julia had encouraged Abby to rent them, she had been too busy to even think about it. Now, as Pauline began to take over more and more of the workload, she decided it was time to start looking for a tenant.

A week later, after several phone calls from interested parties, Abby witnessed a lease prepared by Julia, renting the upstairs premises to a diminutive single lady in her late sixties with pure white hair, twinkling blue eyes and a canary named Daisy. Emma McQueen had arrived in Canada from Scotland with her parents when she was fourteen but one could still hear the brogue in her voice whenever she spoke particularly when she was excited or talking to another Scot. Most of the time, Abby was hardly ever aware of Emma's existence as she came and went via a side entrance to the store that led directly upstairs. It was only when she heard water running, Daisy's occasional chirping or the beginning of the month when Emma paid her rent that Abby was even aware that there was someone else on the premises. Occasionally, when she did think of

Emma, she wondered how she would have gotten along with Henrick, but then it occurred to her that maybe Ginny had already taken a place in his heart.

At the end of June, Dorothy once again asked if Kate could join them at their cottage in Muskoka. Reluctantly but a little relieved that she didn't have to worry about who would look after her daughter while she was working, and with the urging of Kate herself, Abby agreed. At the same time, Julia decided to spend her three-week vacation traveling alone through the western United States and Canada. She had never attempted a trip like this before and it was a sign of her growing independence. Left to her own devices during her leisure hours, Abby was at a bit of a loss but after the first week she made up her mind to use the time by visiting many of the small art galleries in the city, taking in a couple of movies and catching up on her reading.

On a Saturday morning, with Pauline minding the shop, Abby dressed casually in a pair of lightweight jeans, a plain white tee shirt and her favourite blue Keds and feeling very young and carefree; she took a streetcar to the centre of town to W.H. Smith's. She loved to browse through the bookstore and was anxious to find a paperback copy of James Michener's novel 'Hawaii' which she had been unable to afford when it was released two years earlier in hardcover. When she finally saw what she was looking for in the best sellers section, she was excited and was just about to retrieve the book from the shelf when a hand stretched out in front of her and snatched it away. Abby was outraged, whirling around ready to chastise whoever had so rudely reached across and taken the one book that she desperately wanted to read, but the words died in her throat. The man looking down at her and smiling took her breath away. He was at least two inches over six feet, slim with broad shoulders and breathtakingly handsome. Thick black hair flopped casually over his forehead, his eyes were the colour of onyx and his deeply tanned face was rugged but he had a sensitive mouth which drew Abby's attention when he spoke, "Oops, I'm sorry," he said still smiling, "is this the book you were looking for?"

Abby, still mesmerized by the stranger's looks, found his voice even more disturbing. She had always been in love with the refined accent of the English upper class and this was what she was hearing now. She felt herself blush as she stammered, "Er…. yes actually it was, but you can have it."

"I wouldn't dream of it, you were here first and I apologize for my rude behaviour," and he handed the book back to her.

Abby was flustered but took the book and tucked it under her arm, "Thank you, "she said, "I hope you'll find another copy," and started to walk away.

"Hold on," said the stranger grabbing her arm, "maybe I can borrow your copy when you've finished with it."

Abby had the feeling that he was coming on to her, "Excuse me," she said indignantly, "I don't even know you and I have to go."

"Well we could change that," the stranger insisted still holding her arm, "why don't I buy you a cup of coffee?"

"Why would you want to do that?" asked Abby naively.

"So that we can get to know each other better. Look I'm only in town for another two weeks and I'd like to fraternize with some of the natives," and he grinned disarmingly.

Abby couldn't help grinning back, "I suppose a cup of coffee wouldn't hurt, are you suggesting right now?"

"There's no time like the present, there's a nice little coffee shop two doors away. If you're willing, we can pay for your book and be on our way."

"Okay," Abby agreed, "but I can pay for my own book."

Abby could hardly believe that a few minutes later she was sitting across from a man she had met only moments before. He was certainly attractive and she liked the way he was dressed in jeans and a black tee shirt but she struggled to understand why she had accepted his offer so readily. It was so out of character for her but for a brief instant she felt energized by her impulsiveness, a trait that was so much in contrast to her normal regulated existence. Her thoughts were interrupted as the stranger finished spooning sugar into his cup and asked, "What were you thinking about?"

Abby stared into the coal black eyes, "I was thinking that I don't even know your name," she said.

"Well that's easily remedied, it's Simon Fraser and I'm very pleased to meet you," he replied extending his hand towards her, "and you lovely lady are?"

Abby was amused by this formal gesture but shook his hand and responded, "Abby, Abby Harrison."

"Mmmm cute name Abby, I presume it's short for something?"

"Yes, it's short for Abigail but thankfully nobody calls me that."

"Abby certainly suits you," Simon remarked, "did anybody ever tell you what amazing blue eyes you have?

You're obviously Canadian and am I to assume that you live here in Toronto?"

Abby was flattered by Simon's compliment but decided not to acknowledge it, "I've lived here for about fifteen years and before that I lived in Oakfield; it's a small town not too far away. But what about you, you're certainly not from here you sound very English?"

Simon chuckled, "I guess it's not hard to figure out with this accent. Some people consider it a little affected."

"Oh no," Abby protested, "I think it's fascinating, I could listen to you talk all day," then realizing what she had said she blushed with embarrassment.

Simon raised an eyebrow, "In that case why don't we make a whole day of it? I hear it's going to be beautiful tomorrow and we could go over to Centre Island and maybe have a picnic. I'll bring the food and...., "he hesitated when Abby looked startled and sat back in her seat. "I'm sorry," he continued, "I'm being terribly presumptuous; maybe you have other plans."

Abby seemed to relax and shook her head, "No, I don't have any plans for tomorrow, I'm actually free as a bird but it's all a little sudden."

"I know, once again my apologies, but I think I explained I'm only here for another two weeks and then I have to go back to London. Please say you'll come out with me, it will be the highlight of my trip."

"Why are you in Toronto, are you on vacation?"

"Yes, I have some time off but I'd rather tell you all about it tomorrow. Now please, say yes."

Abby couldn't help smiling, "All right, we'll go to the island tomorrow but I insist on helping out with the food."

CHAPTER 30

SUNDAY MORNING, ABBY MET Simon on the dock at the foot of Bay Street. She had declined his offer of a ride home from the bookstore and insisted that she make her own way to the ferry. After such a brief encounter even the remote possibility that she might be making a mistake prevented her from trusting Simon completely. She had no idea that within twenty-four hours her whole attitude would completely change.

Simon wore a similar black tee shirt to the one he had worn the day before, but he had traded his jeans for knee length khaki shorts and Abby couldn't help noticing his muscular legs covered in a fine layer of dark hair. He was still, in her mind, one of the most handsome men she had ever seen and she wondered why he had taken such an interest in her. She had never considered herself beautiful or even pretty, when in fact she was more attractive now at age thirty-five than when she was in her twenties and had received many compliments over the past few years. Wanting to look her best, she had curled her hair, taken great care with her makeup, not wanting it to look overdone, and put on her new white pedal pushers and pale yellow top with it's tiny shoestring straps. When she looked in the mirror she was pleased with what she saw but she was nervous and almost smoked one of Julia's cigarettes, which she had vowed to give up but still kept in a drawer in case her willpower gave out.

On the ferry crossing, the sky was so blue and the water so calm it was almost mesmerizing and there were dozens of small sailboats dotted all over the lake. Rather than spoiling the moment Abby and Simon stood at the rail of the ferry and watched the receding skyline of Toronto in silence. It was only when they had almost reached the dock at the island that Simon took Abby's hand and said, "I hope you don't think I was ignoring you, it's just that sometimes my life is a little hectic and when I find myself in a peaceful situation like this, I just want to drink it all in."

"I completely understand," Abby said gently squeezing Simon's hand, "I'd like to hear all about this hectic life of yours."

"And I'd like to hear all about your life," Simon countered, "let's get off this ferry and find somewhere nice and shady by the water where we can have our picnic and talk."

"Sounds like a wonderful idea," said Abby as the ferry came to a standstill at the landing dock and let out a blast on its horn.

Abby had brought french bread, cold cuts of chicken and roast beef, thick slices of swiss cheese and fresh strawberries while Simon provided a bottle of vintage white wine and a selection of petit fours which he claimed to have bought at a bakery early that morning. During their picnic under a willow tree, where Simon insisted on feeding the swans even though it was forbidden, Abby learned a lot about his life. Simon was thirty-eight years old and a journalist for the Daily Mail. He had a flat in central London and his family lived in Surrey. His father, now retired, had been a member of parliament; his mother was involved with several charitable organizations and his younger sister Brooke was a budding actress and living with her boyfriend. He was currently on vacation visiting his oldest friend Jim, a Canadian, who he had met when they were both attending university in Oxford but he was due to return to London in two weeks to work on a major story involving the Russian race into space.

Abby was impressed but noticed that Simon had not mentioned his marital status even though she was very aware that he was not wearing a ring, "It all sounds very exciting," she responded sipping on her wine, "and is there a Mrs. Fraser in the picture?"

"Yes, my mother," Simon replied with a devilish grin, then he suddenly looked serious, "actually I've never been married although I came close once. Linda and I practically grew up together and our families always expected us to become a couple. We got engaged about ten years ago but it didn't last, I guess we knew too much about each other to make it interesting. Soon after we broke up, she married some chap she met in Paris on vacation and ended up living in the south of France. My parents usually get a card every Christmas, otherwise there hasn't been any contact."

Abby was relieved but still curious, "Hasn't there been anyone else special in your life?"

Simon shook his head, "Not really although don't get me wrong, I'm no saint. I've had my share of lady friends. Anyway that's enough about me, I want to hear all about you now."

Abby was reluctant to tell Simon that she was still married but after she detailed the circumstances and Ed's subsequent disappearance he sympathized with the predicament she was in. His compassion was evident when she tearfully told him about the loss of Daniel but he lit up when she talked about Kate, "I love kids," he commented. "How old is she?"

"She's almost ten, in fact her birthday's coming up really soon and I'm hoping she'll be home by then. She's staying with some friends at a cottage in Muskoka and she just loves it there."

"You must really miss her especially if there's just the two of you. What about your husband's parents, do you ever see them?"

Abby wanted to make one thing very clear, "Oh no we're not alone," she replied as she began to clear up the picnic utensils, "we live at my sister-in-law Julia's house. She's been wonderful to me, in fact I don't know how I would have survived without her. As for Ed's parents, we see them fairly often; they've been very supportive but I know my mother-in-law desperately misses Ed and they've spent a small fortune trying to locate him."

"And is Julia married?" Simon questioned as he began to pack up the picnic basket.

"No, she's divorced from Ed's older brother. I wish you could meet her but she's on vacation at the moment and won't be back for two weeks."

"That's too bad but speaking of meeting people, I'd like you to meet my friend Jim, he's a great guy."

"I'd like that, what does he do for a living?"

"He's an industrial engineer and a good one although that's not what he wanted to do. He always wanted to be a vet but when his father died at an early age, he felt duty bound to take over the running of the family business. By the way, you haven't told me what you do Abby."

Abby beamed as she proudly told Simon all about her transition from a lowly sales clerk in a five and dime in Oakfield to becoming the owner of a florist shop, although she grew sad when she talked about Henrick and Gerda.

Both Abby and Simon learned a lot about each other that afternoon and they were in no rush to catch the ferry back. They spent a lazy two hours after their picnic lying on the plaid rug that Abby had provided gazing at the willow tree branches swaying gently over their heads while they talked about their lives. Occasionally Simon would lean up on one elbow and look down at Abby thinking how pretty she looked and finally unable to contain himself any longer, he bent down and kissed her lightly on the lips. Abby was surprised at her own response; she wanted him to kiss her and scared to death that he might, but when it happened, it seemed so natural and she slid her arm around his neck and kissed him back.

It was almost supper time when they took a stroll around the island laughing at the antics of the ducks, wandering through the animal farm with its horses, cows and goats and browsing through the specialty shops which housed a myriad of tourist treasures. When Abby's stomach began to rumble and she realized how hungry she was, Simon suggested that they go back to the mainland and eat in one of the lakeside restaurants. Supper spent outdoors by the water was one of the most enjoyable times that Abby could remember. Both she and Simon dined on crisp Caesar salads, fresh red snapper covered in a light hollandaise sauce and a heavenly concoction of all kinds of summer fruits covered in thick clotted cream. As the evening wore on and the wine that they shared began to go to Abby's head, she didn't know when she had felt happier. Simon was the personification of every woman's dream, handsome, charming and intelligent with a wicked sense of humour. Abby didn't want the evening to end and when Simon suggested that he drive her home she agreed without any sense of trepidation.

Simon had borrowed Jim's Corvette convertible and they drove to Julia's house with the top down, soft music playing on the radio and Abby's hair blowing in the breeze. Abby was instantly aware of people on the street turning to look at them as they drove by and she couldn't help smiling to herself when she saw two of her neighbour's, who were sitting on their porches, actually get up and stare when they pulled into the driveway. There was no question in Abby's mind about allowing Simon into the house; she couldn't bear to let him go. Once inside, he wandered around commenting on various objects perched on tables and the many photographs displayed throughout the room including several of Kate and Julia, "Well I can see that your daughter is going to grow up to be a beauty just like her mother," he called out to Abby who was in the kitchen making coffee, "and your sister-in-law's not too shabby either."

Abby came back into the living room while she waited for the coffee to percolate, "Not too shabby? I think Julia is beautiful, wait until you meet her."

"Oh I didn't think I was going to be able to," said Simon taking both of Abby's hands.

Abby realized that she had already been fantasizing about their relationship continuing after Simon returned home and the hope that he would come back to Toronto and she lowered her eyes and blushed, "Oh, sorry, that's right, I forgot. She'll just be coming back when you leave."

Simon had always been very astute and easily read between the lines, "Don't worry Abby, I'll be back sooner than you think," he assured her and drew her into his arms and kissed her passionately.

Abby was responding without any reservation when Simon suddenly released her and jumped backwards, "What an earth was that?" he said as he felt something forcing its way between his feet. Then looking down he saw Molly who was now looking up at Abby and meowing, obviously looking for her supper, which was well overdue.

"Well who do we have here?" asked Simon as he gently picked Molly up and stroked her head. "What a pretty creature you are."

Abby sighed, "That's Molly and I forgot all about her supper."

Simon started to walk towards the kitchen still holding Molly who seemed perfectly content to be held by this complete stranger, "Well, we can soon remedy that; where's her food Mom?"

Abby chuckled and fished in the cupboard for Molly's Meow Mix then handed it to Simon who emptied some into Molly's bowl and then slowly lowered her to the floor, "She's a beautiful looking animal," he remarked, "you know Abby, I love kids but sometimes I think I love animals even more."

"I know what you mean," Abby agreed, "they hardly ever answer back and they love you no matter what you do."

"I could be like that," teased Simon as he swung Abby into his arms again.

Abby wriggled out of Simon's grasp and lifted the percolator from the counter top, "Down boy," she said playfully, "time for coffee."

CHAPTER 31

ON MONDAY MORNING, ABBY awoke feeling that her whole world had suddenly changed. Simon had been a perfect gentleman and left, although reluctantly, before midnight after making arrangements to see her the following Friday. Although, it was obvious that they would have liked to have seen each other during the week, Simon had already made an arrangement to drive up to Rice Lake with Jim and spend the next three days fishing. They had intended to leave on Sunday but Jim was more than accommodating when Simon explained that he had met someone he was sincerely interested in and asked if they could leave a day later. He was to return late on Thursday afternoon; meanwhile on the same day Abby was committed to overseeing the flower arrangements for a small wedding taking place that evening. Pauline did not have enough experience to take over for her and she had only just recently begun to expand the business supplying flowers for special occasions and supervising their arrangement. It was already beginning to prove very lucrative and despite the temptation of giving Pauline the responsibility so that she could see Simon, Abby had her reputation to consider and future business depended on her ability to provide her clients with the best service possible.

While preparing toast and coffee for breakfast, Abby pondered on her predicament and decided that it would not be long before she would need to hire additional help in the shop and also invest in a delivery van and driver. She was just about to head out of the door when the phone rang and thinking there might be a problem with Kate; she rushed back to answer it. She whispered, "Hello," while keeping her fingers crossed hoping that this would not be bad news and was surprised when she heard a voice that sounded like music to her ears, "Good morning Abby, how's my lovely lady this morning?"

Abby dropped her purse onto the counter and felt her whole body relax, "Simon?" she asked although she had no doubt it was him, "Where are you?"

"We're about half way to Rice Lake and decided to stop to pick up some supplies. I thought I'd just call to see how you were this beautiful morning."

"I'm just fine but even better now that you've called. I didn't expect to hear from you until Friday."

"I just couldn't resist Abby, I hope I didn't disturb you."

"No, of course not. I was just going out the front door when I heard the phone and I thought something might have happened to Kate."

"Oh dear, I'm sorry if I alarmed you. I should have thought about that before I rang," said Simon genuinely concerned.

"It's fine Simon," said Abby reassuringly, "mothers always tend to fear the worst when their children are miles away."

"I understand Abby, it won't happen again," Simon responded, "Listen Abby, I'd better go, Jim needs some help carrying all these supplies to the car. I'll call you on Friday during the day and maybe I could pick you up from the shop when you finish work."

"That would be perfect," Abby replied picking up her purse, "I'll give you directions when you call," and she proceeded to give him the telephone number at Charlotte's.

CHAPTER 32

THE NEXT FOUR DAYS seemed like an eternity to Abby and she thought about Simon constantly. At night she had trouble sleeping, but woke up feeling ready to face the world knowing that every day brought her closer to seeing him again. Monday evening she wrote a letter to Kate but didn't mention Simon, and on Tuesday she visited Martha and John and they talked a lot about Ed, but there was still no trace of his whereabouts. On Wednesday, when she arrived home exhausted after a very busy day she found a postcard in the mail from Julia. She had just left San Francisco, rented a car and was on her way to Seattle. She was enjoying the experience of traveling alone but hinted that she had met some interesting people along the way. Abby suspected that, knowing Julia, she had probably been approached by a number of men on her trip which was understandable considering how attractive she was. Abby couldn't help smiling thinking about Julia and what a wonderful friend she had turned out to be. Thursday evening, Abby was so busy overseeing the flower arrangements for the wedding that she had to solicit Pauline's help for a few hours and she hardly had time to think about Simon. By the time she got home she was so tired that she took a bubble bath, put on her favourite terry robe, made herself a grilled cheese sandwich and coffee and sank down onto the sofa to watch a rerun of an old Bette Davis movie. Finally, at just after eleven o'clock she made her way up to bed, fell into a deep sleep and woke up on Friday morning ecstatic at the thought that she would be seeing Simon later that day. She had no idea what he had planned for the evening and she didn't really care, just the thought of being with him sent her spirits soaring.

By three o'clock in the afternoon, Abby still hadn't heard from Simon and she was beginning to get anxious. Even Pauline, sensing that Abby's mood had changed, asked if something was wrong, but she just shook her head and continued to fuss with an arrangement of lilies and delphiniums needed for a birthday celebration. Just ten minutes later the phone rang and before Abby had a chance to pick it up, Pauline already had the receiver to her ear. She listened for a moment then turning to Abby with a knowing smile on her face said, "It's for you Abby," and as she passed the phone over she whispered, "Nice voice, very sexy."

It was obvious to Pauline that the call had completely changed Abby's mood and she gathered from what she had heard that whoever had called was coming by the shop later in the day. She didn't like to pry and she respected Abby's privacy, but she was disappointed when Abby said she could leave early and wouldn't get to see whoever had called. Abby had already arranged for her to work the next day and the following Saturday but she had assured her that there would soon be more help and she wasn't expected to work weekends for much longer.

Abby got dressed that morning not knowing what to wear because she had no idea where Simon would be taking her that night. She finally settled on a lightweight white cotton dress with a scoop neck and cap sleeves, which she dressed up with the heavy beaded necklace she had purchased in Kansas City and low-heeled white sandals. When Simon walked through the door at just before six o'clock, she knew she had made the right decision when he let out a low wolf whistle and commented, "Well, look at you, you're a sight for sore eyes, love the dress," and he swung her into his arms.

Abby stared up into the face that she had pictured so many times in the last few days and murmured, "Hi handsome, where did you get that tan?"

Simon chuckled, "Sunbathing buck naked on a riverbank."

"I bet the fish enjoyed that sight," teased Abby.

"Ah the fish," Simon countered, "yes, we actually caught some."

"Sounds like you and Jim had a good time."

"Yes, we did," Simon responded stepping back but still holding both of Abby's hands, "it was a good few days but I missed you."

"I missed you too, in fact I could hardly wait to see you again," Abby admitted without reservation.

"That's fabulous." said Simon and then abruptly released Abby's hands and twirled around to look at the flower and plant displays, "So this is Charlotte's," and he walked towards the window and fingered the leaves of a white hydrangea, "you have a wonderful display here Abby."

"Well, I do my best and one of the benefits of owning my own business is being able to take fresh flowers home all the time"

"Mmmmm..." Simon mused, "I suppose that means I can only bring you chocolates or perfume, in other words, no roses for Abby."

Abby grinned, "I guess you're right, but don't worry I love chocolate," then reaching under the counter for her purse she asked, "by the way, where were you thinking of going this evening?"

Simon scooted around behind the counter and took Abby's arm and then leading her towards the door replied, "Don't you worry, I have that all figured out; supper's in the car."

Abby stopped and looked up at Simon, "What do you mean, did you get take out?"

Simon threw back his head and gave a hearty laugh, "No, my love, I am cooking supper at your house."

Abby had not expected this, "You mean you can cook too?"

"Master chef, my dear." Simon replied bowing slightly, "No seriously, my culinary skills are very limited but I know how to broil a steak and that's all a man needs."

"So, what happened to all those fish you caught?" asked Abby mockingly.

"In the freezer my love, ready to be sacrificed another day. Now let's go home because the thought of that steak is making me hungry."

Simon didn't disappoint Abby, the filet mignon was cooked to perfection and he managed to cook the asparagus until it was tender but not limp. He even tossed together an interesting salad of spinach leaves, mushrooms, hard boiled eggs and onion with a Dijon mustard dressing and supplied a loaf of fresh french bread and a bottle of burgundy wine. Meanwhile Abby had been shooed out of the kitchen and was given the task of setting the table, feeding Molly, who had taken a particular fancy to Simon, and then relaxing on the patio with a martini. Abby was amused at Simon's take-charge attitude but she was enjoying being waited on for a change; it was a whole new experience for her.

It was almost eight o'clock before they actually sat down at the table and by then Abby was feeling a little light headed and more than ready to eat. Simon didn't talk much during the meal; he was obviously a man that enjoyed savouring his food and he wasn't going to be distracted. Meanwhile, Abby was content just to watch him and when he finally put down his knife and fork, which she noticed he still used in the manner of the English, he leaned back in his chair, let out a big sigh and then closing his eyes said, "Ah, that was good even though I do say so myself."

Abby agreed, "It was good Simon, thank you. Now what's for dessert?"

Simon's eyes flew open, "Dessert?" he roared, "You don't expect dessert too, do you?"

Abby just laughed, "Of course, I always expect dessert, where is it?" and she got up from the table and ran towards the kitchen but Simon was right on her tail. Jumping ahead of her he positioned himself in front of the refrigerator door and insisted she go back to the table. Abby tried to get around him but he was far to strong for her and she finally conceded and trudged back to the table pretending to be in a sulk. Minutes later Simon returned triumphantly holding a plate over his head, which Abby soon discovered was a decadent chocolate peanut butter cheesecake. All thoughts of what the number of calories could do to her figure flew out of Abby's head as Simon cut her a large slice and put it on her plate.

Simon watched Abby with amusement as she relished every morsel, "Is that what you had in mind?" he asked playfully.

Abby knew what Simon was thinking, "Why, can you think of anything better?"

Simon got up from the table and walked around the table, "You shouldn't answer a question with a question," and then he lifted Abby out of her chair and hugging her tightly against his chest, kissed her gently on the forehead.

Abby looked up and said with a whisper, "We should do the dishes."

"Later!" Simon whispered back and with that he lifted her bodily into his arms and carried her up the stairs. Their romantic rendezvous almost came to an end before it began because Simon had no idea where he was going and when he opened the door to a cupboard instead of Abby's room, she collapsed into a fit of giggles. It was only seconds later when Simon managed to place her gently on top of her own bed that she realized just how serious this moment in her life was to be. Ed had been the only man that she had ever been intimate with and while she was afraid, she was also excited and she wasn't disappointed.

Simon sensed that Abby was not very experienced and took his time gently making love to her. He removed her clothes slowly, piece by piece, until she was lying naked on top of the covers and he told her how beautiful she was. It was only after he had tantalized her with light feathery kisses all over her body that he finally took off his own clothes and Abby's heart felt like it had turned over. He had the physique of a man who had taken great care of himself with broad shoulders, muscular arms and a chest that tapered down to a slim waist and hips. His skin was naturally dark but even darker now from the sun and he moved with confidence and no trace of self-consciousness. Abby could hardly take her eyes off him and when he lowered himself on top of her she stared into his eyes and murmured, "I want you Simon."

Later when Simon had fallen asleep with his arm draped across her, Abby lay wide-awake reliving every moment they had just shared. She had never felt so desirable and fought to stay awake for fear of losing the sheer feeling of elation that had taken over her mind and body. Simon had brought her to heights she had never even imagined and she was almost embarrassed to admit to herself how naïve she had been. For fear of waking Simon, she hardly dared move but she couldn't resist peering up at his face, which in repose was even more handsome. Finally, she closed her eyes, never intending to sleep but exhaustion overcame her and she could no longer retain any rational thought.

CHAPTER 33

EARLY ON SATURDAY MORNING, Simon's conscious mind began to register with memories of the night before and with eyes still closed but smiling to himself, he reached out for Abby only to make contact with a furry bundle that squealed rather loudly. Simon opened one onyx eye and squinted at two brilliant green eyes staring right back at him, "Molly, you're not exactly what I expected," he murmured softly. Molly reacted by turning her back and snuggling down against Simon's chest and he couldn't help but respond by stroking her silky fur and took pleasure in the sound of her purring. It was then that his sense of smell came into play and the aroma of bacon frying and coffee brewing wafted up from below and he started to think about Abby and their lovemaking of the night before. She had surprised him with her passion, and as he continued to think about her, he began to get aroused, but Molly suddenly put an end to his musings when, without warning she sprang from the bed and raced out of the room.

When Simon appeared in the doorway to the kitchen dressed only in jeans and barefoot with his dark hair tousled, Abby's heart turned over again, "Good morning," she said as she continued to whip some eggs and milk in a bowl, "did you sleep well?"

Simon sauntered over and pressed his body up against her back; he slipped his arms around her waist and replied, "Yes, I slept like a newborn babe, my love."

Abby snickered, "Obviously, you have never had any children."

Simon reached around and took the fork out of Abby's hand, laying it on then counter and then twirled her around to face him and kissed her lightly on the mouth, "Okay smarty pants, I bow to your wisdom. Now what's for breakfast wench because I could eat a horse?"

"No horse available today," Abby teased, "how about scrambled eggs, bacon and home fries?"

"Well, I guess I'll have to settle for that."

Abby punched him playfully on the chest, "Sit down then or you won't get anything and you'd better put a shirt on because I'm having trouble concentrating on my cooking."

Simon ignored Abby's suggestive grin, sat down at the kitchen table with his legs sprawled out in front of him and proceeded to leer at her, "Nice jeans," he remarked paying particular attention to Abby's rear, "don't think I've seen you in those before."

"Just shows how unobservant you are," Abby responded without turning around, "I was wearing them the first time I met you."

"Really?" Simon said drumming his fingers on the table. "Must have been the pretty face that distracted me."

"Good comeback," Abby answered, still trying to concentrate on her cooking.

Simon was about to make another remark when Molly decided that his lap looked rather inviting and leapt up, landing with a heavy thud which startled Simon enough to swear. Abby twisted her head around and smiled when she saw what had happened, "That cat really likes you."

"Believe me I like her too, but I won't if she does that again, I almost lost my manhood."

Abby chuckled as she dished out the eggs and bacon onto a plate and brought it to the table, "That would never do, then I'd have to find myself another playmate."

Simon grabbed Abby around the waist and was about to pull her onto his lap when he remembered it was already occupied, "I can't believe this," he sighed, "I know I'm popular with the ladies but I've never dealt with two at once."

Abby pulled out of his grasp, "Eat your breakfast," she ordered and slapped him playfully on the side of the head.

Simon dug into his breakfast as though he hadn't eaten in a week and Abby thoroughly enjoyed watching him. Now that she was sitting so close to him, she could see the dark stubble on his face and couldn't help commenting, "Mmmm I wonder what you would look like with a beard."

With a forkful of scrambled egg halfway to his mouth Simon grunted, "Well you're never going to find out, in fact as soon as I've finished breakfast I'm off home to shower, shave and change and before you know it, I'll be back here to pick you up."

Abby looked surprised, "Oh, I didn't realize you made plans for us for today."

"Today, tomorrow and the next day," Simon responded grinning.

"And what if I had already made plans?" countered Abby.

"Then you would have to unmake them because I have every minute accounted for."

"Simon, you know I'm working on Monday."

"Yes, I know," Simon conceded, "but we have all day today and all day tomorrow and I know exactly how to take advantage of this fabulous weather and the pleasure of your company."

Abby began to feel a glimmer of excitement, "Where are we going? Are we staying in the city?"

"Simon shook his head, "No way, I have to take Jim's car back to him because he has a date tonight but I'll pick up a rental car and then we can drive to Niagara-on-the-Lake, book a room overlooking the falls and then tomorrow we can go wherever our mood takes us."

"It sounds heavenly," said Abby unable to take the smile off her face as Simon drained the last of his coffee.

When Simon left Julia's house, Abby started rushing around frantically trying to figure out what she should wear. She eventually settled on a pair of powder blue cotton slacks and a pale lemon tee shirt and then she had to decide on what to take with her. She eventually packed a similar outfit for Sunday and from the back of her closet, found a sleeveless aqua dress in a fine muslin type of material with a deep v-neck that she had never worn and a pair of high heeled bone sandals. She was debating whether she should take them in case they went some place where they needed to dress up when she suddenly remembered that she hadn't packed any underwear or a nightgown. Suddenly she was flustered digging through drawers for her best lacy pants and bra and the slinky pink nightgown that Julia had given her for Christmas. It was only after she had thrown every conceivable personal item she could think of including deodorant, toothpaste and cosmetics, into a bag that she suddenly noticed the birth control pills that had long since been discarded sitting in the bathroom cabinet. She breathed a sigh of relief when she remembered that Simon had used protection but she knew she had to be sure that he would continue to do so because there was no way that she wanted to get pregnant.

Twenty minutes before Simon was due to arrive back to pick her up she remembered Molly and immediately felt guilty by selfishly putting her out of her mind. Having never left Molly alone at night before, Abby raced next door to her neighbor Alice Chambers, an elderly widow who had two cats of her own, and pleaded with her to drop in late that night to make sure that Molly was all right and again in the morning to feed her and refresh her water bowl. Abby breathed a sigh of relief when Alice said it would be a pleasure to help her out and to go and enjoy herself, then as Abby walked away blowing her a kiss, Alice smiled and gave her a lascivious wink.

Simon arrived right on time driving a gold Chevrolet Bel Air sedan and wearing white linen shorts and a black short sleeve shirt that really seemed to accentuate his tan. As he stepped out of the car, Abby ran around to the other side of the car, before he had a chance to react, jumped in and called out, "Okay handsome, let's go."

CHAPTER 34

ABBY DIDN'T WANT THE time away with Simon to end. She felt like she was living in another world because she was seeing everything through a different set of eyes.

At Niagara-on-the Lake they trailed through all the specialty shops and then had a late lunch, enjoying fresh lobster salads and wine at an outdoor café before heading to the falls. Abby had been to Niagara Falls once before with Ed and the children, when they were very young, but the excitement she experienced with Simon now had been non-existent then. They walked the perimeter and watched the water thundering down and then ventured out on the Maid of the Mist and got soaked even though they were wearing oil slickers. Holding hands and racing from one side of the boat, as it turned in the eddy swirling around it, they giggled like two teenagers experiencing their first love affair.

Simon made the mistake of not calling ahead to book a room and at the height of the season, there were no vacancies but to Simon, this just meant another adventure, "We'll just drive a little further west and I'm sure we'll find something," he announced with confidence.

In Port Colborne, they found a wonderful old inn called Kent House with a wrap around veranda and bamboo furniture where many of the guests were enjoying afternoon tea. Their room, which overlooked a garden beautifully landscaped with rolling lawns and myriads of flowerbeds, was furnished with an antique pine bed and dresser, a plump chintz comforter with a wing chair in the same material and a stone fireplace. It looked so inviting that Simon was tempted to lure Abby into bed, but not wanting to give the owners any reason to gossip by staying in the room too long in the middle of the afternoon, they unpacked their few belongings and wandered down to the veranda.

Simon was feeling restless after having driven from Toronto and then from Niagara, so when he asked one of the guests if there were any hiking areas, it was suggested that he might prefer to rent a bike and explore the recreational trail along the Welland Canal. Their ride was almost over before it began when they found themselves at the beginning of the trail in Lakeview Park where a concert was playing in the pavilion and they couldn't resist parking their bikes and sitting on the grass while a local group of teenagers sang a medley of show tunes. It was only when Simon nudged Abby and suggested they be on their way that they finally experienced the exhilaration of flying along the trail with the wind blowing in their faces and the feeling of freedom. Abby was exhausted by the time they got back to the inn and when she flopped down on the bed and kicked off her shoes, Simon no longer cared what the natives might think. Pulling off his own shoes, he sank down beside her and murmured in her ear, "Are you going to sleep now my lovely?"

Abby turned and snuggled against him, "What do you think?"

"I think we both need a shower but if we have one now we'll only have to have another later."

"And why is that?" asked Abby coyly.

"Why? Because we're all sweaty but when I've finished with you we'll be all sweaty again."

"Is that right?"

"Yes it is, now come here," and with that Simon rolled on top of Abby and began kissing her passionately.

Half an hour later they were both sound asleep, tired out from their bike ride and their lovemaking and it was only the sound of a bell ringing that eventually woke them. Simon, looking at his watch, realized the bell must have indicated that it was time for supper. Reluctantly he got up, and pulling Abby with him, headed for the shower. This just proved to be another distraction and Abby encountered another new experience when Simon decided to make love to her again.

By the time they had dressed for dinner, Simon was certain they were too late to eat at the inn and thought they should find somewhere else, preferably where there might be some dancing. Asking directions from the owner, they discovered that there was a seafood restaurant with a small dance floor, which overlooked Lake Erie, and they were fortunate enough to get a table even though it was Saturday and very busy. They both had the country pate with hazelnuts then Simon chose the monkfish with an orange sauce while Abby had a creamy shrimp risotto with tiny crab cakes. By the time they topped off their meal with a kiwi lime sorbet with fresh blackberries, they were unable to eat another bite and wondered if they would ever make it to the dance floor.

"I could just sit here and look at you all night," said Simon reaching across the table for Abby's hand, "you look lovely in that dress, by the way."

"Why, thank you kindly sir, and you look pretty sharp yourself," she remarked as she marvelled again at just how handsome Simon was in black slacks and a black shirt with a white linen jacket.

"Why don't I order some more wine and we'll take a spin on the dance floor," Simon suggested.

"I think I'll just have coffee otherwise I might have trouble staying upright."

"Okay, coffee it is," Simon agreed and summoned the waiter with a wave of his hand.

Abby discovered that Simon was an excellent dancer and it was almost closing time when Abby announced that her feet were killing her and she couldn't dance another step. Later they literally fell into bed after dropping their clothes in the middle of the room and Abby realized she never got to wear the nightgown that Julia had given her.

Sunday morning, came too soon, but when it did Simon was raring to go, pushing Abby out of bed and teasing her that she was a lazybones. When she remained on the carpet refusing to move, he picked her up bodily and carried her to the shower where she woke up with a shriek when the cold water came raining down on her.

They had breakfast at the inn at a table for eight and chattered with the other guests, two from the east coast and the other four from France. Abby was surprised when Simon began to converse with them fluently in French and meant to ask him about it later. After breakfast, they spent the morning at the Sugarloaf Marina, watched ships go through the canal locks and then walked along

Nickel Beach and paddled in the water at the edge of the lake. At noon, they munched on hot dogs and fries from an outdoor vendor just off the lakefront area and Simon suggested that they visit the Farmer's Market to buy some fresh fruit and vegetables to take back home with them. It was on the drive back to Toronto that Abby suddenly remembered how easily Simon had conversed with the couple from France that morning, "I didn't realize you were fluent in French," she commented, "where did you learn it?"

Simon kept his eyes on the road but he looked pensive when Abby's question took him back to a time when he felt as free as a bird without a care in the world, "I learned the basics in high school and then after university Jim and I went on a backpacking trip through Europe for a year. After he was called back to Canada, when his father was dying, I stayed on in Paris for the next eighteen months and soon I stopped speaking English completely."

Abby felt like a country mouse listening to Simon, "You are so lucky to have been to so many places, the furthest I've been is Kansas City."

"Don't worry Abby, you've got plenty of time. Maybe you can come and visit me in England."

Abby turned sharply towards Simon to see if he looked sincere, "Are you serious?"

"Of course," Simon answered reaching for her hand, "I'd love for you to see London and to see where my parents live. I grew up there and it's a beautiful place, we have horses and other animals and acres of green fields, I know you'd love it."

"Oh I know I would too," said Abby excitedly, "you've told me so much about your family Simon and I would love to meet them. You haven't told me much about your work though, what exactly do you write about as a journalist?"

Simon fell silent for a moment as though he was considering his reply, "Well, I write about all kinds of things, politics, science, sports, human interest stories, all kinds of stuff. I think I told you, when I get back I'll be working on the Russian space race."

"Does that mean you'll be going to Russia?"

"Possibly but it's not a big deal, I've been there before."

"You have? Where else have you been?"

Simon leaned over and nudged Abby with his shoulder, "You're asking a lot of questions young lady?"

"That's because I want to know all about you," Abby persisted, "so tell me where else have you been?"

Simon sighed, "Ah well if you must know, I've been to Africa, Asia and I've traveled pretty extensively through the States."

"And all this through your job at the Daily Mail?" Abby continued with growing suspicion.

"Yes, now let's talk about something else," Simon insisted appearing to get a little impatient, "I'm on vacation and I don't really want to discuss work."

"One more question please?" begged Abby in a little girl voice.

Simon sighed again letting go of her hand, "Okay what is it?"

"What do you think of Canada? Here we were in a small town in Ontario with not a great deal to offer compared to some of the places you must have seen and yet you seemed to get so involved with everything going on around you."

Simon smiled, “I love Canada,” he replied, “I’ve been out west and down east and all through Quebec and I just love the spaciousness of the place. The people are great too, sort of halfway between American and British although some of you may not take too kindly to that. It doesn’t really matter where I go, there’s always something new to peak my interest. Most of the cities of the world are so commercialized now that sometimes it’s hard to tell what country one’s in but there are differences, whether it’s the language, the food, and the culture. Then once in a blue moon, I find a treasure and this time it was you,” and he reached for Abby’s hand again.

CHAPTER 35

AFTER THEY ARRIVED BACK at Julia's house, Simon dropped Abby off, then left to return the rental car while Abby did her best to try and appease Molly who was distinctly distant after being abandoned all weekend. She had not expected Simon to spend the evening with her and was surprised when he suggested that he pick up something for supper and then they could relax for the rest of the night. She was even more surprised and couldn't believe her good fortune when he proposed that they spend the whole week together before he returned to England the following Sunday. Not wanting to let him out of her sight for a moment, she readily agreed and they became inseparable except for the hours she spent at the shop. Just sharing breakfast with him each morning made the rest of the day a joyful experience, and Pauline couldn't help teasing her about what a good man could do for one's mood. But it was the passionate nights they shared that were so special and as the days passed Abby didn't know how she would be able to bear it after he had gone from the house and possibly from her life forever.

Simon had spent most mornings relaxing on the patio and reading while Molly draped herself contentedly across his lap and he made a point of seeing Jim at least once a day, either for lunch or by dropping in at his office for an hour or so. It was during lunch on Wednesday when Jim proposed that he and his girlfriend, Vicky, get together with Simon and Abby and have supper one evening. Simon was more than happy to make the arrangements and on Friday evening Abby was to meet Jim for the first time.

"Where are we going?" Abby asked anxiously, needing to know what she should wear for such an occasion. She wanted to make a good impression in front of Simon's best friend and she knew that if she were dressed appropriately she would be able to relax and concentrate on the company rather than herself. She also knew that this all seemed rather superficial but she still had a long way to go before she acquired the confidence of someone like Julia.

"We're going to Julie's Mansion," Simon replied, "it just opened last year and I hear the food's really good. It used to be the old Massey house where Vincent and Raymond Massey were raised."

"I see," Abby murmured, "it sounds interesting. I'm looking forward to seeing it."

Simon sensed that Abby wasn't feeling exactly comfortable about meeting Jim and getting up from his chair, he walked over to Abby, who was making coffee, and turned her around to face him, "Look Abby," he said gently, "it's going to be fine, Jim's the finest person you could care to meet and I've only met Vicky once before but she seems like a nice lady. You don't have to dress up but I wouldn't suggest you wear those sexy jeans," and he grinned and kissed her on the cheek.

Abby hung her head, "I guess I'm feeling a little anxious because a couple of days after that, you'll be gone."

Simon put his index finger under Abby's chin and tipped her head up, "I told you I'd be back and I meant it. Probably in September, that's only a couple of months away. I'm not going to forget about you Abby."

Abby was forced to look at Simon but her eyes were full of tears, "I'm going to miss you so much, I've never been this happy."

Simon chuckled, "Well you don't look too happy to me. Now buck up and let's have that coffee before I die of thirst."

Abby learned a lot about Jim before she finally met him. Simon had already told her, on several occasions, what a good friend he had been since their Oxford days but she knew little about his personal life. Vicky, his current girlfriend, had been on the scene for almost two years but it was a casual affair and Simon didn't see it going anywhere. Jim had married at age twenty-five and had a daughter Kelly but his marriage had ended in an acrimonious divorce and his ex-wife and child now lived in Montreal. Jim adored Kelly but didn't get to see her nearly as often as he would have liked because of his difficult relationship with her mother. His first encounter with Angela was on the backpacking trip when he and Simon ran into a group of Canadians wandering through Saint Peter's Square in Rome. They struck up a friendship with the group and traveled through Switzerland and Germany together. When they reached Berlin, Jim got the news about his father and flew back to Toronto while Simon stayed on in Paris. Jim kept in touch with Angela and when she returned to her hometown of Montreal they commuted back and forth for a year before Angela finally got transferred to Toronto. Within six months she moved in with Jim and when they discovered she was pregnant they got married in a hasty ceremony. When Kelly was born, Simon had already returned home to England but Jim wanted him to be Kelly's godfather. However, Angela was not impressed with Simon, believing him to be a bit of a womanizer, and demanded that her cousin Jeffrey be the godfather instead. Simon was disappointed but he had already had his misgivings about Angela and had even suggested to Jim early on that he was concerned about where their relationship was going. It took very little time before Jim realized that he had made a mistake and when he wasn't looking after Kelly, he buried himself in his job to avoid any conflict. It turned out that Angela, who was a sales representative for a cosmetics company, traveled extensively and she often returned to the company's head office in Montreal. By the time Kelly was three years old, and on many occasions in the care of a nanny, Jim suspected that Angela was having an affair and when he finally confronted her she admitted that she too had made a mistake and was still in love with someone she had once been engaged to. There was no saving their marriage even though Jim begged Angela to try for Kelly's sake and when she won custody of Kelly in a malicious court battle where Jim was made to look like he spent all his time at his job, he went through the most depressing period of his life. It was Simon, who pulled him through, flying in from London, talking him through his darkest days and only leaving when he began to see the old Jim start to emerge.

When Abby walked into Julie's Mansion in her yellow summer suit with Simon by her side, she anxiously looked around to see if she could identify Jim from the description Simon had given her, “Can you see them?” she asked.

“No, we’re supposed to meet them upstairs for a drink first. I know they’re here because I saw Jim’s car in the parking lot,” Simon replied taking Abby’s hand and leading her towards the staircase.

Abby noticed the beautiful carpeting and the dark wood paneling and when they reached the second floor, there was an oval shaped banister where one could lean over and look down at the floor below, “What a wonderful old house,” she remarked.

“Yes, it reminds me a bit of home,” said Simon steering her towards the bar.

Just as Abby was about to make another comment on the décor Simon broke away and tapped a man on the shoulder who was sitting at the bar, “Hey there buddy,” he chuckled.

Jim whirled around, stood up and gave Simon a bear hug, “So you finally got here!” he said as he gazed past Simon at Abby who was standing back feeling a little awkward.

Jim didn’t wait for an introduction and stepped forward with his hand outstretched, “And this must be Abby, I’m so pleased to meet you. Come and meet Vicky”

Abby advanced towards the bar as a tall and very attractive redhead rose from her seat smiling, “Hi,” she said, “I’m Vicky, come and have a seat beside me. What would you like to drink?”

Abby couldn’t help liking Vicky. She was outgoing and had a great sense of humour and she made Abby feel very comfortable. Abby remembered Simon commenting that Jim and Vicky’s relationship was only casual and she couldn't help wondering why, when she seemed such an ideal companion. She later learned that Vicky worked for a travel agent and spent a lot of her time visiting resorts all over North America, Mexico and the Caribbean. It sounded like a glamorous life but not the basis for a serious commitment. Meanwhile, she had not yet formed an opinion of Jim who appeared to be quiet spoken and in a deep conversation with Simon about the space race. While he didn't have the movie star looks of Simon, he was an attractive man, around the same height with a slim build, light brown hair and hazel eyes. It was only after they had eaten and had settled down with coffee and liqueurs that he engaged Abby in a conversation about her home, her work and Kate while Simon sat quietly amused knowing that Jim was trying to determine the seriousness of his relationship with her. Later when Jim dropped Abby and Simon off at Julia's house, he seemed sincere when he took her hand and said, "I really hope we get to see you again soon, Abby."

Saturday was a beautiful hot sunny day, but without the humidity of the previous few days and Simon suggested they go to Riverdale Park and have another picnic. Spreading out a blanket under the shade of a maple tree they feasted on smoked turkey, bagels, brie, tortellini salad and fresh peaches, all of which they had enjoyed shopping for at the small specialty store just a block from Charlotte's. Being so close, Abby had not been able to resist dropping into the shop to see how Pauline was coping with the usual Saturday crowd but she made Simon wait outside so that she wouldn't have to put up with any of Pauline's teasing. After the picnic, they were relaxing with a glass of wine when several men in white began to converge on the grass close by and Simon realized that a cricket game was about to begin. He was excited, because he had never seen a match in Canada before while back home it had been his favourite sport and he had been on the winning team at Oxford. Abby thought it looked a little like baseball but listened intently when Simon explained what was going on and even if she didn't understand everything, just listening to his voice was enough.

Abby never wanted to leave the park but by five o'clock, dark clouds had formed and it looked like rain. Gathering up their blanket and the picnic basket, they headed for the streetcar and made their way back to the house just before a storm broke creating streaks of lightning and deafening thunder which caused Molly to cower in a cupboard refusing to come out even for her favourite food.

Abby made spaghetti and meatballs for supper and then sat with Simon on the back patio and watched while the rain pelted down and the clouds looked even more menacing. "I'll always remember tonight," sighed Abby, "it's like an omen."

"I'm not sure what you mean," said Simon staring up at the sky.

"Well it's so dark and dismal, "Abby explained, "like a prelude of things to come."

Simon got up and pulled Abby out of her chair into his arms, "I'll show you what's to come my love, let's go upstairs."

Abby couldn't help chuckling, "I think you have a one track mind."

"But you like the way I think, admit it." Simon countered.

"I love the way you think, just lead the way."

Later that evening as they were lying in bed exhausted after an hour of passion, Abby felt that she would never experience such closeness to another person again, and when Simon suggested they get some sleep because he had to leave early in the morning, she clung to him fearing she would never see him again. It was only after assuring her over and over that he would be back that she finally fell asleep in his arms and didn't wake up until the sun rose just before six o'clock. She nudged Simon, who had turned away from her with his arm now draped across the tail of a half asleep Molly and whispered in his ear, "Simon, it's time to get up."

An hour later after a shower and shave, Simon waived away the suggestion of breakfast but sat drinking coffee at the kitchen table holding Abby's hand and staring at her intently, "I'm sorry I have to leave so early but I have to pick up the rest of my things from Jim's before he drives me to the airport."

"I understand," Abby said softly with tears in her eyes.

Simon squeezed her hand, "Before I go, I have something to say to you Abby. You may not believe this, but I've never met anyone like you before. Sure, I've come in contact with a lot of nice ladies in my travels but I haven't ever felt this connection. I don't know what's going to happen in the future but I know I'll be back as soon as I can because...," and he hesitated, "I think I'm falling in love with you."

"Oh Simon," Abby cried, tears now running down her cheeks, "I'm going to miss you so much and I can't wait to see you again. I hope you'll write me or phone me, I couldn't bear it if I didn't hear from you."

Simon reached over and pulled Abby onto his lap, "Of course you'll hear from me sweetheart and I'm going to give you Jim's phone number just in case you need anything."

"There's no need for that," Abby protested stroking Simon's hair way from his forehead.

"I want you to have it," Simon insisted, "promise me if you need any help for any reason, you'll get in touch with him."

Abby nodded, "All right, I promise."

When Simon left Abby at the front door and stepped into the taxi to take him to Jim's, Abby thought her heart would break. She didn't know how she would get through the day if it weren't for the fact that Julia was arriving home that evening.

CHAPTER 36

ABBY SPENT THE NEXT two hours cleaning up the house and removing any evidence of Simon having been there; she just didn't know how she could explain to Julia how she had allowed a man to stay at the house when she had only just met him.

At noon, Abby made herself an egg salad sandwich and some tea and went out to sit on the patio and just relax and think about Simon. Soon Molly jumped up on the seat beside her, content to lie in the sun and Abby stroked her silky fur and gazed up at the sky hoping to see a plane fly overhead and imagined that Simon was on board looking down at her. She had just finished her sandwich when she heard the phone ringing and thinking it might be Kate she ran to pick it up and gasped when she heard Simon's voice, "Hello Abby, we're at the airport and it looks like my flight has been delayed for about forty minutes, so I just had to call you."

"Oh Simon, I'm so glad you did," said Abby her heart racing, "I'm missing you already."

"I know sweetheart and I'm missing you too but I promise as soon as I get to London I'll drop you a line even if it's only a postcard. After I arrive I'll be driving straight down to Surrey to see my folks for a couple of days before I have to start work."

They continued to talk until Jim interrupted Simon to tell him that they were calling his flight and then it seemed to Abby that he was gone in a flash with barely enough time to say goodbye. As she put down the phone she murmured, "Take care my darling and safe journey."

Facing the afternoon alone in the house was too daunting, so Abby decided to go to Charlotte's and make sure that everything was in order. She felt guilty that she had put her personal desires ahead of business and placed Pauline in a position of responsibility that she may not have been ready for. However, after checking all of the flowers and plants and the paperwork which she had also entrusted to Pauline, she put her mind at rest and realized that she had acquired a trusted and conscientious employee and someone she could rely on again in the future. She also realized that it was time to hire more help and she began to prepare an advertisement to put in the local paper as well as making up a sign for the window. Abby smiled as she penned the words for the sign thinking of the day that she first walked into the shop and met Henrick. So much had happened since that day, she was now the owner of Charlotte's and she had changed in so many ways, improving her appearance and becoming more confident and finally meeting a man who, she had to admit, she had fallen in love with. She had no idea where the relationship would end up; it was far too early to tell and he lived well over three thousand miles away. It was difficult to put Simon out of her mind as she locked up the shop and returned home to make a light supper, feed Molly and settle down before Julia arrived.

At seven o'clock with the dishes done and her clothes put out ready for the morning, Abby settled down to read 'Hawaii', the book that initiated her romance with Simon. She had just finished the second chapter when she heard a car in the driveway and rushing to the window saw Julia getting out of a taxi looking fabulous in white jeans and a crimson tank top. Abby rushed through the front door and leapt down the steps practically bowling Julia over when she threw her arms around her, "Julia, welcome home," she cried, "it's so lovely to see you."

Julia returned the hug and then pulled away smiling from ear to ear, "Well that's a nice homecoming Abby but hold on while I pay the cabbie and get my suitcase."

Abby hopped up and down impatiently then helped Julia drag her suitcase into the house as well as a carry-on bag and another large shopping bag with the name 'Neiman Marcus' displayed prominently on each side.

When they got inside the house, Julia just dropped everything in the hallway and flopped onto the sofa in the living room announcing that it had been a long flight and she could do with a cup of coffee. Abby was only too pleased to wait on Julia insisting that she eat something too and bringing her a large slice of apple strudel.

Julia sipped her coffee and sighed, "Oh that's so good Abby, thank you. Now tell me what have you been up to while I've been away?"

Abby turned away for a moment because she could feel her face starting to flush and then turning back replied, "Not too much but I want to hear all about your trip. Where did you go, what did you do, did you meet anyone nice?"

Julia started to laugh, "Sit down Abby and relax and I'll tell you all about it," and she patted the seat beside her.

Abby sat down, "I'm sorry, I'm just excited to see you."

Julia nodded, "I had a great time but I'm happy to be home again. I drove up the coast from Los Angeles to Seattle then I took the ferry to Vancouver and flew home from there. I love San Francisco and stayed there for three days. I'd actually been there before with Raymond but it was so different being on my own. I got to see so many things that he wasn't interested in and I met a lot of nice people. As a matter of fact, I met nice people everywhere I went and I didn't feel conspicuous or uncomfortable because I was alone. When I first got to Vancouver, I was seriously thinking of flying all the way to Halifax to see if I could hunt Mark down but I realized he had probably come back here by then and there was really no point in starting things up again."

Abby reached over and placed her hand on Julia's arm "You still miss him, don't you?"

"Yes, I suppose I do, but it wouldn't work out. Anyway it's water under the bridge now," she said leaning back into the cushions and taking another sip of coffee.

Abby was still curious, "Didn't you meet anyone special that you could go out with for an evening?"

Julia put her cup down, "As a matter of fact I did, but only when I got to Vancouver. I was sitting in Stanley Park reading a book and a man sat down on the bench and started talking to me. I was a bit nervous at first, although there were a lot of people around but after a while we were laughing together and I could feel the chemistry plus the fact that he wasn't bad to look at."

Abby was all ears, “So what happened next?”

“Well, we made a date to go out to dinner that same night.”

“Tell me more, how did that go? Is this guy single, available or what?”

Julia chuckled, “It was a perfect evening. We sat outside at this marvellous restaurant overlooking the ocean and learned a lot about each other. His name is David Grayson, he's divorced with no children and he's an architect. He's about six feet tall, fair hair, blue eyes and looks a bit like a young Gary Cooper. Now what else would you like to know?” she asked teasingly.

“Well, are you going to see him again, Vancouver's a long way away?”

“Yes, he's coming to Toronto on business in September.”

“Oh,” Abby remarked dropping her eyes and thinking that's when Simon said he would be back.

Julia placed her index finger under Abby's chin and tipped her head up, “What's going on Abby?”

Abby immediately straightened and started to get up, “Nothing's going on.”

Julia grabbed Abby's arm and pulled her back down, “You can't fool me, is everything all right? The minute I mentioned Dave was coming here in September you acted a bit weird.”

“All right, I'll tell you,” Abby replied settling back in her seat, “I met someone too.”

Almost an hour later Julia knew everything about Abby's first encounter with Simon and what had gone on during the previous two weeks including the fact that he had spent the last seven nights at the house. During this whole time she sat quietly listening without interrupting and then when Abby finally broke down in tears as she told Julia about Simon's last phone call, she scooted over and cradled Abby in her arms, "Oh Abby," she said soothingly, "I am so sorry but try not to be sad, think about seeing him again in a couple of months."

Abby looked up trying to focus on Julia's face, "You mean, you're not angry that I let a complete stranger stay in your house for a whole week?"

Julia smiled and shook her head, "Why on earth would you think that? Of course, I'm not angry, I'm just happy that you found someone so special and that he found you. You deserve to have someone in your life Abby and anything I can do to help, well, you only have to ask."

Abby took Julia's hand, "You are so good to me. Here I am rambling on about myself and I've never really even given you a chance to tell me all about your vacation."

"It's okay Abby, I can tell you about it later. You probably want to hear more about Dave, but I don't expect anything to come of it while your relationship with Simon sounds like the beginning of something serious."

The conversation went on late into the evening with Julia continuing to encourage Abby to look on the bright side. When Abby suddenly remembered that Julia hadn't even unpacked, she made her a cup of coffee and a snack and then excused herself to go to bed, but not before Julia announced that she had presents for everyone from her trip.

CHAPTER 37

A WEEK AFTER JULIA'S arrival home, Abby received a postcard from Simon. The minute Abby retrieved it from the pile of mail and saw the picture of the Tower of London, her heart turned over. It was short and sweet saying that he had arrived safely, was on his way to Surrey, would be in touch soon and missed her. He signed it "With love Simon" and there were several kisses. Abby couldn't wait to show it to Julia.

During the next few weeks, Abby was kept busy as her business began to slowly grow. Clients that had used Charlotte's to provide flowers for weddings and other special occasions had passed on Abby's name to friends and family and she could hardly keep up with the orders coming in. After several interviews Abby hired another full time assistant to help out. She had not expected to hire a man but after Peter Groves entered the shop one Friday morning and informed her that he was the best person for the job, she hired him on the spot. Peter was tall, very slim with pale blonde hair, twinkling blue eyes and a very flamboyant manner, which enchanted all the ladies. Julia laughed uproariously when she met him, and the minute she got Abby alone immediately informed her that he was obviously a homosexual. Abby, looked shocked at first and then broke down in a fit of giggles realizing how naïve she had been. At first Pauline showed an immediate resentment against Peter and made fun of his exaggerated mannerisms but within a week he had charmed her with so many flattering remarks that they soon became the best of friends. Abby then leased a van to make deliveries and hired a part time driver, Terry Flynn, a middle aged Irishman with a wife and four children and thankful to be able to make some extra money. Terry was the complete opposite of Peter, short with a heavy build and very masculine, but to Abby's surprise they got along well and now she could afford to relax and have a little extra time to herself.

Two weeks after the postcard arrived Abby received a letter written from Simon's London address. Abby sat quietly on the patio reading the three pages over and over again. Simon had spent just three days in Surrey with his parents and then returned home to spend one day with his sister Brooke before starting back to work at the Daily Mail. He didn't elaborate too much on what he was working on but vaguely alluded to the Russian space race and then reminisced about the time they had shared together. He closed by once again telling her how much he missed her and that he was looking forward to seeing her in September.

After reading the letter through for the third time, Abby rummaged in the small desk in Julia's room looking for some paper and was soon sitting at the kitchen table spilling out her innermost feelings to Simon. Reading her letter through, however, she decided that it might not be what Simon wanted to hear, so she tore it up and started over, this time talking about Julia and the shop and her excitement about Kate's return home.

It was almost the end of August before Kate arrived, seven weeks since she had left for the cottage with the Ward family. While Abby had talked to her several times on the telephone and had even received one almost indecipherable letter with a scribbled drawing of Helen with her beagle Buster, she didn't realize how much she had missed her until she walked through the front door. "Baby," she cried lifting Kate off her feet and hugging her tightly, "it's so lovely to see you."

"Hello Mommy," said Kate squirming a little.

Abby looked past Kate at Dorothy who was standing and smiling at the reunion, "Dorothy, thank you so much, how can I ever repay you? Please come in and have a cup of tea."

Dorothy took a step forward and laid a hand on Kate's head, "It was my pleasure Abby and Kate's such a great companion for Helen. I won't come in if you don't mind; I need to get back and unpack. I dropped Helen off with Colin and they'll be waiting for me."

Kate, who had now been deposited back on the ground, ran and gave Dorothy a hug, "Thank you Mrs. Ward," she murmured and then ran towards the kitchen yelling, "Where's Molly?"

Abby grinned and walked Dorothy back to her car before returning to house to find Kate cuddled up with Molly on the sofa in the living room. Molly didn't look too happy but Kate was hanging onto her for dear life and wasn't about to let her get away. Seeing her mother come into the room she said, "I missed Molly Mommy, why can't

I take her with me next time I go to the cottage? Helen's allowed to take Buster."

Abby sat down beside Kate and gently stroked Molly so that she began to settle down and started to purr, "Well, cats aren't like dogs, honey. They like to stay home and if you let them out, they often get lost because they aren't as smart as dogs."

"Hmmmm, but Molly's really smart. I bet she's much smarter than Buster; he acts really dumb sometimes and he's so slow."

"That's because he's very old Kate, he's almost fourteen. That's like being eighty if you're a person."

"Really Mommy?"

"Yes Kate, so you remember that and the next time you see Buster, treat him nicely."

"Oh I always do Mommy," Kate replied, "I love Buster but I love Molly even more."

Later that day when Julia arrived home they all went out to celebrate at the Dairy Queen and then dropped in on Martha and John. Martha was so happy to see her granddaughter that she insisted on feeding her more ice cream until Abby had to put her foot down.

John had Kate on his lap and was telling her about a fish he caught on their vacation near Rice Lake when out of the blue she asked, "Did you see my Daddy there? He liked to fish?"

John looked helplessly up at Martha while Abby held her breath and then Julia stepped in and said, "I'm sorry Kate, but none of us have heard from your Daddy. Maybe he'll get in touch soon."

Kate looked downcast, “He probably doesn’t even remember where we live any more.”

Abby knelt down in front of Kate and grasped both arms, “I’m sure he remembers honey. He must be some place where he can’t get in touch with us but I know he could never forget you.”

Kate struggled down from her grandfather and pushed past Abby towards Martha, where she buried her face in her Grandmother’s lap, “I’m never going to hear from him again; you’re just all saying that.”

Abby started forward but John shook his head and Julia grasped Abby’s arm and mouthed the word, “Don’t”

There was silence for what seemed like an eternity and nobody moved and then suddenly Kate lifted her head and said, “Let’s go home now, I want to see Molly.”

CHAPTER 38

ABBY RECEIVED A LETTER from Simon two weeks later announcing hat he would be paying a flying visit to Toronto in mid September and would call her with the details as soon as he knew his schedule. Abby had no idea what a flying visit meant, but she assumed that Simon would only be in town for a day or two and while she was thrilled that she would be seeing him again as promised; she was disappointed that their time together would probably be brief.

Right after Labour Day, just after Kate had returned to school, Abby got the call she had been waiting for. Just hearing Simon's voice again with his wonderful upper class English accent made her heart beat a little faster. He was arriving early on Friday evening and Jim was picking him up at the airport but he promised that after he dropped his bag at Jim's place, he would be on his way to see her. Abby didn't ask when he would be leaving again; she couldn't bear to hear the answer.

A day later, Julia learned that Dave was also arriving the following weekend but late on Saturday night and would be staying in Toronto for a week. She was looking forward to seeing him and hoping that they could get together with Abby and Simon on Sunday. She was curious to meet the man who had stolen Abby's heart in such a short period of time.

Abby had no intention of allowing Simon to stay at the house while Julia was there. Kate would not be a problem because Abby had decided that rather than expose her to a relationship that she might not understand, and might even resent, she had made arrangements for Kate to stay with Martha and John for the weekend. Kate was not particularly happy and was upset at having to leave Molly again, but when Martha suggested they go shopping for some new winter boots and a special trip to see Cinderella at a local theatre, she relented.

On Friday, Abby left the shop early, confident in the knowledge that between Peter and Pauline they could handle any situation that arose, and rushed home to prepare for Simon. She wasn't even sure what time he would be arriving, whether he would have had supper or what his plans were for the evening, but she needed to tidy up the house, have a long hot bath and pick through her wardrobe for something to wear. When Julia arrived, just after six o'clock, she found Abby in the kitchen dressed in navy slacks and a powder blue cashmere sweater feverishly wiping smudges off of wine glasses with a tea cloth, "Hi Abby," she said gaily waiving her hand as she passed by her into the living room, "what are you doing?"

Abby hadn't heard Julia come in and whirled around in surprise, "Oh Julia, you scared me," she called out, "I'm just cleaning some glasses, and you're home early."

Julia came back into the kitchen, "Yes, well it's Friday and I thought I'd better just run in and change and then get out of your hair."

Abby shook her head, "There's no need to do that, why don't you stay for a while, I'd like you to meet Simon."

"No Abby," Julia insisted, "this is your night; I'll have plenty of time to meet him tomorrow and in any case I'm going to see La Dolce Vita with Sandy from the office."

Abby turned back to her chore, "Okay that sounds like a good idea, we'll make some arrangement for tomorrow."

Julia stepped forward and placed a hand on Abby's shoulder, "By the way Abby, you look lovely but you need just a little more colour in your cheeks. Also, I just wanted to tell you that if you want Simon to stay overnight; I'm okay with that."

Abby turned and leaned back against the sink, "I couldn't do that Julia; I just wouldn't feel comfortable."

Julia started to walk away, "It's up to you Abby; now I'd better get going or I'll be late for the movie."

At seven o'clock Abby still hadn't heard from Simon and she was chewing on her nails with worry when suddenly the phone rang. It was Jim calling from the airport to tell her that the plane had been delayed, and it was just now arriving and he'd do his best to make sure that Simon got to the house as soon as he could. Abby breathed a sigh of relief and spent the next hour pacing the floor, occasionally petting Molly and sipping on a glass of wine that she had poured to calm her nerves.

At exactly fifteen minutes past eight, she heard a car in the driveway and ran to the window to see a taxi pulling in. She didn't wait to see who it was; she just ran through the front door and down the steps, throwing herself into Simon's arms as he stepped onto the walkway, "Whoa," Simon chuckled as he hugged her back, "I think you must have missed me."

Abby playfully tapped him on the chest with her fist, "Of course I missed you, you big dummy."

"Oh, so I'm a dummy now, am I? Well let this dummy pay the cabbie and we can discuss this further."

Moments later they were in the hallway locked in a passionate embrace until finally Simon held Abby away from him and said, "Let me look at you," and as Abby looked down shyly at her feet, he continued, "you look just as lovely as I remember you. That shade of blue really brings out the colour of your eyes."

When Simon discovered that he would not be meeting Kate that weekend, he was disappointed but understood when Abby explained that Kate still had an attachment to her father and might have trouble understanding their relationship. He also understood why Julia had excused herself for the evening but despite his best effort, Abby was too nervous to allow herself to be lured upstairs to the bedroom. Early on, Abby learned that Simon was due to leave on a work related trip to Washington D.C. on Sunday night and would be returning to London directly from there. This news prompted Abby to become very quiet until Simon cheered her up by telling some of his pathetic English jokes and made plans for them to drive up to Lake Simcoe on Saturday night after a dinner date, which they hoped to arrange with Julia and David.

At eleven o'clock, Abby reluctantly suggested that Simon should leave before Julia got home, and after a very long session of kissing and hugging while waiting for the taxi, Simon eventually made his way back to Jim's.

CHAPTER 39

SATURDAY MORNING WAS A bright but crisp fall morning and leaves were already turning to gold. When Abby woke up and looked out on the back garden, she couldn't help wishing it were still summer and was not looking forward to the Canadian winter. For a moment she felt downcast, but at the thought of seeing Simon in a few hours her mood lifted. Jim had invited her for lunch and she was looking forward to seeing where Simon stayed when he was in Toronto.

Julia was still asleep when Simon picked Abby up in Jim's car. After the movie she had gone to a bar with Sandy, stayed until closing time and then gone on to a party with a group of rowdy Australians they had met along the way. Abby dreaded to think how Julia would be feeling by the time Dave arrived that afternoon and left a bottle of aspirins on her bedside table and a note telling her to drink a lot of black coffee.

Jim's house was exactly as Abby had expected from the outside, as she had often walked through the neighbourhood near Riverdale Park and knew the area. It was attached on both sides and very narrow but surprisingly spacious once she got inside with a glass-enclosed patio at the back leading out onto a very pretty garden with a flagstone walkway. The furnishings were all in earth tones and decidedly masculine but potted plants here and there softened the décor and Abby particularly loved the bookcases which lined two complete walls in the living room and the dozens of colourful paintings that were displayed depicting sea and landscapes.

When Jim noticed the interest Abby was taking in the room, he offered to show her the rest of the house and graciously invited her to join Simon and himself for a glass of wine before lunch. Seated next to the fireplace, Abby couldn't help noticing the photographs on the mantle. There was one of a young Simon with his arm around Jim's shoulders posed in front of the Eiffel Tower and another of a very young, pretty girl with long dark hair who she assumed was Jim's daughter. When Jim returned with three glasses of white wine on a tray, he confirmed that it was indeed Kelly and that he was obviously a proud father despite the fact that he had to admit; she took after her mother as far as looks were concerned.

"There is another member of the family you haven't met yet," Jim announced placing his glass down on a side table.

Abby looked at Simon and frowned while Simon just shrugged his shoulders and then looked up at Jim and winked. Before Abby had a chance to question who else lived there, she heard a rattling noise coming from the back of the house and as Jim walked out of the room he called out, "Oops there he is now, I'd better let him in."

Abby was really curious and whispered to Simon, "Who is it?" but she got her answer before Simon could say a word when a rather scruffy looking dog bounded into the room and placing his paws on Simon's lap, proceeded to lick his face. "Hi there Scamp," Simon said lovingly patting the dog's head, "had a good run today?"

Jim walked through the door and glanced over at Abby who seemed a little unsure of how to react to this unexpected arrival, "This is Scamp, he's rather boisterous but he wouldn't hurt a fly."

Abby tentatively held out her hand towards the dog who turned his attention away from Simon and started sniffing at her fingers, "What kind of dog is he?" Abby asked.

"He's a border terrier; usually they settle down a bit when they get older but he still acts like a puppy."

"I've never seen a dog like him before," Abby commented, noticing the wiry feel of the reddish-tan coat as she ran her hand along his back, "how old is he?"

"He's five," Jim replied and I've had him since he was six weeks old, "it's a bit of a commitment but I can't imagine being without him. Thankfully I have a great neighbour, George Robins, who walks him twice a day for me. George is retired and he likes the exercise, plus he has a dog of his own."

"A dog would be nice," said Abby, "but we have to make do with a cat instead. They're a lot easier to take care of and Kate adores Molly. Everyone should have a pet; even the elderly lady that rents the flat upstairs from my store has a bird. Mind you it's a bit noisy sometimes but it's company for her."

Simon chuckled, "Wait until you come and meet my folks, you'll be surrounded by animals Abby. I hope you like horses?"

Jim looked a little taken aback at this remark but Abby was encouraged that Simon had been sincere when he had mentioned her visiting England, "I love horses," she replied smiling at a particular memory, "but I'm not sure they like me. I tried riding one once and when we crossed a river, he dumped me right off his back. Fortunately it was a very shallow river and my pride was hurt more than anything else."

Both Jim and Simon roared with laughter, "Don't worry," Simon assured her, "I'll teach you how to ride. We have a very gentle mare named Scarlett and I assure you she won't dump you anywhere."

For the next two hours over a lunch of fresh spinach salad with crabmeat, mandarin oranges, red onions & avocado that Jim had prepared himself, the threesome chatted amiably and Abby came to understand the close friendship which existed between Simon and Jim.

After a dessert of strawberry cheesecake and helping Jim clear the table and stack the dishes, Abby confided that she had no idea how she was going to manage another bite that day even though she was aware that they still had a dinner date with Julia and David. Jim suggested they just stay at his house and relax while he dropped in at his office for a couple of hours, and then Simon could take Abby home to pick up some things for their trip up to Lake Simcoe that night and make sure that Julia had recovered enough to join them for dinner.

When Jim left with Scamp at his heels determined to follow his master into the car, Abby sat back in her chair by the fireplace and sighed, "That was lovely Simon; I really like your friend Jim."

"Couldn't meet a better man," Simon remarked, "we've always been there for each other. I just wish he would meet someone and settle down."

"What about Vicky?" Abby asked.

"No, she's not right for him although she's a great girl. She's a lot of fun and he enjoys her company but a committed relationship just isn't in the cards."

"Well, you must know a lot of women, don't you know anyone who might be suitable for him?"

Simon raised an eyebrow, "Now you're fishing sweetheart. I don't know lots of women, at least not the kind Jim's looking for."

"And what kind do you know?" Abby persisted.

Simon wagged his finger at her, "You really want to know don't you? Well, I know old women, young women, ugly women, gorgeous women, fat women, thin women….."

"Stop, stop," Abby cried, "okay I get it; you're just going to keep them all a deep dark secret."

Simon pulled Abby up from her chair and folded her into his arms, "Yes but I won't keep you a secret my love, I've already told my family about you."

Abby pulled away and stared into Simon's eyes, "Really? What have you told them?"

"Ah, now that part really is a secret," he replied teasingly.

CHAPTER 40

DRIVING UP TO THE lake in Jim's car, Abby reminisced about the evening they had spent with Julia and Dave. Julia had rallied after her hangover from the night before and dazzled everyone in a burgundy wool dress with long sleeves and high neck, which clung to her body and showed off her superb figure. Dave had checked into a hotel downtown near the waterfront and had arrived in a taxi at Julia's house just as she had finished dressing, and after introducing him to Abby, they sat down with a glass of wine waiting for Simon to pick them up. Abby learned a lot more about how Julia and Dave had met in Stanley Park and about Dave's job as an architect which took him all over the country. He was obviously a well-educated man and reminded Abby a little of Mark but he was a lot better looking and seemed a better match for Julia.

When they were on their second glass of wine, Abby began to get a little anxious as Simon was almost fifteen minutes late. She had wanted to look her best and had opted for an emerald green shantung suit with a short jacket and nipped in waist, and when Simon finally arrived, she knew she had made the right choice when she opened the door and he let out a low whistle and said, "Sorry I'm late sweetheart but this was worth waiting for. You look fabulous."

Julia was the perfect hostess insisting, that Simon join them while they finished the wine and even providing some hors d'oeuvres which she had been heating up in the oven. The conversation flowed easily and continued after they arrived at Barberian's Steak House and settled down to a three-course meal that left everyone mellow and relaxed.

Simon drove Julia and Dave back to the house and let Abby out to pick up her overnight case and they were now headed north with Abby resting her head comfortably on Simon's shoulder, "Well, what did you think of Julia?" she asked.

Simon kept his eyes on the road and replied, "Well, she certainly is a beautiful woman, and intelligent too. I think Dave is well suited to her."

"I think so too," Abby agreed, "and guess what she said about you?"

Simon glanced down at Abby but her face was hidden from view, "I have no idea, but do tell."

Abby giggled, "She said she thought you were really hot!"

"Really, and what did you say to that?"

"I said she was right, you were hotter than a firecracker," and Abby started to shake with laughter.

"Now I know you're kidding," said Simon seriously.

"You'll never know," teased Abby.

They continued to banter halfway to the lake and then Abby dozed off and didn't wake up until they arrived at the Briar's Inn at Jackson's Point.

On Sunday, after a passionate night of lovemaking and very little sleep, Abby and Simon woke up to a sunny fall day, famished and ready for the substantial breakfast that the inn provided in the beautifully appointed dining room. After breakfast, they rented some fishing tackle and a small boat and ventured out onto the lake but returned to the marina two hours later empty handed. It was then that they learned that the best ice fishing in Ontario was at Jackson's Point but it was much too early for that, "Just our luck," commented Simon with a grin.

A tour of the antique shops in the area and a walk through some nearby woods gave them a huge appetite and they found themselves back at the inn feasting on roasted tomato soup, pan-seared pickerel and whipped potatoes. Abby put down her fork leaning back with a sigh, "I am going to get so fat hanging out with you."

Simon raised an eyebrow, "All the more for me to get my hands on," he teased.

Abby shook her head, "You're incorrigible."

"I know," Simon responded, "but you love it."

It was just after two o'clock when they were ready to leave the lake area and drive home. Simon still had to drop Abby off at home before spending an hour or two with Jim before leaving for the airport. Abby had hoped that Simon would spend all of his time with her and was feeling a little jealous of Jim, but she realized they were the best of friends and so she kept her feelings to herself. When Simon parked in the driveway to say goodbye to Abby, her emotions suddenly got the better of her and her eyes filled with tears, "This has been such a short visit Simon, do you really have to go to Washington?"

"Afraid so my love, it's my job. I have to be there for three days then I'm flying straight back to London."

"What will you be doing in Washington?" Abby asked.

Simon shrugged his shoulders, "Nothing you'd be that interested in Abby, believe me."

Abby felt that Simon was being evasive, "I'm interested in anything you do, tell me about it," she insisted.

Simon hesitated and then replied, "Well for one, I'm going to be interviewing Gus Grissom about the Mercury program. He was the second American to go into space."

"Oh, so you're still working on the same subject?"

"Yes, it's a whole series of articles and it's been drawing a lot of interest from our readers."

Abby looked thoughtful, "I see, and what will you do next?"

Simon smiled and squeezed Abby's hand, "I'm not sure yet; I have a few irons in the fire, but I'll be getting some time off right after the Christmas holidays and I'll be coming back to Toronto for at least a week."

"To see Jim?" asked Abby while praying for a different answer.

Simon laughed, "Yes, to see Jim and Scamp and one other person, but I can't quite remember her name."

Abby hit Simon playfully on the arm, "You are such a tease, but that's almost four months away, it seems such a long time to go without seeing you."

"You can see me in your dreams Abby, and I'll write and phone. Soon you'll be getting ready for Christmas and then the time will fly by. Before you know it, I'll be right back here beside you."

"Oh Simon," Abby sighed wrapping her arms around him, "I'm going to miss you so much."

After a tearful goodbye, Abby discovered that Julia wasn't at home and unable to bear being alone she decided to go to Martha and John's to pick Kate up. Martha persuaded her to stay for supper and while John was playing a game of scrabble with Kate at the dining room table, Abby told Martha all about Simon. In deference to Ed, she was not forthcoming about every detail of their relationship and she expected Martha's reaction to be negative but she was surprised when Martha placed a hand on her shoulder and said, "You deserve to be happy Abby, don't waste your life wondering if Ed will ever come back. It's time you moved on, for your sake and for Kate's."

CHAPTER 41

ABBY SOON DISCOVERED THAT Simon had been right, first there was Halloween and Abby was busy in the shop dealing with special orders for Spider Moms, deep purple carnations and pumpkin containers. There was also Kate's costume to make and this year she had decided to be one of Cinderella's ugly sisters. On Halloween night Abby and Julia had great fun dressing Kate in a dowdy gray dress they had made from some cotton cloth Martha had given them, a black wig with a bun and the ugliest mask they could find, complete with a hook nose, warts and all. Standing back and looking at Kate, carrying a black wicker basket to collect her treats in, they roared with laughter until Kate stamped her foot and informed them that she was supposed to be frightening, not funny.

Christmas was spent, in the usual tradition, at Martha and John's. Julia had left to spend the holidays with Dave in Vancouver and Abby was grateful that she and Kate were with the family, because despite the fact that Ed was missing, she still considered her in-laws, and Julia, the only family she had.

Since Simon had returned to England, Abby had received three letters and three phone calls. He had apologized for not writing more often but explained that as a journalist, his job was to write and he preferred to pick up the phone and hear her voice. Meanwhile, Abby wrote almost every week, and although she tried to phone him once or twice, he was never at home. She often wondered where he was, especially when he called and the reception was so poor. He always claimed to be in London, but there was no way of knowing if that was the truth and Abby suspected that there was more to his job than he was telling her.

When Julia returned from Vancouver, just before the end of December, they decided to have a quiet New Year's Eve and invite Martha and John over for dinner. They spent most of the day cooking, with Julia making her special dish of roast rack of lamb with mint sauce, risotto and asparagus while Abby concentrated on an appetizer of shrimp and artichokes and a decadent dessert of chocolate peanut pie, which was Kate's favourite. The evening with her in-laws left Abby with a feeling of contentment and she was particularly proud of Kate when she insisted that her grandmother sit down while she helped with the dishes. That night, she went to bed in a happy mood, knowing that she would be seeing Simon in just two weeks, only to wake up in the morning anticipating the long day ahead and wishing that she was at the shop, just to make the time go faster.

At breakfast, Abby toyed with her food until Julia asked what the problem was. Abby looked up and shook her head, "I don't think I'm cut out for a long distance romance," she said.

Julia sat down at the table with her coffee cup in hand, "Look Abby, Simon's going to be here soon. I know it's difficult, you have no idea how this relationship is going to end up but you still have Kate to consider. So far, you've done really well and she has no idea what's been going on. Actually, I think it's time you told her about Simon. She's going to be twelve this year and she's growing up fast. She hasn't mentioned her father for a while and even if she's upset at first, she'll get over it. Simon's going to be here for over a week, how do you expect to deal with that? You can't go on lying to her Abby."

"I know you're right Julia," Abby replied, "I will tell her, I promise, I'm just not sure what to tell her."

Julia sipped her coffee, "Tell her the truth; tell her you met a man in the summer and that he's become very special to you. Tell her you didn't mention it before because you know she still thinks of Ed and no one can ever replace him as her father but you hope she'll accept your new friend and be nice to him."

"You're so eloquent Julia, thank you, I'll talk to Kate later today. By the way, how's Dave? Did he call you yesterday, I didn't hear the phone ring all day?"

"Yes, he actually called when you popped out to pick up the milk, I just forgot to tell you."

"You really like him, don't you Julia?"

Julia smiled, "He's kind of nice, but I don't want it to get serious. I'm rather enjoying this long distance relationship; it leaves me to indulge in other interests of my own."

Abby was curious, "Then why couldn't you deal with Mark living in Halifax."

Julia looked sad, "I guess because I was in love with Mark and it made it too hard. That's why I understand how much problem you're having with this thing with Simon, you've obviously fallen for him pretty hard."

"Yes," Abby replied, "I suppose I have and I don't know what I'm going to do about it."

"Don't do anything Abby, if it's meant to be, it will all work out in the long run," Julia advised getting up from the table, "in the meantime, let's not mope around all day, let's go up to Riverdale Park and take our toboggan. The snow is really thick underfoot and even though there are some big fluffy flakes falling, it's not that cold. It'll be lots of fun, so you go get dressed and I'll go up and tell Kate."

New Year's Day turned out to be more fun than Abby expected. They spent hours sliding down the slopes in the park surrounded by dozens of others, either tobogganing like themselves or skiing. They found themselves screaming with excitement and then laughing until their bellies ached every time they tipped over into a snow bank. When they got back to the house, they snacked on hamburgers and hot chocolate and after lunch Julia and Kate opted to build a snowman in the garden while Abby remained indoors reading a book and occasionally glancing out of the window smiling at the sight of her sister-in-law and Kate having so much fun.

After supper that night, Julia signaled to Abby that she was going up to her room so that she could be alone with Kate and have the opportunity to tell her about Simon. Abby was extremely nervous but she sat Kate down on the sofa beside her and told her that a friend was coming to visit them very soon. When Kate asked who the friend was and Abby explained all about Simon, she was shocked when Kate jumped up and said, "That's cool Mom, can I go upstairs now please, I want to play with Molly?"

Later, Abby remarked to Julia, "I should have known Kate wouldn't take this too seriously, I don't know why I was so worried."

CHAPTER 42

ON THE SATURDAY WHEN Simon was due to arrive, Jim called Abby early in the morning and asked her if she would like to go with him to the airport to pick Simon up. Abby was surprised when she got the call and grateful that Jim had been thoughtful enough to consider how happy this would make her. On the drive out, Abby expressed her concern about Kate meeting Simon for the first time and Jim thought he had the perfect solution. His ex-wife was driving in from Montreal and dropping their daughter, Kelly, off at the house later that day for a five-day visit. It had been arranged rather quickly and Jim had not been prepared to take three days off out of his workweek, but he was used to Angela's impulsive behaviour and immediately adjusted his schedule to deal with Kelly's visit. He suggested, after he squared things away with Simon, that Abby bring Kate over the next day and that they all go to a movie together and then somewhere the girls would like for supper. "This will probably distract Kate from thinking about Simon too much," he said.

When Abby saw Simon walk through the arrivals gate, her heart turned over. It always amazed her every time she saw him, how handsome he was and she couldn't help noticing many of the women waiting at the gate staring at him and probably wondering if he was some famous movie star. At the sight of Abby, Simon dropped his overnight bag and ran towards her, then gathering her up in his arms he lifted her up and swung her around murmuring in her ear, "Hello there, beautiful lady, I didn't expect you to be here."

Jim looked on grinning from ear to ear and when Simon finally noticed him standing back from the crowd, he stepped forward to give him the usual bear hug and whispered, "Thanks old chap for bringing Abby, that was a wonderful surprise."

All the way home, while Jim played the role of chauffeur in the front seat, Simon and Abby snuggled in the back seat chattering away happily about the week ahead. Simon thought that bringing Kate and Kelly together was a great idea and he was looking forward to finally meeting Kate after so many months.

The week with Simon went by so quickly that Abby could hardly believe that they were already back at the airport saying goodbye. They had crammed so much into the last few days, tobogganing, visiting the zoo, the museum and the art gallery and going to the movies. Kate and Kelly had taken to each other immediately and Kate fell in love with Scamp the first time he licked her face at Jim's house. Moments before, after he had bounded into the room at the sound of all the voices, she had turned to her mother and whispered, "That's a pretty ugly dog Mom." To which Abby replied, "No dogs are ugly honey and Scamp is so sweet, I know you're going to like him." It was after that, when Kate tentatively held her hand under Scamp's nose and he placed his paws on her knees and licked her face that she fell in love.

Kate's reaction to Simon was a little different, the moment she met him she seemed to lose her self-confidence and could hardly speak. She seemed to be in awe of his good looks and couldn't take her eyes off of him. Meanwhile Simon paid her a lot of attention asking about her school work, what she liked to do in her spare time and showing a genuine interest in a young girl who might possibly become someone very important in his life. Simon's attempt to put Kate at ease and Kelly's admiration for her father's best friend, who she had called 'Uncle Simon' all her life finally brought Kate out of her shell. After their third meeting she confided to her mother, "I think Simon's really cool Mom and he's so handsome."

After Simon left, Abby fell into a depression; she had no idea when she would see him again. He had told her that he was going on an assignment to a remote part of Angola and he would probably have trouble getting in touch with her for a while. When Abby admitted she had no idea where Angola was and wanted to know what his assignment was, Simon told her that Angola was on the west coast of Africa and that it was purely a human-interest story about the farmers in the area. Abby wasn't sure that she believed him but when she pushed him for more information, he cut her off and suggested that she take a vacation in England in the summer and meet his family. Even this did not satisfy Abby and she was apprehensive about where Simon was really going and what the future held for them.

By the end of February when Abby had not heard from Simon, she called Jim to see if he had had any contact but Jim appeared to be nonchalant about Simon's silence and just echoed Simon's explanation that he was in a remote spot and unable to communicate. He assured Abby that if he heard anything, he would call her immediately.

Julia got a little tired of Abby moping around the house and suggested that she take Kate and visit Henrick during spring break. Abby was reluctant to leave Toronto in case Simon tried to get in touch with her but Julia insisted she would contact her if he called or if a letter arrived. Abby then made an excuse that she couldn't leave the shop but again Julia shot her down criticizing her for not having enough faith in Pauline and Peter to run things. Eventually Abby relented and called Henrick who was ecstatic to hear that Abby and Kate were coming to Siesta Key and immediately invited them to stay with him and Gerda's cousins at the house. Just listening to Henrick's voice lifted Abby's spirits and when she told Kate where they were going, she felt almost happy when Kate jumped up and down for joy at the prospect of spending spring break at the beach.

"What will you do while we're away?" Abby asked Julia, one morning at breakfast.

"Don't worry about me," replied Julia grinning, "Dave's coming into town so I won't be lonely."

"Ah so now I know why you wanted to get rid of us," Abby teased.

"Well, I can hardly carry on a romance right under your noses, can I?"

Abby looked serious, "Tell me truthfully Julia, do you really mind sharing the house with Kate and me? Sometimes I think we're intruding on your privacy."

Julia reached over and grabbed Abby's hand, "Don't you ever think that, I love sharing the house with you. It's as much your home as mine and for as long as you like."

Abby placed her other hand over Julia's "Thank you so much Julia, you are so good to me."

"Nonsense," Julia said abruptly getting up from the table, "now let's get these dishes in the sink or we'll be late for work."

CHAPTER 43

THREE DAYS AFTER ABBY and Kate's arrival in Florida, Julia phoned to say that Jim had called to tell her that Simon's father had contacted him. Simon had managed to wire them in England and tell them that all was well and that he hoped to be back home by mid April. Abby was disappointed that the message was so brief but relieved to hear that Simon was safe. In order not to spoil Kate's holiday, she put on a happy face and decided to make the most of the remainder of her stay with Henrick.

Sofie and Willem were wonderful hosts and put Abby and Kate up in the spare bedroom, which was decorated with bamboo furniture and a bedspread with an orchid motif to match the wallpaper. The large bay window overlooked the sparkling blue ocean and they only needed to take a few steps across the paved road to reach the beach. Kate was in her element wanting to spend most of her time in the water while Abby and Henrick relaxed on the sand chatting about their lives and keeping one eye on Kate. Abby confided at length to Henrick about her feelings for Simon and how conflicted she was about the future. Henrick tried to reassure her that no matter what problems they had to face, if it were meant to be, then it would happen. Abby wasn't convinced but felt a little encouraged and was determined that while she was in Florida, she was going to enjoy herself and try not to think too much about Simon. She was happy to see how content Henrick was in his new life even though he missed Gerda terribly. He had a comfortable room with his own television in Sofie's home and he loved to go out fishing with Willem. He had even formed a friendship with two of the men, both widowers, at the golf club and every now and then they would spend an evening at the local bar and reminisce about their former lives and the wives they had lost. The elusive Ginny had yet to be seen and Abby was anxious to meet the woman who had captured a piece of Henrick's heart but it was not to be. The week flew by quickly and there were tears at the airport when Abby and Kate left but she promised Henrick that she would come back again and that she would always keep in touch.

As soon as Abby got back home, she arranged for a huge bouquet of spring flowers to be sent to Willem and Sofie to express her thanks for their hospitality. It was obvious that they were still very much in love and when they spoke occasionally in their native Dutch, Abby would think about how far they had come and how little she knew about the world. Henrick claimed they were the salt of the earth and he would be grateful to them for the rest of his days for giving him a home after Gerda died.

Julia was in a great mood when Abby and Kate finally arrived at the house. She had just said her goodbyes to Dave that morning and had enjoyed a very romantic week with lots of intimate dinners and lazy mornings spent making love and cooking breakfast together. Abby felt that the relationship between Julia and Dave was getting serious but Julia laughed at the idea and said she was just having some fun.

A week later, after having returned to the shop full time and finding that everything had run smoothly, Abby received the long awaited call from Simon. When she picked up the phone and said "Hello" at first there was silence and then a crackling noise and finally Simon's voice faintly calling, "Abby, it's Simon, can you hear me?"

"Oh Simon," Abby replied breathlessly, "Barely, where are you?"

"I'm still in Angola, but I managed to get to Luanda, that's the capital, and I just had to call. How are you?"

Abby strained to hear Simon through the static, "I'm fine, but I've missed you so much and when I didn't hear from you I was worried."

"Sorry sweetheart, but I couldn't get to a phone and getting mail through was just as impossible. You shouldn't have worried though, you must have known you would hear from me."

Abby had tears in her eyes and tried to keep her voice steady, "It's so wonderful to hear your voice; when are you going back to England?"

"I should be leaving for London in a day or two and when I get there I'll call you again. I want you to come over in June and……"

Abby could only hear static and repeated "Hello" over and over again but the connection was lost. Reluctantly she put down the phone and then slumped into the nearest chair and began to sob. It was here that Kate found her a few minutes later, "What's wrong Mom?" she asked putting her arm around Abby's shoulders.

Abby looked up at Kate, her eyes red from crying, "Oh I'm just being silly honey. I just heard from Simon and then he got cut off."

"Maybe he'll call back," Kate suggested.

"No, I don't think so, he's still in Africa and the phones are bad. He'll probably call again as soon as he gets back to London in a couple of days."

Kate hopped from one foot to the other, "I want to see him, when is he coming here?"

Abby smiled and took Kate's hand, "I didn't know you were such a fan."

Kate looked sheepish, "Well, he is kind of like a movie star and I love the way he talks."

Abby shook her head, "I think you have a crush."

Kate lowered her eyes, "No, I just think he's cool."

"Well I don't think he'll be coming back here for a while, but I may be going to England to see him."

"I want to come too," said Kate jumping up and down with excitement.

"I don't think that's possible honey, I'm sorry."

"No fair" said Kate petulantly, "I never go anywhere."

Abby laughed, "Now that's priceless, you just came back from Florida."

Kate tossed her head, "That doesn't count. That's only in America," and with that she skipped out of the room while Abby gazed after her trying to understand how an eleven-year-old's mind worked.

CHAPTER 44

IT WAS THREE DAYS later when Abby got the call she was waiting for. Kate picked up the phone and yelled to her mother who was in the kitchen preparing breakfast, "It's Simon, Mom, he's calling from London."

Abby rushed into the room but had to wait patiently while Kate chattered away excitedly about her trip to Florida and how good a swimmer she was. It was only when Abby put her hands on her hips and frowned that Kate realized she had better hand the phone over, "Here's Mom," she said, "she's getting mad at me. Bye Simon."

Abby shook her head and took the phone from Kate's outstretched hand and then waved her out of the room, "Hi, Simon," she whispered into the phone, "sorry about that but she's been hovering near the phone since I told her you'd be calling. I think that daughter of mine has developed a crush on you."

Simon chuckled, "Well, I'm flattered; she's a great kid and I enjoy talking to her but how are you my love."

"I'm wonderful now that I can hear your voice," Abby replied, "Kate said you were calling from London. How long will you be there?"

"I suspect quite a while, we have a lot of editing to do for the series and then I'm not sure what my next assignment will be. We don't usually have back-to-back assignments out of the country but one never knows. Hopefully I'll be home for at least two months and I'm trying to arrange to get two weeks off in mid-June."

"Does that mean you might come here?" Abby said anxiously as she wound the telephone cord nervously around her fingers.

"No my love, it means I want you to come here. I want you to see London and maybe Paris for a couple of days and then spend a week with my family. Say, you'll come if I can arrange it," Simon pleaded, "I need to see you Abby. I've missed you so much and being stuck in that godforsaken place in Africa gave me a lot of time to think."

Abby's legs began to shake and she sank down into the nearest chair, "Oh darling, of course I'll come. I haven't stopped thinking about you since you left and I can't wait to see you again. I love you Simon, you must know that by now."

"I love you too Abby. I think I started to fall in love with you that first weekend but I guess I've been in denial. I want you with me and Kate too."

Abby was stunned, "I don't know what to say Simon. I want us to be together too but I don't know how, we live such different lives."

"Listen Abby, when you get to London, we'll talk and we'll work something out. It may not happen tomorrow or even a year from now but an ocean can't keep us apart forever."

The next few weeks were a whirlwind of activity for Abby. Abby determined that she couldn't possibly go to Paris and London without a whole new wardrobe and from the sounds of it, Simon's family were affluent so it was important that she felt comfortable in their environment. On several occasions Julia accompanied Abby on her shopping expeditions and every time they returned home laden with bags full of clothes and shoes for every occasion, Kate demanded that her mother give them all a fashion show.

Kate had come to terms with the fact that Abby would be going on holiday without her but only after Abby promised that the next time she went to England, she would take her along and that Julia would take good care of Molly. Julia had offered to look after Kate but knowing that she was deeply involved with a court case, which would probably require hours of extra work, Abby arranged for Kate to stay with her grandparents. Both John and Martha were thrilled to be able to help out as they had seen little of Kate for the last three or four months. Abby had not intentionally kept Kate away but every time she saw John or Martha she felt obliged to talk about Ed, and now that she was in love with Simon, she felt uncomfortable talking to her in-laws about their son.

On a glorious June day, Abby flew directly to Paris expecting Simon to meet her at the airport but at the last minute he had called to say that, because of an urgent problem at the paper, he would be delayed until suppertime and that she was to go on to the hotel and he would get there as quickly as he could. Abby was hoping to sleep most of the way so that the time would go faster but she was too excited, and when the plane started to descend over the roof tops of Paris she could hardly contain her enthusiasm and starting babbling to the elderly lady who had been quietly reading or sleeping since they had left Toronto.

Simon had booked them into the Ritz Hotel. In the taxi taking Abby to the Place Vendome, in the centre of the city, Abby could hardly believe that she was actually in France, but the sights she saw along the way convinced her she wasn't dreaming and when she entered the lobby of the hotel, she was mesmerized by the grandeur of her surroundings. Julia was uppermost in her mind when she looked around at all of the fashionable women and she was thankful that she had been persuaded to update her wardrobe, have her hair re-styled into a shorter shoulder length and paint her nails a striking shade of crimson.

Once in the suite of rooms, Abby was overwhelmed with the furnishings. Her feet sank into the sitting room carpet, pale green dotted with darker green flowers, while all of the upholstery and drapes were gold damask with myriads of velvet cushions in various shades of green and gold. The bedroom was even more elaborate, with a four-poster bed covered in a plump rose comforter, a thick rose and sage green carpet and beautiful lamps with tasselled pink shades, on the mahogany side tables. Abby couldn't wait to see the bathroom, where she found a huge green marble tub set on a pedestal, a matching sink and commode and a rather strange looking object which she eventually learned was a bidet, and a common item in France.

Waiting for Simon was an ordeal but Abby passed the time by unpacking and watching the traffic from the large windows facing onto the Place Vendome from the fourth floor. Changing from her traveling clothes twice, first into a yellow linen dress with matching heels and then again into a pair of comfortable white slacks, coffee silk blouse and flat white sandals, Abby wondered whether they would be going out for supper and whether she might have to change again but as five o'clock approached, all thoughts of what she was wearing slipped from her mind. Standing at the window, with every taxi that drew up, Abby held her breath and as fares were dispatched onto the sidewalk, she let out a sigh of disappointment.

By six o'clock Abby was no longer at the window but sitting in one of the huge wing chairs watching television but this proved to be no distraction as all the stations were in French and Abby's knowledge of the language was limited. She had been fortunate that the taxi driver, the concierge and the bellboy had all spoken excellent English and she felt ashamed that coming from a country, which was bilingual, she had only her schoolbook French to fall back on. Soon she was beginning to fall asleep as jet lag began to take over but she was immediately aroused when she heard the door to the suite open and turned to see Simon walk into the room. As Abby jumped up from her chair, Simon dropped his bag on the floor and raced towards her, "Hello, my love," he murmured as he folded her into his arms, "I'm sorry I'm so late but my plane was delayed. I was going to phone you from Orly but that would just take more time so I came directly here."

"Sshh," Abby whispered, "it doesn't matter, you're here now and we've got two whole weeks to be together."

Simon kissed Abby passionately then holding both her hands pushed her gently away from him, "Let me look at you," he said, "you're just as beautiful as I remember and your hair, it's different, but I like it."

Abby cocked her head to one side, "Do you really like it? Julia persuaded me to cut it shorter and she talked me into getting a whole new wardrobe too."

"Well, Julia has great taste so you can't go too far wrong, now come here and let me hold you sweetheart, I've missed feeling you close to me."

It was almost nine o'clock before Simon and Abby left the hotel to dine at the Deux Magots Café on the Left Bank. After making passionate love for the past two hours they were too exhausted to eat a full meal and enjoyed a light supper of Coquille St. Jacques followed by a lemon meringue tart and a vintage bottle of white Bordeaux. By the time coffee was served both Simon and Abby were in a mellow mood and decided to take a stroll along the bank of the Seine and then a taxi back to the hotel. It was an unusually warm night for June and Abby was glad she had decided not to change and was comfortable in her slacks and sandals. Holding onto Simon's arm, she couldn't believe she was really in Paris and the sight of Notre Dame and the lights of the boats on the river mesmerized her.

Two days later on the plane headed for London, Abby babbled on endlessly about Paris. Simon had taken her to all of the places she had only ever read about, the Eiffel Tower, the Louvre, the Arc de Triomphe and they had even dined at Maxim's, the famous restaurant where unbeknown to Abby, Simon had secured reservations more than two months earlier. Simon seemed to know every corner of Paris and Abby was amazed at his command of the language.

Now they were on their way to stay in Simon's flat and Abby was feeling a little nervous as the plane came into land even though she knew that she didn't have to meet Simon's parents for another four days. Simon lived in a flat on the ground floor of a Georgian terrace house in Mayfair, a particularly affluent area of central London. When Simon opened the door and ushered Abby inside she was overwhelmed with the richness of the décor. The dark hardwood floors were covered in luxurious Persian rugs in brilliant colours of red, green and gold and the sofa with two matching chairs was upholstered in dark green velvet. Mahogany bookcases covered two walls and every shelf was filled with leather bound books while on every table there were various artefacts from around the world.

Abby was especially intrigued by the marble fireplace, which dominated the room and the oil painting of a horse grazing in a green field, which hung above the mantel. She had gazed about her in awe as she came through the door but she was drawn to the painting, "This is a wonderful place Simon," she said, "and I really love this painting."

Simon came to stand beside her and she noticed a tear in his eye as he looked up, "That's Apollo, I grew up riding on his back and he was the gentlest, sweetest animal. He died right after I left home and I always believed he died of a broken heart. I felt guilty about that for a long time but he was twenty-eight years old and his time had come, I really miss him."

Abby squeezed Simon's hand, "Don't you have another horse now?" she asked.

Simon smiled, "Yes, actually I do. Her name's Scarlett, she's only four-years old. You'll get to see her when we get to Surrey."

Abby sighed and walked away from the fireplace, "I'm really nervous about meeting your parents Simon."

"There's no need to be Abby, they're great people and they're going to love you, just like I do."

Abby turned and stared across the room at Simon, "Do you really mean that?"

"Why would you ever doubt it?" Simon replied striding towards Abby and taking her in his arms.

Abby shrugged and sighed again, "I don't know, it just seems all too good to be true. I never ever thought I would meet someone like you. You live in a whole different world and I don't know where I fit in. When I'm not with you, I think about you all the time but we live so far apart...."

"Ssssh......," Simon murmured as he stroked the back of her head, "I told you, I don't know how we're going to work this out Abby. I know you can't just pick up with Kate and leave everything behind right now and I'm not in a position to do that either. All I know is, one day we will be together but in the meantime we have to take every moment we can and enjoy it."

Abby kissed Simon gently on the cheek, "I know darling, I'm sorry I didn't mean to sound ungrateful. I had a wonderful time in Paris and I can't wait to see London. You're right, let's just enjoy every second we have together and I promise I won't be a pain in the neck."

Simon chuckled, "Okay, I'm glad to hear that, now let's unpack and that will give me an excuse to show you my boudoir."

"You're bad," said Abby as she playfully punched him on the shoulder.

After three days of sightseeing in London, Abby was exhausted. They had spent nearly every waking moment visiting all of the famous landmarks, the Tower of London,

Houses of Parliament, St. Paul's Cathedral, Westminster Abbey, Buckingham Palace, Piccadilly Circus and the British Museum. Simon only let up on his role as tour guide on the third day when they relaxed on a bench near the lake in St. James's Park and watched the ducks floating quietly by. It was a pleasant warm day with a brilliant blue sky and Abby wanted to sit there forever but Simon started to get fidgety after an hour.

"What is it?" Abby asked when she noticed Simon was tapping his foot.

"What?" said Simon abruptly, as though she had interrupted his thoughts.

"You're tapping your foot, did you want to leave now?"

Simon stood up and stretched, "Yes, we need to be home by four o'clock"

Abby remained sitting, "And are you going to tell me why?' she asked.

Simon shook his head, "It's a secret."

Abby frowned, "What are you up to now Simon? I don't think I can take anymore excitement for a while."

Simon grabbed Abby's hand and pulled her up, "If I told you it wouldn't be a secret. Now come along or we'll be late."

Abby protested as Simon dragged her along the footpath, "Late for what? Late for what?"

Back at the flat, Simon suggested Abby relax while he made her a nice cup of tea and wandered off into the kitchen. Try as she might, Abby couldn't relax and after two minutes, she was just about to go and see what Simon was up to when the doorbell rang. Abby hesitated and when Simon didn't appear to answer the door, she called out, "Simon, someone's at the door."

When Simon still didn't appear and the doorbell rang for a second time, Abby decided she had better answer it and she was shocked when she opened the door and a tiny blonde girl who appeared to be in her early twenties breezed in and threw her arms around her. "Hello," she said in the same upper class English as Simon, "I'm Brooke, Simon's sister and you must be Abby," she continued as she stepped back and stared into Abby's eyes, "wow, you really are gorgeous. That brother of mine didn't do you justice; he's such a dork. I bet you didn't even know I was coming did you, you look so surprised?"

Abby nodded and stammered, "No he didn't tell me. He said that he had a surprise for me but I didn't know it was going to be you. I'm so pleased to meet you."

"Well, I'm pleased to meet you too Abby," said Brooke now becoming very formal and shaking Abby's hand, "and I love your accent. Now where is that brother of mine?'

"Right here sis," called Simon from the other side of the room where he had been secretly watching the exchange between Brooke and Abby.

Brooke flew across the room and jumped up into Simon's arms, "How's my hunky brother," she yelled kissing him loudly on the cheek.

Simon deposited her gently onto her feet, "Same old Brooke," he said smiling, and then looking at Abby continued, "well, do you like your surprise? This is my baby sister and even though she's a complete pain, I'd miss her if she didn't show up once in a while."

Abby didn't get a chance to respond before Brooke countered, "He says I'm a pain, well I could tell you some stories about him that would make your hair curl, but I'll save those until I know you better," and with that she bounced back to Abby, "I hope we can be friends because Simon tells me you're really special and he's even taking you to see my folks."

Abby was enchanted with this elfin creature with curly white blonde hair, deep brown eyes and dressed all in black from head to toe even though it was summer, "I'd love for us to be friends, "she said, "and it's a wonderful surprise meeting you like this."

Brooke turned to Simon, "I think you've found a keeper here. Now are we all going out to supper tonight because if so I want to pop home and change? I was out shopping on Oxford Street and I need to take a nice hot bath. It was so crowded and I only bought a pair of stockings and this….." and she rummaged in the oversize bag that she had deposited on the floor. Finally, after dumping several items onto the rug while Simon winked at Abby, she stood up and handed a small silver box to Abby. "This is for you," she said.

Abby was flabbergasted, "Why thank you," she murmured as she slowly took off the lid and lifted out a wide gold bracelet embossed with a continuous line of maple leaves, "Oh," Abby squealed, "it's wonderful , but you shouldn't have done this Brooke. Look Simon, isn't it beautiful, it's got maple leaves on it."

Brooke smiled tossing her head, "The salesman told me that maple leaves were a Canadian symbol so I thought you would like it."

"Like it, I love it, thank you so much."

"That was nice of you Brooke," remarked Simon, "now if we're going out later you'd better get off home and get cleaned up."

Brooke stuck out her tongue at Simon and then turned back to Abby, "Don't take any notice of him, he's too bossy. I'll see you at about seven o'clock back here. See if you can get a reservation at Bentley's Simon, I want lobster tonight," and with that she ran out the front door before Abby had a chance to say goodbye.

CHAPTER 45

ABBY LEARNED A LOT more about Simon's family that evening, and was a little less nervous about meeting his parents when she discovered that Brooke would also be in Surrey for at least four days while they were there. She was enchanted with Simon's sister and quickly realized that the siblings had a close bond and a great rapport. Their endless teasing of each other had Abby laughing so much that she hardly noticed the superb supper they were served at Bentley's including lobster thermidore, which was the specialty of the house.

The following day, Abby was on her way to Surrey in Simon's green Aston Martin. Driving to Redhill, Abby had no idea what to expect but as they entered the town's main street, she was fascinated with the myriads of Tudor style shops and intrigued to see where Simon's parents lived. Eventually they left the town behind and traveled for a mile through lush green fields, where herds of fat, brown and white cows were grazing, and then headed down a narrow road bordered by tall hedgerows. It was at the end of the road that Abby finally saw what she could only think of as a mansion. Abby later learned that the house was in the Elizabethan style built in the sixteenth century of local stone and even had a great hall for parties and entertainment. Abby became even more anxious as she stepped out of the car onto the cobbled driveway and looked up at the house, "Oh Simon," she exclaimed, "this is incredible. I had no idea you lived in a home like this."

Simon took her arm and guided her towards the front steps, "We call it Faversham House after one of my maternal ancestors and it may look impressive but let me tell you, it can get pretty draughty in the winter." He was about to continue but stopped as he saw the front door open and his mother and father appear on the top step.

Abby took in the scene as she nervously approached and was immediately transported back to the time she first met Ed's parents, but Roger and Lydia Fraser were nothing like John and Martha. Simon's father was of medium height, with a rather portly figure and a round boyish face with thin brown hair and blue eyes that twinkled behind silver rimmed glasses while his mother was at least two inches taller, and rail thin. Her hair, which was the same color as her daughter's was swept back in an elegant chignon and her eyes were the dark onyx of her son's. She was what would usually be called a handsome woman and wore the traditional dress of the upper class, when at home, of a pencil slim skirt, sweater set and single row of pearls.

When Abby reached the bottom step Lydia Fraser came towards her and hugging her gently whispered, "Abby, welcome to our home, it is so lovely to meet you." Then she turned to Simon and wrapping her arms around him said, "Hello darling, I'm so glad you're here. Your father and I have been so excited waiting for you to arrive."

Simon's father waited until his wife had greeted Abby before he came towards her smiling. He reached out with both hands and captured Abby's right hand between them, "How do you do, my dear? Simon has told us so much about you and Lydia and I are so happy that you can spend some time with us," then calling to Simon he said, "Hello there son, let's all go in the house, it's feverishly hot out here."

Simon winked at Abby as they trooped behind his parents into the grand hallway of Faversham House. Abby gasped when she saw the grand staircase with its deep red carpet and dark wood balustrades and then she noticed the life size portrait of Lydia at the top of the stairs. It was a striking painting of Lydia when she was about Brooke's age. Her hair was a slightly darker shade of blonde and she wore an off-the-shoulder dress of deep blue satin that showed off her delicate face. Abby could see, even from a distance, that she had once been a beautiful young girl and that age had cruelly hardened her features. She reached out and touched Lydia's arm to attract her attention, "What a wonderful staircase Mrs. Fraser and that portrait of you is magnificent, do you mind if I look at it more closely."

Lydia smiled, "I'm afraid the years have taken their toll Abby but, of course, you may go up and look at it. Why don't you wait until we've had tea in the library and then I'll show you your room? In the meantime Christian will take your bags upstairs and one more thing, please call me Lydia."

Abby followed silently behind Lydia while father and son chattered quietly behind her. She couldn't hear what they were saying but from the odd word she thought they were talking about Africa. She had questioned Simon several times about his work there but he had always changed the subject claiming to be tired of work and just wanted to enjoy the moment.

After afternoon tea, which consisted of thin crustless cucumber sandwiches, dainty blueberry tarts and Earl Grey tea served by Tilly, the maid, wearing the traditional outfit of black with white trim, Lydia took Abby upstairs to her bedroom. Simon winked at her again as she exited the library knowing full well that his mother would not allow them to sleep together while under her roof. However, this did not deter Simon too much as his parents slept in the master suite, which was at the end of a very long hallway and a fair distance from all of the other bedrooms. It would not be difficult to creep into Abby's room at night.

On the way upstairs, Abby paused at the portrait of Lydia and marvelled at the depth of colour and the way the artist had effectively shown the light and shade of the satin as it fell in folds from Lydia's shoulders, "This is a remarkable painting," she remarked, "who was the artist?"

Lydia looked rather coy, "I have to be honest," she replied, "It was my first husband, Andrew Markham. I don't suppose Simon told you I was married before but it was very brief. He was a well-known artist here in England and quite a bit older than me. I fell in love with him right after we met and we were married three months later. He had just finished the portrait when he was killed in a riding accident. He fell when his horse stumbled after jumping a fence and hit his head. He never regained consciousness and died two days later. "

Abby took Lydia's hand, "I am so sorry, I had no idea."

Lydia smiled, "It's quite alright my dear. I took a while to get over it and then I met Roger. He could never take the place of Andrew but he's been a good husband and father and given me two wonderful children. He even understands why I want to keep this portrait exactly where it is, in memory of Andrew."

Abby was touched that Lydia had been so open with her, "Thank you for sharing this with me Mrs. Fraser. To be truthful I was so nervous coming here and meeting you but now I feel right at home."

Lydia put her arm around Abby's shoulder, "Good, I am glad you feel that way and please call me Lydia. You know Abby, Simon would never have brought you here if he thought I wouldn't approve. He has always been very respectful to his father and me and we only want what's best for him. By the way, Brooke, who is such a free spirit, likes you tremendously and is looking forward to seeing you again when she arrives tomorrow."

"Oh, I didn't realize Brooke had spoken to you after we had supper at Bentley's. She's a wonderful girl and so funny."

"Yes, and she's a dutiful daughter too and Roger just dotes on her. She doesn't get down here too much but she calls every other day to check in on us and let us know what she is doing no matter where she is. She's been traveling quite a bit with a theatre group and I'm not sure Max is very happy about that."

"Is Max her boyfriend? We didn't see him in London and she didn't even mention him. As a matter of fact neither did Simon."

Lydia chuckled and took Abby's arm guiding her along the corridor to her room, "Yes, Max is the boyfriend. They've been living together for almost a year and to be truthful, her father and I are not too happy about that. He's a rather bohemian sort of chap. I think he's Hungarian or something like that. He's pleasant enough but seems a bit out of place here. I just hope Brooke doesn't decide to marry him."

Just then, they reached the door of Abby's room and Abby gasped again when she stepped inside. The bed was the dominant feature, a huge four-poster covered in the fattest rose comforter she had ever seen and heaped with matching pillows trimmed with ecru lace. The carpet was a deeper rose and all of the furniture a deep mahogany while the mullioned window looked out onto the back of the house where to the left, stood the stables and to the right a magnificent garden landscaped with a small pond surrounded by willow trees and beds and beds of colorful flowers. Abby raced to the window and then twirled around noticing the huge bouquet of vivid purple lisianthus, spikes of pink veronica and gloriously scented white freesias on the bedside table. "Oh Lydia," she sighed, "this is a beautiful room and the flowers are gorgeous."

"Yes, I thought you might appreciate them Abby, Simon tells me you own your own florist shop in Toronto."

"That's right," Abby replied proudly, "it's called Charlotte's. I bought it from a Dutch couple, Henrick and Gerda Vanderveer. I worked for them for a few years and I didn't know anything about flowers when I first started but they gave me a chance. After Gerda died, Henrick wanted me to buy the shop from him but I couldn't afford it so he allowed me to pay him back out of the profits. He's a wonderful old man and now he lives in Florida with some relatives, Kate and I just got back from a visit with him a few months ago."

"What a wonderful opportunity," said Lydia sitting down on the small pink sofa in the corner of the room and patting the seat beside her inviting Abby to sit down too, "but where did the name Charlotte come from and tell me more about Kate."

"Well, Charlotte was the name of Gerda's mother and she named the shop in her memory after they had to leave their parents behind in the war and escape from Holland. As for Kate, I wish she were here with me to see your wonderful house and to meet you and Roger. She's almost twelve now and an exceptional young lady although I'm naturally prejudiced."

"And so you should be my dear," said Lydia reaching for Abby's hand, "Simon told me about Daniel and I cannot imagine how hard that must have been for you. It was hard enough losing my first husband but to lose a child must be absolutely devastating. I don't think I would ever get over it."

"I don't think anyone ever really does but one buries it deep inside and you have to go on especially if you have another child that needs you. Actually, it was my mother-in-law Martha, who snapped me out of my depression and I will always be grateful to her for that."

Lydia nodded, "Under the circumstances, I think it's wonderful that you've kept up the relationship with your in-laws. Has there been any word about your husband?"

Abby looked at Lydia in astonishment, "You know all about that?"

Lydia squeezed Abby's hand, "No need to be embarrassed my dear, we pried the information out of Simon. When we realized how serious he was about you and then he told us you were still married, we were really curious. He was reluctant to tell us, and it wasn't really any of our business, but we love our son so much and we didn't want to see him get hurt. We may come from a different generation Abby but we realize that the world has changed and if you and Simon have to be together without the benefit of marriage, then so be it."

Abby sat staring at Lydia while she spoke hardly able to believe what she was hearing, "I had no idea that Simon had told you so much about me. We've talked about being together some day but we live so far apart and there are so many things to consider particularly Kate and my business. Then I could never expect Simon to leave England, I know his job is important to him although he doesn't talk about it very much."

Lydia stood up abruptly and turned around to face Abby, "I'm sure things will work out for both of you in the end Abby, now let's go back downstairs and see what the boys are doing. I think Simon said something about showing you the stables."

Abby rose from the sofa and followed Lydia out of the room frowning. She was very aware that Lydia had cut the conversation short when she mentioned Simon's work.

CHAPTER 46

IT WAS LATE AFTERNOON when Simon, along with his father, escorted Abby out to roam through the gardens and she delighted Roger Fraser with her knowledge of plants and flowers, even though he was well aware that she was the proprietor of a florist shop. The grounds of Faversham House were his pride and joy and he often worked alongside the part-time gardener they employed, to maintain the beauty of the sweeping lawns, the dozens of trees and myriads of flowerbeds. Meanwhile, Simon was impatiently waiting to introduce Abby to Scarlett and he was not disappointed at her reaction when she reached the stables and finally encountered the magnificent animal that had finally replaced Apollo in his heart. Abby fell in love with Scarlett on sight and marvelled at her shining chestnut coat with the white blaze on her forehead and white socks on the rear legs. Scarlett stood inches taller than most of the other horses in the stable and her muscular body gave her an appearance of great power, but Abby only had to look into the large brown eyes to see the gentleness there.

Roger headed back to the house while Simon continued to give Abby a tour of the stables and introduced her to Quinn, a small, slight man with a thin face and twinkling brown eyes wearing coveralls, a cap and large rubber boots. Quinn was in charge of all of the horses, which numbered seven, and managed the young stable hand Bart, who was nowhere in sight. Quinn shook hands with Abby and echoed Simon's sentiments about Scarlett, "You'll never find a gentler horse ma'am. If you plan on going riding while you're here, I'd suggest you take Scarlett."

"Thank you Quinn, I think I would like that," Abby responded, "as long as Simon doesn't mind."

"Of course I wouldn't mind, we'll be here early morning Quinn so maybe you can get the horses ready. I'll take Bailey out, I bet he hasn't had a good run in a while."

Quinn tipped his cap to Simon, "Right you are sir. His lordship hasn't been riding lately, I think he had a touch of gout last week but he did mention that he was feeling better yesterday."

At Quinn's response, Abby's mouth fell open in astonishment. She had no idea that Simon's father had been knighted and wondered what else she had to learn about his family. She was stunned into silence for the moment but fully intended to ask Simon about his father when they were alone.

Her thoughts were interrupted by the sound of barking and when she turned around she was amazed at the sight of a pack of dogs headed straight towards her wagging their tails and followed by a young lad who she assumed must be the stable hand. She instinctively backed up but Simon laid a hand on her shoulder, "It's okay Abby, they won't hurt you," he whispered gently in her ear.

Abby bent down tentatively as the dogs surrounded her, "My goodness," she said stroking one dog's head, "how many dogs do you have and what breed are they?"

"This is all of them," Simon replied with a chuckle, "there's seven of them altogether and they're all English setters except for the one you've taken a liking to and she's a Springer spaniel named Belle."

"They're wonderful Simon," said Abby standing up while continuing to stare at Belle, "you are so lucky to be surrounded by all these animals."

"Yes I know, I miss them when I'm away from here. It's impossible for me to keep a pet in London so I come down here as often as I can."

Simon thanked Quinn, patted Scarlett gently on the nose and began to walk Abby back to the house. They were only a few feet away from the back entrance when Abby laid her hand on Simon's arm, "Stop for a moment please Simon, I want to ask you something."

Simon raised an eyebrow, "What is it Abby, you look serious all of a sudden?"

"I'm just wondering why you never told me your father had been knighted and if there's anything else you haven't told me."

Simon turned away for a split second and then began to laugh, "Is that it Abby? Well, to tell the truth I never even thought about it. The whole family thinks it's a big joke and we tease Dad about it all the time. The Right Honourable Roger Fraser sounds so bloody pompous. It's no big deal really Abby, a lot of members of Parliament are knighted."

Abby looked skeptical, "And is there anything else?"

Again, there was a split second hesitation before Simon answered, "I can't think of anything of any consequence but if I do, I'll be sure to tell you."

Abby was not appeased by Simon's reply but decided not to pursue her quest for more information other than keeping her eyes and ears open.

Supper was a formal affair, served in the huge dining room with its red flocked wallpaper, mahogany floors covered by an antique rug in shades of red, green, brown and ivory and a magnificent reproduction of Monet's painting 'Wild Poppies'.

Abby was seated next to Simon on one side of the twelve-foot long dining table with Roger sitting opposite and Lydia at the head of the table. Immediately after being seated, Lydia had leaned over and touched Abby's hand, "Forgive us for being so formal my dear, we could eat in the garden room but with all the glass, it's much too hot at this time of the year."

Abby smiled, "No need to apologize Lydia, this is a wonderful room and I love the candelabra and the beautiful flowers on the table. Everything is so elegant here."

"And may I say, you look very elegant tonight Abby," Lydia responded, "that shade of blue is perfect with your coloring."

Abby was relieved and eternally thankful to Julia that she had packed three formal cocktail dresses and had decided to wear the blue chiffon this evening. She would have felt exceedingly out of place beside Lydia who had changed from her skirt and sweater set into a mint green satin shift with tear drop pearl earrings and matching choker. Roger, meanwhile had dressed in a dark green blazer, black slacks and black polo shirt and Simon looked dashing in a black suit with a black ascot tucked inside a white open neck shirt.

The conversation around the table was light hearted with Roger telling the odd joke while Tilly served up three courses, a cream of cauliflower soup, salmon with au gratin potatoes and asparagus and a fresh raspberry tart topped with Devon cream. Abby drank two glass of wine and was feeling mellow and comfortable by the time supper was over and she was reluctant to leave the table. It was Lydia who suggested they retire to the library so that Roger could have his cigar and where they could indulge in a 1940 bottle of B & B from the cellar. Abby later learned that B & B was Brandy & Benedictine and after two small glasses she was hardly able to keep her eyes open. When Lydia noticed that Abby had become very quiet she suggested that she must be very tired and might like to go to bed. Abby looked over at Simon and shrugged, "Sorry to be such a party pooper, but it has been a long day. You don't mind if I turn in, do you?"

Simon stood up and pulled Abby up gently from the sofa, at the same time retrieving the empty glass from her hand, "Of course I don't mind my love, as a matter of fact I'm thinking of turning in myself soon. I'll walk you up to your room in case you get lost."

Abby bade Lydia and Roger goodnight thanking them for their hospitality and then left the library with Simon guiding her through the door. When they finally reached her room Simon took her in his arms and whispered, "I'd better go back down otherwise they'll get suspicious but don't be surprised if you get a visitor later."

"Oh Simon, that would be lovely, but are you sure no one will be able to hear us?'

"Not a chance in hell. First of all this room is far from my parent's room and Dad snores like a leaf blower so

Mother always sleeps with earplugs. Thank God, Tilly and Christian both sleep in the house and can hear if the fire alarms go off. It's only happened once and it was a false alarm but my parents didn't hear a thing."

"Okay, I guess you've convinced me. Now you had better go but I need a kiss to tide me over."

Simon grinned and kissed Abby passionately, "There you are, and that will have to do for a couple of hours."

Abby pushed him away, "Go, before they come looking for you."

Simon backed up along the hallway, "Goodnight fair lady," he called out then, after making a sweeping bow; he turned and headed for the stairs.

CHAPTER 47

ABBY AWOKE TO BRILLIANT sunlight streaming through the window and a loud knocking on her door. Before she had a chance to clear her thoughts and remember where she was, Simon came bounding through the door and swept the comforter off the bed leaving her completely naked. Abby screamed and tried to cover herself while Simon backed away laughing, "Oops!" he said, "forgot about that, sorry love," and he threw the comforter back over her and then jumped in beside her.

Abby burrowed down in the bed and muttered, "What's the time? It can't be time to get up yet."

Simon tried tickling her as he replied, "It's seven o'clock and it's a glorious day. I thought we could go for a ride before breakfast."

Abby groaned, "Can't we go after breakfast, I'm tired?"

"I'm not surprised you're tired after your performance last night," Simon teased.

Abby peeked out from under the covers as she remembered the hours they had spent making love after Simon had crept into her room, "Are you sure nobody heard us?" she asked anxiously.

"Everybody heard us, it's the talk of the house. As a matter of fact my mother and father were so inspired they had the best sex they've had in years."

"Liar, liar," Abby screamed as she swung a pillow at Simon's head.

Simon jumped up and ran to the door, "Okay have it your way but wait until you see them at breakfast. Now get up you wanton woman and put on some clothes. I'll meet you at the stable in half an hour."

Abby started to protest but Simon had already closed the door behind him.

The ride through the lush green fields and through the woods surrounding Faversham House was exhilarating even though Scarlett kept a steady pace. Abby was surprised how, after the first few tense moments, she was able to relax and just go with the rhythm of the horse as she cantered gently along. Meanwhile Simon tagged along beside Abby for most of the time but then decided to give Bailey his head and allow him to jump over the hedgerow and race down to the river.

It was just before nine o'clock when they arrived back at the stable where Quinn took charge of the horses and Simon and Abby headed back to the house for breakfast.

Abby was apprehensive when they entered the dining room and encountered Roger and Lydia at the table. She still wasn't absolutely sure whether Simon was joking about disturbing his parents during the night and breathed a sigh of relief when they both looked up and almost simultaneously said, "Good morning Abby, how was the ride, did Scarlett behave herself?"

Abby turned and gave Simon a smug look and then sat down, "Good morning, yes Scarlett was as gentle as a lamb. It's a wonderful day and it's so beautiful here, I can't get over how green the grass is."

"Yes, everyone comments on that," said Lydia, "I think Simon should take you for a drive through the countryside around here. You would really appreciate it Abby, especially knowing all you do about flowers and plants."

Roger interrupted to ask, "How did you sleep Abby? I always find it difficult to get a good night's rest in a strange bed."

Abby lowered her head in an attempt not to look at Simon again, "I slept very well thank you Roger, although I didn't expect to get woken up at the crack of dawn by your dear son to go riding."

"Best time of the day," Simon protested, "and you know you enjoyed it once you got those lazy bones out of bed."

Lydia chuckled, "Don't let him rankle you Abby, he's always been incorrigible."

"Right," said Simon, "and I only get worse when I'm starving. What's for breakfast Mother?"

"Now who's being lazy," said Roger shaking his head, "everything's on the buffet as you well know." Then turning to Abby he continued, "Please help yourself my dear to whatever you want and Tilly will be in any minute with fresh coffee."

Abby made her way to the buffet set up on one long wall of the dining room to find covered dishes containing all the ingredients of a typical English breakfast, sausages, bacon, scrambled eggs, fried tomatoes and toast with fresh butter, marmalade or blackberry jam.

Abby took just a little of everything while Simon piled his plate until it was almost overflowing and then called out to Lydia, "No baked beans Mother?"

Lydia rolled her eyes at Abby, "No not today, sorry son. I think you have quite enough there to keep you from dying of hunger and anyway you need to save some space for lunch today. We are actually going to set up a table in the gardens and have a sort of picnic."

"Oh that sounds wonderful Lydia," said Abby, "do you do that often?"

"No actually we don't," Lydia replied, "but today is a special occasion, not only are you here as our guest my dear but we got a phone call while you were out riding and Brooke is on her way here with Max."

Simon put down his fork looking a little surprised, "I didn't think she was coming down until tomorrow and did she have to bring Max?"

Lydia glanced over at her husband before replying but he was buried in the local newspaper and did not look up, "Well there was a change in plan and she wanted to spend more time with Abby. As for Max, he is Brooke's boyfriend. Simon whether you like it or not, I want you to be pleasant to him."

Simon grunted, "Huh, I'm always pleasant to him although I don't see what Brooke sees in him. Maybe if he got a proper job I'd have more respect for him."

Abby was curious, "What does he do for a living?"

Simon shrugged his shoulders, "He writes poetry, or thinks he does."

Lydia leaned over and placed her hand on Simon's arm, "Now then son, let's not be too harsh, he has had one book of poems published."

"Yes, but I'll be damned if I understand a word of them", protested Simon.

"Nevertheless that's quite an achievement and you should give him some credit."

Abby intervened, "Surely Simon as a writer yourself. you must know how hard it is to get anything published. Incidentally, I'd love to read some of your articles while I'm here."

Abby immediately noticed the exchange of looks between Simon and his mother as Lydia quickly rose from the table, "I must go and see what's keeping Tilly with that coffee, you must be dying of thirst by now Abby."

At the same time Simon got up leaving half of his food and announced that he forgot to give Quinn some instructions about Bailey, "I'll be back in a few minutes," he said.

Abby remained quietly at the table picking at her scrambled eggs and glanced over at Roger who was still buried in his paper, "Excuse me Roger," she said.

"Yes, my dear," Roger responded peering over his glasses.

"Did I say something to upset everybody?"

"What's that dear? I'm afraid I wasn't paying much attention."

"It doesn't matter," Abby replied, "I think I'll skip coffee and go out for a walk. Will you tell Simon I'll see him later?"

"Of course my dear, enjoy yourself and make sure you have some good walking shoes on," and with that Roger resumed his reading.

Abby didn't return to the house until almost noon. She had walked for what seemed like miles with the highlight of her journey, a visit to a local church. St John's was built in 1846 and had gone through many renovations but it's magnificent spire stood out majestically against the clear blue sky and Abby spent almost twenty minutes inside exploring every nook and cranny. Not a particularly religious person, she found it comforting to sit for a while in one of the pews and consider her dilemma. She was convinced that Simon and his family shared a secret but she didn't want to jeopardize her relationship with Simon by prying or by confronting the issue. Ultimately, she knew she would have to know everything about this man she had fallen in love with if they were to have a future together, but for now she decided to let sleeping dogs lie.

As Abby approached the house, she noticed a rather racy looking red car in the driveway and assumed that Brooke and the mysterious Max had arrived. She decided to run quickly up to her room and change her clothes before lunch and hoped to avoid any member of the family before she had a chance to make herself presentable. Twenty minutes later, wearing a cornflower blue sundress with white high-heeled sandals, she made her way tentatively down the stairs just in time to encounter the rest of the family heading out of the library towards the dining room. Brooke noticed Abby immediately and came rushing forward with her arms outstretched, "Abby, how wonderful to see you again," she said excitedly, "you look amazing."

Abby hugged Brooke and then held her at a distance taking in the pale blonde curls and the white muslin dress with the myriad of frills that reminded her of an angel who was only missing her wings, "Hello Brooke," she responded, "it's great to see you too and I love your dress."

Simon looked on with amusement while Roger and Lydia continued on to the dining room and Max stood back quietly smoking a cigarette.

"Where were you Abby?" Simon asked finally coming forward. "We thought we might have to start lunch without you."

Abby smiled and gave him a peck on the cheek, "I went for a walk and ended up at a church. It was so peaceful there and I decided to stay for a while and take a look around."

"Must have been St. John's," offered Brooke, "it's a lovely old church with all those stained glass windows. Too bad you won't be here next Sunday or you could go there for the service with my parents."

"Yes, it is too bad," replied Abby looking sadly up at Simon.

Brooke suddenly remembered that she had neglected to introduce Max and beckoned him over, "Abby," she said, "I'd like you to meet Max; I've told him all about you by the way."

Max approached Abby with his hand outstretched, "I'm very pleased to meet you Abby."

"Thank you Max, it's a pleasure to meet you too," Abby replied formally while observing the young man who stood before her. She couldn't help noticing, that although short in stature he was rather attractive, very slim with almost shoulder length dark hair, hazel eyes, an aquiline nose and sensitive mouth. He was entirely in black from head to toe just as Abby had imagined a poet to dress.

As Abby started to take a step backward Lydia appeared at the dining room door, "Are you children coming to lunch or not?" she called out, "The soup's getting cold."

CHAPTER 48

AFTER LUNCH, WHICH WAS a light-hearted affair with everyone making small talk except for Max who was very quiet, Simon and Abby took a bicycle ride down to the river. Roger and Lydia were in the gardens of Faversham House tending to one of the rose beds while Max and Brooke had elected to do a little horseback riding. All four young people had agreed to meet later in town for supper and then spend some time at one of the local pubs, where a rather colourful fellow well known as Freddie Fiddler often entertained the patrons with a lively tune on the violin. Resting on the river's grassy bank, Simon pulled Abby towards him and kissed her gently on the mouth. A yellow butterfly landed on Abby's foot but she made no attempt to drive it away, "Look Simon," she said, "isn't it beautiful."

"Yes, it is and you're beautiful too. In fact I don't think I've ever seen you look so radiant."

"That's because I'm so happy darling. I love it here and I love being with you, in fact if it wasn't for Kate I'd never want to leave."

"It's not quite real though, is it Abby?" said Simon staring out across the water.

"I don't know what you mean," Abby responded feeling a small sense of alarm.

Simon turned towards Abby and took her hand, "This is where I grew up but it's still a fantasy even to me. Even though I come here quite often it doesn't even feel like coming home, it's more like a vacation. I guess I've grown out of it Abby and my home is in London now. I've been to a lot of places in this world and Redhill just doesn't seem real any more."

"I'm not sure I understand Simon. You spent your childhood here and your parents live here, how can you say it's not real?"

Simon stood up and pulled Abby up with him, "I can't explain it and I don't think I want to try."

Abby felt a growing frustration and pushed Simon away from her, "Why do I get the feeling that every now and again, you just shut me out. What's going on Simon, what are you not telling me?"

Simon sighed and pulled Abby into his arms, "Nothing is going on sweetheart; there's nothing to tell except that I love you dearly."

Abby shook her head, "Why don't I believe you? It's like you're leading a secret life that I know nothing about."

Simon chuckled, "Maybe I have three wives tucked away somewhere and a bunch of kids, but there's always room for one more."

Abby punched him lightly on the shoulder, "You're incorrigible and not very funny but I guess I'm stuck with you."

Kissing Abby passionately, Simon responded, "Right sweetheart, you're stuck with me for good."

That evening at the Dog & Duck public house, Abby had a wonderful time. She was with the man she loved and got along with Brooke like a house on fire. Even Max loosened up after a couple of glasses of ale and amused them by reciting limericks, one after the other, until they were all laughing uncontrollably. They dined on typical pub fare, shepherd's pie, bangers and mash and bubble and squeak and then relaxed listening to Freddie Fiddler as he played his lively music and the patrons stamped their feet and cheered every time he finished a tune. By ten o'clock, after three gin and tonics, Abby was so mellow she didn't want to move and eventually Simon and Max had to haul her out of her seat and guide her gently to the laneway where Simon's car was parked. Max offered to drive and once in the rear seat, with her head on Simon's shoulder, Abby promptly fell asleep.

Waking up in the morning with a slight headache, Abby couldn't even remember coming back to the house and had no idea how she ended up in bed in her nightgown. Later she discovered that Lydia had intercepted them and taken over, insisting that she take Abby upstairs and have Tilly help her undress Abby and put her to bed. Abby was mortified when she discovered what had happened and thinking that Lydia would think a lot less of her she sought her out to make her apologies.

"Lydia, I am so sorry about last night," she said humbly, "I can't ever remember having so much to drink that I couldn't remember what happened. I do hope you will forgive me for all the trouble I put you through."

Lydia was as gracious as ever, "My dear," she said putting her arm around Abby's shoulders, "there's no need to apologize. You're on vacation and a little indulging never hurt anyone. You were probably having such a good time you didn't even realize how much liquor you had."

Abby smiled, "Well we did have a wonderful time. Max made us laugh so much with his silly poems and it got so lively when the music started. Everyone was so friendly and they all seemed to know each other. I've never been to any place like that in Toronto."

"I know exactly what you mean Abby, it's a whole different world here. Roger and I love it and we could never live in a big city. I'm thankful though that London isn't very far otherwise we would hardly ever see Simon or Brooke."

Abby shook her head; "I can't imagine having Kate going off somewhere when she grows up. I hope that when the time comes she settles down close by. I don't think I could bear it if I didn't see her on a regular basis."

Lydia removed her arm from Abby's shoulders and took her hand, "That time is a long way off Abby and you don't know what's going to happen with you and Simon. I know your relationship is serious but I can't see him moving to Canada even though his best friend Jim is there too. It might mean you moving here and then what about Kate?"

Abby could feel the tears welling up in her eyes, "I don't know what's going to happen Lydia. I do know that I love Simon with all my heart and I want to be with him but we live worlds apart."

Lydia squeezed Abby's hand. "Whatever will be, will be my dear. Just have faith that in the end everything will be all right."

CHAPTER 49

ABBY COULD HARDLY BELIEVE how quickly the days passed and suddenly it was Friday afternoon. They were leaving Faversham house in a couple of hours in order to be back in London and closer to the airport for Abby's flight home on Saturday morning.

Abby and Simon were sitting having tea and buttered scones in the library with Lydia and Roger and reminiscing about the past few days. "I can't thank you enough for your hospitality," said Abby, "you've both been so kind to me and I've enjoyed every minute of my stay here."

Roger took his wife's hand and squeezed it gently indicating that he wanted to respond, "We've loved having you here my dear and we hope you'll come back and see us often. I know that Brooke feels she's made a new friend and I even heard Max commenting what a breath of fresh air you are."

"I'm surprised you listened to Max's opinion about anything, Dad," Simon remarked with a little sarcasm.

"Now son," Roger countered, "I got to know Max a little better while he was here and anyway I realize that if Brooke cares so much about him, then maybe we've been selling him short."

Simon chuckled, "No prejudice there Dad, you always were a push over when it came to Brooke."

"I like Max," Abby intervened, "he has a really good sense of humor and he's very intelligent. I noticed he was a little moody at times but most artistic types are like that."

Simon frowned, "I just think my sister could do a little better, that's all."

Lydia nodded, "You could be right Simon but let's not spend all afternoon discussing Max. I want to hear what you two young lovebirds have planned for this evening after you get back to London."

Abby blushed imagining cozying up with Simon in his London flat but Simon saved her any embarrassment, "Well, by the time we get back it will be getting a little late but not too late for a nice meal at Wilton's."

Lydia sighed, "Wilton's, oh I love it there, they have the best seafood in London. I hope you made a reservation Simon otherwise you'll never get a table."

"Not to worry mother, I made a reservation three weeks ago. I couldn't risk Abby missing out on the fabulous scampi or their great sherry trifle."

"Mmm, I envy you Abby," said Lydia, "I almost wish Roger and I were coming with you but I wouldn't want to spoil your evening. I'm sure you want to spend your last night alone together."

Simon glanced at Abby with a sad expression, "Yes mother this evening is rather special. I can't believe Abby is flying home tomorrow and I'm going to miss her."

Abby couldn't help herself as her eyes started to tear up and Lydia immediately came to sit beside her and patted her shoulder, "There, there Abby," she whispered, "don't be upset. You'll be back soon, I just know you will."

Simon nodded in agreement, "Yes, of course she will and I'm planning another visit to Toronto in September."

"Why don't we make some plans now?" Lydia suggested, "Christmas is a lovely time in Redhill and last year we even had snow. We always decorate the whole house and the neighbourhood children go from house to house singing carols. You could come back for the holiday Abby and bring Kate with you."

Abby looked up at Lydia with surprise, "Are you serious Lydia? That sounds absolutely wonderful and Kate would be in heaven. She's already miffed at me for not bringing her with me this time and I think she has a crush on Simon."

"Great idea," Simon commented, "we could take Kate on a hay ride and if you're here long enough we could take her to all the London tourist spots, it would be a great education for her."

Abby clapped her hands together; "I feel so much better now; thank you so much all of you, now I don't feel so sad about going home. Knowing I'll be back in a few months makes me much happier."

"So you will come back with Kate?" asked Lydia.

"Yes, of course, nothing would keep us away. Thank you, thank you," said Abby hugging Lydia and kissing her gently on each cheek.

CHAPTER 50

THE FOLLOWING DAY ON the flight back to Toronto Abby couldn't help thinking about the time she had spent with Simon and his family. Lydia had given her one of her favourite Barbara Cartland romance novels to read but she found it impossible to concentrate. The previous evening in London was uppermost in Abby's mind as she thought about the wonderful food they had enjoyed at Wilton's and the hours of love making afterwards in Simon's flat. It was the early hours of the morning before they both fell asleep when Simon confessed that for the first time in his life he was deeply in love and wanted to find a way that they could be together. He even suggested moving to Toronto temporarily and had no concerns about getting a position on one of the local papers, but eventually he wanted to return to England and make a permanent home there with Abby. Abby's mind was in a turmoil thinking about how Kate would react having to leave the place she had always known and giving up the shop would become a whole other problem. She had worked so hard to make her business a success and through the experience, she had finally gained her independence and self-confidence. No real concrete plans had been made about the future, but they had both agreed to think about it seriously and hoped to come to some decision when Simon visited Abby in September.

When Abby walked out of the arrivals gate after the long overseas flight, she found Julia and Kate waiting with open arms. There was a lot of hugging and many tears before they collected Abby's baggage and set off home. Kate wanted to know everything and kept up a barrage of questions before Julia had to intervene, "Kate, why don't you wait until your mother gets home and has a little rest and then I'm sure she'll tell you everything. She must be very tired after flying so far and I bet the first thing she'd like is a good cup of coffee."

Kate looked a little sullen as Abby squeezed her hand, "It's all right honey," she said, "but Aunt Julia's right, I am a little tired. As soon as we get home and I change into something comfortable and have that coffee, I'm going to show you all of my photos and then you can ask me whatever you like."

Kate looked up at Abby in surprise, "You, have photos already?"

"Yes, Simon knew this place where I could get them developed really quickly and I have pictures of his parents house in Surrey and all of his family, even his horses and dogs."

"Oh, fabulous," cried Kate, "I can't wait to see them."

"I can't wait either," echoed Julia, "by the way Abby, did I tell you, you look fabulous; you got some real colour while you were away and I love that outfit."

Abby looked down at the white bell bottoms she was wearing with the peasant blouse embroidered with tiny red and blue flowers, "Brooke picked it out for me when we went shopping one day in Redhill. She has a great fashion sense and looks great in everything, wait until you see her photo."

Abby arrived home to find Molly greeting her at the front door. This was so unusual that she immediately picked her up and stroked her soft grey fur, "Hello Molly," she murmured, "did you miss me?" Molly's response was loud purring as she relaxed in Abby's arms.

"She's such a big suck," said Kate coming into the hallway, "she probably wants her supper."

"We'll all have supper soon," remarked Julia depositing Abby's suitcase inside the front door, "and while I'm getting something together and making you that coffee, maybe you'd like to change, Abby."

"Yes I would, thanks Julia," replied Abby depositing Molly on the floor and retrieving her suitcase.

While Abby headed upstairs to slip into a pair of cotton slacks and a sleeveless top, Julia slipped a lasagne that she had prepared earlier, into the oven and filled up the percolator. Meanwhile, Kate decided to telephone her friend Helen to tell her all about her mother's arrival home.

Abby had always been a very organized person and decided to unpack before coming back downstairs and she wanted to find the photos to show Kate. Fifteen minutes later with coffee mug in hand, Abby was sitting with Kate and Julia at the dining room table handing over the photos one by one. Julia was mainly interested in Faversham House, the Fraser's and the mysterious Max, "He looks rather interesting," she remarked, "is he an artist?"

"He's actually a poet," Abby replied, "I found him very attractive but a little too short for my liking. I want to know what you think of Brooke?"

"I think she's really pretty," Kate interjected, "and I love her hair."

"I have to agree," said Julia, "she's so dainty and she has a lovely face. In fact Abby, the whole family is good looking."

"Yes, especially Simon," said Kate with a dreamy look on her face.

Julia glanced over at Abby and grinned, then rolled her eyes.

"Where are the pictures of the animals?" demanded Kate.

"Well here's Scarlett, she's Simon's horse but he let me ride her because she's so gentle. Oh, and here are the dogs."

"Oh wow," said Kate, there are so many of them, "what kind of dogs are they?"

"Let me see," replied Abby, "six of them are setters and the one in the middle there is Belle, she's a Springer spaniel."

"You're so lucky Mom," Kate sighed as she slumped back in her chair, "I wish I'd been there."

Abby looked across at Julia and winked, "Well honey," she said placing her hand on Kate's shoulder, "I have some news for you, Mrs. Fraser has invited us to come for Christmas."

Kate sat bolt upright, "You mean, you and me? Really Mom?"

"Yes, the two of us and I told her we would be delighted."

Kate clapped her hands together, "Will Simon be there too and can Aunt Julia come as well?"

"Yes of course Simon will be there and I'm sure the Fraser's would love to see your Aunt Julia but she might have other plans."

Julia nodded, "That's right Kate, although it's very sweet of you to think of me."

"I can't wait," said Kate, "how many months is it until Christmas?"

"Now, now, let's not wish our lives away and anyway Simon is coming to visit us in September."

"Hoorah," yelled Kate, "and can we go and see Jim and Scamp and will Kelly be here ....?"

"Whoa," Abby interjected, "settle down, September is a couple of months away but I'm sure we'll see Jim and Scamp, I'm not sure about Kelly."

"Well, I guess as long as Simon's here, that's okay," said Kate solemnly as she got up and left the table.

Abby shrugged as she looked at Julia, "Make sure you wash your hands before supper," she called out.

CHAPTER 51

IT ONLY TOOK ABBY a few days to fall back into her normal routine and she quickly discovered that Pauline and Peter had done an excellent job of looking after the shop while she was away. This took a tremendous weight off of her shoulders because she intended to spend more time with Kate during the summer school break. When Abby was at Charlotte's, Kate was with her grandparents or with her friend Helen at the Ward's house, but when Abby took the odd day off, they would often go swimming at Sunnybrook, take a stroll along the boardwalk at the Beaches or borrow Julia's car to take a drive in the country.

Abby was counting the days to September when she would see Simon again and she was in contact with him regularly either by mail or by telephone. Most of their conversation centred on their feelings for each other but apart from Simon's upcoming visit, they didn't talk about the future. They both needed some time alone to consider the impact on their lives if either one of them left their home country and settled thousands of miles away. For Abby, it was particularly daunting because she had spent all of her life in Ontario while Simon had traveled extensively and had even lived in Paris when he was a young man.

Abby was reluctant to discuss the prospect of moving to England with Kate but she did subtly suggest that Simon might soon be coming to Toronto for an extended stay.

"You mean he's not going back when he comes in September," said Kate, her eyes wide open in surprise.

"No honey," Abby replied gently, "he will be going back this time but he may come back later and even get a job here."

"Not before Christmas though?" Kate questioned, already worried that their planned trip to England would no longer happen.

"No not before Christmas, Kate," Abby chuckled, "we are still going to visit the Fraser's, I promise."

Kate breathed a sigh of relief, "Oh good, because I've told everyone I'm going and Grandma thinks it's wonderful and she wishes she and grandpa could come too."

"Is that what Grandma said? Well I wish they could come too Kate, but that's just not possible and anyway Grandma didn't really mean it."

"I know but I think Grandma and Grandpa are always sad at Christmas because they miss Daddy."

This was the first time that Kate had mentioned her father in a long time and Abby's heart went out to her, "I'm sorry honey, I didn't know you were thinking about Daddy; you must miss him too."

Kate shook her head, "Not really Mom, but sometimes when I'm in bed at night I wonder where he is and what he's doing."

"Oh honey," said Abby taking Kate's hand, "we don't know where he is and I wish we did. If you ever want to talk about Daddy, you know I'm here to listen. He was a good man but after your brother died, he just lost his way."

"I know Mom," Kate said sadly, "I'd just like to know where he is, that's all."

Simon arrived in the middle of September when Toronto was experiencing some warm fall weather. Jim and Abby greeted him at the airport and once again Jim stood back while his closest friend gathered Abby in his arms and joyfully swung her around and around, "Hello, my pretty lady," he said loud enough for others waiting in the arrival area to hear. Jim looked around and could see the smiles on peoples' faces and he couldn't help smiling himself, it was good to see Simon so happy.

Back at Jim's house as the threesome came through the front door, Scamp bounded along the hallway and threw himself at Simon wagging his tail furiously. Simon immediately dropped his bags and ruffled the dog's wiry coat, "Hello Scamp, how's my boy," he said. Scamp continued to jump up and down and eventually Jim had to calm him but even though he crouched down quietly on the carpet he never took his eyes off of Simon. As it was now early evening and Simon had eaten on the plane, Jim brought out a couple bottles of beer, a glass of white wine for Abby and a plate of sausage rolls. "Let me know if you guys want anything else," he said, "I can always make some sandwiches."

"Couldn't eat another thing old chap," Simon replied, "and I had two glasses of scotch on the plane so I had better just stick with this one beer."

"How was the flight darling?" asked Abby clutching Simon's hand as they sat side by side on the sofa.

"Well, I was coming to see you sweetheart so it was pretty exciting."

Jim intervened, "How long are you staying this time Simon?"

"Three whole weeks, if you can put up with me for that long."

"Oh I think I can manage that," Jim responded grinning, "but I know you wanted to spend some private time with Abby so providing you'll take care of Scamp, I'm taking off next Saturday for a few days."

Simon looked surprised, "Of course I'll look after Scamp, but you don't have to do that."

"I know that, but you're not the only one with a lady friend you know."

"Oh I see, are you going somewhere with Vicky?"

"As a matter of fact I am, we're driving up to the Laurentians, and it's supposed to be really pretty this time of the year. By the way, we're taking Vicky's car so you can use mine."

Abby smiled up at Jim, "You're such a thoughtful man Jim; Simon's so lucky to have a friend like you."

"Well I can't get rid of him so I figure I'd better treat him well," Jim said playfully, "maybe when you take him off my hands I won't have to put up with him anymore."

Simon raised his beer bottle, "Amen to that", he said.

CHAPTER 52

FOR ABBY, THE NEXT three weeks passed far too quickly and even though she took one whole week and several odd days away from the shop, she felt she just hadn't spent enough time with Simon. When she was away from him she thought about him all the time and couldn't wait to see him again, but she knew she had to give him some space to spend some time alone with Jim and to explore the possibility of moving to Toronto.

It was while Jim was away in the Laurentian's with Vicky and Abby was staying at Jim's house that Simon brought up the subject of leaving England. "I've done an awful lot of thinking about our situation," he said as he sat beside Abby on Jim's cozy living room sofa with Scamp at his feet, "I have a contract with my paper back home which expires in March next year and then I'm free to leave without any problem. I already know they want me to sign another contract but I've told my boss that I'll probably be moving on."

"What did he say?" asked Abby.

"Well, he wasn't too happy but after I told him about you, he understood."

"You really told him about me?" Abby said looking surprised.

"Yes, of course, sweetheart, I told you in June that I wanted us to be together and I meant it. I know you have at least two very important reasons to want to stay here, at least for now. You still have Charlotte's to run and then, of course, there's Kate. There's no way I would expect you to separate her from her school and the friends she's made here."

Abby threw her arms around Simon's neck, "Oh Simon, I've been so worried about what to do. I could have given up the shop but I couldn't just uproot Kate at this stage in her life."

Simon stroked Abby's hair, "It's all right, I understand and that's why tomorrow I'm going to start seeing what opportunities there might be at The Globe & Mail or The Star."

"I'm sure they'll want to snap you right up but where will you live?"

"Jim offered to let me stay here but sooner or later I'll have to get a place of my own so that we can spend more time together. I'd like us to live together Abby but I know that isn't possible under the circumstances."

Abby hung her head, "You mean because I'm still married and it just wouldn't be right. If only I knew where Ed was I could start divorce proceedings."

"Have you considered the fact that he might be dead?" Simon whispered.

"Yes," Abby replied, "I have but I would have to prove that. If he can't be traced after seven years, then I think I can declare him officially dead but I'm not sure."

"How would you feel about me trying to track him down, after all, I've done a lot of investigative work in my time Abby?"

"Oh, could you Simon, I would be so grateful? I know that John and Martha would like to know what happened to him. Martha cries over him all the time and I feel so badly for her."

"Yes, it must be really hard for your in-laws. Maybe I can help and I expect Kate would like to know what happened to her father. She's a great kid Abby, you've done a good job of raising her on your own."

Abby bent down and stroked Scamp's head, "I can't take all the credit Simon, I couldn't have done it without Julia. She basically took us in when we had nowhere else to go; she encouraged me to go into business for myself and she always has time for Kate."

"Yes," Simon agreed, "She's obviously been a great friend as well as your sister-in-law and she's smart too."

Abby gave Simon a sideways glance and grinned, "You forgot to mention beautiful."

Simon slowly nodded his head, "Can't argue with that but you're more my type."

"Very diplomatic my love," said Abby chuckling.

David Grayson flew into Toronto a few days later to collaborate on the design of a new high rise building in the financial district. As Julia's birthday was the next day, the timing was perfect and they decided to celebrate at Julia's house. Julia suggested that Abby invite Simon, Jim and Vicky and that rather than cooking a meal, she would have it catered.

Kate spent the evening at the Ward's feeling a little left out but preferred to spend time with Helen than a bunch of grownups. As she left the house trotting along behind Dorothy Ward, she called out to Abby who was waving from the front step, "Don't all get drunk now." Abby just shook her head and disappeared into the hallway quietly shutting the front door and smiling to herself.

The evening went without a hitch and it was just after midnight when Julia's guests departed and she was left alone with Abby.

"That was a fabulous evening Julia," said Abby giving her sister-in-law a hug.

"Yes it was nice," Julia responded," I can't believe all the lovely gifts I got. The crocodile purse you got me is wonderful."

"I thought you'd like it and it will go with your new fall suit but what about the ring that David gave you?" she asked raising one eyebrow.

"Now don't get any ideas," Julia replied, "It's just a friendship ring."

"Mmm.... pretty fancy friendship ring," teased Abby.

"That Vicky is a bit flaky, don't you think?" said Julia changing the subject.

"Yes, she is. I like her but I don't think she's right for Jim, in fact I think you're more his type."

"Oh so your matchmaking now," laughed Julia tossing her head, "well I'm going to bed before you start getting serious."

After Simon had been in town for almost two weeks, he surprised Abby with the announcement that they were flying to Quebec City for the weekend and staying at Le Chateau Frontenac. He had already secretly arranged for Julia to take care of Kate so that Abby would be free to leave Toronto. They spent two days wandering the streets of the old city, browsing the myriads of shops tucked away along the narrow cobble stoned streets and eating in the wonderful French restaurants that provided delicious food including tender medallions of veal in a cream sauce, duck l'orange, peppercorn steak and enticing desserts like chocolate profiteroles and rich caramel custards.

Their suite at the hotel was luxurious, and when they eventually made it back after an exhausting day, they fell tumbling onto the huge king size bed and spent hours making love and talking about the future. Abby felt like they were back in Paris and it brought back so many sweet memories that she wished they could spend a few more days but it was not to be.

Just before leaving to return to London, Simon told Abby that he had managed to arrange a meeting with the Globe and Mail. They were always looking for people with a lot of experience and wanted to talk to him again early in the New Year when his contract was about to expire. He felt very positive about the outcome and anticipated moving to Toronto in late March.

Abby was over the moon even though she knew they would not be living together. Just having Simon in the same city on a permanent basis was more than she had ever expected. Simon was just as enthused, "I can't wait to settle in one place for a while Abby and then we'll be able to see each other all the time. Eventually I'd like for us to get married but I know there's a lot to be resolved before that can happen."

Abby looked surprised, "Is that a proposal Simon?" she asked.

"Yes my love, it's a proposal but there's no ring yet," he teased, "but I promise I'll buy you the biggest diamond you've ever seen and it won't look like the ring Dave gave to Julia.

"That was just a friendship ring, Simon," Abby retorted.

"I know, I was just being smart. You know I love you Abby and I hope you'll say yes to my proposal. I can't promise that I'll want to stay here in Canada but we won't move to England until the time is right for you and Kate."

Tears formed in Abby's eyes as she threw her arms around Simon's neck, "Of course I accept Simon, I love you so much and don't care where we live as long as we're together."

CHAPTER 53

SIMON'S PROPOSAL RANG IN Abby's ears over and over after he returned to London. The scene at the airport had been particularly difficult and Abby couldn't control her emotions. She clung to Simon at the boarding gate and stood sobbing as his plane lifted off from the tarmac. Julia had offered to drive them and it was Julia that Abby leaned on for comfort as they made their way home.

"I can't believe he's gone," Abby whispered, "it feels like he just got here."

"I know," Julia agreed patting Abby's hand, "but try and think about the future now. Christmas will soon be here and then you and Kate will be off to England. You'll have a wonderful time Abby and then in March, Simon will be back for good."

Julia caught a glimmer of a smile as Abby murmured, "You're right, I should be thinking about all the wonderful times ahead but I miss him so much already."

"Okay enough of this gloom and doom," scolded Julia, "let's pick up Kate from Helen's house and we'll all go to the Dairy Queen like we used to and each have a gigantic sundae with the works."

Abby chuckled, "What would I do without you Julia, you always know how to cheer me up. "

Over the next month Abby settled down again into the routine of running Charlotte's and spending time with Kate in the evenings and on weekends. One Sunday they even visited Jim, at his invitation, and took Scamp for a walk in the park. Being with Jim made Abby feel even closer to Simon even though she had already received three letters and one hour long phone call. It was during the phone call that Abby learned Simon would be going back to Africa to finish his series for the Daily Mail. She was relieved to learn that this would be his last assignment overseas and that he would be working out of his London office once he got back. She was not happy to hear that he would be out of touch for at least three weeks because of the remote area he would be in.

The day that Simon left for Africa he made another call to Abby and told her again how much he loved her and how much he was looking forward to the future. When he finally rang off after whispering, "Bye, my love I'll be in touch," Abby hung up the phone and lowered herself into the nearest chair quietly weeping. She couldn't bear the thought of having no contact with Simon for three weeks, it seemed like a lifetime.

Abby threw herself into running Charlotte's in an attempt to make the time pass and three weeks after Simon's last call she was counting the hours until she heard from him. Two days later, after the scheduled date of his return, she was a nervous wreck.

"Why hasn't he called?" she moaned to Julia hoping she would have a logical answer.

"Well, his plane is probably delayed Abby, all kinds of things could have made him late getting in."

"You're right again and I know I'm being silly but I can't bear this waiting."

"Why don't you call his flat then, "Julia suggested, "or his family? Better yet, why don't you call Jim and see if he's heard anything"

"Do you think he'd mind me bothering him?"

"No, of course not but he probably hasn't heard anything either."

Abby placed a call to Jim but there was no reply and she spent another two hours wringing her hands before contacting him again. Jim was just as surprised as she was that Simon hadn't been in touch and agreed to call the Frasers' later that day. He didn't want to disturb them considering the time difference and promised he would ring Abby back as soon as he had any news.

Julia persuaded Abby to do a little gardening to take her mind off Simon but with the cold weather approaching Abby found little to occupy her outdoors and spent most of the time raking the leaves. Just before supper time, Jim called to say that the Frasers' hadn't heard anything either but they were not worried because it was common for transportation to break down on the remote roads and Simon probably missed his plane. They were certain he would arrive soon and asked Jim to tell Abby not to worry. This did not appease Abby and twenty-four hours later, she became frantic.

"Why is Mom so miserable," Kate whispered to Julia as soon as Abby left the table after supper that evening.

"Well, she hasn't heard from Simon and she's worried that something may have happened to him," Julia replied keeping her voice very low.

Just then Abby appeared in the doorway, "What are you two whispering about?" she demanded.

Kate jumped up from her chair tipping a sleeping Molly off of her lap, "Nothing Mom, I have to get on with my homework," and she rushed past Abby with her dirty dishes, deposited them in the sink with a clatter and then ran quickly up the stairs before Abby could say another word.

Abby looked at Julia and shook her head, "You were talking about Simon weren't you?"

"Yes, we were," Julia replied with a sigh, "but I think you should try and take your mind off him for a while. Why don't we watch the Dick Van Dyke Show, that should cheer you up?"

"I just can't," Abby replied burying her head in her hands, "I think I'm going to phone Jim again to see if he's heard anything."

Just at that moment, the phone rang and Abby looked startled as Julia leapt up from her seat, "I'll get that," she insisted.

Abby listened intently as Julia responded to whoever was on the other end of the line but before she could determine what the call was about Julia had rung off and turned slowly towards her, "That was Jim, he's coming over here," she said softly.

"Why, why is he coming here? What is he coming to tell me," Abby cried out.

Julia took both of Abby's hands, "I honestly don't know Abby but he would rather talk to you in person than on the telephone."

Abby pulled away and sagged against the wall, "Something terrible has happened to Simon," she said as she began to quietly cry.

Julia encouraged Abby to sit down while they waited for Jim and tried to comfort her but Abby was too distraught.

When the doorbell finally rang, Abby held her breath while Julia let Jim in. He looked haggard when he entered the living room and gently lowered himself into the seat across from Abby.

"It's not good news Abby but we mustn't give up hope," he said softly.

Abby appeared to recover her composure and sat upright, "Has there been a plane crash?" she asked.

"No," Jim replied, "and I guess I should start at the beginning Abby."

Abby frowned, "I don't know what you mean but I've had a feeling for a long time that all of you have been keeping a deep dark secret."

"You're right Abby," Jim admitted, "we have been keeping a secret but we all had good intentions. If things had gone as planned. Simon would have moved here in March and you would have been none the wiser."

"What are you trying to tell me?" Abby insisted, her voice rising in frustration.

"Simon isn't just a regular journalist Abby, he's a war correspondent. He's been on the front lines so many times and his life has constantly been in danger but we always thought he was indestructible. He's been covering the war for independence in Angola and he and his cameraman never showed up in Luanda to catch their flight back to England. They have people on the ground looking for them but it's a remote region and overrun with militants. They could be anywhere Abby, they could be holed up somewhere; we just don't know yet."

Abby got up and walked over to the window, "He's got to be out there somewhere," she said gazing up at the sky.

"I'm sorry Abby, but I hope you can understand why Simon didn't want you to know what he was doing"

Abby turned with her eyes flashing, "I'm not a child Jim, Simon had no right not to tell me and you went along with his lie."

Julia walked over and put her hand on Abby's shoulder, "Don't take it out on Jim, Abby," she said gently, "he was only going along with Simon's wishes. Jim's right, you may never have needed to know the danger that Simon was in. It's ironic that something like this happened now when in a few months he would no longer be in harm's way."

Jim walked over and hugged both women, "Don't give up hope Abby. Simon is a force to be reckoned with and if anyone can get out of a tricky situation, he can."

CHAPTER 54

THREE DAYS LATER BROOKE called Abby from London but there was still no news of Simon's whereabouts. Jim had spoken to the Frasers' two or three times and through Lydia, Brooke had learned just how distraught Abby was. When Abby first picked up the telephone and heard the crackle of the overseas line, her heart missed a beat and then she recognized Brooke's soft English voice, "Hello Abby, is that you?" she asked.

"Oh Brooke, yes it's me." Abby replied breathlessly, "Have you heard anything?"

"No, I'm afraid not, the Mail had been in touch with us on a regular basis and they're doing all they can to find them. It's all over the news here and in the papers. None of us are giving up hope and you mustn't either Abby. I believe Simon is coming home, I just have to believe that," she said bravely but Abby could hear Brooke's voice beginning to break.

After the call, Abby telephoned Julia at her office to ask her if there was anywhere in the city where she could buy newspapers from other countries. Julia immediately recalled Lichtman's News located downtown, a bookstore that specialized in selling foreign newspapers, and she agreed to go there after work to see if she could get a copy of the Daily Mail, "You know, even if I do find one, it will probably be an old edition," she reminded Abby.

When Julia arrived home that evening, it didn't matter to Abby that the newspaper was two days old, the photograph of Simon featured prominently on the front page was enough to almost tip her over the edge. She read the headline over and over again, "Simon Fraser Missing in Angola" and reread the story several times trying to imagine the life that Simon had been leading. She learned that the war of independence from the Portuguese had been going on for some time and Simon had been in the thick of it on many occasions as chief war correspondent for his paper. This was to be his last assignment before resigning from his job at the Daily Mail. The article gave a history of Simon's achievements during his years with the paper and a lengthy background about his family, focusing mainly on his father, Roger Fraser. Abby felt like she was already reading his obituary and cried bitterly as she ran her fingers gently over the photo which showed him in army fatigues looking even more handsome than she ever remembered.

The next morning after Julia had left for her office and Kate had gone to school, Abby sat at the kitchen table toying with some pancakes that Julia had made in an attempt to entice her to eat. She knew she wasn't being fair to Peter and Pauline expecting them to run Charlotte's without her help but she couldn't concentrate on anything other than Simon. She had just gone into the kitchen to tip her uneaten breakfast into the trashcan when the doorbell rang. Abby looked startled and was reluctant to answer but when the bell rang again she walked tentatively to the door and opened it. Jim stood on the doorstep and for a moment just stared at Abby, then he stepped forward and took her in his arms, "I'm so sorry Abby," he murmured.

Abby felt her body go numb as she whispered, "He's dead isn't he?"

Jim stroked her hair, "Yes, I'm afraid so Abby, let's go inside," and he guided her gently into the living room where she slumped onto the sofa.

"Tell me everything Jim, please," she begged.

Jim sat down beside her and took her hand, "Lydia called me and I came straight here. I can't believe how stoic she was. They found the jeep that Simon and his cameraman were driving. It was burned out but neither of them was in it and then they found their bodies close by. From what Lydia told me they were in the wrong place at the wrong time and got caught in the crossfire."

"How did they die Jim?" Abby whispered.

"You don't really want to know the details Abby." "Yes I do so please tell me," Abby demanded,

Jim squeezed Abby's hand, "They were both shot in the head from behind."

"Abby shook her head trying to get the image out of her mind, "Do you think they suffered?"

"No, I don't think they felt anything. That's one thing that Lydia kept repeating over and over again, I think it gave her a lot of comfort to know that."

"What happens now Jim?" Abby asked gazing up at him, her face covered in tears.

"Well they're bringing Simon's body back to England and he'll be buried in Redhill. Lydia is going to let me know when the funeral is. They still have to make all the arrangements."

"I want to go," Abby whispered.

"Of course, we'll go together Abby. As soon as I know the details I'll let you know and I'll book our flights. For now though, Abby I don't think you should be on your own. Would you like me to stay for a while or do you want me to call Julia to come home?"

Abby got up and began to wipe away her tears, "No, I'll be okay Jim. I don't want to bother Julia and I'm sure you have other things to do. I'd really rather be alone right now."

"Are you sure?" Jim questioned, rising to his feet, "I can stay and we can talk, it might make you feel better."

Abby shook her head, "You're such a thoughtful man Jim and here I am thinking all about myself when Simon was your best friend; you must be devastated."

"I guess I was always prepared for something like this knowing the dangerous situations Simon got into. I'm going to miss him a lot; I couldn't have wished for a better friend."

After Jim left, Abby took to her bed and that's where Kate found her when she got home from school, "What's wrong Mom, are you sick?" she asked, dropping her schoolbooks on the floor beside Abby's bed.

"Come and sit beside me Kate," Abby said gently, "I have something to tell you."

"It's something bad, isn't it?" said Kate nervously.

"Yes, I'm afraid it is honey," Abby replied.

CHAPTER 55

ONE WEEK LATER, JIM and Abby were on a flight across the Atlantic. For Abby, it had been a time of tremendous grief and she was still in a state of denial. It was hard to believe that she would never again see the vital, handsome man she had fallen in love with. She would never feel his touch or listen to his wonderful voice and she would never be able to dream about their future together. After all she had been through, with the loss of Daniel and the failure of her marriage, she had finally found happiness with the man of her dreams only to learn that happiness was fleeting. Kate was Abby's one salvation and she had marvelled at the way she had handled the news of Simon's death. She had climbed into bed beside Abby and hugging her mother tightly murmured, "You know Mom, Simon is with Daniel now, so he won't be alone any more."

Abby stroked Kate's head, "But Simon didn't even know Daniel honey."

"Everyone knows everyone in heaven Mom and they have fun. One day when I go to heaven I'll see Simon and Daniel and if you go there before me, I'll see you there too."

Abby, who was not a religious person, started to sob, "Where did you learn all this Kate, you never went to church?"

"Helen told me," Kate replied, "she goes to church every Sunday and her Dad teaches Sunday school."

"Would you like to go to church too, Kate?"

"Uh uh, I don't think so. Anyway we learn a lot of stuff in school."

Abby snuggled closer to Kate, "You are so precious to me," she whispered, "I don't know what I'd do without you."

Jim glanced at Abby and noticed that her eyes were closed. When they had first boarded the plane, she had been nervous and clinging to his arm and after they were finally seated, she couldn't stop talking about Simon. He realized how distraught she was and slowly in his quiet gentle way, he made Abby feel more at ease. He encouraged her to eat, ordered her a glass of wine and asked the stewardess to bring her a blanket. Even in his own grief, Jim was the perfect gentleman.

Arriving in London, Jim rented a car and they immediately drove to Redhill. It was late and they were both tired but they were anxious to get to Faversham House. As Jim pulled into the driveway at just before eight o'clock in the evening, it was Brooke who ran down the steps to greet them. She threw herself into Jim's arms and almost knocked him off his feet, "Oh Jim, it's been so long. It's so lovely to see you, thank you for coming."

Jim pushed Brooke away so that he could get a good look at her, "My goodness," he said, "you get prettier every time I see you."

"And you get more good looking," Brooke countered then she noticed Abby standing quietly beside the car. She stepped forward and took hold of both of Abby's hands then pulled her into her arms, "Abby, I am so sorry," she whispered.

As hard as she might, Abby couldn't stop the tears, "I should be saying that to you Brooke. He was your brother and I know how close you were."

"Thank you Abby, now let's go into the house. We were expecting you a little earlier and we've already had supper but Tilly has a casserole warming in the oven for you."

"Thanks Brooke," said Jim following her up the steps while gently guiding Abby with the palm of his hand on her back.

Lydia stood in the hallway as they came through the front door and ran forward to gather Jim and Abby in her arms. Tears ran down her cheeks as she welcomed them, "I am so happy you are both here," she said, "but I wish it was for a different reason."

The next morning, the day of the funeral, Abby woke up just before dawn and thought about the night before. Roger had been waiting to greet them in the library and Abby had been shocked to see how much he had changed. While Lydia still looked immaculate and Brooke as lovely as ever, even though they were both dressed in somber black, Roger was bundled up in a thick flannel robe and slippers and appeared to have lost weight. Lydia had confided that she was worried about him; he had taken Simon's death very hard and she wasn't sure he would recover.

Abby had questioned again why she had not been told about the dangerous work in which Simon had been involved and for a brief moment even displayed a hint of anger that she had been deceived. Lydia, however, understanding Abby's disappointment that she had not been confided in, quietly explained how much Simon loved her and wanted to protect her and she finally acquiesced.

An hour later, Abby rose from the bed ready to face the day ahead and to say a last goodbye to the man she had loved so dearly.

CHAPTER 56

THE FUNERAL WAS HELD at St. Matthews Church and Abby was amazed at how many people were in attendance. There was Simon's extended family of cousins, aunts and uncles and his friends from London and even overseas. There were his co-workers from the Daily Mail, reporters from television and radio and Max, who had arrived that morning to support Brooke.

The service in the great church seemed interminable to Abby and she couldn't take her eyes off of the ornate walnut casket with its lid thankfully closed. She wanted so desperately to see Simon's dear face one more time but not like this.

The weather service had called for rain and Abby had imagined a scene in the cemetery with dozens of large black umbrellas adding to the gloom of the day but it was not to be. Though cool, the skies were a bright blue and the sun lifted many lagging spirits at a time when all seemed gray. As the casket was lowered into the ground, Jim took Abby's hand and squeezed it gently. She looked at him and smiled then releasing her hand walked slowly forward and tossed a red rose she had been holding into the grave, "Goodbye my love," she whispered.

Back at Faversham House Tilly, with the help of a local caterer, had laid out a feast for all of the guests and an hour after Simon had been laid to rest, it seemed like a party was in full swing. Abby looked around her in disbelief remarking to Brooke, "How can they carry on like this, everyone looks so happy?"

"They're celebrating Simon's life, he would have wanted it this way," she replied.

Just at that moment, Jim called for silence and with glass in hand spoke about the friend that he would never forget and then proposed a toast to his memory.

Everyone raised their glass quietly uttering, "To Simon", while Abby remained tight lipped unable to speak and with tears rolling down her face. Brooke placed an arm around Abby's shoulders and gently drew her close, "Don't cry Abby," she whispered, "Simon's in a better place now."

Brooke's effort to comfort was of no avail and Abby broke away, running out of the door and upstairs to seek sanctuary in her room. This was where Lydia found her fifteen minutes later lying prone on the bed and weeping into the pillow.

"Abby, I want you to get up now," Lydia said softly, "let's go for a walk."

Abby turned and looked up at Lydia, her eyes red and swollen, "I don't want to go for a walk; I want to stay here."

"That's not a good idea Abby, you shouldn't be alone. I thought we'd go down to the stables and see Scarlett."

Abby raised herself up on her elbows, "But what about all of your guests?"

"They can look after themselves quite adequately," Lydia replied, "in any case Brooke is quite capable of playing hostess and it will force Roger to start interacting a bit more. He's been so withdrawn lately and understandably so but he needs to start paying attention to others again."

"I don't know how you do it Lydia," Abby remarked getting up from the bed, "how do you hold it together?"

"Well my dear, it's not easy but if I focus on the people that are dear to my heart that are still here, I don't have time to think about those that aren't. Now let's go Abby, grab your coat because it's chilly and I'll get mine from the hall closet."

At the stables, Abby and Lydia were met by Quinn, "Afternoon ma'am, afternoon Miss," he said politely tipping his cap.

"Good afternoon Quinn," Lydia responded, "we've come to see Scarlett; how is she today?"

"Oh, she's right as rain ma'am. I had Bart take her out for a run this morning and she worked up a real appetite. She'll be pleased to see you."

"Thank you Quinn, we'll just go along and take a look at her."

"Er...excuse me ma'am", said Quinn falteringly, "may I ask you how my Lordship is? We haven't seen him here at the stables for quite a while."

"I know Quinn, but he's doing a little better and I hope to cajole him into poking his nose outside within the next few days. It's just been really difficult for him."

"I'm glad to hear that ma'am, now if you'll excuse me I had better get on with my chores."

"Certainly Quinn, come along Abby," said Lydia taking Abby's hand and leading her to Scarlett's stall.

At the sight of the great chestnut mare. Abby felt as though her heart would break all over again. This was Simon's beloved horse; his pride and joy and now her master would no longer ride her through the fields and woods ever again. Abby stroked the soft head between her ears and looking into the large brown eyes whispered to Lydia, "Do you think she knows?"

"I don't think so," Lydia replied, "horses are very intelligent creatures but don't forget Simon didn't see her every day. Quinn and Bart are here all the time and they see that she's well looked after and gets lots of exercise."

"I suppose you're right," sighed Abby walking to the next stall and noticing Bailey, the horse that Simon had ridden when she had visited with the Frasers' before.

"Let's walk down to the river," Lydia suggested and started to walk out of the stables into the field beyond.

Abby followed a few steps behind and as they walked in silence, she marvelled at Lydia's courage in the face of losing her only son. When they reached the river and looked out across the water, Lydia finally spoke, "I hope you know that you are always welcome here Abby. You were very special to Simon and just because he's gone, it doesn't mean that you'll be forgotten. We'd like you to come back one day just as we planned. I know Christmas will be too soon and I'm not sure how we are going to celebrate the holidays this year but maybe one summer you can come back with Kate."

Abby's eyes teared up again, "You are so kind Lydia, thank you so much. I would love to come back and see you all again and I know Kate would love it here too."

"Good, I'm glad," said Lydia, "and one day even if you meet someone else the invitation still stands."

Abby shook her head violently, "No, I'll never meet anyone else, I don't even want to."

Lydia took hold of both of Abby's hands, "Look at me Abby", she demanded, "That's silly; you are young and beautiful and you have years and years ahead of you. Yes, Simon was unique and you'll never meet anyone like him again but everyone is unique Abby. There's someone else out there for you and one day you'll find him. When you first came here, I told you about my first husband Andrew. After he died I thought I would never get over it but then I met Roger. I also told you that he could never replace Andrew but he's been a good husband and a good father to Simon and Brooke. Now, I could have shut myself away and wasted my life but I chose to take another chance. You took another chance with Simon after your marriage broke up, Abby, and now you have to do it again."

Abby hugged Lydia and kissed her on the cheek, "I know you're right Lydia; I just don't know if I'll ever be ready; that's all."

CHAPTER 57

TWO DAYS LATER, JIM and Abby were on their way back to Toronto. Lydia had begged them to stay longer but Abby wanted to go home and Jim had an important project he was working on. They were both in a much lighter mood on this journey even though their hearts were heavy. After lunch was served and Abby had consumed two glasses of wine, she felt too restless to read and just felt like talking.

"What do you really do Jim?" she asked.

"I assume you're talking about my job?"

"Yes, Simon told me you were some kind of engineer."

"Yes, an industrial engineer"

"And what does an industrial engineer do?" Abby persisted.

Jim chuckled, "You're going to find this all very boring."

"Why don't you let me decide that?" asked Abby.

"Well, we study plans and designs for manufacturing facilities. We also study machinery, analyze production costs, develop maintenance standards, determine human resources and conduct time studies. Shall I go on?" he said with a smile.

"You mean there's more?"

Jim laughed out loud, "Told you it was boring, didn't I? Now you tell me what you do. I know you own a flower shop so I guess you pick flowers and put them in pots."

Abby knew he was teasing but pretended to be indignant, "That is certainly not what I do," she said haughtily, "I purchase the flowers and plants, help with some of the arrangements, organize special orders for weddings or other occasions and take care of all the financial end of the business. It's a lot of work."

"Oh, and who runs the shop when you're not there? The place must fall apart."

Abby knew Jim was still being playful but she suddenly felt a little sad again, "Okay, I'm not indispensable. I've got two wonderful assistants and a driver and they've been so supportive. I don't know what I would have done without them, but now I have to get back to reality and start pulling my weight again."

Jim grew more sober, "Maybe that's the best thing you can do for now Abby, throw yourself into your business. I find work always helps to take one's mind of one's troubles."

"Yes, you're right Jim and then of course I still have Kate who is even more important to me than Charlotte's. I feel that I've been neglecting her so much lately and even when Simon was alive I often felt guilty spending time away from her."

"Abby, I have to tell you something," Jim said as he flagged the stewardess down for more wine, "kids think a lot more of their parents when they see them as role models. That doesn't mean someone who stays at home all day cleaning house and dishing out meals. It means someone that is involved in living; someone that is truly their own person and not just there to take care of others. Seeing a parent passionate about their job, their hobby or even a relationship is inspiring to a child. It gives them insight to what they might be able to achieve for themselves. Just because you've spent some time away from Kate doesn't mean that the time you do spend with her isn't meaningful and don't forget she also has Julia and Julia's no slouch."

Abby smiled as she accepted another glass of wine from the stewardess, "You're right, Julia's no slouch; she's one smart cookie and I owe her a lot. Anyway, I understand what you're saying Jim, but I still think I should try and spend more time with Kate."

"Well, I hope you will both come and visit me the next time Kelly's here. I know that the two girls got along really well and I have to admit it's a lot easier for me when Kelly has someone her own age close by."

"That would be lovely Jim, thanks for suggesting it. By the way, who's looking after Scamp right now?"

"My old neighbour next door, I told you about him before. He takes Scamp out for a walk when I'm at work and any time I'm away he takes him to stay in his house. It's a real godsend because a dog is a bit of a commitment."

"Hmm," Abby mused, "not like our Molly, she seems quite content on her own."

"Yes, well we don't want to emulate Molly do we?" said Jim.

Two hours later after a brief nap brought on by the amount of wine she had consumed, Abby realized they were landing in Toronto. She had arranged for Julia to pick them up at the airport and drive Jim right to his front door. The minute she stepped through the arrivals gate, she could see Julia waving frantically from behind a large group of people waiting for their own friends or relatives.

"Where's Kate?" Abby yelled as she pushed through the crowd.

"Hi, how are you both?" Julia responded grabbing Abby in a bear hug and then stepping forward to give Jim a peck on the cheek.

"We're fine," said Abby impatiently, "but where's Kate?"

"She's at home with a bit of a cold but Martha's with her, so you don't have to worry."

"Are you sure it's just a cold?" Abby asked anxiously.

"Yes, I'm sure," Julia replied, "now let's go get your luggage and get out of here."

CHAPTER 58

THE NEXT FEW WEEKS were the most difficult Abby had ever been through. She had already had to accept the fact that her only son had been killed in a senseless accident, but now she had also lost the one man who she had truly thought she would spend the rest of her life with. She had never been a religious person and now found herself questioning the existence of God on a daily basis and when Martha suggested that she go to church on her first Sunday home, she vehemently refused.

Julia and Kate did their best to comfort Abby and try to shake her out of her depression and even Peter and Pauline began to feel the strain of working with her. The running of Charlotte's had been their responsibility whenever Abby took time away from business and yet they were now subjected to being treated as though they were incapable of completing the most menial tasks. It was difficult to sympathize with Abby, even knowing how depressed she was when away from the shop, while during business hours she took on the role of a taskmaster. She stood over Pauline while she arranged the simplest bouquet, hovered while Peter dealt with a customer, demanded that any shipments received be checked at least twice and became obsessive about the length of time it took Terry to make a delivery.

Martha came into the shop one day to purchase some flowers for a sick neighbour only to find that Abby had stepped out on an errand. It was only natural that she wanted to know how Abby was coping and immediately sensed that neither Peter nor Pauline wanted to talk. After much coaxing, she managed to discover how much Abby's behaviour was affecting them and in that moment she decided to do something about it. At seven o'clock that same evening, Julia was surprised to see Martha standing on the doorstep, "Hi Martha, I didn't know you were coming over tonight," she remarked.

"Where's Abby?" Martha asked pushing past Julia into the hallway.

Julia was shocked at Martha's behaviour, "She's upstairs in her room, why is something wrong?"

Martha turned and nodded her head, "I would say there's something wrong, wouldn't you? I was in the shop today and from what I see, Abby's treating the staff pretty shabbily. She needs someone to set her straight."

Julia stepped forward and took Martha's hand, "Don't you think she's been through enough?" she asked gently, "She's been so depressed since Simon died."

"Depressed? That's not the impression I got; she's been ruling the roost with Peter and Pauline and I seriously think they're on the point of quitting."

"I had no idea that was going on at Charlotte's. When she's here, she spends most of her time in her room and when she does come out, she hardly ever utters a word. I've tried talking to her and even Kate, bless her, has done her best to cheer her up but it's useless."

"Sounds like a regular Jekyll and Hyde to me. Incidentally, where is Kate? I would prefer she wasn't here right now."

"She's at Helen's house but she should be back in about an hour. Why, what are you going to do?"

"I'm going to give Abby a piece of my mind," Martha announced as she turned to go up the stairs. Julia held out her hand to stop her only to realize that it was too late. Abby stood at the door to the living room surveying the scene.

"What's going on?" she demanded.

"Ah," said Martha as she took Abby's arm and guided her over to the sofa, "come and sit down Abby, we need to talk."

Abby looked nervous, "What about?"

"I think I'll go and clear the supper dishes," Julia announced.

"I prefer that you stayed Julia," said Martha, "after all Abby's behaviour affects you too."

"Wait a minute," said Abby trying to get up, "if you've come here to give me a lecture, I'm not interested in hearing it."

Martha pulled Abby back down again, "Well, you're going to hear it young lady. For your information I was in your shop today and I didn't like what I heard."

Abby looked indignant, "What do you mean? What have those two been saying about me?"

"Don't you get on your high horse with me missy. Nobody volunteered any information; I had to drag it out of them. You've been acting like a little dictator around there and you'll be lucky if you have any staff left if you carry on like that. Then I come here and find out that you're holed up in your room and not talking. What's the matter with you Abby, you've been through a lot worse than this, you lost a child for God's sake."

Abby covered her face with her hands, "Please don't Martha," she begged.

"I've said it before and I'll say it again Abby," Martha continued, "you can go on moping about and being difficult for the rest of your life or you can stop right now and start being human again. You still have Kate to consider. When Daniel died, you left that poor child to cope by herself for a year and now you're doing it again. She's coming into her teenage years and she needs you more than ever. You can't expect Julia to take over the reins; you're her mother so start acting like one."

Abby started to cry, quietly and then her sobbing increased until her whole body was trembling. Julia ran forward to comfort her but Martha waved her away, "Let her cry, it will do her good."

Kate never saw her mother that night. Right after Martha confronted her and she had broken down in tears, she rushed to her room and crawled under the bedcovers. Martha had persuaded Julia not to go after her but to let her think about what she had said in the hope that her state of mind would improve.

The next morning when Julia came downstairs early, to prepare breakfast for Kate before she left for school, she was surprised to find Abby up and already dressed making coffee and setting the table. Abby looked up as Julia entered the kitchen, "Good morning Julia," she said with a smile, "did you hear Kate stirring up there?"

"Yes, I heard her in the bathroom. Are you okay Abby?"

Abby nodded, "Yes I'm fine, we'll talk over breakfast."

Just then Kate crept quietly into the room, "Hi Mom," she said, "you're up early today."

"Yes, I know honey, I wanted to talk to you and Julia before you left today."

Kate looked wary, "What about Mom?"

"Let me get you some breakfast and then I'll tell you but don't worry everything's going to be all right. Now what would you like eggs, pancakes?"

Kate looked at Julia and rolled her eyes, "I usually have cereal Mom."

"I know but today is special so let's have something different. Julia, will you help me please, I don't want Kate to be late for school?"

When they finally sat down to breakfast of scrambled eggs, bacon and toast, Kate could hardly contain herself, "Okay Mom what do you want to talk about?"

"Well," Abby replied laying her fork down, "I just wanted to tell you both that I know I've been absolutely miserable to live with lately and want to apologize."

"There's no need to apologize," Julia whispered.

"Please let me finish, Julia." Abby insisted taking Kate's hand, "Your grandmother came here last night while you were at Helen's and she told me a few home truths. This isn't the first time that she's brought me to my senses; she's a very strong woman and I wish I were more like her. Anyway, I know Simon's gone; no amount of grief will bring him back and you don't deserve to have a mother who's moping about all day. As for you," she said turning to Julia, "I really am sorry, you've been so patient with me and I couldn't wish for a better friend. I just hope you'll forgive me."

"Of course I forgive you," said Julia graciously, "but what are you going to do about Peter and Pauline?"

Abby thought for a moment, "I think I'll sweep in there today with a box of donuts and be as sweet as pie."

Julia chuckled, "They may think you've gone off your rocker."

"Oh I'll have a talk with them first thing this morning. I think I've just been keeping them at arm's length because I couldn't stand them fussing over me. They must think I'm a real ogre if they even considered leaving and they've been so supportive all the times I've been away. I hope they'll give me another chance," she said sadly.

Kate patted Abby's hand, "Oh Mom they're not going to leave you. How could you think such a thing?"

"Well, I've been pretty mean to them and I wouldn't blame them if they quit but I think I could talk them around."

"Now you're being silly," Julia said, "there's no way either one of them is going to abandon you."

Abby got up from the table, "I guess you're right. Well I'd better get moving otherwise I'll be really late. Finish your breakfast Kate, then make sure Molly's got enough food and water before you leave."

"Okay Mom." Kate replied nibbling on her toast. "Will you be home early tonight?"

"Yes honey," Abby answered realizing just how late she had been staying at the shop every day, "in fact, I was thinking of taking you out for supper tonight and I hope you'll come too, Julia."

"Love to," said Julia as she rose from her seat and started to clear the dishes.

CHAPTER 59

OVER THE NEXT FEW months, Abby did her best to put on a brave face and during those times when she felt particularly downhearted she would come up with an excuse to take herself away from Kate, Julia and Charlotte's. Sometimes she would go shopping, even though her heart wasn't in it, but a new outfit always seemed to lift her spirits. Sometimes she would go to a movie and try to get lost in the story playing out on the screen and often she would just go for a walk.

Christmas had been the most difficult even though she had been especially busy in the shop and Julia had made sure that she was occupied over the holiday. On Christmas Eve, Julia hosted a party at the house and invited Jim, his daughter Kelly and the Wards' along with Kate's closest friend Helen. David was in town visiting from Vancouver, so in all there were six adults and three children plus Scamp who had snuck out when the front door opened and who Jim didn't have the heart to leave behind.

Abby was subdued but happy to see Jim and to be able to talk to him about Simon and the Fraser's. Brooke had called Jim earlier that week to wish him a happy holiday, to report that her parents were in good health and to ask after Abby. She was leaving for a few days vacation in Paris with Max but had promised she would call Abby soon after she got back. Abby had been hoping to continue her connection to Simon's family and Brooke's message encouraged her to make a call to Lydia the next day.

Julia had set up a rather unique Christmas Eve buffet, mostly to accommodate the children. There were hot dogs, hamburgers, pizza and fried chicken and for dessert, a decadent chocolate cake. Knowing that the next day they would be expected to dine on a traditional turkey dinner, the adults were more than happy with the more simple fare and consumed their fair share of wine and beer. Scamp was in his element, being fussed over by everyone and receiving scraps from the table, but when Molly wandered into the room, to everyone's amusement, he cowered behind the nearest chair.

All in all, the evening was a great success but Abby went to bed that night relieved that it was over and that she only had to get through one more day surrounded by people.

Christmas morning, Abby got up early suspecting that Kate would be up at the crack of dawn to open her gifts. It had been after midnight when she had been able to smuggle the packages out of her room and put them under the tree and she was looking forward to seeing Kate's reaction.

Julia arrived in the kitchen a few moments later, awakened by the smell of coffee, "Merry Christmas," she said giving Abby a hug, "what are you doing up so early?"

"Oh, I couldn't sleep any longer and I expect Kate will be down any minute."

At that very moment Kate appeared in the doorway, "Hi Mom, Hi Aunt Julia," she said sleepily, "is it morning yet?"

Julia chuckled, "Yes, but barely. Sorry if I woke you up sweetie."

"That's okay," Kate responded yawning, "it's so dark though, I thought it was the middle of the night. Can I open my presents now, please Mom?"

Abby turned from the counter where she was pouring coffee, "Not just yet honey. Let's all have some breakfast and then we can all open our presents."

Kate's patience was rewarded when she opened the first package from her mother. It was beautifully wrapped in gold foil with a huge red satin bow and inside was the outfit she had raved over a week earlier. Kate loved clothes and she wasn't disappointed when both Abby and Julia went overboard with shoes, socks, boots and a new parka. Later they piled into Julia's car and spent the rest of the day at John and Martha's. David had also been invited and he arrived just in time to be seated for one of Martha's famous Christmas dinners with turkey, ham, roast potatoes, sage dressing, carrots, sprouts and a brandy soaked Christmas pudding.

Julia was thankful that Raymond wasn't there even though their divorce had been amicable. She just felt that it would have been a little awkward with David there too, especially now that she was beginning to have some serious feelings for him. Even Abby had noticed a change in Julia when David arrived in town this time. She seemed more responsive to his attentions and Abby began to wonder where the relationship was going and what it would mean if they decided to get together on a permanent basis. Maybe Julia would consider moving to Vancouver. That would mean selling the house and the thought of Julia moving away disturbed Abby. She had supported her through thick and thin and she would miss her terribly.

David returned home right after the holidays and despite Abby's fears, she decided not to question Julia about her plans for the future. After a week passed without Julia even mentioning David, she breathed a sigh of relief, settled back into her normal routine and began to think about the next few months and the prospect of spring break when she would have to make arrangements for Kate while she worked.

Despite talking to Lydia and Brooke on two or three occasions when they tried to persuade her to come back to England in the summer, Abby couldn't face the idea of spending a vacation at the Fraser's without Simon. She assured them that one day she would take them up on their offer and bring Kate with her but she felt it was too soon. Her concern about spring break was resolved late in February when she received a call from Henrick. He invited her to visit him again in Florida for a week and she realized this was a perfect opportunity to actually take a break herself and take care of Kate at the same time.

As the holiday drew near, Abby actually felt excited at the prospect of seeing Henrick again and Kate was counting down the days. Abby had always thought of her old boss as a rather wise old man and he had been full of sympathy and understanding when he had heard about Simon's death. Now Abby was looking forward to be being able to talk to him face to face and learn how he had coped with losing Gerda after so many years.

On their arrival in Siesta Key, once again Willem and Sofie welcomed Abby and Kate into their home. Abby shed a few tears as Henrick embraced her and murmured in her ear, "It's so lovely to see you my sweet girl." He was like the father she had never had and she felt such comfort in his arms but it also reminded her that she wasn't the only one without a father. At that moment she wondered again where Ed was and if she would ever hear from him again.

Abby was anxious to talk to Henrick but Willem had arranged all sorts of activities during the first few days and they went out to dinner each night to a couple of the local restaurants noted for their seafood. It was on the fourth day that Abby finally found herself sitting on a beach chair beside Henrick while Kate paddled at the edge of the ocean looking for shells. Abby was feeling the effects of the sun and rubbing lotion into her legs when she felt Henrick looking at her. She looked up smiling, "What is it, do I have cream on my nose or something?"

Henrick laughed, "No, I was really thinking how pretty you look but I also think you've lost a little weight and I just hope you're taking care of yourself."

Abby sighed, "Now, you've seen me at every meal since I've been here and did it look like I was starving myself?"

"No, that is true; you have had a good appetite but I suspect you weren't eating too well before you came here."

"Well, I can't deny the fact that I didn't feel like eating too much after Simon died but being here with you has been so relaxing. I have to admit this is the first time I've felt at peace with myself for months."

Henrick leaned over and touched Abby's hand, "I am so glad to hear that my dear; I have been worried about you."

"How do you get over it?"

"You mean losing someone you love?"

"Yes, my time with Simon was so brief, but you and Gerda were together for so long. I just don't understand how you could go on living without her."

Henrick shook his head, "My dear, dear Abby what choice did I have? Life has to go on no matter how hard it may seem at the time. Gerda would have wanted me to go on living and she would want me to be happy. When I first lost her I thought my world had come to an end but I managed to make a new life for myself thanks to Wilem and Sofie. Yes, an old man like me was able to start over and believe it or not, I'm happy again. You have to count your blessings Abby. You've got Kate and she's precious and you have Julia and one day you'll meet someone else."

"No," Abby protested, "I'll never meet anyone like Simon again"

"That's right," Henrick agreed, "but you will fall in love again Abby, trust me. He may not be as handsome or as exciting but there will be other reasons why you'll want to spend the rest of your life with him. I never thought anyone could ever replace Gerda but then I met Ginny. She's nothing like Gerda but she's fun and she makes me laugh and she's pretty sexy too."

Abby's mouth dropped open, "Why Henrick, you devil, I thought you were too old for that kind of thing."

Henrick snorted, "Ha, you young people, you think you know it all."

CHAPTER 60

JULIA NOTICED A CHANGE in Abby when she returned from her vacation. She was beginning to take notice of what was going on around her rather than living her life like a robot. Charlotte's became the centre of her attention and she began to expand the business. While Peter and Pauline ran the shop she threw herself into promoting her special occasion services and by the fall, she was inundated with orders for weddings and anniversary parties. She declined all requests for funeral wreaths; she just couldn't bear to associate herself with anything related to the death of a loved one.

While Charlotte's took up most of Abby's time, she made sure that she was always home on weeknights to have supper with Kate and when business didn't take precedence she made the effort to spend quality time with her on weekends. Kate was becoming a young lady and had developed a particular interest in fashion. Her favourite pastime was window-shopping with her mother and occasionally when she saw an outfit that caught her eye, Abby would surprise her by dragging her into the store and buying it for her on the spot. Kate never took advantage of the fact that her mother had become a successful businesswoman and could now afford to be generous. She had the common sense of someone much older and Abby felt a tremendous pride. She had lost both her father and her brother and at times even Abby had emotionally abandoned her, but she had survived without any apparent effect. Little did either Abby or Kate know that they were about to lose the most stabilizing force in their lives.

One Friday evening in October, just after the Thanksgiving holiday, Julia seemed to be on edge and picked at the turkey casserole that Abby had prepared.

"What's the matter?" asked Abby frowning. "You've hardly eaten anything."

"This is yummy," remarked Kate, "don't you like it Aunt Julia?"

Julia looked up and smiled, "The food is wonderful but I'm feeling a little anxious. I must confess I have something to tell you both and I've been dreading it all week."

Abby grabbed Julia's hand, "What is it?" she cried. "Are you sick, please don't tell me you're sick."

Julia shook her head, "No, nothing like that."

"Then what? It's bad, I can tell," said Abby releasing Julia's hand and getting up from the table.

"Sit down Abby," Julia demanded in a voice that made Kate jump.

Abby sat down reluctantly and stared at Julia with tears in her eyes expecting the worst.

"Now," Julia continued, "I suppose there's only one way to say this. I've decided to marry David and I'm moving to Vancouver."

Abby looked horrified while Kate slumped back in her chair. "I had no idea things were that serious between you two," said Abby, "when did all this come about?"

"This last weekend." Julia replied. "He proposed to me last Christmas but I wasn't ready and I almost broke up with him then because I didn't think it was fair to continue our relationship when I wasn't prepared to make a commitment. Then in the summer when we spent two weeks together in Europe I came to realize how compatible we were. I know it was incredibly romantic, especially in Venice, and I tried not to let that colour my judgment so I was still not certain. Then when I saw him again in September and again this last weekend, when he asked me to marry him again, I decided to accept his proposal."

Kate looked excited, "Are you having a big wedding? Are you going to wear a long white dress? Can I be a bridesmaid?"

Abby kept very quiet while Julia laughed, "No, we are not having a big wedding and I'm not wearing white but you can be my bridesmaid and your Mom can be my matron of honor."

"Whoopee," cried Kate, "isn't it neat Mom?"

"It's wonderful honey." Abby whispered.

"I think your Mom is having a little trouble getting used to the idea honey," Julia said looking wistfully at Kate.

"Well, it is a bit of a shock," Abby agreed, "but I'm really happy for you, if that's what you want. I'm just upset that you'll be moving so far away. Somehow I had a feeling that this might happen but I kept putting it to the back of my mind. Kate and I will be lost without you; you've been so good to us and we love you so much."

Julia got up and put her arms around Abby, "I love you too, and I promise we'll see each other often. I'll probably come with David when he has business in Toronto and you and Kate can come and visit me any time you like. We plan to get married here in the New Year. I meant it when I said I wanted you both to be in the wedding party but it will be a small wedding with Martha and John, a few co-workers and one or two of David's friends."

"What about his family?" asked Abby.

"Unfortunately, his father died when he was in his teens and his mother will try to be here but she has rheumatoid arthritis and finds it very difficult to get around."

"Can Jim come too?" Kate interjected.

"Of course, if your Mom would like him to," Julia replied looking questioningly at Abby.

"It's sweet of you to ask that honey," Abby remarked, "I'm sure he would like to come and maybe he'd like to bring Vicky."

"Hmmph, I guess that's okay," Kate said grudgingly, "but it would be better if he could bring Scamp."

Abby looked at Julia and rolled her eyes, "Tell me Julia," she said, "what do you intend to do about the house?"

"Well, I thought about keeping it and just asking you to pay for all the utilities and taxes or you could buy it from me if you wanted to. I promise I'll give you a really good deal Abby."

"That's way too generous Julia and I'd like to think about it but I can tell you now, I don't want to move. Even though you own this house, Kate and I have always thought of it as our home and we want to stay."

"That's fabulous," said Julia, "I was hoping you felt that way. Take your time and when you make up your mind about buying the house or not, just let me know."

CHAPTER 61

CHRISTMAS THAT YEAR WAS a particularly busy one for Abby. With the expansion of her business, she had so many orders for private parties that she was overwhelmed and had to hire part-time staff to help out. It was during this period that she decided to promote Peter to manager of the shop and gave him carte blanche to look for another assistant. Pauline had always been dedicated to Abby but she had a family to think about and Peter, being single with no commitments, was the ideal person to take over.

On Christmas Eve, after giving some last minute instructions to Peter, Abby raced to the stores to do some last minute shopping. Usually she was organized and bought all her Christmas gifts early in December but Charlotte's had taken precedence and she now only had less than two hours to make her purchases. Luck was with her when she found a beautiful silver and onyx bracelet for Julia; a cherry red velour robe for Martha and an argyle sweater for John, but finding something for Kate proved to be a little more difficult. Finally, she settled on a pair of jeans in the latest style and a white cable knit top with a polo neck and prayed that Kate would like it. She knew just how fussy Kate had become about her clothes and didn't want to disappoint her.

Christmas morning, Abby, Julia and Kate spent the morning alone celebrating with a special breakfast and opening their gifts. It was a bittersweet time, each knowing that this would probably be the last Christmas they would be spending together in this house. Although Abby had made up her mind to buy the house outright, it was unlikely that Julia would ever come back to visit without David and it would never be the same again.

That afternoon they enjoyed the traditional Christmas dinner with Martha and John and chattered endlessly about Julia's upcoming wedding, which was taking place at the end of January. The ceremony was being held in a small chapel with a reception in a private room at The Royal York Hotel. Julia had already chosen her outfit, a short rose silk empire style dress and matching silk stiletto pumps. She had decided not to wear a hat but to wear her hair in a chignon adorned with a single pink flower.

David had elected not to fly to Toronto over the holidays. He was involved in a project with a deadline of just two days before his wedding and their three-week honeymoon in Hawaii. However, Julia had been on his mind a great deal and on Christmas Eve, she received a small parcel containing a beautifully wrapped velvet box. Inside was a heart shaped diamond necklace and a heartfelt note with an explanation that the necklace was only a little something for Christmas and the next velvet box would contain the engagement ring that he would deliver to her personally. Kate could hardly wait for January to end. She was so excited about the wedding even though she was sad that Julia would be living so far away. She had never been to a wedding before and thought it was all incredibly romantic.

Finally the big day had arrived and although it was bitterly cold and a blanket of snow covered the ground, the sun was shining and the ice on the trees sparkled like a thousand miniature fairy lights. The chapel held about thirty guests, most of them being Julia's co-workers and their wives from her law firm and four of David's close friends from Vancouver. Martha, looking sophisticated in an emerald green suit with a triple row of pearls, sat with John in the front pew and next to John sat Jim who had accepted Julia's invitation but had not brought Vicky with him.

David's friend, Adam, stood up for him and nudged him playfully when he stumbled over his wedding vows and Abby and Kate, both wearing similar pale yellow dresses, stood beside Julia and giggled when she dropped the wedding ring as David was attempting to put it on her finger. In spite of the minor mishaps, the ceremony went well and everyone raced to his or her car, to escape the cold, while haphazardly throwing rice at the happy couple. It was at the reception that Abby finally had a chance to talk to Jim, "How are you?" she asked giving him a hug, "We haven't seen you for a while."

"Well, I've been pretty busy with work and I took Kelly away on a skiing vacation at Christmas while Angela took off somewhere with her boyfriend."

"You sound a little bitter, is something wrong?"

Jim shook his head and smiled, "Sorry, I didn't mean to sound that way. It's just that sometimes I think Kelly would be better off living with me than with her mother."

Abby was surprised, "Are you sure Jim? What makes you feel that way?"

Jim beckoned to a passing waiter bearing a tray of canapés, "She just leaves her alone far too much, that's all. Look Abby, this is supposed to be a happy occasion so maybe we can talk about this some other time. "

Abby sensed that Jim was feeling a little depressed and touched his hand, "I'd like that Jim and I'm a good listener."

Jim smiled as he took some canapés and offered one to Abby, "May I say that you look incredibly lovely today and Kate looks so grown up."

"Why, thank you kind sir and what do you think of Julia?"

Jim glanced over at Julia who was gazing lovingly into David's eyes, "She's a knockout, and she looks so happy."

"She is, and I'm happy for her but we're going to miss her terribly."

"Martha told me that Charlotte's is thriving and that you're buying the house. I think that's wonderful Abby, at least I'll know where to find you."

Abby frowned, "What on earth do you mean? I always intended for us to stay in touch; I've just been so busy with Christmas and the wedding."

"Just kidding," said Jim grinning, "now how about raiding the buffet, I'm starving?"

"Love to," Abby replied, "but tell me, where's Vicky? I thought Julia invited her too."

"Vicky is no more," Jim replied with a sigh, "she met someone on one of her trips to the east coast and now she's madly in love."

"I'm really sorry to hear that," Abby responded, "you two had been going out for a long time."

"Too long actually, she was great fun but not someone I could really get serious over. Now come on," he insisted, grabbing Abby's hand and steering her across the room, "let's eat before all the food is gone."

It was midnight when David and Julia left the reception to retire to the room they had booked for the night before leaving for Hawaii the next day, but not before they woke Kate. She had fallen asleep on one of the comfortable sofas that were scattered around the perimeter of the room. Julia had left all the furniture behind and had packed her personal possessions to be forwarded on to her so there was no reason for her to go back to the house. After the honeymoon, she would be returning to her new home with David in Vancouver. Abby knew that it would be the last time they would see each other for a while and she tried desperately to hold back her tears while Kate threw her arms around Julia's waist and wouldn't let go. It was only after Julia made them promise they would come out for a visit in the summer that they finally parted and it was then that Jim suggested Kate probably needed to go home.

"You're right," Abby agreed, "she's never been up this late before."

"I'll give you a lift," Jim offered, hoping that Abby would accept but he was disappointed when Abby replied, "That's really kind of you but Julia left me her car. I'm not really used to driving but I think I can manage to get home in one piece."

Jim had been attracted to Abby the first time he met her but had always pushed any romantic thoughts to the back of his mind. His loyalty to Simon had always taken precedence but Simon was not a factor anymore. On this night, he felt he couldn't just let her go, "Why don't you and Kate come over for a visit next Sunday, I know Kate would love to see Scamp?"

"Oh can we, can we Mom?" Kate begged tugging on Abby's dress.

Abby patted Kate on the shoulder and smiled, then turned to Jim, "Thank you, we'd like that but it will have to be the Sunday after because it's John's birthday next weekend and Martha's invited us for supper."

"Oh dear," Jim responded dejectedly," and the weekend after I'll be out of town on business."

"Well, why don't I call you," Abby suggested, "and maybe we can get together after that?"

Kate groaned, "Not fair, I want to see Scamp."

Abby grinned at Jim, "Look, we have to go, we'll see you soon," and with that she gave him a quick hug, waved goodbye and was gone.

The house seemed empty without Julia and Abby found it difficult to arrange her schedule to accommodate both Kate and her business, but after a week of rushing home early and feeling exhausted, because of the increased pressure, Dorothy Ward came to her rescue. She was so used to Kate spending time at her home with Helen that she even agreed to let her eat with the family three nights a week so that Abby could take her time at the shop or even take some leisure time for herself. Abby was grateful and so relieved that her spirits lifted and she was looking forward to John's birthday celebration. She was also looking forward to seeing Raymond again and curious about the new lady in his life. Although the divorce between Raymond and Julia had been amicable they had chosen not to socialize and now that Julia was in Vancouver, he had no hesitation about attending his father's party.

Abby wore a lavender dress of fine wool and paid particular attention to her hair which had grown quite long and fell in soft curls past her shoulders.

"You look really pretty Mom," Kate remarked.

"Well, you look pretty too," Abby responded surveying Kate from head to toe. She could hardly believe that she was now fourteen years old, almost as tall as Abby herself and looking more and more like a young lady. "Wait until Grandma and Grandpa see you in that blue dress and don't forget Uncle Raymond will be there."

Kate frowned, "I suppose it will be nice to see him but I can hardly remember what he looks like. Is he coming by himself?"

"No honey, he's bringing his girlfriend, I think her name's Connie."

"What does she look like?"

"I've never met her so I have no idea." Abby replied checking her watch, "Now come along Kate, let's get our coats otherwise we'll be late."

The party went without a hitch. Martha had invited several of John's co-workers and their spouses and some of their neighbours. Kate had been apprehensive about spending time with so many grownups and was relieved to see that the Johnson's, who lived next door, had brought along their fifteen- year-old son Alex. Kate had never been shy around boys and within minutes of meeting, they were happily chatting away in a corner munching on some of Martha's homemade hors d'oeuvres. Meanwhile Abby was catching up on Raymond's latest news and being introduced to Connie who was the complete opposite of Julia. Where Julia was tall and slim and would be considered, by many, to be a beautiful woman, Connie was short, slightly overweight and plain but Abby soon learned that she was extremely outgoing and had a wonderful sense of humour. Raymond seemed to dote on her and Abby couldn't help but feel a little envious. The following year she would be turning forty and even among this crowd of people, she suddenly felt terribly lonely.

CHAPTER 62

THE FOLLOWING DAY, BEING a Sunday, both Abby and Kate took their time getting up. They hadn't made any plans for the day and, while eating breakfast, were just discussing what to do when the phone rang.

Abby was surprised to hear Martha's voice on the line so early and felt an immediate sense of alarm, "What is it Martha, is John okay?"

"John's fine," Martha replied speaking very softly, "but I need you to come over to the house this morning and I think it would be better if you didn't bring Kate."

"What? I don't understand," said Abby a little impatiently.

Martha lowered her voice even more so that she was almost whispering, "Abby, Ed's here and he needs to see you."

Abby felt as though her heart missed a beat and she lowered herself slowly onto the closest chair, "I'll be there as soon as I can," she said and then slowly hung up the phone.

"What is it Mom?" asked Kate coming over and putting her hand on Abby's shoulder.

Abby hesitated and then turning to Kate said, "Oh, nothing to worry about honey. Grandpa sprained his ankle and Grandma needs me to help take him to the hospital."

Abby had no idea how she came up with a story so quickly but she couldn't let Kate see her father before she had spoken to him herself and when Kate begged to come along, Abby insisted that she would only be an hour and she had to stay home and look after Molly.

"That's dumb," Kate protested, "Molly looks after herself all the time." But Abby could not be persuaded to change her mind.

On the drive to her in-law's house, Abby was shaking. She had no idea how she was going to react to seeing Ed after all this time. She was relieved that he was obviously alive but angry that he had deserted them without a single word for almost seven years. She had actually been considering declaring him dead so that she could be a free woman and now he had shown up on his parent's doorstep. As she approached the house, Martha came out to greet her and wrapped her arms around her quietly crying, "He's really here, Abby. He's alive."

"Where is he?" Abby asked, gently pulling out of Martha's arms and reaching out to wipe the tears from her face.

"He's in the living room with John. He's changed Abby, he doesn't look the same any more and you'd hardly recognize him."

Abby followed Martha into the house, hung up her coat in the hall closet then proceeded to the doorway of the living room where she stopped in shock at the sight of her husband who was slowly turning to face her. His hair was the same shade of red, but with streaks of grey, falling almost to his shoulders and he had a full beard and moustache. Always stocky but not really overweight, he now carried at least an extra thirty pounds which had settled mostly in his mid section and his clothes were those one would expect a lumberjack to wear with a tartan shirt, jeans and heavy leather boots.

"Hello Abby," he said and his voice was unmistakable.

"Hello Ed," Abby replied without moving, "I would never have known you."

John got up from his chair, "I think you two need to talk so Martha and I are going into the kitchen," and he patted Ed gently on the back as he left the room taking Martha with him.

"Please come in and sit down Abby," said Ed stretching out his hand towards her.

Abby hesitated and then walked slowly over to the sofa and sat down, all the time keeping her eyes on Ed who lowered himself into the chair opposite her.

"Nothing I am going to say is going to excuse what I did to you and Kate but I want you to hear me out Abby."

"I'm listening Ed," Abby responded without any emotion.

Ed stared at Abby noticing the way she sat upright and expressionless, "You're looking good Abby and I like your hair like that. You haven't aged a bit."

Abby shook her head in frustration, "I'm waiting for an explanation. Let's get this over with."

Ed sighed slowly rubbing his hands together, "When Daniel died, I felt like dying too and I just couldn't shake the depression. I know you were hurting too, Abby, but I just couldn't help you and I'm sorry for that but you've proved you're a stronger person than I am. When I started drinking, it dulled the pain but I couldn't stop and when you left me, that's when I ran. I drank and gambled away every penny. I took what was rightfully yours Abby and I knew I could never get you back. That's when the depression got so bad that I ended up on the street and then I didn't want anyone to find me because I had become such a pitiful creature. I know I sound like I was feeling really sorry for myself but I'd reached a low point and I seriously considered just ending it all. Then I met someone who offered me a chance at a new life far away from here and I ended up at a logging camp out west. That's where I've been ever since Abby and even though it's taken me a while to get rid of my demons, I've finally found some happiness."

"And why are you here now Ed? What brought you all the way back to Toronto?" Abby asked dispassionately.

Ed bowed his head, "I want a divorce Abby. I've been living with a woman for the past three years and I want us to get married. She's pregnant Abby and she wants us to be a proper family."

"You mean like our family," said Abby sarcastically.

Ed leaned forward in his chair, "Please Abby, I don't blame you for being bitter. I've been a terrible husband and I know you've been through some really hard times since I left. Mom told me all about the man you were going to marry……"

Abby held up her hand, "Stop, just stop. Don't you dare talk about my life; it's none of your business. You can have your divorce and the sooner the better but I do have one thing to ask, what about Kate?"

Ed shook his head, "Mom, showed me photos, she's a beautiful young lady and I expect she's probably forgotten all about me by now. I think it would be better if she knew nothing about my being here because once I leave I'll not be coming back."

Abby got up from the sofa, "Fine, send me the divorce papers and I'll sign them," she said then turned to walk out the door.

"Abby, please let's not leave it like this," Ed called after her but he was too late. Abby threw on her coat, called out to John and Martha that she was leaving and a few minutes later she was on her way home to Kate.

When Abby turned into the driveway she was surprised to find Kate waiting on the doorstep. "What are you doing out here?" she demanded as she stepped out of the car.

Kate waited for her mother to reach her and then replied, "Grandma phoned, she wanted to know if you'd come back and then when I asked how Grandpa was, she didn't even answer and said she had to run. What's going on Mom?"

Abby put her arm around Kate's shoulders, "Let's go inside and we can talk; it's freezing out here."

Once in the warmth of the living room Abby suggested that Kate sit down. She knew that her daughter deserved to know the truth however painful it might be.

Kate looked frightened and was grasping a cushion in front of her protectively, "Is it Grandpa, did something really bad happen to him?"

Abby knelt down in front of Kate and placed her hands gently on her knees, "Grandpa is fine Kate, I'm so sorry I lied to you."

Kate frowned, "Why? Where did you go and why is Grandma looking for you?"

"I went to Grandma's house but not to take Grandpa to the hospital and I left rather suddenly so they probably want to talk to me about what happened."

"What did happen Mom?"

Abby got up, sat down beside Kate and took one of her hands into her own. "I went to see your father," she whispered.

Kate's eyes opened wide as she realized what Abby had said, "You mean he's here, he's at Grandma's house?"

"Yes, and we all thought it would be best if we didn't tell you about it but I can't lie to you Kate. Your father only came here because he wants a divorce."

"But where's he been? I don't understand," cried Kate her voice rising in frustration, "doesn't he want to see me?"

"Oh honey, I think he does but he thought it would be better if you just forgot all about him." Abby replied gently. "He's changed, Kate, you wouldn't even know him if you saw him. He had a very hard time after your brother died and he couldn't face us so he ran away. For the past few years he's been living out west and now he's found someone he wants to spend the rest of his life with."

Tears started to form in Kate's eyes, "So, he doesn't really care about me at all. He just wants a divorce so that he can marry someone else and then I suppose they'll have their own kids."

Abby sighed, "Well, to be truthful honey, they're already expecting a baby and that's why your father wants to get married now."

Kate jumped up from the sofa and stood with her hands clenched at her sides, "I hate him; I never want to see him again as long as I live."

Abby got up and gathered Kate into her arms, "Don't say that Kate. Maybe one day you can forgive him and have some kind of relationship with him. Please come and sit down I need to tell you something."

Once Kate had calmed down, Abby continued, "I've never talked to you about my childhood but I think we should talk about it now. I always told you that my parents died when I was very young but that wasn't true. My father was too young to get married and his family disassociated themselves from my mother and her family. Right after I was born, my mother ran away and we never heard from her again and so my grandmother looked after me. Then when she died her two sisters brought me up. Aunt Lillian was like a mother to me especially after Aunt Adeline died too and I loved her dearly. We had a wonderful life together and I'll always be grateful for the things she taught me, like empathy, compassion, patience and so many other things. When she passed away in my arms I thought the world had come to an end but I survived and then I met your father. So many people have been taken from me, Kate, but I've survived all of the heartaches. When your brother was killed I was more depressed than at any other time in my life and I have always regretted how I neglected you. Then when Simon died I didn't think I could bear it, but I did. I guess what I'm trying to tell you Kate, is that life can be hard but no matter what problems come your way you can overcome them and be a better person and the one thing that Aunt Lillian taught me that has meant more than anything is forgiveness. I may have reacted impulsively when I saw your father today but I forgave him long ago and you must too just as I would forgive my mother if she ever appeared in my life again."

Kate shook her head slowly, "You mean, you'd really forgive your mother when she ran away when you were just a baby?"

"Yes, I would Kate because she was so young and probably terribly frightened and didn't realize what she was doing. Who knows, maybe she thinks about me now and again and maybe she's even tried to find me."

"Why don't you try and find her, Mom?"

"I've thought about it Kate, but maybe she doesn't want to be found so I'm leaving well enough alone."

"Why didn't you tell me all this before?"

"I wanted to be sure you'd be old enough to understand and I want you to let your father go Kate. I've forgiven him and I want you to do so as well. Maybe, like I said, one day you can have a relationship with him but give it some time."

"But how will I know where he is?"

Abby smiled, "Oh, that's simple, I don't think Grandma and Grandpa will lose touch with him again and that reminds me I should phone them before they start to worry."

Kate gave Abby a hug, "I'm glad we had this talk Mom. I guess I can live without a father after all this time."

"Yes, and even without a father figure you can still be an extraordinary person Kate."

"Why are men such a pain Mom?"

Abby chuckled, "That's my girl, smart enough already to know a thing or two about the opposite sex."

CHAPTER 63

ONE EVENING TWO WEEKS later, Abby got a call from Jim inviting her and Kate over for supper the following Sunday and after a moment of hesitation, Abby accepted. She had only ever thought of Jim as Simon's best friend but now there seemed to be a stronger connection. He was the only person close to her that she could really talk to about Simon and even though she was still in contact with the Frasers', they were too far away to be of any great solace to her.

When Kate heard about the invitation she was thrilled and eager to know if Kelly would be there. "Jim didn't mention her I'm afraid honey", said Abby, "so I don't think she's coming down this weekend but at least you'll see Scamp."

"Oh, that's super Mom, I love Scamp. Can he come here again one day? He's so scared of Molly, it makes me laugh."

"Oh I think that can be arranged, but we'll have to see how busy Jim is. Sometimes he has to go out of town."

"He's lucky; I wish I could go to a lot of different places."

"Well you can when you get a little older. You can go anywhere you want to if you make up your mind to it.

Don't be like me Kate; I never went anywhere until after I got the shop."

"I know, but you can go to lots of places now. Aunt Julia said we could go and visit her in Vancouver and you told me we could go to England one day."

Abby looked sad, "Yes, well that was when Simon was alive but it would seem a bit strange going there on vacation now."

Kate shook her head, "You told me that Mrs. Fraser said you could come back and stay with them and bring me too, please Mom, can't we go in the summer?"

Abby sighed, "I just don't know Kate, I think we should visit Aunt Julia first and then maybe next year we can think about England.

"Really Mom?"

"Yes really, now enough talk, it's time you went to bed young lady, you've got school tomorrow."

The Sunday spent with Jim was full of activity and even though Kelly wasn't there, Kate had a lot of fun with Scamp. They went for a romp in the park and Kate giggled with delight as he chased the squirrels and rolled around in a puddle covering himself in a layer of mud. After they got back to the house, they gave him a bath and got soaked when he jumped out covered in suds and started to shake himself vigorously. It was all they could do to get him back in the tub and all the while Kate laughed uncontrollably while Abby perched on top of the toilet thinking what a happy scene Jim and her daughter made. It was almost like they were a family but when she realized where her thoughts were leading she drew herself up with a start and suggested they might all want something hot to drink after Scamp's antics. Two hours later, much to Kate's delight, they were sitting in the front row of the cinema loaded down with pop and popcorn watching "My Fair Lady". Both Abby and Jim had tried to dissuade Kate from sitting so close to the screen, and they envisioned an evening nursing sore necks, but she was so excited that they didn't want to insist and spoil her fun.

When the movie finally ended and they were on their way back to Jim's house, Kate couldn't stop chattering about how wonderful it was and then she started singing "The Rain in Spain" over and over again in a bad English accent causing Abby to look helplessly at Jim and grimace.

Jim had already prepared a chicken casserole for their supper and served it with a tossed salad. Dessert was one of Kate's favorites, chocolate mousse covered in whipped cream and so delicious that she had to have seconds. Abby was impressed with Jim's culinary skills, not being a great cook herself, and commented, "This is wonderful Jim, I wish I could cook but I just don't seem to have the knack for it."

Jim was modest, "Thank you, Abby, but this was easy to put together. I'm not sure I could produce anything too elaborate."

"Well it may have been simple but it tasted heavenly and we really appreciate you going to all this trouble."

"Yes," Kate chimed in, "it was great Jim. Can we come visit you again soon?"

"Of course," Jim replied looking intently at Abby, "I would love that."

CHAPTER 64

THROUGHOUT THAT SPRING AND early summer Abby and Kate returned to Jim's home twice and he accepted Abby's invitation to visit at her house on two other occasions. Soon it became evident that the friendship between Abby and Jim was beginning to change. Kate began to notice the subtle way that Jim would stare at her mother when she wasn't looking and occasionally she caught the way Abby would gently reach out and touch Jim's hand.

One night when Abby slipped into Kate's room to say goodnight and after another day spent at Jim's house, Kate decided to broach the subject, "Mom," she asked, "you really like Jim, don't you?"

Abby sat down on the side of the bed, "Yes, of course I like him honey."

"No, I mean you really, really like him."

"What are you trying to say Kate?"

"Well, I think he more than likes you because I see the way he looks at you and I wouldn't mind if he was your boyfriend."

Abby chuckled, "Oh Kate, I think you've got it all wrong. I think Jim is a wonderful man, he's kind and generous and easy to talk to but he's just a friend."

"It's because of Simon, isn't it Mom? You can't get over him so now you're going to spend the rest of your life all alone."

Abby squeezed Kate's hand, "No honey, it isn't like that. I loved Simon so much that after he died I thought I would never ever want to be with anyone else again but now I don't feel that way and one day I'm sure someone will come into my life."

Kate pulled the comforter over her head and mumbled, "I think he's already here Mom."

A week later, they received an invitation from Julia to visit her in Vancouver at the end of July and after making all the necessary arrangements with Peter to run Charlotte's and for Martha to take care of Molly, Abby accepted the invitation. Abby decided that in order to give Kate a real treat they would extend their vacation by a few days and fly to Calgary and then take the train trip through the Rockies. Kate was ecstatic, hardly sleeping a wink, and constantly peering out of the window at the mountains that seemed to climb into the sky.

The sight of Julia at the train station caused Abby to break down in tears, she was so happy to see her sister-in-law again. Julia was wearing a white cotton jumpsuit complete with a red sash and red sandals. With her dark hair and glowing tan, she looked wonderful. Abby felt like a poor relation in her comfortable traveling clothes but Julia thought she looked fabulous, "Let me have a look at you both," she said holding them at arms length, "I can't believe you've traveled over six hundred miles on that train, you both look great."

"You're too kind, as always, Julia," Abby responded, "but personally I'd give my eye teeth to take a bath right now. By the way, where's David?"

"Oh he had to go into his office for a meeting but he'll be back early. Let's go find the car and get you two back to the house so that you can clean up and have a rest."

The vacation out west was a brand new experience for both Abby and Kate. Other than to sleep, they spent very little time at Julia's home which was a large four-bedroom grey stone house decorated in a traditional style and with a huge back garden shaded by towering maple trees. Julia had taken the week off work and on most days David joined them on their sightseeing tours to Grouse Mountain, Stanley Park and the zoo. One day, they took the ferry to Victoria, had afternoon tea in the Empress Hotel then visited the Undersea Gardens and on another, they took the Rocky Mountaineer train trip to Whistler. At night, they would often eat out, usually in the trendy Gastown area, but on the last night Julia cooked up a fabulous feast of fresh lobster, risotto and asparagus and they all laughed merrily at Kate as she struggled to crack open the lobster claws and then happily munched away with butter dripping from her chin.

Saying goodbye to Julia was difficult but both Abby and Kate were in great spirits and full of happy memories as they boarded the plane back to Toronto. Kate already had her notebook out recording every little detail of their trip so that she could tell her friend Helen all about it and she could hardly wait to get the dozens of photos developed that they had taken.

Jim had offered to pick them up when they arrived back but Abby had already made arrangements for Peter to meet them and she was anxious to know how business had fared while she had been away. She was relieved to learn that everything had run smoothly and asked Peter if he would mind stopping at her mother-in-law's house so that they could pick up Molly. Martha was eager for Abby and Kate to stay for a while so that she could hear all about their holiday but Abby bowed out and promised to visit within the week. She just wanted to get home, unpack and put her feet up after the long journey.

They arrived home to find a pile of mail lying on the mat just inside the door but Abby had no time to deal with it until later and it wasn't until after supper when Kate was already tucked up in bed that she remembered the stack she had casually thrown onto the hall table. She discarded the exceptional amount of flyers, announcing all kinds of special deals, into the wastebasket and concentrated on the envelopes that remained. Most were bills but one was a large brown envelope postmarked ten days prior while another was an invitation size lavender envelope with a UK stamp. She gingerly opened the large envelope first already anticipating what it would contain. She was not disappointed when the first page appeared to be a letter from a lawyer in Fort Nelson, BC followed by pages of legal documents. These were the divorce papers that she had been expecting and she simply had to sign them in the presence of a notary public and her marriage would be over. She breathed a sigh of relief and turned to the lavender envelope that she knew had to have come from the Frasers' even though there was no return address. Abby walked slowly into the living room and sank into a chair when she read the invitation. Brooke was marrying Max and she had been invited to the wedding.

CHAPTER 65

ABBY TOSSED AND TURNED throughout the night desperately needing sleep but unable to shake off the thoughts that kept running through her head. The wedding ceremony was to be in mid September at St. Matthews, the same church where she had endured one of the saddest days of her life and now she was expected to be in that same place celebrating the marriage of Simon's sister. To add to her dilemma, Lydia had enclosed a brief note suggesting that she bring Kate and she had invited them to stay at Faversham House for as long as they wished.

As dawn broke, Abby made up her mind that she would decline the invitation, citing business commitments and Kate's new school year and with the sound of the alarm, she rolled out of bed feeling at peace with her decision. She also decided that she would not mention the invitation to Kate and at breakfast, prior to getting ready for work and shipping Kate off to the Wards', she tried to keep the conversation light. It was when the phone rang and Kate answered it, mouthing 'Jim' to her mother that she realized her secret might be uncovered.

Listening to one side of the conversation it was obvious that Jim was asking Kate all about their vacation and she breathed a sigh of relief when Kate handed her the phone. “Good morning Jim, you’re an early caller,” she said a little defensively.

“Sorry Abby, I hope I’m not disturbing you but I wanted to welcome you home. Kate tells me you had a wonderful time but I’m not surprised, by the way how’s Julia?”

“She’s fine and very happy, I think she and David are a good match. They have a lovely home and they took us to so many places.”

“That’s wonderful Abby. There’s another reason why I called though.”

“Oh, what’s that?” Abby said with mounting apprehension.

“Well I was wondering if you received your invitation to Brooke’s wedding.”

“Yes. I did,” Abby replied rather abruptly, “and I’m not going.”

There was a moment’s silence on the other end of the line before Jim said, “Oh, I’m sorry to hear that Abby, may I ask why?”

“I’m too busy with Charlotte’s and Kate goes back to school at the beginning of September.”

There was a another moment of silence before Jim responded, “Are you sure that’s the real reason you aren’t going Abby?”

“I’m not sure what you mean, what other reason could there be?”

Jim’s voice softened, “Look Abby, I know how difficult you feel it might be but I know how much Brooke wants you to be there and Lydia is looking forward to meeting Kate. Why don’t you reconsider?”

Abby was aware of Kate staring at her as she replied, "I don't want to discuss this now Jim, if you don't mind. Perhaps we can talk later, why don't I call you tonight?"

"Okay Abby, but in the meantime promise me you'll think about it."

"I've been thinking about it all night Jim, bye for now," and as Abby gently placed the phone down she turned to Kate who was obviously burning with curiosity.

"What's going on Mom? What are you too busy to do and why can't you talk about it now?"

Abby sighed, "I guess you'll find out one way or another so I might as well tell you, we received an invitation to Brooke's wedding."

"Brooke? Who's that?" said Kate frowning.

"Sorry, Brooke is Simon's sister and she's getting married to Max in September."

Kate's eyes lit up, "You mean in England Mom?"

"Yes, in Redhill where Simon's parents live but we're not going Kate."

"Why can't we go? You said you would take me there one day," Kate demanded her voice rising.

"You heard me on the phone," Kate replied, "I'm busy at work and you can't miss the beginning of school."

Kate jumped up from her chair and stamped her foot, "It's not fair, you said you would take me to England one day. Peter can run the shop and it won't matter if I miss a few days of school. I don't believe that's the reason you won't go, it's because of Simon isn't it."

"Sit down honey, please," Abby begged, "I know you're angry and I'm sorry and you're right it is about Simon. It's hard to explain but I don't think I can bear to see Brooke get married in the same church where we attended

Simon's funeral. Not only that but I'll be thinking that it's probably the same place where Simon and I would have been married. Do you understand Kate?"

Kate reached out and took Abby's hand, "Yes, I think I do Mom but I still think we should go. Please think about it some more."

Abby nodded, "Okay I will, I promise, I'll phone Jim back tonight and talk to him about it, but no more pressure from you young lady, okay."

Kate grinned, "Okay Mom, now you'd better get cracking or you'll be late for work."

"Oh dear," Abby chuckled, "can't be late or I'll be in big trouble."

That evening Kate couldn't resist asking Abby when she would be phoning Jim but Abby wouldn't be pushed and waited until Kate was safely upstairs in her room. Abby was surprised to learn that Jim was taking Kelly to the wedding and that he would be staying at Faversham House for ten days. His ex-wife was more than happy to get their daughter off of her hands while she went on her own vacation to Greece with her latest conquest. Realizing that Kate and Kelly would be good company for each other, Abby's resolve started to crumble and by the time her conversation with Jim ended she was at the point of changing her mind.

Kate was delirious with excitement the next morning when Abby informed her that after talking to Jim and a second sleepless night she had decided that they would go to the wedding after all. Kate's mood quickly caught on and Abby felt a positive change but she still had some trepidation about the trip.

August quickly slipped by and at the beginning of September Abby settled any business issues that might come up while she was away, shopped for a gift for Brooke and Max and searched high and low for suitable outfits for Kate and herself. By concentrating on a gift that was uniquely Canadian, Abby found a limited edition print by Robert Bateman of two trumpeter swans and after spending a small fortune on the frame, she was sure that she had made the right choice. Finding two outfits was a little more difficult but after some suggestions from Julia, who was thrilled that Abby had accepted the invitation, she settled on a simple low-cut rose silk dress for herself and a pale yellow organza dress for Kate with a full skirt and square neckline.

Kate was thrilled with her dress and begged Abby to buy her shoes to match, but Abby was still practical by nature and compromised with a pair of low-heeled white sandals. This appeared to satisfy Kate and for the third or fourth time that week, she was on the phone chattering away to Kelly about the wedding and despite the long distance charges, Abby was happy that the girls were forming such a bond. Kate was already excited about going to England but after learning that Kelly was going too, she was over the moon. The only disappointment was that they wouldn't be traveling together as Jim was leaving earlier on a flight via Montreal so that he could connect with Kelly at the airport there and even though she would be returning to Toronto with Jim, they were scheduled to fly back three days after Abby and Kate.

CHAPTER 66

ABBY AND KATE LEFT Toronto very early on a cool September morning. Abby was still apprehensive about the trip but put on a brave face for Kate who was thrilled to be traveling across an ocean to Europe. The trip itself was uneventful and they arrived at their London hotel late in the evening. Jim, who was already in Redhill, had booked them a room for three nights near Green Park so that Kate would have the opportunity to visit the city and Abby had already planned to take her to many of the most famous tourist spots. In two days they visited the Tower of London, Westminster Abbey, the Houses of Parliament, Buckingham Palace and the British Museum. Kate, who had always been interested in history, was overwhelmed and Abby was forced to buy roll after roll of film to satisfy Kate's need to photograph everything so that she could show her schoolmates back home.

On the third day just before noon, Jim arrived at the hotel with Kelly driving Lydia's sedan. He was to take them back to Redhill and Abby, feeling genuinely happy to see him, realized that she no longer dreaded her return visit to Faversham House.

On the trip into the country, Kate sat in the back seat with Kelly and while Kate babbled on about London, Kelly countered with her excitement about the Frasers', the house, the grounds, the horses and the dogs. Meanwhile, Abby relived the previous two days telling Jim all about the places they had visited, how much Kate had enjoyed it, and how grateful she was that he had persuaded her to come. As Jim listened, occasionally glancing at Abby and admiring how lovely she looked with her hair curling gently over her shoulders and the deep blue of her dress that brought out the colour of her eyes, he realized that he was beginning to feel a lot more than friendship for this woman who had been so much in love with his closest friend.

They finally arrived in the town of Redhill and Abby felt a sense of comfort recognizing so many familiar places. It was only when they passed the church where she had suffered through the deep sadness of Simon's funeral that she felt a sinking in her stomach. Jim immediately noticed her mood change and gently touched her hand, "Brooke and Max are going to be married in St. Matthews, Abby."

Abby turned abruptly, "I know and I can't understand why they chose that church."

"I can. The family have always attended services there and they want to think of it as a place where joyous events can take place as well as sad ones."

Abby was silent for a moment and then nodded, "I suppose you're right, I just think it's going to be hard setting foot in there again."

Just then Kate chimed in, "When will we be there please, how much further is it?"

Jim glanced over his shoulder and smiled, "Getting a little anxious, are we? Well, let me see, we should be there in about two hours."

"No way," Kate protested, "I'll be starved to death by then."

Abby chuckled, "He's teasing you, we should be there in about ten minutes."

"Hurrah," Kate yelled while settling back in her seat and continuing to chatter with Kelly.

The arrival of Abby and Kate at Faversham House caused quite a commotion. As they drove up to the front steps, Lydia, Roger and Brooke came rushing out of the front door to embrace Abby. It was an emotional reunion and there were tears in Abby's eyes. Kate stood back quietly surveying the scene feeling a little uncomfortable until Lydia stepped forward and gave her a hug saying, "So you're Kate. How lovely you are, just like your mother. I am so happy to finally meet you, welcome to our home."

Kate smiled and murmured, "Thank you so much Mrs. Fraser, I'm excited to be here."

Lydia then took her hand and drew her towards the steps, "This is my husband Roger and my daughter Brooke. Now let's all go inside, I'm sure you could all do with a cup of tea."

Kate raised her eyebrows and followed Abby and the Frasers' inside. Meanwhile Kelly lagged behind with Jim who did a little jig and whispered in an affected British accent, "Got to have the proverbial cup of tea, what!"

CHAPTER 67

THERE WERE SEVEN BEDROOMS at Faversham House as well as the maid's quarters while Quinn, who was in charge of the horses, lived on the grounds in a small cottage with his wife Birdie. The Frasers' occupied the master bedroom while Brooke and her closest friend Marsha Hampton, who was the maid of honour occupied the one next door. Two elderly couples, friends of the Frasers' who had arrived earlier, took up two guest rooms on the floor above, Jim and Kelly each had one to themselves and Abby and Kate shared a room. Abby breathed a sigh of relief when Tilly showed them into their room and she realized that it wasn't the same one where she had spent so many nights with Simon. Meanwhile, Kate was feeling very grand having a maid unpack her clothes and show her where everything was. She had never been in a place like Faversham House before and she couldn't wait to see the rest of it. Once Tilly left them alone, she beamed at Abby and said, "Mom, you didn't tell me how great it was here. Did you see that staircase and all those paintings? Boy, these people must be really rich."

Abby laughed, "Well, I think you can say they have a little more than we do honey but you haven't seen anything yet. Wait until you see the dining room and the sunroom and the grounds are just gorgeous. I'm a little tired but if Mrs. Fraser doesn't mind, I'm sure that Kelly would love to show you around."

Kate clapped her hands together, "Oh can I go and ask her now Mom? And I want to see the horses especially Scarlett, oh may I, please may I?"

"Yes, of course, go downstairs but don't run and don't get lost. Go back to the library where we had tea and I'm sure Mrs. Fraser will let Kelly take you around. Jim might want to go with you in case you get off the beaten track, in fact I would be happier if he did."

"Okay I'll ask him. You know he really likes you Mom, I saw the way he looked at you when we were driving here."

"Don't be silly Kate, now run off and just explain that I'm having a little rest but I'll join everyone for supper."

"Is this going to be like a bridal supper Mom, after all it's the night before the wedding."

"No honey, we're just having a regular supper for the people that are here now. Max couldn't get here until the morning because he had some business commitment in London and Brooke didn't want anything fancy without him."

"I think Brooke's so pretty Mom, she's so dainty and I love her hair, it's almost white."

"Yes, she is lovely and she has a lovely personality too. Now are you going to go and let me have some rest?"

"Okay, I'll go now and come back in time to change for supper."

"Good, and don't forget your manners especially in front of the Fraser's guests."

The following morning at dawn, the house was a beehive of activity with the arrival of Brooke's wedding dress, her hairdresser, the florist and the caterers. Lydia normally liked to cook for herself and Roger or have Christian, the butler, help out when they had two or three guests, but there would be about fifty people at the reception and she decided to hire professional help.

Abby watched the florist place the flower arrangements in the grand hallway and the dining room and the meticulous way they decorated the stairway where Brooke would be descending before making her way to the church. She had been involved in so many weddings and she wondered how Peter and Pauline were coping at Charlotte's.

Max arrived with his brother Colin just before noon and was immediately whisked upstairs to Jim's room where he was to change and stay out of Brooke's way until he saw her at St. Matthews.

Abby suggested that Kate and Kelly went to the stables and spend more time with the horses so that they would not be in the way. They were happy to leave and promised to be back in time to change and leave the house at two o'clock, but Kate was disappointed that she hadn't even had a glimpse of Max. When Kate finally met Max as she bounded in the front door with Kelly, her mouth dropped open. He was standing in the hallway dressed in a dark blue suit, crisp white shirt and sapphire blue tie with his dark hair curling over the back of his collar. Later she was to describe him to her mother as "Yummy." Abby was amused and suggested that she would be even more impressed if she could see him in his regular clothes.

The wedding went off without a hitch and Brooke looked like an angel. She wore a strapless white satin dress that clung to her slim body and gardenias in her hair, and as she walked down the aisle on Roger's arm, both Abby and Lydia had tears in their eyes. Meanwhile Max stood at the altar with Colin at his side glowing with pride as he watched Brooke approach. There were no other attendants except for Marsha who looked stunning in an apple green gown that complimented her fiery red hair.

Back at the house, after the wedding, the reception got into full swing and because the weather was so warm the guests spilled out onto the grounds where the caterers had set up a huge buffet table. Kate and Kelly gaped at the amount of food and were immediately drawn to the desserts, which included, strawberry tarts, chocolate silk pie, cheesecake and fantasy fudge cake. It was only after both Abby and Jim insisted they first eat some chicken, ham and other vegetables or salad that they grudgingly agreed to stay away from the dessert table until later.

As afternoon turned into evening and the light started to fade, a trio of musicians arrived to play and encourage the guests to dance. A small wooden dance floor had been set up on the grass near the house and there were fairy lights around the perimeter. Soon several couples were dancing to some of the most popular songs of the day. It was when the trio started to play "Unchained Melody" that Jim asked Abby to dance and he held her closer than he had intended but he couldn't help himself.

"You look absolutely lovely tonight Abby," he said. "That color rose really suits you."

"Thank you Jim," Abby replied smiling, "you look pretty good yourself. But how about Brooke, didn't she look beautiful?"

"Yes, she certainly did, Max is a lucky guy. In fact he's lucky to have married into the family, Roger and Lydia are great people."

"Yes, they are and I wish Simon had been here to see his sister get married. He wasn't that crazy about Max but I like him now that I've got to know him a little better, I think he'll make her happy."

Abby stepped back and looked into Jim's eyes, "I really want to thank you again for talking me into coming. It's been wonderful seeing everyone and I hope I'll be invited back again one day."

Jim drew Abby back into his arms, "As long as you're with me Abby, you can be sure you'll be coming back."

Abby wasn't sure what to say but she felt comfortable and safe and above all, happy. Meanwhile, Lydia who was observing them from a table at the edge of the dance floor turned to Roger and remarked, "I sense the beginning of a romance."

Just before midnight, Max and Brooke, now wearing a flowing powder blue dress, left to stay at a local hotel before flying to Paris the next afternoon. When Abby embraced Brooke and wished her a happy life, she was dumbfounded when Brooke whispered, "Jim's a great guy Abby and Simon would have approved. Good luck," and then she was gone, sliding into Max's green jaguar and waving giddily at everyone as they drove away.

When Abby finally got to her room in the early hours of the morning, she found Kate fast asleep having worn herself out disco dancing with Kelly and two of the young lads from town. She climbed into bed physically exhausted but her mind wouldn't shut down and she couldn't stop thinking about the remark that Brooke had made and the times that Kate had dropped gentle hints about Jim. Slowly her thoughts began to focus on the man himself and she had to admit that her relationship with him had changed. She had liked him from the moment they had met and admired him for his concern about Kelly. Simon and Jim had been like brothers and when Simon died, Jim had helped her through the terrible tragedy even though his heart must have been breaking too. Like Kate, she had also noticed how he looked at her lately and how closely he had held her when they were dancing. She smiled as she snuggled down under the covers and looked forward to the days ahead.

CHAPTER 68

BOTH ABBY AND KATE were late for breakfast but Roger, Lydia and their houseguests were still in the dining room having coffee. Brooke's friend, Marsha, and her husband Gerald had already left to return to London along with Max's brother and Jim and Kelly were nowhere to be seen. After serving Kate and herself with scrambled eggs, sausages and fried tomatoes from the buffet table, Abby sat down and quietly asked, "Where are Jim and Kelly?"

Lydia passed the toast to Abby and replied, "Oh, they were up at the crack of dawn and went riding."

Kate dropped her fork onto her plate with a clatter, "Not fair, I wanted to go, why didn't they wait for me?"

Before Abby could admonish Kate for being rude, Lydia responded with a smile, "We didn't want to wake you, Kate. After all that dancing last night, we thought you might need your sleep."

"But Kelly was dancing just as much as me," Kate protested.

Lydia shrugged her shoulders; "Well, then I guess she got over her jet lag long before you did."

"Can I go after breakfast please Mom and will you come with me?" Kate begged reaching across and touching her mother's hand.

"Yes, of course honey, as long as we have Mrs. Fraser's permission," and she looked over at Lydia for approval.

"No need to ask my dear, while you're still here for the next couple of days, you can do whatever you choose. Our friends here will be leaving at noon today and then Roger and I are going into town for the rest of the day to do some shopping and have supper out. The house will be all yours and I've asked Christian to prepare lunch and supper so you won't go hungry."

"That is so kind of you Lydia, and I'm sorry I haven't been able to spend more time with you," she said looking over at the Fraser's guests.

Don Campbell, who had known Roger most of his life, nodded, "Well maybe we'll see you again one of these days my dear. In any event, it's been a pleasure meeting you and Kate, we've heard so much about you from Lydia."

Abby felt so comfortable that she took her time at the breakfast table and entered into a lively conversation about the British monarchy and the rampant speculation on who Prince Charles would marry. Meanwhile, Kate toyed impatiently with her food and practically ran from the room when Abby took a final sip of her coffee and rose from the table.

Arriving at the stables, suitably dressed in jeans and heavy sweaters, as the morning was cool, Kate begged to ride Scarlett but Quinn advised against it and while Abby rode Scarlett, Kate rode a pure white mare named Bianco. They had a glorious ride across the fields and through the woods eventually resting by a stream and by the time they turned back, the temperature had risen and the sun was shining brightly in an almost clear blue sky. Kate loved the verdant green of the English countryside and the late summer flowers that were still blooming and she had felt so free riding with her mother but she had been hoping they would come across Jim and Kelly on the way. She was soon to learn that they had gone in a completely different direction and by the time they reached the stables, they were already back rubbing down their horses.

For the rest of that day and the next, Abby and Jim spent most of their time with the girls, riding, swimming in the river, taking the dogs for walks and shopping in town and Abby felt more and more as though they were a family except that at night, she slept alone.

Kate didn't want to leave especially as Kelly was staying on for a few more days and Lydia had graciously suggested that they stay as long as they liked but Kate needed to go back to school and Abby had business commitments.

The night before they were due to leave, Abby couldn't sleep so she took the stairs down to the sunroom and slipped through the sliding door into the garden. It was a beautiful clear night and warm enough that Abby felt comfortable in her silk robe. She walked out onto the grass in her bare feet, stared up at the myriad of stars and sighed, then hearing a footstep on the pathway nearby her hand flew to her throat and she whirled around only to see that it was Jim.

"Sorry, I didn't mean to startle you, beautiful isn't it?" and his gaze swept across the grounds then settled on Abby's face. He no longer had on the more formal attire he had worn at dinner with the Frasers' and now wore a pair of faded jeans and a light blue cashmere sweater.

Before Abby could reply he took a step forward and said, "Are you sure you're warm enough, I could fetch you a jacket?"

"I'm perfectly fine thanks Jim," Abby responded. What are you still doing up?"

"I guess, like you, I couldn't sleep so I thought I'd come down and get some fresh air."

"It is lovely here," Abby remarked, "Kate doesn't want to go home and I must admit, I wish I could stay a few more days."

"Yes, Lydia mentioned that you would like to stay but I understand why you have to get back. Kelly is going to miss having Kate to chum around with."

Abby looked directly into Jim's eyes, "Will you miss us too Jim?" she asked, then immediately wished she could disappear.

Jim took another step forward and took Abby's hand, "That goes without saying Abby, in fact that's why I couldn't sleep. I've been thinking about you a lot."

Abby lowered her eyes, "I've been thinking about you too," she whispered.

Jim reached out and tipped Abby's chin up so that he could see her reaction, "It's more than that Abby, I think I'm falling in love with you."

Then he was kissing her, gently at first, and then more passionately until Abby broke away and shook her head, "We need to slow down Jim, and I don't know if I'm ready for another relationship."

Jim held her at arm's length, "No pressure Abby. When we get back to Toronto, let's see where we go from here but I need to see you and as often as you'll let me."

Abby smiled and stroked Jim's cheek, "I think that's a wonderful idea."

CHAPTER 69

THE NEXT DAY, WHILE Kate was out for a last ride with Kelly and Abby was in her room packing, there was a knock at the door. Abby thought it was probably Tilly asking if she could help and was surprised to find Lydia standing there.

"Oh, it's you Lydia," she said, "what a nice surprise. Do come in I was just packing up the last of our things."

"I didn't mean to disturb you my dear," Lydia said as she crossed the room to perch on the edge of the bed, "I just wanted to have a few words alone with you before you left."

Abby sat down beside her and frowned, "Is something wrong?"

"No, of course not. I just wanted you to know how much we enjoyed having you and Kate here and you will always be welcome. I know it wasn't easy for you to come back after Simon died but he wanted you to be part of the family and we want to think of you that way too. Both Roger and I know how happy you made our son and we'll always be grateful for that."

Abby started to respond but Lydia held up her hand and continued, "You know Abby, Jim has been like another son to us. We've known him since Simon first met him at university. He spent many weekends here and all of the holidays except when he went home to visit his father. Even when he went back to Canada, after he finished his education and then got married, he came back here often. We never liked Angela, she's a self-centered, selfish woman but we tolerated her for Jim's sake. Nobody was surprised when the marriage fell apart but one good thing came out of it, and that was Kelly. She's a wonderful girl, adores her father and it's too bad she has to live with her mother."

"Why are you telling me all this," Abby asked with a puzzled look on her face.

Lydia turned and covered Abby's hand with her own, "Because I think there may be some chance of a relationship between the two of you and nothing would make Roger and I happier. Don't throw away that chance Abby just because Jim was Simon's closest friend. I know Simon would want you to spend your life with someone who would take care of you and love you just much as he did and Jim's the finest young man I know. It's pretty obvious that he already feels something deeper than just friendship for you Abby, any fool can see that."

"I'm not sure what to say Lydia except that Brooke made a comment about Jim just as she was leaving and Kate's been dropping hints every now and again. One thing I can tell you, last night Jim and I had a talk and we agreed to see each other when we get back to Toronto."

Lydia sighed, "Well, that's a start and I'll keep my fingers crossed but I think a lot of what happens will be up to you Abby. Just don't close your heart off. Who knows, maybe you'll be back here together very soon, I do hope so."

Abby grinned. "I think you should have taken up a profession as a matchmaker Lydia, but anyway we'll see what happens."

Lydia got up to go but Abby grasped her arm "Don't go just yet. I'm glad you're here because I wanted to give you something."

Lydia watched as Abby took a small box wrapped in gold foil off the dressing table and handed it to her.

"What is it? Lydia asked as she carefully took off the wrapping.

"Just a small token of my appreciation for everything you've done for Kate and me."

Lydia was delighted to find a marquisite pin in the shape of a bow lying in a velvet box. She looked at Abby with tears in her eyes and then stepped forward to embrace Abby and kiss her gently on the cheek, "It's absolutely beautiful my dear, I shall treasure it always, thank you so much."

Lydia turned to leave and then turned back again, "Oh by the way, I meant to tell you earlier but plans have changed for getting you to London. My sister Pamela lives in Mayfair and she's invited me up for a few days so I'll be driving you. It doesn't make sense for Jim to go all the way there and back again and now that he doesn't have to, he's arranged to take Roger and Kelly down to Brighton for two days. Kelly loves the ocean and the sea air will do Roger good."

Abby felt a little disappointed that Jim would not be taking them to the airport and that surprised her but she shook off the thought and focused on how much Roger would enjoy the time away, "What a wonderful idea," she commented, "I'm sure they'll have a great time and you and I will have lots to talk about on the drive up."

When it finally came time to leave just after noon, Abby successfully hid how terribly sad she felt. She hugged Roger, Jim and Kelly and busied herself hustling Kate into the car while Lydia sat patiently at the wheel. As they pulled out of the driveway she couldn't help focusing on Jim who was looking at her intently with a gentle smile on his face. Meanwhile Kate was hanging out of the window yelling at Kelly, "Don't forget, you invited me to Montreal."

"What was that all about?" asked Abby.

Kate shrugged, "She said I could go and visit her one of these days."

Lydia looked over at Abby and remarked, "Hmmm, I expect her mother might have something to say about that."

CHAPTER 70

WHEN ABBY AND KATE arrived home they immediately unpacked and then left to pick up Molly at Martha's. Abby wanted to wait until the next day but Kate was whining constantly about seeing her beloved pet and Abby finally gave in although she was dog tired and just wanted to relax.

Martha and John were happy to see them but, understanding they needed to rest, didn't pressure them to stay for very long. Kate joyfully found Molly sleeping on a chair in the living room and scooping her up in her arms, covered her with kisses. Molly wasn't particularly pleased to be disturbed and then pushed inside her carrier for the ride home and she meowed all the way but once inside the house she was soon back in her favourite spot, on top of Kate's bed.

It wasn't long before Kate joined Molly leaving Abby in the kitchen sorting through the mail and it was only minutes later when the phone rang and she immediately recognized Peter's voice when he said, "Hi Abby, welcome home."

"Hi Peter," she replied cheerily. "We haven't been in very long. Kate insisted that we pick up Molly and she just went up to get some sleep. What's up, why are you calling? Is everything at Charlotte's okay?"

"Everything's fine at the shop Abby but you had a visitor that I thought you should know about."

"A visitor, at the shop? Who was it?"

"Well, that's just it, we don't really know. She wouldn't give her name and when we told her you were on vacation she just left. Then the next day she came in again and asked when you'd be back."

"Well, maybe it was just a customer that wanted to deal directly with me."

"No, I don't think so. We asked her if we could help and she said she hadn't come to buy anything."

"Well what did she look like?" Abby asked getting more and more curious.

"Actually she looked a bit like you Abby but quite a bit older and she didn't look very well. She was very pale and spoke very quietly."

Abby's heart began to race, "Did you tell her I'd be back at the shop tomorrow? Did she say when she was coming back?"

"Yes, we told her when you'd be here but she didn't say anything, she just left."

Abby paused and then said, "All right Peter, thanks for calling. I'll see you in the morning."

Peter hesitated and then asked, "Have you any idea who this woman is Abby?"

Abby abruptly replied, "No, goodnight Peter," and she gently put the phone down and sank onto the nearest chair. She sat there for what seemed an eternity with all sorts of scenarios rushing through her head. Could this be her mother, the woman that no one had ever really discussed with her, not even Aunt Lillian? And what if it was, what could she possibly have to say to her? On the one hand, a small part of her hoped she was right and on the other, she hoped the woman never came back again, but what then, wouldn't she always wonder who she was?

Abby didn't sleep much that night and was anxious to get to Charlotte's in the morning. Kate protested loudly about having to go back to school without even having one day off to settle back home but Abby eventually pushed her out the door promising to finish work early and take her out to supper.

During the morning there was a lot to catch up on. Peter had booked three orders for floral arrangements for weddings that week and had a contract for Abby to consider providing fresh flowers to the home of a prominent politician who lived in Rosedale. In spite of the amount of work she had to do, every time somebody stepped through the shop door, Abby held her breath until Peter finally asked, "You're waiting for that lady who came here while you were away aren't you Abby?"

Abby looked up in surprise from where she was leaning over the counter, "Oh, I'm sorry Peter, yes I guess I am a bit intrigued, can't you tell me anything more about her?"

Peter shook his head, "Not really. I already mentioned that she looked a lot like you only she must have been around sixty. She seemed real secretive and wouldn't even leave her name. Who do you think it might be Abby?"

"I have no idea," Abby responded rather sharply, "let's just forget about her, she probably won't come back anyway," but inwardly she was more curious than ever.

At four o'clock, unable to concentrate, Abby decided to leave for the day and take an hour or two for herself before

Kate returned from the Wards' where she was visiting after school. She was just stepping onto the sidewalk and checking in her purse for her keys when she heard a woman's voice whisper, "Abigail, is that you?"

Abby looked up, startled to find, directly in her path, a woman with short dark hair that framed a face exactly like her own except for the pallor and the deep wrinkles around the eyes and mouth. She was about an inch shorter than Abby and wore a loose fitting burgundy wool coat and clutched a large back purse to her chest,

Abby managed to stammer, "Yes, although most people call me Abby. What can I do for you?"

The woman hesitated and then replied in a quiet voice, "Could we please go somewhere and talk. I promise not to take much of your time and I did see a coffee shop in the next block?"

Abby stepped back, "But what is this all about? I don't even know you, who are you?"

"Please," the woman begged, "spare me a few moments, it's important."

Abby paused not sure what to do then answered, "All right but I need to go back inside for a moment, why don't you go ahead and I'll meet you there."

The woman started to walk away and then turned back, "You will come, won't you?" she asked.

"Yes, I will," Abby said and darted into Charlotte's.

Peter looked up in surprise, "Forget something Abby?" he questioned.

Abby ran behind the counter pretending to look for something while she gathered her thoughts and ignoring Peter then minutes later she was out on the street again heading for the coffee shop and trembling with anticipation.

The woman glanced up from the table where she was seated with her hands folded around a mug of steaming coffee, "Thank you for coming," she said as Abby sat down.

"What's this all about?" Abby demanded becoming more anxious.

"Wouldn't you like something to drink?" the woman asked.

"No, I just want to know what it is you want. I know you came to the shop while I was away and wouldn't leave your name. Why is that, please tell me?"

The woman bowed her head and then looking back at Abby whispered, "My name is Rose Barrows, and I used to be Emily Parkinson, I'm your mother Abigail."

Abby, who had been sitting tensely in her chair felt her body go rigid, "I thought as much," she said with an edge in her voice, "but that doesn't tell me what you want."

The woman reached across the table but Abby snatched her hands away and put them in her lap under the table, "I am asking you again, what is it you want?" she said.

"I understand this must be a shock to you and I don't blame you for being angry but please hear me out."

Abby sat back, "Go on, I'm listening."

The woman continued, "I don't know what my Mama told you about me but I was only fifteen when you were born. Back then, if you had a baby out of wedlock, you were an object of cruel gossip, especially in a place like Oakfield. I was so ashamed I just wanted to die but I ran away instead. When I crept out of the house in the middle of the night, I had no idea where I was going. I had no money to buy food, shelter or clothes, all I had were the clothes on my back. I started walking and kept on walking for hours until I was so exhausted and hungry that I sat down on a patch of grass at the edge of the road and fell asleep. That's where Sam Barrows found me."

Abby shifted in her seat trying to imagine what this woman, who claimed to be her mother, had gone through, "Go on," she said quietly.

"Sam was on his way home to his farm carting two pigs in the back of his truck when he saw me lying on the side of the road. He woke me up and asked me what I was doing there and I didn't know what to say so I didn't say anything. He thought I was deaf, or dumb, or both and I looked such a sorry sight that he put me in the truck and took me with him. I was scared but I was so hungry and so tired that I didn't have the energy to fight and he seemed like a nice man. It turned out that I was really lucky that day. Sam took me home to his wife and they fed me, found me some clean clothes and allowed me to sleep for as long as I needed before they tried to question me about who I was and where I came from. From the time I woke up and the time they discovered I was awake, I had come up with a plan so that they could never send me back to Oakville. I told them my name was Rose Austen. I picked the name Rose from the wallpaper, which was covered in roses, and Austen was for my favourite author Jane Austen. Later I became Rose Barrows."

Abby interjected, "Did they try and find your family?"

"No, not after I lied and told them that my parents beat me and I couldn't go back. I begged them to just let me go and wander the streets rather than send me back home. Ruby, Sam's wife, was worried what the neighbours would say. They were off the beaten track but they couldn't keep me hidden forever. Then Sam came up with a plan, he claimed that I was his cousin's child and she was too sick to take care of me any more. Funnily enough everyone believed him and they felt sorry for me, they even brought me clothes that their own children had grown out of. In time Sam and Ruby treated me like their own daughter and I forgot what Mama even looked like but I never forgot about you Abigail."

Abby chose to ignore Rose's last remark, "Tell me about my father."

"There's really not much to tell. His name was Tim Richardson and we were both in the same class at Madison High. He lived just a few doors down from our house and we would walk to school together every day. I thought we were friends and I trusted him, then one day, knowing that I loved animals, he lured me into a small wooded area claiming that he'd seen a stray cat there the day before. He forced himself on me and you were the result."

"What did he look like?"

"He was a good-looking boy, you have his eyes. As for what happened to him, well he went unpunished. He claimed that I was the one who seduced him and I couldn't prove otherwise. Mama didn't want any scandal, so she stopped me from making a fuss and as soon as they found out I was pregnant his family moved out of town. It didn't stop people talking though and I felt like a pariah so that's why I ran. When I went back to Oakfield recently, I found out that your father had died of a heart attack just after his fortieth birthday so I guess there was some justice after all."

"You said your name was Rose Barrows, did the Barrows' adopt you?"

"No, they had a son Lucas, he was nineteen when Sam found me and he still lived at home. He wasn't too happy at first having a stranger thrust into their midst but it didn't take long before he stopped looking at me as a charity case. It was just after my seventeenth birthday when he finally told me that he'd fallen in love with me and a year later we were married. Some folks frowned on the union thinking we were related by blood but we closed our ears to the gossip and made a life for ourselves."

"Did you have any children?" Abby whispered.

"Sadly, no," Rose replied, "Lucas wanted a child so badly and I thought God was punishing me for abandoning you, but I couldn't tell him that. We led a very simple life, Lucas continued to help Sam on the farm and I made a little extra money making hand knitted goods for a local store. We were happy in our own way, despite the fact that we only had each other, then when Lucas was only thirty-five, he had a terrible accident that left him unable to walk."

Abby gasped, "My goodness, that's awful, how did it happen?"

"A tractor ran over his legs and mangled them. He almost died and in the days after the accident, we were sure we were going to lose him." Rose hesitated then continued, "May God forgive me for saying this but he would have been better off dead. He changed from a sweet and thoughtful man into a bitter, pitiful and spiteful human being and living with him was like living with the devil. I wanted to run away so many times but I couldn't leave him like that and I'd already run away from my responsibilities once before, I just couldn't do it again. He lived for another miserable twenty years and then I was finally free."

"What did you do then?" Abby asked now totally intrigued by Rose's story.

"I sold the house Sam had bought us when we first got married, moved into a small place in the village and got a job in the local library. I was fairly content but lonely and I'd never stopped thinking about you and wondering where you were. After two years I went back to Oakfield to look for you but I soon found out that Mama, Aunt Lillian and Aunt Adeline were all dead and nobody knew what had happened to you. Someone thought you'd got married and moved here to Toronto and when I realized that I didn't even know your married name and I lost all hope of finding you, I gave up and went back to my lonely life."

Again Rose paused and then lowered her head, "Six months ago, I found out I had terminal cancer and that's when I knew I had to find you before I left this world."

Abby's hand flew to her mouth, "Oh no, I'm so sorry."

Rose reached across the table again for Abby's hand and this time Abby didn't recoil.

Rose continued, "I went back to Oakfield determined to find you and I finally learned that you had married a man named Edward Harrison. I packed up my belongings and moved to a small flat here and started my search but then I got so sick from the treatments I was getting that I didn't think I could continue. God must have had pity on me and decided to give me another chance because I got my strength back and managed to track you down. I found out you were no longer with your husband and you had a daughter and I just had to see you and tell you how sorry I was for leaving you. I hope you will find it in your heart to forgive me and I promise that if you do, I won't bother you again."

While Rose was talking, tears were forming in Abby's eyes and she remembered the conversation she had with Kate about her father and the need to forgive. She grasped Rose's hand with both of her own, "You were only fifteen," she said, "just a child, the same age as my Kate."

Rose started to sob and Abby rose from her chair to gently usher her out onto the street and away from prying eyes, "I want you to come home with me," she said.

CHAPTER 71

AFTER ABBY GOT HOME and had settled Rose comfortably in the living room with a cup of tea, she telephoned Dorothy Ward to ask if she could keep Kate there for an hour or two longer. Dorothy was pleased to oblige and even offered to let Kate stay and have supper with Helen. Abby was relieved to be able to spend more time with Rose before she met Kate and when she returned to the living room she found her standing near the fireplace, "You have a lovely home, "she said, "and so close to the lake. It must be wonderful in the summer months."

"Yes it is," Abby replied, ""it used to belong to my sister-in-law Julia but that's a long story."

"I'd love to hear about it Abigail, in fact I want to know everything about you. I missed out on all those years and if I could share them with you now, it will make me very happy."

Abby patted the seat beside her, "Why don't you come and sit down, we'll have lots of time to talk, I promise?"

Rose walked over shaking her head, "Not so very long I'm afraid, I don't know how much longer I have, it could be weeks, it could be months, the doctors can't seem to give me a straight answer."

"Surely there's something they can do? If you need to go to a specialist, perhaps I can help."

"I'm afraid not," Rose said sadly, "I've seen so many doctors, had chemotherapy and radiology but nothing seems to be helping. It's in the pancreas and the survival rate is almost zero. My one regret is that I didn't look for you years ago and now we have so little time. I really hope we can spend some of that time together Abigail and I would love to meet Kate."

Before Abby could respond Rose continued, "I noticed a photo of Kate on the mantle, at least I assume it's her. She's lovely and very much like you."

"Yes, everybody remarks on the resemblance but then it appears to run in the family," Abby said smiling as she pushed a stray curl away from Rose's forehead.

"Who is the little boy in the other picture, is he a relative?" Rose asked glancing up at the mantle.

Abby sighed, "That's Daniel, my son, he was killed in an auto accident."

Rose put her hand to her throat, "Oh Abigail, I am so sorry, how ever did you get over it?"

"It took a long time, destroyed my marriage and alienated me from Kate but thankfully I mended my relationship with my daughter and now we share a good life together. I owe a lot of my recovery to my mother-in-law." Abby paused and then took Rose's hand, "Really Rose, there is so much to tell you but let's not do that tonight. This has all been a bit of a shock and I'll need to tell Kate about you before I can let you see her. It isn't every day that someone acquires a brand new grandmother."

"I understand perfectly," said Rose as she stood up, "I should be going and let you get some rest."

"I'll drive you home," Abby offered.

"Thank you but no, I prefer to walk a little and then I'll take the streetcar. I have so much to think about now. I didn't really expect you to react the way you did and I can hardly believe I'm here in your home."

Abby walked Rose to the door, handed her a card with her telephone number and then kissed her lightly on the cheek, "Call me tomorrow and I'll arrange for you to meet Kate. Goodnight Rose."

When Kate finally arrived home at eight o'clock, she found Abby sitting in the sun room staring out at the garden, "What are you doing in here Mom, she asked, "it's almost dark out?"

Abby turned and smiled, "Come and sit down," she said, "I have something wonderful to tell you but it's also really quite sad."

The next evening, Abby and Kate met Rose at a small downtown restaurant. Kate had been shifting about nervously in her chair waiting to see the woman who claimed to be her grandmother but when Rose finally walked through the door, there was no mistaking the resemblance.

Abby got up to greet Rose and bring her to the table, "This is Kate, "she said and then slipping her arm around Rose's shoulder she said, "and this is Mrs. Barrows."

"It's lovely to meet you," Rose said nervously as she sat down.

"Hello," Kate responded and then blurted out, "Are you really my grandmother?"

Rose smiled, "Yes I am and I'm so happy to find out that I have a granddaughter, especially one as pretty as you."

"Well," said Kate without reservation, "I can't call you Mrs. Barrows and I call my other grandmother Gran, so I'll just have to call you Nana."

Abby started to laugh, "And I thought this was going to be awkward," she said.

Two days later, Jim called after arriving back in Toronto. He was anxious to see Abby but soon discovered that somebody else had taken precedence in her life. He listened while Abby excitedly told him about Rose and was genuinely sorry when he heard that she was terminally ill. He suggested that it would be best if he left her to spend as much time as possible with her mother and offered to do anything to help if she needed him. Abby hung up the phone thinking what a kind and thoughtful man he was and she was disappointed that they had not made any arrangements to see each other.

During the next few weeks, Abby, Kate and Rose spent many hours together and Abby even introduced Rose to her in-laws. Martha and John were the perfect hosts, knowing how little time Rose had left.

From their many conversations, Rose soon learned all about Abby's life and the people who had such an impact on her, particularly Ed, Julia and Simon. She realized that Abby had, in many ways, a much harder life than her own and she begged her to open her heart to new experiences while she was still young and the possibility of a new relationship.

Abby reminded her that she was almost forty and Rose just laughed, "You are so young Abigail and you have so many years ahead of you. You shouldn't be alone."

Rose never mentioned Jim although she had heard all about him from Kate. She wisely thought that trying to push Abby into his arms might have the opposite effect.

When Rose became seriously ill after a session of chemotherapy, Abby moved her into the guest room and hired a day nurse to look after her while she was at Charlotte's. In the evening and on weekends she tended to Rose just as she had with Aunt Lillian over twenty years earlier. Even Kate did her part sitting on Rose's bed with Molly lying gently beside her and reading from Rose's favourite book, "Pride and Prejudice."

Abby thought that the treatments Rose was getting would have a positive effect, even though the side effects were brutal, but it was not to be. Exactly ten weeks to the day that Abby had been reunited with her mother, Rose was taken to the hospital and the prognosis was grim. The doctor told Abby that he didn't expect Rose to last through the night and suggested that if there were other family members, they should be there. Abby didn't want Kate to see how deathly ill Rose was but Martha insisted on bringing her to the hospital and all three sat vigil at Rose's bedside.

At three o'clock in the morning, Abby noticed Rose open her eyes and attempt to speak. Abby immediately grasped Rose's hand and bent down so that she could hear her even though her breathing was so laboured, "Thank you my darling daughter for making my last days on this earth so happy," Rose whispered.

Abby looked at Rose with tears streaming down her face, "Thank you for finding me Mama," she whispered back and then laid her head on Rose's chest as she took her final breath.

CHAPTER 72

THE NEXT TWO DAYS flew by in a flurry of activity and Abby had no time to mourn. She had discovered that Rose had been a religious woman and she vowed to give her life closure with a small chapel service before she was cremated.

Rose had been in regular contact with Sam and Ruby Barrows but had never disclosed the fact that she had a daughter or that she was terminally ill. Now, with Jim's help, Abby managed to locate Sam and after a painful conversation where they both shed a few tears, he promised to attend the funeral service with Ruby.

On the day of the funeral, Abby arrived at the chapel early and sat with Kate in the first pew quietly gazing at the casket completely covered in white roses and thinking how sad it was that she had been allowed so little time with her mother. It wasn't long before she heard footsteps and turned to see Julia and David standing in the doorway and it took just seconds before the two women were in each other's arms with Abby finally breaking down and sobbing uncontrollably. It was only when Martha and John arrived that she managed to pull herself together and broke away to attend to her other guests.

Jim soon arrived with Kelly and Abby's staff from Charlotte's including Peter, Pauline and her driver Terry Flynn. Rose had visited the shop often after that first occasion, usually to meet Abby for lunch, and Peter had come to enjoy her gentle nature and sense of humour.

Just before the minister arrived the Wards', with Kate's friend Helen, entered the chapel and as Abby stepped forward to greet them, she noticed three more people standing back in the shadows. It took only a moment to realize that the elderly couple dressed in simple clothes and looking very uncomfortable were the Barrows' so she side stepped the Wards' with a wave of her hand and introduced herself, "Hello," she said, "I'm Abby, Rose's daughter. You must be Sam and Ruby?"

The man nodded, "Yes ma'am, pleased to meet you. Just sorry it's such a sad occasion."

"Please come and sit down," Abby said ushering them towards the front of the chapel, "the service will be starting soon and we can talk afterwards. We are having a small gathering at my home and I would like you to join us."

"It would be our pleasure ma'am," Sam replied.

Once the Barrows' were settled, Abby turned back to see who had followed them in and when she recognized who it was she ran forward with her arms outstretched, "Henrick," she called out, "I can't believe it's you," and she fell into his arms.

Henrick stroked Abby's hair, "Yes, it's your old friend and I couldn't stay away. I wanted to be here for you Abby."

"Oh it's so wonderful to see you but when did you get here? Where are you staying?"

"I got here last night but I wanted to surprise you. I'm only here for one more day and then I have to get back. Sofie is very sick and Willem is having trouble coping."

"I'm so sorry to hear that but you have to stay at the house tonight and then we can talk. Everyone's coming back after the service but later when they all leave, we can have some time to ourselves."

Henrick nodded, "I'd like that Abby, I want to hear all about your mother."

"And I'd like to tell you all about her," Abby replied proudly.

The service was short and poignant with Kate reading a poem that she had composed to honour her grandmother. Abby managed to stay calm but Jim noticed how drawn she looked and the sober black suit she wore only added to her pallor. Almost everyone stood silently as the hearse drove away carrying Rose's body to the crematorium. Abby and Kate laid their hands gently on the casket and said their final goodbyes before the door of the hearse closed and Sam stood quietly, hat in hand, with tears streaming down his face.

A half hour later just as everyone reached Abby's house, an enormous box arrived via special delivery containing a huge bouquet of dahlias in vivid colours of red, burgundy and orange. Abby immediately recognized Lydia's distinctive handwriting on the note tucked into the bouquet and she quietly shut herself in the bathroom so that she could read it in peace. "I know this is like sending coals to Newcastle," Lydia wrote, "but these flowers are from the garden. We just wanted to brighten a day that must be terribly sad. Just know that our thoughts are with you. All of us send our love, Lydia, Roger and Brooke."

Abby was touched that the Frasers' had sent the flowers and she knew that Jim must have told them of her loss. She emerged from the bathroom and looked around at everyone gathered in the living room and she could hardly believe that Julia, David and Henrick had traveled so far to be with her. She noticed that Henrick was in deep conversation with Jim while Kate was sitting with Julia holding her hand and chattering with excitement. Abby suspected that she was boring Julia to death with the details of their trip to England. She never seemed to tire of talking about it.

Abby managed to spend quite a bit of time with the Barrows' but it was obvious they felt out of place. She learned that they were so used to their country life that coming to the city was quite an ordeal but they wanted to be there for Rose. Sam confirmed the story that he had found Rose on the side of the road and that they had taken her in. They were fearful for years that someone would discover their secret but they really believed that Rose came from an abusive family and had no idea that she had given birth to a baby. Abby thought it was ironic that they had all experienced the loss of a child. The Barrow's had lost Lucas, she had lost Daniel and even Rose, in her own way, had lost her own child by abandoning her soon after she was born. Despite the sadness of the occasion, Abby found herself smiling and even laughing when Molly decided that she liked the look of Henrick and decided that his lap was a good place to park. Kate was about to shoo her away but Henrick discouraged her and seemed perfectly content stroking the cat's soft fur while she purred with delight.

Julia and David were staying in a downtown hotel and returning to Vancouver in two days, so before they left the house, they arranged to go to dinner with Abby and Jim the following night. The Barrows' took their leave just before Julia and David, anxious to get on the road, and a little later, all the guests left except for Henrick.

"Well, I'm glad I came my dear girl," said Henrick still sitting contentedly with Molly, "at least I got to meet the young man I've heard so much about."

Abby looked puzzled, "What do you mean?"

"The young man that was here, Jim," Henrick replied.

"I don't understand," said Abby shaking her head, "what have you heard about him?"

"That's for me to know and for you to find out," said Henrick teasingly.

"Mmmm, I suspect Kate might have something to do with this," Abby pondered while staring accusingly at Kate who was looking guilty.

"Anyway," Henrick continued, "I like the young man, he seems like a decent chap."

"He's not so young," Abby countered, "he's forty -two."

Henrick roared with laughter, "Ha, when you're as old as me, sixty-two is even young!"

Abby was grateful for the light-hearted conversation and decided not to talk about Rose until the next day. Henrick's plane wasn't due to leave until noon so they would have plenty of time to chat and Abby had experienced enough sadness for one day.

The next morning, after a restful sleep which Abby hadn't expected even though she had been physically and emotionally drained, she prepared breakfast and after

Kate had gone off to school she sat with Henrick and told him all about Rose. She had known so little about her but in the few weeks they had spent together, she had come to recognize so many of her wonderful traits, compassion, sincerity, courage and patience and Henrick noticed the pride in her voice when she no longer called her Rose but referred to her as her mother.

Abby drove Henrick to the airport and spent a tearful goodbye in the departure lounge vowing to keep in touch. She drove home slowly along the highway and past the lake finally feeling a sense of contentment even though she had just suffered the fourth great loss in her life.

When she arrived home, she found a letter sitting on the doormat and was surprised when she realized that it was from Ed. He wrote that Martha had telephoned him to tell him about her mother and he wanted her to know how sorry he was to hear her sad news. He also enclosed a photograph of his young son, a sweet looking child with light blonde hair, who he had named Dane. Abby stared at the picture with mixed emotions. She no longer felt any bitterness towards Ed and was pleased that he had made a new life for himself but she was a little resentful that the wonderful son they had shared had been replaced by a boy with an obviously similar name and a child that she would probably never even get to meet.

Dinner at Jim's favourite Italian restaurant the following night was a light-hearted affair. Julia was determined to take Abby's mind off of the loss of her mother and for the most part, she succeeded. It was only when it was time to say goodbye that Abby fought back an overwhelming sense of sadness. Julia and David were returning to Vancouver early the next morning and Abby knew she wouldn't be seeing them again for quite some time.

On the way home Jim, sensing that Abby's mood had changed, suggested that she should take a break, "I've been thinking Abby," he said, "why don't you take a few days off. A friend of mine has a cottage up in Muskoka and I'd love to take you there for a long weekend."

Abby continued to stare out of the window, "I can't leave Kate now, she just lost her grandmother."

"I wasn't suggesting you leave her. We could take her with us; in fact I'll call Angela and ask if Kelly can stay a few more days and then she can come too. The girls would love it there even at this time of the year."

Abby was silent for a minute then turned back from the window, "It does sound like a wonderful idea and I really do need a couple of days away. These last few months have been difficult even though there were so many good moments. My grandmother and my aunts never talked about my mother and I never asked about her. I rarely ever thought about her and had no great desire to ever meet her. When she walked through the door at Charlotte's I had no idea that we would become so close in such a short time." Abby hesitated and then continued, "Sorry, I didn't mean to ramble on. If Kelly can come with us, we would love to come for the weekend."

Jim smiled, "That's great, I'll call Angela first thing in the morning. I'm sure she'll be quite happy for me to keep Kelly here."

"Why do you say that?" Abby asked.

"Well, Angela has never been too interested in domesticity and she's hardly what one would call maternal. Since we've been divorced, she's had several boyfriends and her latest relationship appears to be fairly serious so she's spending more and more time away from home. Kelly even hinted to me that she would like to leave Montreal and come here to live."

"And how do you feel about that?"

Jim glanced over at Abby, "Frankly, I would love it but it would mean disrupting her education. I'm really not sure what to do."

"Would Angela let her go without a fight?" Abby asked.

"Actually, I think she'd be glad to get rid of the responsibility. She's not a bad woman, she's just immature and ironically I think that's what attracted me to her in the first place. She seemed so childlike and vulnerable and I just wanted to protect her but after a while it got tedious. I thought having a child would help her to grow up but it didn't."

"I'm so sorry Jim, it must be difficult not having Kelly with you."

"Yes, well there's a possibility that could change," Jim responded as he pulled into Abby's driveway.

Abby laid her hand on Jim's arm, "I'd like to talk some more, why don't you come in for a nightcap."

"I'd love to," Jim replied turning off the ignition and stepping out of the car to walk around and open Abby's door.

Once inside, Abby offered Jim a brandy and they settled on the sofa disturbing Molly who stalked out of the room in disgust with her tail in the air.

"Where's Kate?" Jim asked.

"Oh she's at her grandparents. What about Kelly, is she at home?"

"Yes, but she'll be fine. I have my neighbour keeping an eye on the house and if anyone tries to break in they'll have to deal with Scamp."

Abby chuckled, "I thought Scamp was a pussy cat."

"He is until someone threatens me or Kelly and then he turns into a tiger."

Abby started to break up with laughter, "I can't imagine that."

Jim reached over and lifted Abby's chin, "You look so lovely when you laugh," he said, "in fact, you look particularly beautiful tonight."

Abby looked down at her favourite cornflower blue dress and blushed knowing that she had worn it deliberately to impress him. In fact, she had gone to a lot of trouble to look her best, curling her hair so that it fell to her shoulders gently framing her face and paying special attention to her make up. Obviously her efforts had paid off and she leaned forward and kissed him lightly on the lips, "Thank you kind sir," she said.

Soon they were in each other's arms and kissing passionately but moments later Jim pushed Abby gently away, "I had better leave," he whispered as he got up.

Abby shook her head, "I know you have to go but I really would like you to stay."

Jim took both of Abby's hands in his own and helped her up, "I would love to stay Abby but tonight is not the right time. When I do stay, I want to wake up in the morning with you beside me."

Abby wrapped her arms around him, "I understand, I really do and I would like that too. Go home to Kelly and call me tomorrow after you speak to Angela."

CHAPTER 73

THE WEEKEND IN MUSKOKA was a great success. Angela had happily agreed to allow Kelly to stay with her father for a few more days and the two girls were in their element despite the cool weather. They explored the woods on rental bikes, tried their hand at archery and went boating on Lake Rosseau with Jim and Abby. On Saturday night, they all attended a local barn dance and laughed over and over again at their pathetic attempts to line dance.

After the girls collapsed in their room that night, Jim and Abby sat, wrapped in blankets, on the porch swing, sipping wine and gazing up at a crystal clear sky illuminated with a myriad of stars.

"It's absolutely beautiful here and so peaceful," Abby remarked.

Jim shifted a little closer and said, "You're beautiful Abby."

Abby smiled and grasped Jim's hand, "Don't start something you can't finish," she teased.

"Oh well, you can't blame a guy for trying," Jim replied as he leaned over and kissed Abby on the side of her mouth.

"Is that the best you can do?" Abby taunted.

Jim didn't reply but took Abby's glass and put it with his own on the side table, gathered her in his arms and kissed her fully on the lips. Abby suddenly felt a desire that had escaped her for a long time and as she ran her hands over Jim's back she said, "Please don't stop."

Jim pulled away, "We have to stop Abby, I want you so much and I think you want me too but I told you the other night, I want us to spend the whole night together and we can't do that here."

Abby left rather reluctantly a few moments later and slept badly, tossing and turning and obsessing over her conflicted feelings for Jim. Her recent physical attraction to him surprised her although she had always thought him to be better than average looking but she couldn't get past the fact that he had been Simon's closest friend. While she had no doubt that intimacy between them was imminent, she wasn't sure that she could ever feel a deep love for him or for any other man.

On Monday after their Muskoka weekend, Jim called to make arrangements to see Abby the following Saturday and it was Abby who suggested that Kate could stay at her grandparents so that they could spend some time alone. It was only after Abby hung up the phone that she had misgivings but she had no intention of backing out of what was obviously going to be their first night together.

On Friday, after her morning shower, Abby took a long hard look at herself in the mirror. She turned this way and that, looking for any flaws and for the most part was satisfied with her reflection that showed no signs of love handles, sagging breasts or cellulite. She breathed a sigh of relief and then suddenly remembered that her lingerie collection was more than a little outdated and needed a boost. She made up her mind to shop that evening and soon after she left Charlotte's she was downtown purchasing two sets of lacy underwear and a sheer silk nightgown.

Jim had tickets for the advance showing of the film 'Dr. Zhivago' but first they were to have dinner at a small French restaurant close to his home. Abby was excited and decided to wear her black cocktail dress with its long sleeves and low neckline. Her hair was piled on top of her head and she wore a triple row of pearls around her neck. Jim whistled when he picked her up at six o'clock and she curtsied slightly then threw her short mink jacket over her shoulders. As Jim guided her to the car he whispered, "You look good enough to eat," and Abby countered with, "Well, you could always skip dinner you know."

Throughout their meal of succulent pork tenderloin wrapped in bacon served with apples and potatoes in a calvados cream sauce, they kept up the banter, joking back and forth with the odd innuendo that made Abby more apprehensive about the night ahead. Even in the theatre, while the movie was exceptional and had received rave reviews, Abby was having trouble concentrating and was glad when the final credits rolled.

They were both quiet on the drive back to Jim's house until he asked, "Are you tired Abby?"

"No," Abby replied, "I'm just winding down. It was a perfect lovely evening and I want to thank you."

"I'm glad you enjoyed it but the night is still young and I have some wonderful cognac at the house. You are coming home with me, aren't you Abby?"

Abby nodded, "Yes, of course, and maybe we can have some coffee too?"

"Whatever your heart desires, I aim to please."

Abby started to laugh a little nervously as she realized they were entering Jim's driveway but her anxiety disappeared when Scamp came bounding out of the door and nearly knocked her over.

Jim bent down and patted the dog's wiry head, "How are you doing there fella, did you miss me?"

Scamp just wagged his tail happily and followed Jim and Abby into the living room.

While Jim excused himself to make coffee and pour cognac into two large brandy snifters, Abby settled on the sofa and when Jim returned carrying a tray, he found that Scamp was occupying the other half of the sofa with his head on Abby's lap. She was obviously enjoying it because she was stroking his back and murmuring in his ear.

Jim put the tray on the coffee table then stood with his hands on his hips, "Okay buster, that's my seat," he said.

Scamp opened one eye but didn't move and Abby grinned while holding onto Scamp with one hand protectively.

Jim looked at Abby and shook his head, "It's either him or me, take your pick."

"Then I think I'll stick with Scamp, he's not so talkative," Abby teased.

Jim threw up his hands, "That's it," he said, "he's gone," and he picked Scamp up bodily and unceremoniously dumped him on the large wing chair by the fireplace. Scamp growled but settled down with eyes closed and ears twitching while Abby observed him and giggled with delight, "He's so adorable, I could watch him all night."

Jim sat down and handed Abby her glass, "That's not an option, he's banned from the bedroom when I have a guest."

"Aha!" said Abby, "So I gather you entertain ladies frequently."

Jim grinned, "Every other night at least."

Abby smiled and then looked serious. "You know I'm a little nervous, don't you Jim? I've only been with two other men in my life."

"There's no need to be nervous, I won't do anything you don't want me to, I promise you that. I respect you Abby, you're not like anyone I've ever known before."

"Thank you Jim," Abby whispered taking his hand, "by the way, I really don't want anything more to drink, why don't we just go up to bed?"

When morning came, Abby awoke early and for a moment had no idea where she was. As her mind cleared, she realized that she was in Jim's room and she turned over to watch him sleeping. His face, in repose, was devoid of all lines and with his hair falling over his forehead he looked almost ten years younger. Abby thought about the night they had shared and what a gentle and considerate lover he had been. She had been surprised at how muscular he was after always seeing him fully dressed and always appearing to be so slim and he had been just as impressed with her body. He made her feel beautiful, complimenting everything about her and she almost felt like a young girl again, not a woman approaching forty with a fifteen year old child.

She was just beginning to drift off when Jim opened his eyes and whispered, "Are you awake Abby?"

Abby rolled over slowly and smiled, "Yes, I've been awake for a while."

Jim stretched one arm out and pulled Abby towards him, "Come here woman," he demanded, "I want you beside me."

Abby snuggled up with her head on Jim's chest and they lay quietly in each other's arms before falling asleep again.

CHAPTER 74

A FEW WEEKS LATER, Abby was snowed under with requests for special Christmas floral decorations and she still had her own shopping to take care of. Since the Muskoka weekend, she had seen Jim on several occasions and spent many wonderful intimate hours at his house but had no opportunity to spend another night. Martha had been sick with bronchitis and Abby was reluctant to allow Kate to even visit her grandparents, let alone stay over. It was a situation that left both Abby and Jim feeling frustrated and as time went on Abby realized how much deeper her feelings for Jim had grown since their first night together.

Martha was still not well over the holiday and Abby persuaded her not to go to all the trouble of preparing her usual elaborate turkey dinner. Meanwhile, Jim suggested that everyone gather at his house and he would do all the cooking with a little help from Abby. Having sampled some of Jim's homemade meals, Abby had no doubt that he was as good a cook as Martha, if not better, and she smiled to herself when she compared him to Simon who could hardly even boil water. Time and time again, she found herself comparing them and wondered how they came to be such good friends considering how different they were. While Simon was adventurous and impulsive, Jim was conservative and somewhat a creature of habit but he was also thoughtful and always considerate of other's feelings, unlike Simon who tended not to even notice when others were sad or in a despondent mood. Abby had always admired Simon's free approach to life and had no doubt of his love for her but at the same time she never felt entirely secure. With Jim she knew she would have a stable future and the more she thought about it the more she came to believe that perhaps that was what she really needed. Jim had already told her that he loved her but he had not hinted at any future plans and Abby suspected he understood that she wasn't yet ready to consider any serious commitment. Meanwhile Kate had other ideas and was constantly commenting how great it would be if Abby married Jim and Kelly moved to Toronto, then they could all be one happy family.

Jim excelled himself preparing a turkey with all the trimmings and a homemade pumpkin pie while Abby provided shortbread, rum balls, sugared almonds and all the traditional holiday treats. Christmas was quiet compared to other years, only six people sat around Jim's dining room table, Jim, Abby, Kate, Kelly and John and Martha. Abby had hoped that Julia and David would be visiting for a few days but they had been invited by David's younger brother to spend two weeks at his vacation home in Mazatlan, Mexico and Julia couldn't resist the temptation of eighty degree weather in the middle of December.

Raymond was also absent from the scene. John and Martha hadn't seen their oldest son in quite some time and they felt some resentment against Connie who appeared to control his comings and goings. They were reluctant to face the fact that she might one day be their daughter-in-law and wished he had met someone more like Abby. As for Ed, they had never met his new wife or got to hold their new grandson but they were hopeful that Ed would bring him to visit before too long.

Martha, while still feeling a little under the weather, was well enough to enjoy the food on her plate and grateful for not having to play the hostess for the first time in years. She commented to Abby on more than one occasion what a fine young man Jim was and what a perfect couple they made.

With the demand for floral decorations over the holiday and New Year's Eve parties, Abby was exhausted. Jim had suggested they go out for dinner at a sophisticated supper club but Abby just wanted to stay home. Meanwhile Kate had been invited to a teen party at Helen's house and was bubbling over with excitement when she left home but also a little reluctant to leave her mother on such an important night.

Kelly had returned to Montreal by train two days earlier after begging her father to let her stay longer and Jim was also feeling a little abandoned. When Abby invited him over for a home cooked meal he accepted with enthusiasm and arrived on her doorstep with not one, but two bottles of wine and a large box of truffles.

"Are you planning to get me drunk?" Abby asked as she pulled him into the hallway.

"Well, now you come to mention it, it might be fun," Jim replied.

Abby punched him playfully on the arm, "First you have to eat my cooking and I have to warn you, I'm no Julia Child."

Jim followed her into the kitchen, "Smells good whatever it is but I don't see any pots or pans."

"That's because it's all in one big pot in the oven."

"Ah, so it's a casserole?"

"It's called Chicken Potato Bake and it's got cheese, chicken, sour cream and potatoes in it. I followed the recipe exactly so it had better be good."

"So how long before we eat," Jim asked, "I'm feeling a bit famished?"

"Sorry but it needs another hour. I've got lots of munchies in the living room so you won't starve to death."

An hour and a half later Jim and Abby were on their second bottle of wine and feeling very mellow having forgotten all about the food. It was only when a strong smell of burning emanated from the kitchen that Abby jumped up and rushed to retrieve her Chicken Potato Bake from the oven. Jim was standing behind her as she cried out, "Oh my goodness, it's burned to a crisp," and started to cry. Jim, on the other hand, began to laugh hysterically and Abby looked at him with a puzzled expression, "Why are you laughing? Our dinner is ruined, a fine celebration this is turning out to be."

Jim wrapped his arms around her, "As long as I'm with you, that's all I need Abby."

"But you said you were famished," she protested.

"I was, but not any more. Anyway we can always order in Chinese or a pizza if you prefer."

"Are you sure you don't mind?" Abby asked tearfully.

"I told you, as long as I'm with you, I'm happy."

One week later, Abby was at Charlotte's in the back room helping Peter to unpack some flowers when she heard the front door open. She asked Peter to attend to the customer but a moment later he was back, "It's Kelly, she wants to see you."

Abby looked up in shock, "Kelly, are you sure?"

Peter put a hand on Abby's arm, "Yes but she looks a little worse for wear."

Abby rushed out to find Kelly with her head bowed and hands clasped in front of her. She had on a pair of jeans, heavy boots and a parka and carried a knapsack over one shoulder. It was her hair that gave her a disheveled appearance. Her normally straight and shiny locks were dull and windblown.

"Kelly what are you doing here," Abby asked as she placed her hands on Kelly's shoulders.

Kelly looked up and Abby could see dark circles under her eyes, "I ran away and I'm not going back."

Abby guided Kelly to the back room and sat her down, "What happened Kelly and how on earth did you get here from Montreal?"

"My Mom's going to marry Marco and they're going to live in Italy. My Mom said I had to go with them but I'm not going, I'm just not and they can't make me."

"You still haven't told me how you got here," Abby repeated softly.

"I crept out of the house last night and I walked for about five miles then I hitchhiked as far as Kingston."

Abby gasped, "You hitchhiked, oh my God, Kelly anything could have happened to you."

Kelly shook her head, "I was okay, I got a ride with a family. When they dropped me off at Kingston, I found a park and slept in some bushes for a couple of hours, I was so tired. Then I got another ride all the way here with a sweet old lady who was visiting her grandson and she brought me right to your door. I didn't want to go to Dad's office, he would have freaked out."

While Kelly was talking, Abby was remembering Rose's story of running away and being rescued by Sam, "We have to phone your mother Kelly, she must be frantic by now."

Kelly shrugged, "I doubt it, she's too busy with Marco to bother about me."

Look," Abby suggested, "let's go to my house and I'll call your father then he can phone your Mom."

"Please don't let him make me go back home," Kelly begged, "I want to stay here."

Abby helped Kelly up from the chair, "We'll see what we can do, "she promised.

Jim was surprised when Abby called and he learned of Kelly's escapade. He dropped what he was doing and hurriedly drove to Abby's house, "Where is she?" he asked anxiously when Abby opened the door.

"She's in the kitchen, I made her a sandwich. Try not to be too hard on her."

Jim brushed past Abby and sighed with relief when he saw Kelly at the kitchen table. Kelly wasted no time in jumping up and throwing herself into her father's arms, "Daddy, please don't make me go back. They can't make me move to Italy, I'll just run away again."

Jim stroked Kelly's hair, "Don't worry honey, you're not leaving the country so unless your mother changes her mind, you're stuck with your old man."

Kelly looked up smiling despite her tears, "Really Daddy, I can stay with you?"

"Well I have to call your mother first and let her know you're okay and then we can discuss what's going to happen."

Abby looked over at Jim and nodded, "Why don't you call Angela from the living room now and we'll just sit here until you are through?"

Jim released Kelly, "Thanks Abby, that's a good idea; I'll call her now."

It seemed like ages before Jim returned to the kitchen. He had been disturbed to discover that Angela, aware that Kelly had run away, had not been overly concerned. The conversation ended in a shouting match that could clearly be heard in the kitchen and resulted in Jim's determination to keep Kelly in Toronto.

The next day, Angela agreed to pack up all of Kelly's belongings and ship them on the next train. Two weeks later she married Marco in a civil ceremony and moved permanently to Italy.

Kate was thrilled to hear that Kelly would be staying with her father and even more resolute that they should all be one happy family. Meanwhile, Abby formed a close bond with Kelly, fully aware that she felt abandoned by her mother and needed someone to take her place, and she went out of her way to help Jim with any issue he had in parenting a fifteen-year-old girl, at the same time encouraging Kate and Kelly's friendship.

CHAPTER 75

IT WAS MID-SUMMER WHEN Jim decided to ask Abby to marry him and on a warm July evening, after dining on an outdoor patio overlooking the lake, he finally popped the question. The emerald cut diamond Jim placed on her finger, before she had even accepted his proposal. overwhelmed Abby. She kept staring back and forth between Jim and the ring until Jim couldn't stand it any longer, "Abby are you going to answer me, I'm dying here?"

Abby grinned and leaned across the table to kiss him on the forehead, "Yes, I'll marry you, you're not getting this little bauble back that's for sure."

Jim bounced up and gathered Abby into his arms oblivious of the other diners observing the scene with some amusement, "Materialistic little madam," he whispered. Suddenly applause broke out and Abby blushed while Jim turned and bowed twice before sitting down again.

Kate and Kelly were both over the moon when they heard the news and peppered Jim and Abby with questions about the wedding and the new living arrangements. This prompted them to examine what would be best for everyone and they finally concluded that they should start afresh.

The wedding date was set for mid October and, two months earlier, Jim and Abby put both their homes up for sale. Abby felt a degree of sadness about leaving the house she had shared with Julia but she was excited about starting over.

Jim, Abby and the girls spent hours looking at houses all over the city and fell in love with a Queen Anne style house in the ritzy Rosedale area. It had four bedrooms, two bathrooms, a huge kitchen and an enormous walled garden dominated by century old willow trees. Abby was nervous about investing in so much in property but with their combined incomes Jim convinced her that they could easily afford it and that the house would appreciate in value so they had nothing to lose.

Abby had wanted to marry at City Hall and avoid all the fanfare but pressure from the girls and Julia, who was overjoyed at the news, soon changed her mind. The wedding took place at a small chapel and it seemed as though all the guests who were at Rose's funeral had come back to celebrate, with the exception of the Barrows.. Julia and David arrived from Vancouver and Henrick flew in from Florida but this time he was accompanied by Ginny who he had finally set up house with.

Abby wore a short ivory silk dress with spaghetti straps and flowers in her hair and John, appearing very statesmanlike in a black suit and red tie, walked her slowly down the aisle. Following nervously behind, Kate and Kelly looked very grown up in mint green satin while Martha struggled to find a tissue to wipe away her tears. Abby only had eyes for Jim waiting with the minister, dressed in a midnight blue tuxedo and accompanied by his best man, Graham Barker, a friend he had known and worked with for years. She didn't notice the two people sitting at the back of the chapel until the ceremony was over, and she was walking back down the aisle on Jim's arm so she was surprised when he suddenly stopped and motioned to her to look to her left, "Look who's here Abby," he said.

Abby gasped when she recognized the Frasers' and releasing herself from Jim she ran towards them, "Lydia, Roger, oh my goodness I can't believe you're here," she cried.

Lydia embraced Abby, "We wouldn't have missed Jim's wedding for the world especially knowing he was marrying you Abby. We didn't tell you we were coming because we wanted to surprise you."

"Oh you've done that all right," Abby said gasping for breath and holding her hand to her chest, "it's so wonderful to see you both."

Roger took Abby's hand in both of his own, "We'll talk later, my dear, but right now I think your other guests are waiting to throw the traditional rice and take some pictures."

Abby turned back reluctantly until she saw Jim's face. His smile portrayed so much love for her at that moment that she felt a deep emotion and knew that she had found her soul mate.

Settling into the new house was an adventure and even with many of the pieces of furniture both Abby and Jim brought with them, they still needed to redecorate many of the rooms and add additional pieces. Kate and Kelly each had their own bedroom adjacent to each other and they were allowed to pick their own paint colours and furnishings. Kate's room was feminine, all pink and flowery while Kelly preferred deep dark blues and a more modern theme. Considering their difference in taste, both in décor and clothes, it was amazing that they became closer than most sisters and thrived in each other's company. Meanwhile even Scamp and Molly had come to terms with each other, which meant that Molly ruled the roost and ignored Scamp even though he tried on many occasions to make friends with her. Molly had always preferred to stay indoors and spent most of her time in Kate's room while Scamp loved to play in the back yard and be taken for walks in Rosedale Park.

Because of the move to the new house and the need to ensure that Kelly was settled, Jim and Abby decided to forego a traditional honeymoon and take the girls on vacation at the next Spring break. After pouring through travel brochures featuring exotic locations, Jim brought everyone down to earth by suggesting that they all go to the east coast. Both Kate and Kelly were disappointed after imagining themselves lying on a beach in Aruba or somewhere equally romantic until Jim pointed out that there was lots of time for that and they needed to see their own country first.

After flying to Halifax, they rented a car and traveled throughout Nova Scotia and New Brunswick, eventually arriving in Maine. It was their first vacation as a family and one they would never forget. Just riding along in the car was lots of fun with everyone singing or playing games and they took dozens of photos including several of the girls striking goofy poses or making faces at the camera.

Soon after their return to Toronto when everyone had settled back into their normal routine, Abby got a call from Julia. They had just finished supper when Abby heard the phone ring and rushed to answer it, "The Matthews's residence," she sang out.

Julia chuckled, "That's so good to hear Abby, you certainly sound happy."

"Julia!" Abby cried. "How are you? I've been meaning to call but we just got back from vacation. It was absolutely wonderful and I'm sending you some photos as soon as they're developed."

"That's great Abby," Julia responded, "I'll look forward to seeing them. How are Jim and the girls?"

"They're all fabulous, I couldn't be happier Julia. Kate adores Jim and he's such a good father to Kelly. Anyway, enough about us, I want to hear about you. Anything exciting happening?"

"Actually yes, I do have some news."

"Good, I hope?" Abby asked apprehensively.

"The best Abby, are you sitting down? Dave and I adopted a baby."

Abby gasped, "Oh my goodness. When? How? Why didn't you tell me before?"

"Well we applied to adopt some time ago but I didn't want to tell anyone in case it fell through then it actually happened, Abby, and now we have this incredible little daughter."

Abby was in shock, "Oh that is so amazing. How old is she and what's her name? Tell me all about her."

Julia laughed, "I knew you'd be excited for us. She's nine months old and her name is Sarah. She's a little small for her age but the paediatrician assures me she's perfectly healthy and she's got blue eyes and fuzzy blonde hair. Her birth mother was only sixteen so she gave her up for adoption and she's been in a foster home since the time she was born. I can't tell you how happy we are Abby, I never dreamed of having a child of my own but it was Dave who convinced me to adopt."

"But how are you managing with work Julia?"

"I quit Abby. I figured being a mother to Sarah was more important, at least until she starts school. Dave is thrilled; he loves having me at home and I love it too. Who would have thought I'd get a kick out of sleepless nights and dirty diapers?"

Abby snickered, "Wait till she gets to the terrible two's, that's when the fun really begins."

Julia sighed, "Yes, that's what everyone tells me but that's a long way off so I'm not going to worry about it now. Anyway Abby I have to run but I just had to call and tell you our news and I hope to get to see you soon. Obviously I'm a little tied down at the moment but let's not leave it too long before we make time for a visit."

"We won't Julia, I promise. I can't wait to see Sarah. Tell Dave how thrilled I am for both of you."

"I will Abby, you take care and say hello to everyone. Love you."

"Love you too," Abby whispered and gently put the phone down.

When she returned to the kitchen Jim looked up at her expectantly, "Who was that, you sounded excited about something?"

Abby told Jim and the girls all about Julia's call but Jim noticed that she seemed a little subdued. Meanwhile Kate thought it was fabulous news and was thrilled when she realized that she now had a cousin. It was after the girls had both gone to bed that Jim questioned Abby's change of mood, "What's wrong Abby, I thought you were pleased about the adoption."

Abby sighed, "I am pleased but I guess I'm a little envious too."

Jim got up from the wing chair where he had been reading the paper and moved over to sit next to Abby on the sofa, "Surely you don't mean you're envious about the idea of getting up two or three times a night, heating up formula and worrying yourself into a frazzle every time baby gets the sniffles?"

Abby took Jim's hand and smiled, "It's really not that bad. Do you think I'm too old to have another child?"

Jim let go of Abby's hand abruptly, "Whoa there Abby, we never discussed having children."

Abby got up and started pacing, "I know but that didn't stop me from thinking about it and now after hearing Julia's news I can't help thinking about it again."

"But what about Charlotte's, Abby? You know we can't afford for you to stop working, we went over all that when we bought this house."

"I know, you're right," Abby replied, "let's just forget about it."

CHAPTER 76

ONE MONTH LATER JIM came to the realization that Abby had not put the idea of having another child out of her mind. She went overboard buying outfits and toys for Sarah and it was obvious that she was becoming obsessed with anything to do with babies. Jim finally decided to confront her and was surprised to learn that she had already planned a way to stop working full time and still be able to afford the house. Peter had approached her on one or two occasions about buying into Charlotte's and if she sold him half of the business, she could pay down a good part of the mortgage. She had never taken a salary, living only off of the profits that would now be cut in half, probably more considering they would need to hire someone to replace her. Nevertheless, if they also cut down on some of their household expenses, Abby was convinced they could manage.

Jim was dumbfounded, "You're really serious about this, aren't you?"

Abby nodded, "Yes I am, I know we can work it out Jim but I'm not going to pressure you. I know it's a lot to ask but promise me you'll think about it."

Jim hesitated before replying, "I will Abby but give me some time, I'm not sure I can adjust to becoming a father again."

A week later after Abby had maintained her silence on the subject but was obviously brooding enough for the girls to notice, Jim made an announcement. They were gathered around the kitchen table enjoying an extravagant Sunday brunch when he held up his hand to silence the girls chatter and said, "How would you like to add another member to this family, maybe a little brother or sister, because we're going to have a baby?"

Abby's mouth dropped open and Kate and Kelly screamed in unison, "What?"

Jim repeated very slowly, "We are going to have a baby."

Abby was smiling now as Kate babbled, "I don't believe it, when? How long have you known?"

Abby leaned over and stroked Kate's head, "We aren't pregnant yet honey but we hope to be soon."

Kelly looked from Jim to Abby and back again, "Does this mean.....?"

Jim laughed as he interjected, "Yes we still have sex Kelly even though we may be ancient."

Kelly blushed and Abby started to giggle. "It's okay Kelly, you needn't be embarrassed, your Dad's just teasing you."

Kate piped up, "If you're going to have a baby, I want a sister."

"I'm afraid we can't pick and choose," Abby said, "and anyway we don't even know if I can get pregnant now, we'll just have to wait and see."

Kate stuck her chin in the air, "Well I guess you'll just have to try really hard to make a baby even if you are old."

Jim and Abby looked at each other and collapsed into fits of laughter.

In August, just a few weeks short of Abby's forty-first birthday, Abby's doctor confirmed that she was three months pregnant. It was no surprise because she recognized all the symptoms having gone through two previous pregnancies even though it had been so long ago. She continued to work at Charlotte's right up until the eight month but with the thirty extra pounds on her slim frame and a backache that wouldn't seem to go away, she finally relented and agreed to stay home until the baby was born. She had already sold half of Charlotte's to Peter and he had proved to be a worthy partner. Abby knew that he was a dedicated worker and he didn't disappoint her when he completely took over management of the shop and hired a part timer to assist Pauline.

Jim doted on Abby calling her three or four times a day from his office and making sure that the girls helped out with the household chores.

In February, one week before Abby's due date they were still talking about names for the baby. "I'd like to call her Emily Rose if it's a girl," said Abby, "Emily was my mother's real name and Rose was the name she took when she ran away and the name I knew her by."

"Mmm.... Emily Rose Matthews?" Jim mused. "I like it."

"Good, I'm glad and now that that's settled, it's only fair that you get to choose a boy's name. What about naming him after your father."

"My father's name was Paul and I wouldn't mind that as a second name but not as a first."

"Why not, Paul's a nice name? You never talk about your father?"

"Don't I? Sorry, I guess I resented him a little even though he brought me up on his own after my mother died. I was only three so it must have been difficult for him. We always had a well kept home with plenty of food on the table and he made sure I had a good education."

"Then why the resentment, I don't understand?" Abby asked frowning.

"Well, he was a difficult man to get along with. He didn't communicate too well on a social level but he was brilliant in business and built up the company from scratch. I never had one single real conversation with my father and I never wanted to follow in his footsteps, but when he died I felt obligated to carry the business on. I know I shouldn't feel the way I do but I had other dreams."

Abby put her arms around him, "I'm sorry honey, I know you wanted to be a vet but you're not really unhappy with your work, are you?"

Jim visibly brightened, "No, I actually like it and the guys I work with are great. Speaking of guys we still haven't picked out a first name for a boy but I do have a suggestion."

"What is it?" Abby asked with some apprehension.

"I'm not sure how you'll feel about this but I'd like to call him Simon."

Abby stared open mouthed for a moment and then laying her head on Jim's shoulder said, "I think that is the most generous and wonderful idea, thank you darling."

Five days later in the early hours of the morning, Simon Paul Matthews was born. He weighed eight pounds six ounces and had dark hair just like his mother.

CHAPTER 77

ONE YEAR AFTER SIMON'S birth the family, including Martha and John celebrated his birthday and Julia even flew in from Vancouver with Sarah. It wasn't the first time that Abby and Julia had had the opportunity to admire each other's children. Julia had visited three months earlier when she accompanied David on a business trip and brought Sarah with her. Jim had been amused to see how the two women had doted on the youngsters and he was filled with pride when Julia had commented what a well-behaved and lovable baby Simon was. At one-year-old his features had changed and it was evident that he was going to grow into a handsome boy. Both Kate and Kelly were enchanted with their half brother and were always ready to baby-sit any chance they got.

Later that day, after all the party decorations had been put away and the dishes washed, Abby sat down in the living room with Julia and a well deserved cup of coffee. The babies were down for a nap and Jim had chauffeured the girls to a friend's house for a sleepover. Molly was in her usual spot in Kate's room and Scamp was sleeping under the dining room table. It was so peaceful after all the noise that Abby let out a deep sigh and stretched her legs out on the sofa, "Well, I think that went well, Martha and John seemed to enjoy themselves. I'm glad it's over though, I really needed a few moments to unwind."

Julia chuckled, "Well enjoy it while you can because naps don't last for too long."

"I know and it's funny because although I enjoy these quiet times, I get a little anxious when Simon sleeps too long."

Julia nodded, "I was exactly the same way when Sarah was younger, I guess we'll always worry about our kids to some degree."

"Mmm you've got that right," Abby mused, "but anyway tell me, how's David? How does he enjoy being a father?"

"He absolutely loves it. I just wish I could have given him a child of his own but he's told me over and over again that it doesn't matter and that Sarah is his own."

Abby could see the radiant look on Julia's face, "I can't believe how things have changed since we first met. Here you are, a first time mother and here I am, with a son again when I never imagined having more children after Daniel died."

Julia got up and squatted on the ottoman next to Abby, "Are you really happy Abby?"

"Oh yes, I can honestly say I am. Jim is a wonderful husband and father. He always puts the children and me first and I truly love him with all my heart. Kate adores him too and having Kelly here is just like having another daughter. I'm so happy, but I'm scared Julia."

Julia grabbed Abby's hand, "What are you scared about? Do you think something dreadful is going to happen? That's silly Abby."

"Maybe, but it all seems too good to be true."

Six months later Abby's words came back to haunt her.

Everything had been going smoothly. Simon was thriving, the girls were doing well in school; Jim was working on a major contact and Charlotte's was bringing in a good income under Peter's management. Abby, however, was feeling a little sluggish and Jim had even teased her once or twice that it was all because she had gained a little weight. Looking in the mirror after her morning shower, she couldn't help noticing that all the weight gain was in her stomach and that afternoon after purchasing a home pregnancy test she breathed a sigh of relief when the test was negative.

Two weeks later she woke in the middle of the night in excruciating pain and not wanting to wake Jim, she tried to crawl out of bed. In her attempt she collapsed onto the floor and screamed in agony immediately waking Jim who was at her side in seconds, "What is it Abby?" he cried cradling her head. "What's wrong darling?"

Abby started to moan, "It's my stomach, please do something Jim, I can't stand this pain."

Jim reached for the telephone on the bedside table, "I'm calling an ambulance, just hang on."

Chaos erupted when the ambulance arrived and Kate and Kelly were roused from their beds. They wanted desperately to go to the hospital but were forced to remain behind to look after Simon.

Abby, slipping in and out of consciousness, remembered leaving the house on a stretcher, seeing the girls' worried faces and hearing Scamp barking as the ambulance pulled away with its siren screeching. Every now and then she would feel Jim's hand holding her own and feel the paramedics checking her vital signs and she remembered Jim's worried face as they wheeled her away from him and into the operating room.

The operation revealed a massive abdominal cyst that had slowly filled with fluid over a period of weeks and then twisted on its slim neck putting Abby's life in danger. The doctors drained four quarts of fluid, successfully removed the cyst, and gave Abby a clean bill of health. She had been fortunate that the cyst had not ruptured.

In the recovery room, Abby opened her eyes and saw Jim's face hovering over her. "Hi Honey," he whispered stroking the damp hair away from her forehead, "how are you feeling?"

Abby's eyes filled up, "It's cancer, isn't it? I'm going to die, I knew it was all too good to be true."

"No, no, " Jim protested, "it was nothing like that. You're going to be fine. It was just a cyst but it's all gone now. The doctor will explain everything to you but I promise, you have nothing to worry about and you'll be out of here in a few days. Right now, you need to get some rest."

Abby fell asleep and woke up hours later to find that Jim was still sitting beside her bed and watching over her. It was then that she started to really count her blessings. She was alive and alert and had her whole life to look forward too.

Five days after the operation, Abby was anxious to get home to her family. She left the hospital on a beautiful sunny morning, leaning on Jim for support, and settled into the passenger seat of their car for the drive home. She was content to sit and gaze out of the window only interrupting her thoughts to assure Jim that she was feeling fine. Turning onto the tree-lined street where they lived, she felt a lump begin in her throat and then she saw them, her whole family waiting on the front step. There was Kelly cradling Simon in her arms, Kate hanging on to a squirming Molly and Scamp ready to pounce forward to greet his mistress.

Jim smiled as he turned to Abby and saw the tears forming in her eyes, "Welcome home darling," he whispered.